Her heart felt as if it was skipping beats. She was breathless as if she'd been running in the past few minutes instead of hiding in his room.

Her hand moved, the fingers splaying. She closed her eyes, the better to sense him. Although she had sketched out her father's plans, she had no talent at drawing. For the first time, she wished she could take charcoal and paper and draw him as she felt him.

No doubt it was the influence of the mural of Rome, but she saw him as a gladiator, naked but for strips of leather, his eyes deadly intent. This man would fight for his life, would combat anything or anyone set against him.

He frightened her at the same time he excited something in her, a wish, a desire, a need to be someone different. Daring Martha. Beautiful Martha. Martha, who incited a man's yearning.

His breath was on her cheek now and she knew she should step away. Instead, she held herself still.

"Shall I kiss you, creature of my dreams?"

Romances *by* Karen Ranney

KAREN RANNEY

The English Duke

AVON BOOKS

An Imprint of HarperCollinsPublishers

HarperCollins
PUBLISHERS
Since 1817

THE ENGLISH DUKE. Copyright © 2017 by Karen Ranney LLC. All rights reserved. Printed in the United States of America. No part of this book may be used or reproduced in any manner whatsoever without written permission except in the case of brief quotations embodied in critical articles and reviews. For information, address HarperCollins Publishers, 195 Broadway, New York, NY 10007.

First Avon Books mass market printing: April 2017

ISBN 978-0-06-246689-1

17 18 19 20 21 QGM 10 9 8 7 6 5 4 3 2 1

To Duncan—for being everything.

The
English
Duke

Chapter 1

July, 1871
Griffin House, England

$\mathcal{M}$artha York stared down at the letter her sister had just handed her.

For months she'd been trying to satisfy her father's bequest. He'd asked her to see that his work was given to the Duke of Roth. That's all. Except it hadn't been easy, had it?

She'd been writing to the duke for nearly a year and never received an answer. Not a note. Nothing dictated to a secretary. Not one small sliver of information. She'd kept writing and he'd kept ignoring her.

"Aren't you going to open it, Martha?" Josephine asked.

She nodded, staring at the distinctive emblem on the reverse before removing the seal.

Part of her never wanted him to write back. There, a bit of honesty. She hadn't wanted to relinquish all her father's precious diaries, all his prototypes, all his notes.

"What does he say, Martha?" Josephine asked. "Has he invited us to Sedgebrook? Has he?"

Martha frowned at her sister. "Of course he hasn't."

"But what has he said? Are you going to read it to us?" Josephine asked, her glance encompassing their grandmother.

Gran didn't say a word, but she was looking over at Martha. Normally, nothing could divert her attention from her crochet work.

"He says he doesn't want Father's bequest. He does send his condolences on Father's death. A year late."

"He has to take it," Gran said calmly. "Shall we just send everything in a wagon? He'd have no choice but to accept everything."

"I wouldn't be able to live with myself if something happened to Bessie," she said, referring to her father's latest prototype. "Why he thought the duke would want it, I've no idea."

"They were friends," Gran said. "Matthew didn't spare the time for many people."

Martha only nodded. Gran's son, their father, had been a hermit, but a happy one. He went to the cottage situated at the end of the lawn every day, content to tinker there surrounded by his inventions, and allowing his imagination to take him where it would.

The unlikely friendship between Jordan Hamilton and her father had begun before the man had become the Duke of Roth. He'd been a naval officer then, curious about her father's work, and writing with his questions. That had sparked an intense correspondence, one that lasted until pneumonia had taken Matthew suddenly and unexpectedly.

"At least he finally deigned to answer my letter," Martha said. "Which is the most he's done all these months. He probably got tired of me writing."

"What are you going to do?" Gran asked, her crochet work forgotten on her lap.

"I could simply keep writing him until he agrees to come here."

"Or we could take Father's bequest to him," Josephine said.

Martha glanced up at her sister.

"That's out of the question," she said, staring down at the distinctive handwriting. She knew it well. She'd read every one of the duke's letters to her father.

She hadn't expected him to repudiate her father's gift. Doing so was worse than a slap in the face. His ignoring her letters ridiculed the relationship that Matthew York had valued so much. She'd thought the Duke of Roth had felt the same, but evidently he didn't.

"Why is it out of the question?" Josephine asked.

"Josephine, please sit," she said, looking up at her sister.

Each time Josephine passed in front of her, perfume wafted in her direction. Ever since her mother had departed Griffin House, Josephine had taken to wearing Marie's favorite French perfume. It was, according to her sister, a sophisticated fragrance. Martha thought it was overbearing and too flowery.

Perhaps Josephine wore it to remind her of Marie. No doubt that was the same reason her sister gravitated to the Rose Parlor. Her mother often sat here, staring out at the lawn, her gaze impenetrable and almost troubling to witness.

The room was filled with all those things Marie loved, but evidently not enough to remain at Griffin House. Needlepoint sat in a frame, patiently waiting to be finished. Needlepoint pillows were arranged on the sofa. Footrests upholstered in needlepoint sat at their feet while needlepoint pictures of flowers framed in gold hung on one wall. Even the draperies had needlepoint tiebacks.

She couldn't help but wonder if Marie truly had an affinity for needlepoint or if it was only an outlet for other feelings.

The Rose Parlor had been decorated by her stepmother. The sofa and love seat, as well as the curtains that framed the view of the back lawn and the lake were pink. The pillows that weren't covered in needlepoint were pink as well. The round carpet beneath her feet consisted of overblown lush roses—in pink, of course—with a contrasting green border.

Josephine loved the room. Martha felt slightly bilious in it. Gran didn't seem to mind, being as involved in her crocheting as Marie had been in her needlepoint.

As for herself, when she wasn't in her own room, Martha was in her father's cottage. Although not quite a laboratory, it truly wasn't an office, either. Instead, it was a combination of the two with tall skinny windows looking out over the lake.

She was his assistant and one of her tasks was to record his thoughts and experiments for the ages as well as to serve as his sounding board.

He'd been a good man, a truly inventive one. If he was more involved in his pursuits and less his family, perhaps that was to be expected.

No one, least of all her, had been that surprised when Marie had hied off to France six months after his death. According to the letter she had written Josephine, she was madly in love with a French count.

Of course I will send for you, my love, she'd written. *As soon as Pierre and I are settled at his estate. You will love the château. It's so much more to my taste than Griffin House ever was.*

Marie was French, a fact that Josephine seemed to recite more and more often of late. As if being half-French was something preferable to being completely English.

"Well?" Josephine asked. "What are you going to do?"

Martha looked out at the lake, placid in the July morning, remembering her father's words. "Wherever there's a mystery, you can't help but feel excitement. Always seek to find a mystery. The sheer act of solving it will keep you happy."

The mystery that had occupied her mind ever since his death was finding how that final experiment had been successful. He'd been so happy when he'd come in from the storm. He'd been drenched but ecstatic, telling her that his vessel had leveled off, heading directly for the target.

But he hadn't told her how.

In this instance there were no notes. No thoughts or idle speculation. Nothing to give her any clue.

She was determined that his life's work would be finished, even if she had to turn over all his notes and work to the duke.

"We have to go," Josephine said, interrupting her thoughts. "It's what Father would have wanted. Besides, it's the Duke of Roth! Can you imagine, Martha? We could see Sedgebrook!"

She stared down at the letter again.

Jordan Hamilton, the Duke of Roth, had a great deal to answer for, not the least of which was putting their household into disarray. His words were curt, almost to the point of rudeness, and made her even more determined to fulfill her father's wishes. Like it or not, Matthew York had wanted the Duke of Roth to have his notes and Bessie, his latest invention.

For years she'd been her father's assistant. She was the only one who knew what he wanted, who could pull the exact notes he needed from the volume of his work. She'd been the only one to help him with his experiments. No one else could take apart the reciprocating engine he'd devised, a clever thing run by compressed air, or the hydrostatic valve, and the most important piece of all—the pendulum balance that kept the ship at a certain depth.

She'd spent months categorizing all the parts, carefully labeling the inventions. With the help of the footmen, she'd packed everything away in wooden crates, ready for the duke to come and get them. Several of her father's devices had shown promise, like the light that followed the path of water and the photographs capable of absorbing the colors of its subject.

But it was the York Torpedo Ship that had fascinated her father and the once naval officer Jordan Hamilton.

"What are you going to do, Martha?" Gran asked.

Martha glanced at Josephine, who was practically dancing in place in front of her then over at her grandmother.

"I see nothing else to do, Gran, but to take Father's work to him."

"You can't mean to do it alone, Martha," Josephine said. "You can't do such a shocking thing."

She looked up at Josephine. "No less shocking than all of us descending on Sedgebrook."

"Nevertheless," Gran said, packing up her crochet work in the special bag designed for it, "that's exactly what we shall do. I'll not have you go alone."

She frowned down at the letter again. The penmanship was perfect. Yet the duke had not explained why he'd ignored all of her letters. Evidently he hadn't even opened them. Otherwise, he would have known that her father asked for him, even on his deathbed.

She didn't want to visit the Duke of Roth. She couldn't forget all those occasions when her father had weakly asked, "Has he answered yet? Is he coming?"

Each time she had to tell him the news that there hadn't been any response. All she could do was hold his trembling hand in hers and will him to be stronger.

Wishing for something doesn't make it come about; she'd learned that lesson in those terrible days. She'd been powerless to prevent his gradual fading away until the last breath had almost been a relief.

"Very well."

"Does that mean we're going?" Josephine asked.

"Yes," she said, the word uttered reluctantly.

"DID YOU LOSE it?" Unspoken was the word *again*.

"Yes, I lost it, Reese," Jordan said.

There, a fair attempt at an equitable tone. No one needed to know he was furious.

Another failure. Just one more to add to the stack.

The damn thing had sunk like a rock to the bottom of the lake. Just like the other two.

"Shall we call it a day and have a whiskey?"

He glanced over at his friend.

Reese Burthren had unexpectedly descended on

him two weeks ago and didn't look to be in a hurry to leave. Normally, Jordan wouldn't object to his friend's presence. In fact, it had been enjoyable having another person to talk to at Sedgebrook. The footmen always looked a bit uncomfortable when he talked about gyroscopes and fin angles. Lately, however, Reese had begun to watch his experiments and offer criticisms about his *toy*—Reese's word.

"Be my guest," he said now. "I'll join you when I'm finished here."

Reese didn't budge from his stance at the end of the dock, which meant he was going to stay there as long as Jordan did.

Turning, he forced a smile to his face and addressed Reese. "But not necessarily today," he added. "We'll have that whiskey."

Jordan made his way to where his majordomo, Frederick, stood.

The man was blessed with a stubborn nature the equal of his own coupled with an English bulldog's tenacity. Because of Frederick, no one bothered him. No visitors interrupted his study. No solicitation of any sort ever reached him. No staff problems hounded him. Nor did any shop owners, desirous of their payments. For that alone Frederick was worth his not inconsiderable annual salary.

Frederick had been with the family for most of his life, beginning his apprenticeship as an eager footman. What Frederick had lost in height over the years he'd gained in girth. The man was a living example of John Bull, stout, middle-aged, affable, and a pragmatist. His face was almost always florid, his hair graying but kept rigorously in place by a concoction the housekeeper had devised for him.

Frederick was one of the few people among the staff who knew how dire his financial situation was, yet Jordan knew he would never divulge the information to anyone.

"Ask for volunteers among the footmen," he told Frederick. "Tell them there will be a reward to the one who locates the ship."

Frederick nodded. "Yes, Your Grace."

He knew he'd get enough volunteers, footmen eager to get out of polishing the silver. Not that there was much left of it. His father had managed to keep Sedgebrook solvent by selling a great many portable items.

He, himself, was getting rid of the horses his brother had worked to acquire. One sale a month was enough to keep the staff.

He stared out at the lake, intent on the ripples the wind was creating, anything but think about money at the moment.

"What do you think went wrong?" Reese asked.

"Something in the guidance system. I need to review my calculations."

One of Reese's eyebrows winged upward. "Will it help?"

"In other words, do I know what the hell I'm doing?"

"Not quite," Reese said, smiling.

"The answer is evidently not," Jordan said.

He'd refer to his notes, find out where he'd gone wrong. For now, however, he'd pretend a conviviality and bury his disappointment somewhere Reese couldn't see it.

They'd been friends at school, had renewed their friendship later at the War Office. He and Reese had both been assigned to the Topographical & Statistics

Department, he as a naval officer and Reese as a civilian. His duties were to collate military statistics, with a concentration on the Crimean War. Reese had been tasked with ensuring that the archival maps of the region were correct. They'd dreamed of glory in their respective posts but had never found so much as a hint of it.

Yet his work had opened up another avenue for him, something in which he'd found an abiding interest. The Russians had come up with a small device they called a torpedo in the Crimean War that was used as a mine in the harbors. Rumors persisted they were inventing a mobile mine, thereby creating a devastating weapon. When he'd overheard a superior officer discussing York Armaments and the newest work by Matthew York, he'd been intrigued.

Little did he know, five years ago, that the York Torpedo Ship—or his own invention, the Hamilton Torpedo—would keep him from going mad.

"How many does that make?" Reese asked as they walked toward the boathouse.

"Three," he said.

With any luck, Reese would cease questioning him. He'd give his friend the task of selecting a bottle of wine for dinner from his father's wine cellar. Only one more example of a Hamilton spending money they didn't have.

"Don't you have the material to build another one?"

He debated trying to explain to Reese how much time it took to bend and hammer the copper to a smooth shape, build another engine, not to mention the guidance system and propeller. He might be able to make Reese understand, but the other man would never realize the emotional toll each failure cost him. It was better to keep his thoughts to himself.

"Well, it doesn't really matter, does it?" Reese said, his tone affable.

Jordan grabbed his walking stick and began the slow and painful journey to the end of the dock.

The past year had been difficult. When he'd been laid up in bed he spent hours occupied with plans and sketches. During the months of learning to walk again, he'd kept his mind from the pain with thoughts of leveling devices and timing mechanisms. The idea of developing a workable torpedo had taken on the importance of a quest.

"Yes," he finally said. "It matters."

Chapter 2

"How much farther?" Josephine asked.

Martha waited, but when Gran didn't say anything, she spoke up. "You asked the question five minutes ago, Josephine. We're supposed to reach Sedgebrook sometime this afternoon."

"It would have been faster if we could have taken the train," Josephine said.

Her sister had said that, too, at least three times since they'd started the journey this morning. She bit back her impatience. Josephine was excited, that's all.

They hadn't left Griffin House during the past year because of the mourning period for their father. Josephine might also be anticipating seeing Sedgebrook, one of the great houses of England. Martha might have been enthusiastic about seeing it as well if she wasn't nearly overwhelmed by regret.

A wagon filled with her father's notebooks, Bessie, as well as the other prototypes for the York Torpedo Ship, and the rest of the inventions he'd worked on for the whole of his life followed them at a slower pace. From time to time their coachman stopped on the side of the road to give the wagon time to catch up.

Her father would no doubt approve of this journey. She could almost hear his words.

Martha, I'm sure there's a reason he never wrote. And one compelling him to refuse my bequest. You need only be patient for the answer to be revealed to you.

She had a great deal of patience when it came to devising a tiny chain to stretch between the propeller and the gyroscope. She could sit for hours painstakingly forming the links with a tool and a magnifying glass. However, she didn't have the same kind of tolerance for the duke's actions.

He'd harmed her father and she wasn't about to flippantly forgive him.

Although at one point he'd been interested in her father's advances in torpedoes no doubt he'd changed his mind over the past year. Perhaps he was now involved in races, hunts, balls, and dinner parties. Something more fascinating to him than the product of a man's mind and imagination.

She'd never been more disappointed in one person in her entire life.

The man she'd come to know in letters to her father had probably never existed. The eager young naval officer had disappeared to be replaced by a duke who looked down his nose at anyone of lesser rank.

She didn't want to meet the Duke of Roth. She certainly didn't want to speak with him. Nor would she be burdened with corresponding with the man ever again.

Josephine, on the other hand, looked ecstatic about the upcoming meeting. Excitement pinkened her cheeks and made her eyes sparkle like jewels.

Her grandmother, dressed in black, which was the only color she'd worn for as long as Martha could remember, sat beside Josephine. Her sister was wearing a dark blue high-waisted traveling dress. Martha's attire was similar but not as fashionable since her dress was at least three years old while Josephine had recently freshened her wardrobe. Martha's bonnet was the match of her grandmother's, not as flattering as the hat her sister wore, a small, attractive bit of straw and feathers set forward as if to accentuate the perfection of Josephine's face.

Josephine's brunette hair was swept up and away, the better to reveal her beauty. Her eyes were deep green, the color of grass. Martha's were a muddy brown and nondescript, a word she thought applied to the rest of her.

She and Josephine were of a height, but her sister's figure was perfect while hers was slightly heavier in the bosom.

Marie had once made the comment that Martha was of English peasant stock, the perfect form for giving birth and suckling a dozen children. She'd been eighteen at the time and had only stared, hurt, at her stepmother.

"Oh, Martha, we can't all be beauties. Besides, we both know you'd be happier being your father's assistant for the rest of your life. Balls and soirées are not your cup of tea."

She could still hear Marie's trilling laugh and the words that had proven to be unfortunately prophetic. She wasn't the type for a season. Look how disastrously it had turned out.

She'd had three offers. The first was from a young man who'd been served up like a salmon on a salver by his mother. He'd spoken fewer than seven words during the whole of their acquaintance.

Finally, in desperation, she had asked him, "Why do you want to marry me?"

The poor thing had answered, "Because Mama says I must."

She'd prevailed upon her father to decline his offer immediately.

Her second suitor had been a friend of a friend of the family. He'd been entirely suitable in many ways. He made a good income in the City. He was presentable and nearly handsome. He was, however, so dictatorial that she couldn't tolerate five minutes in his company. When he wanted a glass of punch he decided she should fetch it for him. He wanted to go smoke a cigarillo and didn't even explain why he abruptly left. He told her the colors he preferred in her dresses and how her hair should be arranged.

She was not going to be dictated to by a husband. Her father had raised her to believe her mind was the equal of any man's. She didn't have to be subservient. Unfortunately, her suitor didn't understand the idea of a woman refusing him.

"Of course we'll marry," he said. "You're not entirely a beauty, Martha. Plus, I understand you've put your mind to things not womanly in nature. However, a house full of children will rectify that, I think."

She'd come close to coshing him over the head with something heavy. It was Gran who'd saved her from doing bodily injury.

The third supplicant for her hand had made no effort to conceal the fact that he was penniless. He was an earl, quite lovely to look at and charming. She was almost inclined to accept his suit, but for the fact she caught him with a maid on the terrace. The discovery had added to her knowledge in two ways. She evaluated men with a jaundiced eye now and she'd seen the actual act. He hadn't been the least discreet and she'd been an unwilling voyeur.

But for a chance encounter, she might have been married to the lecher.

Josephine had ignored everything she told her about a season in London. Her warning about it being boring, endless, and painful from time to time, given that her shoes pinched and her corset was laced entirely too tight, had fallen on deaf ears.

Her sister would probably enjoy London since she was Martha's opposite.

Josephine was beautiful and personable, exhibiting no hesitation when it came to social situations. Granted, the past year had been devoid of most encounters outside of the family, a complaint Josephine uttered often.

Her sister seemed to have resented their father's death—or its timing—especially since it coincided with what would have been her introduction to London. Save for that tragedy, she might already be engaged at the moment. Or, at the least, sighing over some young peer.

It would be only a few months until Gran took her sister off to London to be paraded in front of the wolves of the Marriage Mart like a wealthy sheep. Josephine would, no doubt, handle herself well. Her sister had a great deal more inclination to flirt and to charm than she did.

She was, perhaps, too literal, a fault she shared with her father. When someone told her the world was crashing down around their heads, she looked up at the ceiling. She didn't speak in hyperbole. Nor did she understand the need for drama. Just state the facts, add some research to back up your hypothesis, and a solution would become obvious.

"I really don't see why it takes so long," Josephine said.

Her grandmother closed her eyes. Martha couldn't help but wonder if Gran was trying to ignore Josephine.

Amy only clutched the handle above the window. Poor thing was looking increasingly pale. Her grandmother's maid had been with her for decades and was considered as much a friend as a servant. Amy also had a sunny nature, one that went perfectly with her round face and cute nose. She was most often smiling, at least when she wasn't traveling. The rocking motion of the carriage, even their well-sprung vehicle, set her stomach to rolling.

Martha sent her a bracing smile that Amy returned wanly. She'd accompanied them on this journey for Susan's benefit, another fact about which Josephine complained. The two girls shared a maid, Sarah, who'd been left at home.

"It's not as if Amy is proficient at hair, Gran," Josephine had said.

"She doesn't need to be," Martha interjected. "We aren't remaining at Sedgebrook. We'll be there long enough to deliver Father's bequest and that's all. We'll remain overnight at an inn, then turn around and come home."

Regardless of the initial plans, Josephine had packed not one valise but three, insisting she needed everything, even for an overnight journey.

Martha blew out a breath and concentrated on the scenery. They were crossing a bridge now, quite a wide structure with a slight arch. She sat up, trying to peer through the struts for a view of the river. She'd expected a calm, easy-flowing stream and was greeted by a rushing torrent cascading over the rocks bordering it and looking as if it was racing to be somewhere on time.

"Are we almost there, Gran?" Josephine asked, her voice sounding petulant.

"How should I know, child?" her grandmother asked. "I've never been to Sedgebrook, either. Charles said we should reach it shortly after midday and since it's about that time, I would think we are close."

Martha had heard her father talk about Sedgebrook in rapturous terms quite unlike him. He'd seen the Duke of Roth's seat once, as a boy, but he'd never forgotten the sight.

"It isn't simply the size of the place, Martha. There's its dominance over the countryside. You can see the house for miles before you reach it."

He was right. As the carriage came over the rise, Sedgebrook appeared on the horizon almost like the sun at dawn. According to her father, work began on the house in 1653. It took a hundred years to finish Sedgebrook, or the lifetimes of three Dukes of Roth.

Sedgebrook was built of a yellowish stone that had mellowed over the centuries. Near the roofline the color was deeper, almost brown. The house was an open square, with wings to either side, the baroque design adding a flamboyant touch. The main section was adorned with an enormous and opulent dome that was duplicated in smaller proportion on each of the wings. Statues of knights adorned the roof edge, appearing like a frozen army ready to defend.

The Hamiltonian Hills behind the house had been

named for the family and shone bluish gray as they approached. According to her father, the thousand acres surrounding Sedgebrook were comprised of paved walks, and two temples fashioned in the Greek style—the Temple of the Four Winds and the Temple of the Muses. Woodlands flanked the house, leading up to the terraces beside Hamilton Lake, a good distance away.

From here she could see dramatic swaths of blue-and-yellow flowers planted in seemingly random fashion. Although she wasn't familiar with some of the names, she knew bluebells and rhododendrons well enough to identify them. No doubt the formal gardens that had so impressed her father were behind the house.

Josephine gasped beside her. Even Gran looked surprised, and she was rarely impressed by anything.

Her own home was as much a paean to her family's success. In the case of Sedgebrook, however, she thought the Hamilton family might've gone a bit overboard.

It took an hour to reach the graveled approach, the carriage slowing as they entered the open square before the main building.

Twin staircases met at the top landing in front of double doors that looked like hammered metal. The urns situated on every other step on both staircases were filled with bluish flowers.

Beside her, Josephine sat up straight, her eyes sparkling with acquisitive interest.

Their father had refused Josephine nothing. She wanted for no bauble, gown, slippers, toy, or amusement. Anything she desired was instantly hers. More than once Martha had wondered what Josephine

would have done if they'd suddenly become penniless.

Matthew York's death had no effect on the family
fortune. There was no title to go to a remote second
cousin. No long-lost relative stood in the wings an-
nouncing he'd been given the brunt of the inheritance. No, it had been divided into four parts, equally
shared by Gran, Josephine, Marie, and Martha.

Perhaps Marie expected to inherit the majority of
the fortune. On learning of the contents of the will,
her stepmother had what she could only describe as a
temper tantrum. To say Marie was disappointed was
to vastly understate the obvious. After her emotional
outburst was over, she sulked for days and would
hardly speak to anyone.

"It's not the money," Gran said when Martha expressed her confusion. "It's the power. Now she can't
force anyone to do as she wishes."

Gran had smiled, then, and it occurred to Martha
that the expression was a particularly triumphant one.

Not long after that day Marie had decamped from
Griffin House for France.

Still, the sum they'd each inherited was more than
they could spend in their lifetimes. With the freedom
her father's money would give her, she could finish
his work. She needn't get permission to hire the services of a clockmaker or obtain approval for more
copper plates to be delivered to her father's cottage.

Josephine, too, had plans for her fortune. A magnificent, if delayed, debut in London and a husband.
If necessary, she'd buy him.

What a pity the Duke of Roth couldn't be purchased. From Josephine's gaping wonder, she'd quite
fallen in love with the house.

They pulled in front of the staircases, but no servant raced down the steps to greet them. In fact, it looked as if their arrival hadn't even been noticed.

She'd been so annoyed at the duke's letter that she'd sent him a terse response in reply. *The York family will be arriving by carriage on July the twelfth to deliver Matthew York's bequest to the Duke of Roth.* It was a perfectly bland letter, structured so as not to reveal her irritation.

Would he remember they were to arrive today? Would he care?

Josephine was using a handkerchief to dust the tops of her shoes. She'd already inspected her face in the carriage mirror, adjusted her hat, and ensured her appearance was as pristine as it could be after being in a carriage for the majority of the day.

Her sister would always be beautiful regardless of the circumstances.

As the carriage rocked to a halt, Josephine turned to her.

"Don't worry, Martha," she said, smiling. "I shall charm the duke. After a few minutes in my company, he'll be grateful we've come."

She didn't know what annoyed her more: Josephine's brash confidence or her suspicion that her sister was correct.

"YOUR GRACE, A carriage is approaching."

Jordan looked up from his whiskey to see Frederick standing at the door of his library.

At the moment his majordomo was looking as disgruntled as he felt.

"A carriage?"

"Yes, Your Grace."

Damn, he'd forgotten.

"The York family," he said. "They said they'd be here today and they are."

"The York family?"

He glanced over at Reese seated in the twin of the wing chair he occupied.

"Matthew York's family," he said. "He and I conferred about the ship I'm testing. A brilliant man."

"I didn't realize you knew York. The world lost a great inventor when he died."

Reese's comment sparked his own interest. His friend had evidently been aware of the older man. Had Reese known about Matthew's work on the torpedo ship?

"Why is his family visiting?"

He stood. "Hardly visiting. They're bringing me Matthew's bequest. Evidently, he wished me to have his notes and work. I don't want them." Reaching for his walking stick, he began the laborious and overly painful process to reach the door.

Reese kept pace with him, no doubt thinking it a kindness. He wished the other man would go on ahead, but he was doomed to fail in that just like he'd done keeping the York family away.

Walking was a horror for him, but at least he could do it now. The doctors had been doubtful he'd be able to from the beginning. He'd finally found a physician who was more optimistic. Or perhaps Dr. Reynolds had lied better than the others.

"It's a matter of time, Your Grace."

Time. How easily the physician had uttered those words. Time. It had taken time, all right. Ten months, two weeks, three days to get upright and shuffle one foot in front of the other. He still didn't do it well. Nor would he, a judgment his ordinarily optimistic doctor had offered him on his last visit.

"You've already accomplished much more than was thought possible, Your Grace. You should congratulate yourself instead of wishing for more."

"It isn't *more* that I want, Dr. Reynolds. I want to be able to walk without a limp." Without requiring a cane, or a walking stick as his housekeeper so quaintly phrased it. He wanted to be able to cross the room without people turning to stare at him, marking his passage, and noting how the effort to do so evidently pained him.

"Your leg was shattered, Your Grace. There's muscle damage and more. I consider it a miracle you're not confined to a wheeled chair."

"Then your idea of a miracle and mine differ greatly," he said.

He would have consulted another physician, but Dr. Reynolds was his third and the only one who'd given him any hope. The man had also furnished a tall, burly Swedish sadist by the name of Henry who insisted on pummeling him on a daily basis, stretching his leg over his head until he wanted to scream from the pain. But if anyone deserved the credit for his walking again, it was probably Henry, damn the man. If he'd made that remark, Henry would have smiled and insisted on another session.

He'd made Henry his valet, reasoning the man could learn another skill and he could save on the expense of a manservant. Henry was still learning how to care for his clothes, but since Jordan eschewed social events, he didn't give a flying farthing if his cravat was tied correctly. In addition, most of the maids at Sedgebrook sighed after Henry. The man had a handsome face and a remarkable physique coupled with a ready smile.

Jordan finally made it to the door.

"Go on ahead and greet them," he said, hoping Reese wouldn't insist on remaining with him each agonizing step. "Otherwise, Frederick will send them away and I'll have to sort through hurt feelings."

"God forbid," Reese said, smiling.

"They're only staying for a moment," he added. "As long as good manners dictate they remain."

He'd offer them tea, but hoped they'd decline. An hour at most and they'd be gone. In a few days Reese would leave and he'd finally be alone. He wasn't in the mood for visitors or even a friend at this point.

Chapter 3

No one greeted them as the carriage stopped. Finally, Charles descended from his driver's perch, came around to the door and opened it, holding out his arm.

Martha left the vehicle first so she could help Gran.

"What should we do?" she asked after Josephine joined them. "Do you think he's home?"

"Someone is," Gran said, glancing up at the entrance to Sedgebrook.

As a tall man came down the steps, Josephine pushed forward.

The man who approached them had an agreeable-looking face, one disposed to smiling as he was doing now. Although his hair was brown, it was a lighter shade hinting at blond. His deep brown eyes were warm, making Martha wonder if his character was kind.

He was certainly a fine specimen of manhood with his broad shoulders and long legs.

"Good afternoon, Your Grace," Josephine said, making a spectacle of herself by performing a deep curtsy better served for the queen.

To her surprise, the man laughed. "I'm not the duke, miss."

"York," Josephine said. "Miss Josephine York."

"I'm Reese Burthren, His Grace's friend. May I escort you inside?"

Martha looked up at the top of the steps. Now another tall figure stood there.

Did he think himself too important to descend the staircase or could he simply not be bothered to greet visitors?

She couldn't imagine the man's arrogance, standing as he was at the top of the steps, a pasha waiting for her to approach him.

Very well, if the mountain would not come to her, then she would go to the mountain. Brushing past Mr. Burthren, Martha approached the staircase. After grabbing her skirt with one hand, her other on the wide banister, she mounted the twenty-six steps, her head bent to gauge her footing. She didn't pay any attention to the landing, at least not until the last three steps. Then she raised her head to find him watching her.

She almost fell down the stairs.

As it was, she was certain her mouth dropped open and her eyes widened. The man standing there was the most handsome creature she'd ever seen.

Her pulse was behaving in a bizarre fashion, leaping and racing. She felt as if she'd been running, not merely climbing a few steps.

She wanted to be able to manage time, to keep the moments still so that she could study him. His hair was black and thick, cut shorter than was fashionable. He was clean shaven. His flashing blue eyes looked capable of shooting sparks of disdain at her. If she could really halt time, she'd press her fingers against his high cheekbones and the hollows they

created. His face was stern, those full lips bracketed
by lines, his jaw squared. Each feature was perfect,
but together they formed a magnificent face, one as
commanding as a bust of Julius Caesar, but far more
attractive.

Never once had she considered what a man might
look like naked. Not even her three suitors. If she had,
no doubt she would have been struck dumb with re-
vulsion. But this man gave her thoughts of those scandalous statues in the London museum she visited last
year. She'd almost wanted to reach out and touch the
cold marble, feel the musculature of the thigh, cup a
buttock with her palm. Her own reaction had been
so scandalous that she'd been ashamed of herself, exactly as she felt right at the moment.

Here she was, standing at the top of the steps of
Sedgebrook, staring at a stranger and wondering if
he was as handsome without his clothes as he was
attired in a severe black suit.

The color favored him, but Lucifer probably looked
good in black.

"You must be the Duke of Roth, are you not?" Josephine said breathlessly.

Martha glanced to her left to find Josephine standing there. She must have raced up the steps in order
to be the first to greet the duke.

"How utterly delightful to meet you," she said.
"We're here to bring you Father's bequest," she continued, further irritating Martha. "We couldn't possibly send it by messenger, and although everyone
employed at Griffin House is reputable, we would
be beside ourselves if anything happened to all his
work."

Josephine had not once expressed an interest in

what their father did when he was alive. In fact, Martha was certain that if she mentioned the York Torpedo Ship Josephine would only look at her blankly and have absolutely no idea what it was.

The duke bowed slightly. "Thank you, Miss York, but I don't want your father's work."

Was he truly the unbearably insufferable creature he seemed to be? What a shame to have such a loathsome character living inside such a delightful package.

Martha stepped forward, her hand on Josephine's arm, poised to pull her sister back if she dared to interrupt.

"I'm afraid you don't have a choice," Martha said. "The wagon will be here shortly. I don't know if you know this, Your Grace, but my father held you in great esteem." She sent him a look she hoped he understood: *she didn't*. "His last words were of you. He spoke glowingly of your friendship, yet you couldn't be bothered to send condolences when he died."

"Miss Martha York, I presume," the duke said, his voice a low baritone.

She was not going to allow him to know that even his voice affected her.

What was wrong with her? She was being as foolish as those girls she'd met in London during her season, giggling over a man, whispering about his attributes—and they hadn't been speaking of his fortune.

"I'm afraid His Grace was ill," Mr. Burthren said from behind her. "For some time."

The duke shook his head. "It's all right, Reese. I don't need you to fight my battles for me."

What an odd way to put it. She was not engaged in a battle with the duke; she was just pinning his ears back because he'd been insufferably rude. In addition, his actions had hurt her father, which was unpardonable.

Mr. Burthren stepped forward, Gran's hand on his arm. Evidently, he'd been assisting her up the steps, something she'd not thought to do.

"This is Mrs. Susannah York," Mr. Burthren said. "Accompanied by her granddaughters Miss Martha York and Miss Josephine York."

"You've made an outing of it, I see," the duke said.

"Hardly an outing, Your Grace," Martha said. "We've traveled one whole day to get here."

"A train trip is only an hour or so, Miss York. Are you given to much exaggeration?"

Her grandmother disliked trains, thinking them a blight on the countryside, noisy, dirty, and beneath the dignity of York women. An irony, considering a great deal of their wealth came from railroads. Gran ignored that fact as well as the main source of their income: armaments.

She was not going to explain her grandmother's idiosyncrasies to the duke.

"Regardless of the distance or the time," he said, "the trip was wholly unnecessary."

"To you, perhaps, Your Grace. I am simply fulfilling my father's wish. He wanted you to have his research, his papers, and the latest prototype of the York Torpedo Ship. Had I known he wanted you to have everything, I would have counseled against it. I would've added my powers of persuasion, such as they are, to change his mind."

"Do you not think me worthy?"

Oh dear, why had she made that remark? Well, in for a penny, in for a pound.

"You don't even seem to care he died."

If she hadn't been studying him so intently, she might have missed the slight change of expression in his eyes. Just for a moment it looked as if she saw regret behind the flatness of his gaze. Or she could simply be mistaken.

"You must accept my apologies, Mrs. York," he said, turning slightly to address her grandmother. "Mr. Burthren was correct. I was unwell and didn't know your son had passed."

Gran nodded, but instead of speaking, she placed her hand flat against the middle of her chest and let out a slight gasp.

"Gran?"

Martha stepped closer as Gran moaned.

"What is it?"

She placed her arm behind her grandmother, supporting her.

"She needs to sit down," she said, glancing toward the duke.

"I fear the stairs were too much for me," Gran said, her voice sounding breathless.

Her grandmother was looking entirely too pale, almost the same color as Amy who came up the steps behind her. Gran was not a young woman and the past year had been a difficult one for her, with her son's death and her daughter-in-law's abdication of any responsibility.

Amy moved to assist her grandmother while Josephine still stood there smiling at the duke like a dolt.

"Please," Martha said.

She half expected the duke to forbid them admittance to his home. Instead, he nodded toward Reese.

"Would you see them to a convenient parlor?"

Thankfully, Josephine stopped staring, goggle-eyed, at the duke. Reese offered his arm to Gran again and she placed her hand on it, allowing him to lead her into the house through the massive double doors. Josephine followed, smiling brightly up at a portly servant in a dark blue suit who stood as still and as straight as a statue.

Martha followed, glancing back at the duke.

A man's character was revealed within moments of meeting him. The trick was to pay attention, listen, and make judgments based on what he said and how he acted. She understood everything there was to know about the Duke of Roth within seconds of their greeting. He was an arrogant, miserable person, rude, and unconcerned for anyone but himself.

Unless she'd been completely wrong.

The duke followed them, but slowly and obviously painfully. He was using a walking stick she hadn't seen until now and leaning heavily on it. His left leg seemed to be fine, but his right dragged behind him.

She stopped herself from offering help even as the words trembled on her lips.

He glanced up to find her staring at him. His face firmed. He straightened, his shoulders squaring, but he didn't look away.

The glance they shared was strangely intimate, as if she'd come upon him at his most vulnerable. The moment elongated, became almost painfully awkward. She wanted to ask what had happened. He said he'd been unwell. Had he been referring to his leg?

She wanted to apologize, but wasn't sure why. For seeing him limp so badly? For misjudging him? The lines bracketing his mouth were evidently not caused by disdain as much as pain.

"Thank you," she said, wanting to connect with him in some way. "A few minutes is all we need. Just time for Gran to rest. The wagon will be here shortly with my father's things. As soon as it's unloaded, we'll be gone."

He didn't offer a comment in response. Instead, he only nodded.

She understood, finally, that he wasn't going to move as long as she was watching him. She turned and followed Gran and Josephine inside the house.

BLOODY DAMN HELL and all the saints. The last thing he'd wanted was for Martha York and her family to show up on his doorstep.

She's an invaluable asset to me, Hamilton, her father had often written. *Martha knows as much about the York Torpedo as I do.*

Bloody damn hell. He didn't need her here. He didn't need York's work. Not his notes. Not his insight. Nothing. He'd do it on his own, damn it, or die trying.

He stood there, his leg throbbing, forever reminding him of his limitations.

Now he had four of them in his house. Plus Reese.

One of the reasons he'd enjoyed York's friendship so much was because the man hadn't made any demands on him. He might write and suggest an answer to a problem Jordan was experiencing, but he wouldn't expect an answer immediately. Nor would he have descended on Sedgebrook as his family had done.

One thing he had to say about Martha York, she didn't give up. When she'd first written him, he'd been surprised. He'd never corresponded with any of Matthew's relatives. Perhaps he'd suspected the news she wrote and didn't want to face it. Perhaps he simply didn't want to be bothered with anyone else— recovering from his injuries had made him insular and centered in his own misery. He'd ignored each of her letters until he'd finally opened one. His immediate emotion on reading her words was shame. What he'd suspected was true. Matthew had died. His second feeling was a deep sadness. If anything, the older man was a mentor, understanding his need to know why, to create.

Yet he didn't want Matthew's bequest. Perhaps part of it was a vague feeling he didn't deserve to be the recipient of the man's intelligence and talent. A greater part was a desire to accomplish the development of his invention on his own.

He'd been labeled since birth, a spoke in a wheel, a cog in the whole. He was a Hamilton of Sedgebrook, a second son still expected to make a difference in the world, to matter. He was a naval officer with a purchased commission, but still required by his own sense of honor to accomplish and achieve.

His invention was the one thing solely his, belonging to no one else but him. Granted, Matthew had steered him in the right direction several times, but he'd put in the long hours, redone the calculations hundreds of times, experimented with various types of pendulum devices.

"Are you coming in?" Reese asked from the doorway. "I've settled them in the Rococo Parlor and ordered refreshments."

Jordan nodded and took another step. Reese couldn't stop himself from sending him a look of sympathy. He didn't know what was worse, pity from his boyhood friend or his home being invaded.

Chapter 4

$\mathcal{H}$ow are you feeling, Gran?" Martha asked, moving to sit on the odd-shaped sofa next to her grandmother.

Gran was leaning her head back against the carved wood, her eyes closed. In that moment she looked older than her years.

She should never have decided to come. If anything happened to Gran it would be her fault.

"Tea would help," Gran said, opening her eyes and smiling at Martha. "It's nothing, child. I'm simply a little worn-out. That's to be expected. If I could only rest for a bit, I'll be fine."

Mr. Burthren had escorted them here, smiled broadly, and then excused himself saying he would order refreshments. If they weren't delivered in a few minutes, she would go in search of something for Gran herself.

"It's an odd room," Gran said, looking around her. "What did Mr. Burthren call it?"

"The Rococo Parlor," Josephine said, taking one of the chairs near the sofa.

Martha stared up at the ceiling. An entire fresco was painted there, one of an elderly man leading a crowd of scantily clad women toward a mountain. Beneath the fresco, white stucco in fantastical shapes formed a border around the room, ending at columns on all four corners. The pale blue silk walls were decorated by a half dozen paintings, each a landscape filled with people either picnicking or resting beside a tree or near a brook.

Everywhere she looked, the detail was slightly more than she expected: statues of shepherdesses holding their skirts high as they beckoned sheep with tiny little horns, fanciful birds with long brass feathers adorning the tools next to the fireplace.

"It's French, I think," Gran said. After a quick look at Josephine, she didn't say anything further.

"I think it's a delectable room," Josephine said, looking around her like a child who'd been granted entrance to a confectioner's shop and told she could have anything she wished.

Would the duke join them? Martha doubted it. He'd not been pleased by their appearance and probably wished they'd disappear as quickly.

The poor man. She doubted he'd be happy about her compassion, either.

Gran suddenly moaned and slumped to her side.

"Gran? Gran? What's wrong?"

She grabbed her grandmother's wrist, felt a strong pulse, but wasn't reassured because the older woman moaned again.

"What is it?" Josephine asked, coming to stand in front of Gran. "Is she sick?"

Her sister was always in command of the obvious. Martha bit back her annoyance and looked around the room.

"Go summon someone, please," she said to Amy, gesturing to where the bellpull hung from the ceiling.

She bent and placed Gran's feet up on the sofa. She

rested her hand on her grandmother's ankle, wishing she had a pillow and something to cover her. Wishing, too, that she wasn't suddenly overwhelmed by fear.

JORDAN MADE HIS way slowly—since it was his only speed of late—to the Rococo Parlor.

The room had been a present from his grandfather to his wife, who'd evidently cherished both the gesture and the place. It was one of the smaller rooms at Sedgebrook and the decorations only made it seem more crowded.

Ever since he was a boy he avoided the room. Reese, for some reason, liked the parlor. Just because they were best friends didn't mean they agreed on everything. Lately, they found common ground in precious little.

The grandmother was on the ornate couch being fanned by her maid. Both granddaughters turned to look at him when he entered.

Mary, one of the Sedgebrook maids, hesitated at the doorway. He moved out of her way, allowing her to enter with a tray of tea and refreshments. Mary was a good sort, an affable girl, someone who always smiled at him. Not once did she send him a glance of pity and unless he asked she didn't offer to help him in any way.

His passage through the corridors and rooms of Sedgebrook was done like an arthritic octogenarian, but at least his servants didn't look as if they were going to cry when viewing him.

Like Martha York was doing right now.

"How are you feeling, Mrs. York?" he asked.

She didn't answer him. Instead, Martha spoke up.

"She isn't feeling well at all, Your Grace."

Martha had a curious voice. A little lower than normal, almost slumberous in tone, reminding him of a woman on waking in the morning. What a fool he was. There was no reason for him to think of rumpled sheets and marathon bouts of lovemaking, especially around the York woman.

He looked away and decided he wouldn't glance in her direction again.

The younger girl—what was her name again?—stood and approached him.

"I'm afraid Gran is feeling poorly, Your Grace. Whatever shall we do?"

Good manners dictated he offer accommodation, a meal or two, and time for the older woman to recuperate from the journey. He felt as far from good manners as he was from understanding why it was that all of them had descended on him.

Reese would say he was being rude. He was being rude. He didn't wish them to be his houseguests. He didn't want them here. He didn't want his life or his routine disrupted, especially by people he'd not invited to his home.

People he'd tried his best to avoid.

He glanced over to find Martha frowning at him, an expression he found preferable to her look of pity. He was damned if she was going to feel sorry for him.

He was the Duke of Roth, after all. The owner of Sedgebrook, one of the finest houses in Britain. Weren't those the two points the solicitor had emphasized when Jordan had unexpectedly ascended to the title?

"Of course, Your Grace, the coffers aren't quite as full as they once were," he'd added.

Any fool knew what profligate spenders his father and brother had been. What he'd inherited was a ruinously expensive house, a title, and hell all else. The disposition, turning nastier by the day, was all his. Perhaps he did have a reason for it, but the angels of his better nature appealed to him to at least remember his manners.

Stop being an arse.

"You will stay with us, then, at least until you're feeling better," he found himself saying. He forced an agreeable expression to his face and wondered if he looked as pained as he felt.

Mrs. York lifted her hand, evidently with some effort, and waved it in his direction.

"We couldn't possibly be an imposition, Your Grace," she said weakly.

Josephine smiled.

Martha stared up at the ceiling.

"Of course you must," he said. "I won't hear of your leaving until you're back to yourself. If you'll pardon me, I'll go and make arrangements now."

He wanted away from them. As far away as he could get, knowing that politeness—drilled into him by his nurses and nanny—would dictate he saw them again shortly to ensure they were comfortably settled.

Turning, he made his way out of the room and down the corridor, knowing his peaceful life had been irreparably destroyed, at least for the next few days.

"Your Grace."

He stopped, halted by Frederick's appearance.

"The wagon is here, sir."

The wagon. Oh, yes, the bequest he didn't want.

"Send it around to the stables, Frederick," he said. The sooner he accepted the gift, the sooner the three of them would be gone. With any luck, Mrs. York would recover quickly and yearn for home posthaste.

"Shall I have it unpacked, sir?"

"Yes, but leave it in one of the unused stalls."

He never went to the stables anymore. Putting the contents of the wagon there would mean he didn't have to see any of York's work.

Frederick bowed slightly to him as he always did, taking his look of consternation off down the corridor.

She'd taken away the pleasure he'd felt in his invention. Did she know it? Did the sober and pitying Martha York know she'd single-handedly ruined the whole of it for him?

He didn't know who he was angrier at, her or York for going and dying on him.

Dear God, please don't let the grandmother die, too. He could just imagine the chaos that event would induce.

WHEN MARTHA LEARNED of the duke's arrangements, she almost threw her hands up in exasperation. Her grandmother was feeling faint. The last thing she needed to do was to climb yet another set of stairs to the guest suites located on the second floor.

The duke, however, exonerated himself by sending the housekeeper and four footmen to the parlor. Gran was convinced to lie down on a contraption of canvas sheeting supported by two poles. In that manner, her grandmother was carried up the gilded sweeping stairs.

"We put your grandmother in the Florence room," the housekeeper said as they followed at a sedate pace behind the footmen.

The woman had introduced herself minutes earlier

as Mrs. Browning. A singular name, since it seemed everything about the woman was brown. She had curly brown hair, warm brown eyes, and wore a dark brown dress with brown shoes. At her neck was a cameo, again in shades of brown, revealing the silhouette of a young woman.

"I'm having the Palermo and Naples rooms prepared for you and your sister, unless you would prefer to share a room."

The last was said in the form of the question. Martha shook her head.

"If it isn't too much trouble," she said. "Two rooms would be fine."

She'd never shared a room with Josephine and she didn't want to start now, even in difficult circumstances. Josephine was a chatterbox intent on sharing her opinion about a great many subjects, including anything she saw or felt. Unfortunately, a great many of those opinions were complaints. Nothing was quite as perfect as Josephine thought it should be.

The fact that Josephine had not said one word since the duke had left them was an aberration, one that had her glancing back at her sister. Josephine's eyes were wide as she was taking in their progress up the stairs and down the corridor. Evidently Sedgebrook had done for her what no amount of pleading could: made her cease complaining.

"His Grace has sent for the physician," Mrs. Browning was saying. "Dr. Reynolds doesn't live far away."

Her estimation of the duke's character went up another notch. "Please convey my thanks to him for that. I'm sorry we're such an imposition."

The housekeeper didn't disagree with Martha's assessment, only smiled gently.

"These things happen, don't they? I'm sure your grandmother will be fine in a day or so. And then you'll have all this to look back on as an adventure."

She would just as soon have stayed at Griffin House, but she didn't explain to the housekeeper why they were here. Nor did she say a word about the duke and his stubbornness. If he'd agreed to come and get her father's bequest, she wouldn't have had to travel here in the first place. Consequently, Gran wouldn't have been worn-out.

At least half of the blame was his, a comment she didn't make.

The footmen hesitated halfway down the hall. Mrs. Browning made her way to a door, opening it to reveal the guest chamber set aside for Gran.

The room was richly appointed, with rust-colored curtains matching the bed drapes and counterpane. All of the furniture was beautifully carved mahogany and looked as if it would endure for hundreds of years.

She thought she understood why the rooms were named after cities in Italy when she saw the mural painted along one wall of the Florence room. Her suspicion was verified when Mrs. Browning escorted her to the room assigned to be hers. Here one wall was decorated with scenes of the Mediterranean and the Bay of Naples.

She stood there for a moment, marveling at the detail the artist had provided. Clotheslines stretched between the buildings, so realistically drawn she could almost hear the flapping of the shirts in the afternoon breeze.

"The 10th Duke of Roth painted all of these. His Grace's brother. He so loved Italy. It's where the poor soul died. I think he would have painted every room at Sedgebrook, but he was taken from us too soon."

She wanted to ask more about the artist duke, but thought any questions would be too intrusive. After all, she was only a guest and a reluctantly hosted one.

"We keep country hours at Sedgebrook," the housekeeper said at the door. "Dinner is at seven. Would you like me to send a maid to direct you to the dining room? Or would you prefer trays in your rooms?"

Dinner in their rooms would entail extra effort on the part of the staff and she didn't want to be any more of a burden. When she said as much to the housekeeper, the woman smiled.

"It's one and the same, miss. Either a place at the dining table or a tray, it's no bother. It's what you prefer."

"A tray would be ideal, then, Mrs. Browning."

She wished they weren't a day away from Griffin House. If Gran didn't hate trains so much, Martha would have made the arrangements for all of them to return home in a private car, leaving Charles to bring the carriage at his own pace. She didn't want to agitate Gran, however, so it was best if she just bided her time, and was patient—as difficult as it was—allowing circumstances to play out.

After the housekeeper left, she went to the room across the hall.

Josephine answered her knock with a broad smile.

"Isn't Sedgebrook the most wonderful place in the whole wide world, Martha? Can't you just imagine the balls we could have here? People would come from all over England to attend. It's so empty-feeling now, as if it wants to be filled with people."

"Gran is ill," she said. "That's where your thoughts should be, Josephine."

"Why should I worry? You do it so well for both of us."

She didn't have a response to Josephine's barb, but it didn't matter. Her sister carried on with her self-absorbed monologue.

"Of course, the duke is lame, but a title could go a long way to making a woman forget certain things. What a pity he isn't as handsome as Mr. Burthren."

Josephine was wrong. The duke wasn't lame. How rude of her to call him so. He'd been injured, which was obvious. He was in pain, which was a certainty as well, at least to anyone who cared to look. He was also proud and didn't like for people to see him maneuver with his walking stick.

What had happened to him?

Her father had told her that Hamilton had recently come into the dukedom at the unexpected death of his older brother. She didn't know any more than that. Nor had she ever considered he might be handsome or arresting. Or that she would have such a profound reaction to him.

"I'm going to go sit with Gran," Martha said, determined not to think of the duke any further. "I've asked the housekeeper to bring us a dinner tray."

"I think that would be the height of rudeness, Martha. I think we should take dinner with our host."

She didn't remind Josephine that the Duke of Roth wasn't happy about them being there. Insisting on sharing a meal with him would be like poking a stick in the eye of a wounded bear. No, it was best if they simply kept to themselves.

Josephine, however, wasn't happy about her decision. She sent her more than one annoyed glance as they made their way down the corridor to the Florence room.

To her surprise, her grandmother was sitting up in bed, watching as Amy was unpacking a trunk.

"When did you have a trunk loaded onto the coach?" Martha asked, surprised.

"One must always plan for contingencies, Martha."

"It looks as if you've planned for a week, Gran, if not a fortnight."

Her grandmother only smiled at her, the color back in her cheeks.

"Are you feeling better?"

"A trifle," Gran said.

Attired in one of her lace-trimmed nightgowns, her grandmother looked none the worse for wear propped up in the grand Italian-style bed. The mahogany headboard behind her was richly carved with grapes and vines, the dark wood a perfect backdrop for her snowy white hair and blue eyes.

If she didn't know any better, she would think Gran was feigning illness. Yet it would be so unlike her grandmother that Martha immediately dismissed the thought. Perhaps the trunk was only a sign of Gran's practicality showing once again.

When the knock came, Martha answered the door. A maid stood there with a tray of tea and crackers.

"I was feeling a bit peckish," Gran explained. "It will tide me over until dinner."

Josephine plopped down on the chair next to the window.

"She won't let us go down to dinner with the duke,"

she said. "She's a martinet, Gran. You have to do something about her."

"We haven't been invited to dinner, Josephine," Martha said, conscious of the maid's presence in the room.

Thankfully, Josephine didn't continue with her complaints. Instead, she began to describe the wonders of her room to Gran, who listened with great interest.

Gran really did look as if she felt better. Had the spell at the top of the steps been something temporary or had it been a warning sign of another, more serious, condition? Hopefully, the duke's doctor would allay her fears and they could return home to Griffin House tomorrow.

"He's not married, is he?" Josephine asked. "I'm certain we would have heard about a duchess if he were. Of course, there's his atrocious limp."

Truly, didn't Josephine notice the maid?

The girl left, no doubt ready to tell tales of the York women and their gossip.

"Surely His Grace will ask you to dinner soon enough, Josephine," Gran said as Martha returned from the door. "And find you charming."

The imp of suspicion popped its head up again. She studied her grandmother, but Gran avoided her look, choosing to lean back against the pillows, place her linked hands on her chest, and smile at Josephine.

Was this Gran's idea of matchmaking? Surely not. Yet a great many things had happened in the past year she would never have considered, such as her stepmother leaving Griffin House for France without a backward glance and the strange bequest she'd tried for a year to honor.

She hoped the physician arrived quickly. She'd pull him aside and ask if there was any way her grandmother could travel. With any luck the physician would agree that the train would be acceptable and they could be quit of Sedgebrook as soon as possible.

"I'm sure I shan't like what they serve for dinner," Josephine was saying now.

Josephine would complain about Heaven. *Dear God, could the feathers of my wings be a little whiter? There's gold near the tips. Could we have more fluff in that cloud over there? Does St. Peter have to announce the names of the newly arrived in such a loud voice?*

"I'm sure if you don't like what they serve we could ask for something else," she said. "Perhaps some broth, or toast."

"No lamb," Josephine said. "I shall never eat lamb."

Martha only nodded. "No lamb."

The knock on the door was a reprieve and when she went to open it found the housekeeper standing beside a tall thin man in a blue suit. His beard was cut close to his face, but his mustache was easily twice the width of his mouth and curled up on the ends. His brown eyes were kind and amused, as if he found the world a delightful, if puzzling, place.

"Miss York, this is Dr. Reynolds."

Thank heavens. They were one more step closer to getting home.

Chapter 5

$\mathcal{I}$'ll be damned if the woman is going to die on me," Jordan said, staring down into his bowl of soup.

Cook had made his favorite potato soup, but the York women had stolen his appetite. At least they weren't at his dining table.

"Dr. Reynolds says the grandmother needs to rest. She's suffering from exhaustion. She shouldn't have come. If she hadn't come, she wouldn't have exhausted herself." He glanced at Reese. "Do you think that's amusing?"

"I think your reaction to the women is amusing, yes. I've never seen you so out of sorts."

"I have a reason. I'll be damned if the woman is going to die on me," Jordan repeated. "Not here. Not now. Not at Sedgebrook."

"You can do a lot of things, Jordan, but I don't think even you can command the Almighty."

"It has nothing to do with the Almighty," Jordan said. "And everything to do with Martha York."

One of Reese's eyebrows winged upward. "Miss York?"

"She wouldn't leave well enough alone. She insisted on writing me every few weeks. When I didn't answer, did she do as any sane person would do?

Infer from my silence that I didn't wish to correspond with her? No, she just wrote me again. If I hadn't finally answered her, my library would have been papered with her letters."

"Did you read them?"

"Of course I read them," Jordan said.

When Reese didn't say anything, he continued. "I don't want Matthew's bequest, so I thought ignoring her would be enough. Little did I know that she was the most stubborn woman on the planet."

"You've met your match, then."

He put down his spoon and picked up his glass of wine.

Reese smiled. "It wasn't an insult, Jordan. Your tenacity is one of your better traits. Why not accept York's gift? I thought you liked the man."

Jordan sat back in his chair.

"I did," he said, giving Reese the truth. "Very much. I respected him, probably more than any other man I've ever known."

"Even your father? Or Simon?"

"My father died before I really got to know him and Simon was always involved in his interests. He was either running around Europe studying painting or exploring Italy. When we saw each other I think he was vaguely surprised that he had a brother."

"He was much older than you, wasn't he?" Reese asked.

His friend had been strangely intrusive of late, and incessantly curious.

"Eleven years," he said, hoping that Reese would drop the subject of Simon.

"At least your brother left Sedgebrook from time

to time," Reese said, putting an end to his wistful thought.

"He was enthralled with Italy," Jordan said. "He would have remained there year-round, I think, but for twinges of duty. It didn't strike often. He stayed in London and partied when he was home."

"A party or two wouldn't be a bad thing for you. Consider yourself fortunate to have been visited by attractive women, or didn't you notice Josephine York? It would be good practice to talk to her."

"I noticed. I'm not dead. Badly damaged, yes, but not dead. And I don't need any practice. I've had numerous occasions to talk to beautiful women."

"Not lately," Reese said.

"No," he admitted. "Not lately."

"They're heiresses."

"Are they?"

Reese smiled. "The richest in England."

"York Armaments," Jordan said, nodding.

"It's as if Providence delivered them up to you."

Jordan sat back and regarded Reese. "What are you saying? I should convince one of them to marry me? What possible inducement could I give them?"

"The same one you'd give if you went to London to find a wife. You're a duke and the owner of Sedgebrook. Or did you miss that acquisitive glint in the pretty one's eyes?"

"They're both pretty," Jordan said. "Just in different ways."

Reese didn't say anything.

Granted, the older sister wasn't as brightly attractive as the younger one, but Martha had something else. A soberness, perhaps. Or maybe it was strength.

She was decidedly opinionated. He knew that first-hand.

Her hair was interesting. And her eyes. You could tell exactly what she was thinking just by looking at her eyes.

"Martha was instrumental in helping her father," he said, feeling a curious wish to defend her to Reese.

"Was she?"

He nodded. "She was his assistant, I understand. I'd venture to say she knows as much as Matthew about the York Torpedo Ship."

"Why not use the situation to your advantage?"

"In what way?" Jordan asked.

"Perhaps Martha could help you solve your sinking problem."

"I doubt she would," Jordan said. "You didn't see the look on her face when she talked about her father's bequest. Miss York is as annoyed with me as I am her."

He was not about to ask for her assistance with his problem. He would figure out what was causing the vessels to sink. Either one of the seams hadn't been correctly fused or there was a problem with the steering mechanism. As it was, every single one of his torpedo ships had headed straight for the bottom of the lake.

"Matthew figured it out," he said.

Reese took a sip of his wine, then sat back in the chair.

"He got his vessel to work?"

Jordan nodded. "That's what Martha wrote. She didn't tell me how, though."

"Would she share that information?"

"I doubt it," he said.

No, he was definitely not going to seek her help. He didn't want to be the recipient of another of her pitying looks. Or worse, her opinion that he was an idiot. He suspected she wouldn't hesitate to tell him.

He glanced at Reese, saw his smile, and wondered what was amusing his friend so much.

MARTHA COULDN'T SLEEP, despite the mattress being soft and luxurious. Her dinner had been wonderful: potato soup, roast beef with a selection of vegetables, and a perfect pudding at the end. Even the wine had been superlative, but then it would've been. No doubt the Duke of Roth demanded the best of everything.

She finally gave up the effort to sleep and slid from the bed, grabbing her wrapper and donning it before going to the window. The moon was bright enough she could see it through the curtains.

Gran's and Josephine's rooms were on the other side of the corridor and faced the expanse of lawn leading to the woods surrounding Sedgebrook. Her view was of the lake now silver with moonlight.

Perhaps she should have been surprised to see a man standing there on the short dock. A moment later she saw the walking stick and knew it was the duke. Had she somehow known he'd be there?

She didn't attempt to shield herself but stood in the middle of the window watching him. What did he see, looking out over the expanse of the water? Was it pain keeping him awake? Or something else? An unrequited love, perhaps? Did he mourn the loss of someone?

Since she was up, she should go and check on Gran and see if the medicine Dr. Reynolds had given her was working.

"She should be fine," the doctor had said after his examination. "A few days of rest is what I would recommend before traveling back to your home. I've given her a restorative tonic in the meantime."

Had the physician conveyed that information to the duke? If not, she'd have to do it herself in the morning. He would not be pleased, if his reception was indicative of his mood.

She wished he wasn't standing there. She didn't think she'd ever seen anyone quite as alone as the Duke of Roth. She wanted to comfort him in some way, go and stand before him and wrap her arms around his waist, lay her cheek against his chest. His arms would reach out and embrace her.

What a foolish creature she was being. He would no more comfort her than she would do something so forward as to embrace him.

The somber, studious man whose letters she'd read had become firm and fixed in her mind. Yet the image had been shaken because he turned out to be devastatingly handsome. What did that make of her?

She lost track of how long she stood there, moving back only when he turned and slowly made his way back to the house. She stood to the side of the window, not wanting him to see her, and feeling a deep sorrow for him with each punishing step.

JOSEPHINE SURVEYED THE armoire and the dresses Amy had hung there. Tomorrow she'd wear the pale blue dress with the embroidery details.

Martha's interference meant she hadn't been able to see the duke tonight, but there was always a chance she would encounter him in the morning. She wanted to look her best.

Sedgebrook was like a fairy-tale land, one corridor after another leading to a series of unimaginable rooms. She'd already decided she was going to explore the whole of it tomorrow, whether or not doing so would be acceptable or categorized as rude.

She wanted to see everything, all the various parlors and sitting rooms, plus the inner workings of the house. She wasn't going to concern herself with the acres surrounding Sedgebrook. There was time enough to acquaint herself with those after she became the Duchess of Roth. No, for now it would be enough to memorize the placement of the public rooms. Then she'd learn where the duke slept.

First, however, she'd pick out a likely confidante. She'd find a young maid who would be suitably pleased by a little flattery, not to mention a gratuity. That way, she would be informed of the duke's movements and habits, as well as gaining entrance into places normally reserved for the family.

After all, that's what she'd be in little enough time.

Josephine smiled at herself in the mirror, pleased with her appearance. The idea of failing to acquire Sedgebrook never entered her mind. She always got what she wanted, one way or another.

Chapter 6

$\mathcal{M}$artha finally slept, but fitfully, her dreams waking her often during the night. They featured the duke, but not as she'd seen him earlier, a man alone on the dock. The man she imagined wasn't troubled by a limp but walked easily, spoke often, and charmed effortlessly with his smile.

She woke finally, staring up at the ceiling and feeling a strange sense of loss. Closing her eyes didn't bring back her dreams. She was awake and now that she was, there were things to do.

After she dressed, in her only other garment, a lavender dress she'd chosen because it was loose and comfortable, she went to her grandmother's room to see how she'd spent the night.

Breakfast had already been brought to Gran on a tray. Someone had put a bright summer flower in a small vase and Gran and Amy were discussing whether or not the roses should be pruned at Griffin House.

Her grandmother didn't look the least bit ill, but Martha didn't remark about the color in her cheeks or the fact that the empty plates revealed her appetite was healthy.

After Josephine joined her, they were led by one of Sedgebrook's maids down the grand staircase.

Josephine was looking around, taking in the expensive appointments, the brass-and-crystal chandeliers, the curiosities set inside the niches along the wall. She seemed to note the thickness of the carpet beneath her feet, the gilded frames of the portraits lining the hall. Martha could almost see her tallying up the cost of everything in her mind.

She truly wished the doctor hadn't prescribed three days of rest for Gran. The quicker they left Sedgebrook the better.

Their breakfast was to be served in the Morning Parlor, a sunny room on the east side of the house. The walls were hung with a patterned yellow silk replicated on the cushions of the chairs around the mahogany rectangular table.

The gold-framed sketches hanging on the wall caught her eye. At first she thought the artist duke might have drawn them, but they seemed to date from the time of Sedgebrook's construction, each detailing a section of the great house and the gardens as they were being built.

Breakfast was served buffet style, the silver chafing dishes placed on the sideboard along the wall. She wondered if the leftover food would be going to the staff or to the poor. As it was, it looked as if Sedgebrook's cook thought she would be feeding a small army this morning.

She and Josephine helped themselves before taking a place at the dining table. Despite the fact that her sister kept glancing toward the doorway, they weren't joined by anyone. They might have been guests in a luxurious but empty hotel.

Josephine kept up a running commentary about Sedgebrook, her enchantment with the house not only evident but troubling. When their breakfast was finished, Josephine stood.

"I'm for a walk," she said, placing her napkin on the table and standing. "It's a beautiful day."

"I'd prefer you sit with Gran."

Her sister didn't say anything, just gave her a faint smile. She knew what the look meant—Josephine was going to do what she wanted. She also suspected Josephine wasn't going walking as much as exploring.

"It would be rude to wander through Sedgebrook without permission, Josephine."

"Of course it would," her sister said. "You don't need to lecture me on manners, Martha. I'm not the one who seems to annoy the duke."

She hadn't annoyed him, not personally. No doubt he'd been irritated at the situation, but not at her. At least he shouldn't have been.

There was only one thing she needed to do today— ensure the duke understood where her father's notes were located and how to translate his journals. In addition, if the duke had any questions about the remainder of her father's inventions, she wanted to be able to answer them.

She needed to find Charles and let him know about the change of plans. Plus, she might as well go ahead and send the wagon driver home.

She found one of the maids industriously cleaning a carpet runner in the hallway not far from the Morning Parlor and asked for directions to the stables. She found her way outside only after navigating a series of corridors, getting lost, and asking for guidance again.

The stables were located some distance away and built of the same yellowish stone and tiled roof as the main house. She was surprised at the size of the complex, but then everything at Sedgebrook was a little larger than it needed to be. A large fenced paddock was to the right of the building. Beyond was a grassy valley where a few horses were grazing.

Their carriage and the empty wagon sat in a graveled area to the left of the main building. Inside, she stopped a curly-headed stableboy and asked for the stablemaster only to be told he was taking breakfast at the house. When she asked if he knew Charles or their wagon driver, the boy was willing to go in search of both men.

"Does the duke have a workroom nearby?" she asked before he left.

"A workroom, miss?"

"A place where he works on his torpedo ship," she said. At the boy's blank glance, she realized she needed to rephrase her request. "I need to know where they put the contents of the wagon we brought."

He surprised her by turning and walking to the end of the row of stalls, pointing to one.

"Right there, miss."

She walked to where he stood and glanced inside.

To her shock, all her careful planning and packing had been for nothing. Her father's journals were stacked every which way on top of the crates. Cards with notes in his handwriting spilled out onto the packed earth floor. Bessie, the last prototype of the York Torpedo Ship, was propped up in the corner, the crate buried in hay. Two of the other crates were half-open, their contents spilling out.

Had the pendulums been damaged? What about the gyroscope that had been her father's last purchase?

She stared at the destruction, her anger building. She'd spent hours packing everything, worrying about the damage that might occur to the delicate scientific instruments. All for nothing. Only for the Duke of Roth to take her father's work and treat it like so much manure.

"Where does the duke work?" she asked, trying to contain herself. "Where is his laboratory?"

"Miss?"

"Where does he spend his days?"

He looked toward the main house.

"Does he never go out on the lake?" Had she misunderstood everything? Did the man have no interest in the torpedo ship?

"Oh, yes, miss. Or he's in the boathouse."

"Where is it?"

He gave her the directions and she thanked him, grateful she'd been able to be civil before emotion overtook her.

The path to the boathouse was wide and graveled, but a far distance from the main house. Each step seemed to push against the boundaries of her anger.

How dare he?

How dare he treat her father's bequest so shabbily?

How dare he insult her father's memory in such a way?

Being the Duke of Roth did not give him the right to impugn the honor of another human being, especially not such a good man as Matthew York.

Her father was well respected in scientific circles, in business, and as the head of the company bearing their name. His invention could save lives, could end wars early, could help England retain its dominance over the seas.

And what had the Duke of Roth done? Thrown it away. Treated it as if it was nothing more than a child's old toy, well-worn and broken.

If she hadn't been so angry, she might have stopped to marvel at the view of Sedgebrook's lake, the lawn manicured down to the banks, the blooming wildflowers along the path, and the breeze smelling of water and fish. If she hadn't been in such a hurry to reach the duke, she might have even taken advantage of one of the benches situated at a picturesque spot and taken in the scene.

Instead, she increased her pace when she saw the boathouse. The structure sat on a small rise, the dock jutting from the first floor out into the lake. The second floor was dotted with windows, a terrace, and a white ornamental railing.

She marched to the door of the building and opened it, quickly taking in the workbenches and shelves filled with material and equipment. The area was neat and orderly, unlike her father's cottage when he was deeply involved in a project. It became a function of her day to go behind him and straighten up his mess.

Do you need this, Father? Shall I put this up? Can we throw this in the rubbish?

She was not going to cry. She was most definitely not going to cry in front of the arrogant, unkind, beastly Duke of Roth.

"What are you doing here, Miss York?"

She heard him before she could see him, her eyes taking a moment to adjust to the gloom after the bright summer morning.

He was sitting at the long workbench stretching the width of the room. Next to him sat Mr. Burthren.

"How could you?" she asked. "How could you simply toss all my father's work away?"

"I beg your pardon?"

"You should," she said, nodding emphatically. "You truly should. You've been very kind when it came to my grandmother, Your Grace, and I appreciate your hospitality. But you've been beastly about my father and his work and I don't appreciate it one whit. How could you?"

He didn't say a word. Not one word. Not one word of explanation. Not one single syllable to try to make her understand or to defend himself. He simply kept silent, looking at her with his handsome face stern and unmoving.

"I could hate you at this moment," she heard herself saying. "I could. Do you know that on his deathbed my father spoke of you? Some of his last words were for you. 'Have you heard from Hamilton? Has he written?' But you didn't write. You didn't come. And now, Your Grace, now you've done the worst you could do. You've thrown all his work into a stall in your stable."

Turning, she left the boathouse, her anger spent, tears she'd pushed back now winning the battle. She brushed them off her cheeks, overwhelmed by grief.

"Miss York!"

She was not going to pay any attention to Mr. Burthren. He was going to say something she didn't want to hear, words that would be critical and no doubt correct. She shouldn't have spoken in such a way to the duke, their reluctant host. She really shouldn't have lost her temper.

"Miss York!"

He was gaining on her and, short of gathering up her skirts and beginning to run, she had no option but to stop, turn, and face him.

"You've been crying," he said, his warm brown eyes filled with concern.

"Yes, Mr. Burthren, I've been crying. Go ahead and lecture me about my rudeness. I no doubt deserve it."

"I didn't follow you to lecture you, Miss York, but to bring you back to the boathouse. His Grace wishes to talk with you."

"I don't wish to talk to him. I've said everything I wish to say."

"He deserves a hearing, don't you think?"

"No," she said, turning and beginning to walk away again.

"There's a reason he didn't want your father's bequest. Aren't you curious why?"

She was not going to listen to the man. She kept walking.

"No," she said. "I'm not. I would have thought he'd be thrilled to accept everything my father wanted him to have. Evidently, he doesn't care. No doubt he thinks it's all worthless."

"That's not the case, Miss York, I can assure you."

She stopped again, turned, and looked up at him.

"Then I don't understand," she said. "Why put everything in the stable?"

"Because of his honor," he said.

It was such a strange answer she didn't move.

"Jordan has a rather well-developed sense of honor," he continued. "Overdeveloped, perhaps. If he has one overriding flaw, that's it. Other people might be able to get away with telling a lie, but he doesn't. Nor can he abide anyone in his circle who does. In school his nickname was Saint Jordan. Not a positive sobriquet, by the way."

"I haven't asked him to lie, Mr. Burthren."

He smiled. "No, of course you haven't. Jordan's honor doesn't limit itself to honesty, Miss York. He dislikes subterfuge of any sort. Or cheating. He was the first to report a boy for cribbing on an exam."

She frowned at him, still not understanding.

"He thinks taking your father's notes and his vessel would be like cheating," he said.

"Why?"

"Because he didn't do the work on the torpedo ship himself."

"He and my father communicated about Bessie every week," she said. "He knows everything about it."

"I understand your father got the vessel to work."

She nodded.

"A great achievement," he said.

"Not as great an achievement as you think, Mr. Burthren. He didn't share the information with anyone."

"Not even you?" he asked, sounding surprised.

She shook her head. "He was saving the information for the duke. That's why giving him my father's notes wouldn't constitute any advantage. The information isn't there."

"Then perhaps you could tell him that."

"I see no reason to have to explain anything to the man."

"Don't judge him too harshly, Miss York. The torpedo ship has been the one thing occupying him for the last year."

She wanted to ask about the duke's accident and why he walked with a limp, but she didn't. First of all, she didn't want Mr. Burthren to know of her interest. Second, it would be rude to talk about the man behind his back—just as they were currently doing.

"Perhaps you could add your expertise to Jordan's work," he said. "As long as you're here. It might be a form of collaboration."

She glanced at him, wondering if he was being sarcastic. Not many men would welcome a female into his sphere of work.

"He truly wants to apologize."

"He has no intention of apologizing," she said, certain of it.

"He told me, 'Go and get her, Reese. I have to explain.'"

"That doesn't constitute an apology."

He didn't answer.

If she returned to the boathouse it would be for her father and not the duke.

Taking a deep breath, she brushed the remnants of tears from her face and nodded.

"For a moment," she said. "Just a moment."

He didn't say a word, merely kept her company as they retraced their steps. At the door to the boathouse he stayed back.

"I'll be here if you need me," he said.

Once more she nodded, opened the door, and stepped inside.

Chapter 7

This time when Martha entered the boathouse she made more of a study of the interior. The ceiling was high, the beams overhead soaring into darkness even on this bright summer morning. Rows and rows of shelves were carefully labeled with the contents and dates. Near the door to the dock, now open to the sparkling water of a sun-drenched lake, were copper forms she recognized as the initial stages of a torpedo ship.

The workbench had two lanterns set on either end. Now extinguished, they served as proof of long nights spent in experimentation.

There was nothing about the boathouse leading her to believe the duke enjoyed spending time on the lake. No boats sat in the bays. No fishing gear stood in the corner, ready to be used. This structure was surprisingly like her father's cottage in its dedication to a task, that of invention and discovery.

"Thank you for coming back," he said.

She turned her head slowly. He was still seated at the workbench, his right hand holding a curling tool. His left held a piece of copper fixed with a small set of gears.

"Mr. Burthren said you wanted to apologize. I told him I didn't think you would."

"Would you have spoken that way to him?" he asked, not looking at her.

"I beg your pardon?"

"Would you have said the same things to him that you did to me?" He studied the part in his hand, crimped a flange of metal, then examined his work.

"I don't know," she said, confused. She hadn't expected the question.

"Women don't. They see something in Reese's eyes, I suppose. They think him kind. Or compassionate. Or understanding. Something I lack."

Since she agreed with that comment, she remained silent.

"I knew your father a great many years," he said. "I was introduced by someone in the War Office."

"I know that. You corresponded and asked him some questions. He was impressed by your knowledge and your curiosity."

"I liked him," he said, surprising her. "More than any other man I've ever met. I would even consider him a mentor."

"Which makes it even less understandable why you would ignore him when he needed you and treat his work with such disdain."

He glanced over at her, answering the second part of her accusation. "Not disdain, Miss York. Never that. I read your letters. I just didn't respond to them. I should have. At least I should have told you how much I regretted Matthew's death. What he meant to me."

She was not going to cry again.

"Your bringing Matthew's work here means that

whatever I achieve from this moment forward won't be mine. He already found the answer. It would be his victory. His torpedo ship."

"No," she said. "He found the answer, but he never told anyone."

His scowl was impressive, but she wasn't cowed by the Duke of Roth.

"I don't understand," he said.

"That last day," she explained. "He found the answer, but he was saving the information for you. But you never came."

"He never told you?"

She shook her head.

"I've tried to recreate what he'd done, but I'm not certain what it was. I think it had something to do with the gyroscope. Or maybe even the pendulum, but none of my experiments have succeeded."

The duke smiled and she had the curious thought that it was fortunate he hadn't smiled before now. Otherwise, she would have acted like a besotted idiot. His face altered and softened. His eyes warmed.

Although improbable and no doubt uncommon, she understood how someone could fall in love at one glance.

"You've been working on your own?"

She nodded.

"Why?" he asked.

"Why not?" she countered. "Are mysteries only to be solved by men?"

"Is that how you think of it? A mystery?"

"Yes." A short answer and the only one she was going to give him. At least until he smiled again. Then she might confess anything.

"Are you angry he didn't tell you?" he asked.

A question she'd never before considered. She gave him the truth, quickly spoken.

"I wasn't angry," she said. "I was hurt. But it was your collaboration and I understood that. What I didn't understand was why you never came."

"Forgive me," he said softly, surprising her yet again.

Just when she thought she had him labeled and categorized, he popped out of his little box and demanded she take another look.

"What happened to you? Were you recovering from your injury?"

"I'm sorry your father died," he said, which was an answer, of sorts. He had no intention of discussing his leg.

Nor should she have asked. She wished she hadn't voiced her curiosity.

She turned to leave, but was stopped by his comment.

"He often wrote about you," he said.

She truly wanted to cry, and she wouldn't allow herself to do so.

"Do you really not know what he discovered?"

In the past few minutes she'd been buffeted by emotions: sadness, regret, compassion, and now irritation again.

"No," she said, turning to look at him once more. "I don't. It should work. It doesn't. I haven't found the answer why. Perhaps you'll have more success."

"Reese suggested that I ask you to help me," he said.

"He said the same to me."

In the silence she studied the shelving around them. Everything was carefully marked, stacked by size and date. Below the shelves were slots for materials including the sheathing to be hammered into the final ship's form.

"I could show you the latest adaptations to Bessie," she finally said.

"Bessie?"

"It's the name of his latest prototype." She smiled. "He named all of them. But you'd have to move my father's things in here." She pointed to an empty space on the far side of the boathouse. "You have room."

He didn't say anything for a long moment. Accepting her help would give her something to do for the three days they were forced to remain at Sedgebrook. Also, she could show him her father's other inventions, explain his notes, perhaps give him an appreciation for the bequest.

"Are you still angry?" he asked.

She linked her fingers together and looked at him. He confused her, excited her, made her think things no proper woman should consider. He also enraged her and hurt her feelings more than any man she'd ever met. Yet she had no intention of telling him the whole truth. Her emotions were hers and right at the moment she didn't want to share them.

He studied her in the shadowed light as if she was a puzzle he'd been given to solve. Her father had often worn the same expression. Copper sheathing, gun powder, and pendulums were much easier to understand than people.

Was he as much a hermit as her father had been? She had the feeling that the answer to understanding the Duke of Roth was tantalizingly close. All she needed was a little more time.

He was evidently not willing to give it to her.

She ended their stalemate by nodding, turning, and heading for the door.

"I'm used to working alone," he said, as she was stepping over the threshold.

"Mr. Burthren was with you earlier," she said.

"He doesn't understand that I prefer solitude. He doesn't like being alone, I suspect, which is why he's unable to accept that state in others."

"Do you have no one transcribing your thoughts? Making notes of things to check?"

"No."

With one hand on the door frame, she glanced over her shoulder.

"Are you not willing to alter your workday a little?"

"No," he said. "I find I don't like change. Not recently."

"Then there's nothing more to say, is there?"

"Yes, there is," he said. "Don't go."

She stopped and glanced back at him.

"I'd be grateful for your help, Miss York. As long as you understand I'm not given to extraneous conversation."

She bit back her smile. "Neither am I, Your Grace."

"Then shall we muddle through? I'm certain we can tolerate anything for a few days."

She didn't know if that was an insult or not.

"Will you help me retrieve my father's things?"

"No."

"No? Because it's not a fitting job for the Duke of Roth?"

"Tell the majordomo, Frederick, that you need assistance. He'll assign someone to help you."

He once more occupied himself with studying the part in his hand.

"I'll return after I talk to your Frederick."

"I'll expect you," he said, not looking at her.

She should walk away from the boathouse and spend the rest of the time at Sedgebrook with Gran. She should not be feeling a surge of anticipation about returning to spar with this strange and unsettling duke.

Yet she knew she'd be back as soon as she could arrange it.

WHAT THE HELL had he done?

He should race after her—not that he could—and tell her he'd changed his mind.

His boathouse was off limits to women. Or to anyone he didn't want there. He endured Frederick's presence or that of a footman from time to time. Nor had he any choice with Reese. His friend simply appeared and veiled—or not so veiled—hints didn't affect Reese.

He was also surprisingly powerless against Martha York's studied indifference. He knew for a fact that it masked a determined character.

He wanted to know what she knew. Even more startling was his curiosity about her. Did she understand the principles guiding the torpedo ships? Did it fascinate her as much as it did him?

She was different from most women he'd known. She didn't seem to care much about her appearance—witness the windblown condition of her curly hair. Or the fact that she'd not worn a hat in the morning sun. She obviously didn't fear browning her skin because it already had a healthy glow, not the pale and pasty hue so favored among London beauties.

Nor was Martha York a coy female. She didn't mince words but came out and said what was on her mind.

She'd pinned his ears to the wall, hadn't she? He'd never been excoriated quite so completely.

He remembered Matthew's comments about her London season.

They do not understand her, those London men. They seek someone who would charm them. Martha doesn't wish to charm them. She wants to know what they think. Are their thoughts weighty or interesting enough?

He couldn't help but wonder if Matthew had described Martha correctly. Or were his words only those of a fond and biased father?

He'd find out in the next three days.

THE MAID'S NAME was Constance and she was a sweet thing, if not exceptionally bright.

It had taken Josephine less than five minutes to convince her that, as a guest of the duke's, she should have access to the closed private rooms, especially the Conservatory.

The girl had proven to be surprisingly informative about some of the furniture in the Duke's Parlor. Evidently, the housekeeper lectured the staff on the history of their surroundings, the better to appreciate the items they tended.

Josephine swept through the third floor after realizing it was set aside mostly for servants' quarters and some storage over the north wing.

The second floor was comprised mostly of bedrooms and newly renovated bathing chambers. Constance had been fulsome in her praise for the new boiler and the special building built for it. Josephine smiled in earnest appreciation, the better to encourage the maid to divulge other secrets of Sedgebrook.

From Constance she learned where the duke's suite was located. The grand staircase intersected the guest rooms from the family quarters and she made mental notes of the directions.

She would give Constance a little gratuity at the end of their explorations and hint that any information about the duke would be appreciated even more.

Of course, the girl would be one of the first changes she made once she became the Duchess of Roth. It would never do to keep a servant who knew too much.

Chapter 8

$\mathcal{M}$artha made her way back to the house and up the stairs to the second floor. Before she sought out Frederick she'd go and check on Gran and, while she was at it, make sure Josephine hadn't gotten into any trouble.

Perhaps she should be as concerned with her own behavior. After all, she was going to put herself within working distance of the Duke of Roth. He was too handsome for her, too charming—when it was obvious he didn't mean to be—and too intriguing.

She wanted to know how he'd been injured, why he felt it so necessary to achieve something of his own, and what he thought about her father's advancements.

Not one of those questions was commonplace. Nor had she learned the answers from reading his letters. She'd learned how his mind worked when reasoning out the problems inherent with the torpedo ship, but she wanted to know more.

The only way she was going to satisfy her curiosity was by working with the man.

She reached Gran's room and knocked softly. When her grandmother answered, she pushed in the door, unsurprised to find her sitting up in bed, reading, a pot of tea on the nightstand, and biscuit crumbs on a plate.

Amy was sitting in the chair by the window. At Martha's entrance, she folded the garment and stood.

"You sit here, Miss Martha," she said. "I'll just go and get some more biscuits."

She smiled at Amy and thanked her.

The windows in the chamber were open to let in the summer breeze. The sunlight formed a large square on the carpet and in the middle of it sprawled a fat orange striped cat.

"That's Hero," Gran said.

Martha edged past the sunlight, but Hero didn't move, merely remained in his position of half on his back and half on his side, allowing the sun to bathe his hairy belly.

"Why Hero?" she asked.

"He's quite the mouser, I understand, and the father to countless litters. There's one in the barn right now."

Evidently, Gran had made friends with the staff.

"You look like you're feeling better," she said.

Would her grandmother admit to playing ill? Or should she say something about her suspicions? This journey to Sedgebrook was a perfect opportunity for Josephine. The duke was young, handsome, and unmarried. Josephine was his perfect foil. She was young, beautiful, wealthy, and desirous of marriage.

"I am," Gran said. "I think there's something magical in the tonic Dr. Reynolds gave me. I need to make sure my doctor has the same formula."

She wasn't going to second-guess the physician, but it didn't seem as though Gran truly needed to rest for three more days.

"Are you absolutely certain you don't feel up to going home tomorrow?" she asked.

Her grandmother closed the book she was reading and studied her.

"Why? Is there some reason you want to leave, Martha?"

She shook her head.

In three days a great deal could happen. She could become even more fascinated with the duke. Josephine could make a nuisance of herself exploring Sedgebrook.

"How is Josephine faring?"

She glanced at her grandmother.

"She seems quite taken with Sedgebrook," Martha said.

She'd known, ever since she was a girl, that where Josephine was concerned, she always came second place. Josephine's needs came first.

As a child she used to be afraid of thunderstorms until Josephine awoke terrified. Everyone in the household flocked to her room to comfort her. Occasionally, one of the maids would notice that she was standing in her doorway wishing she wasn't alone. She'd learned to depend on herself. Her father had often commented that she was the most self-reliant female he knew.

She never told him why.

Another lesson she learned because of Josephine: she might call Marie mother, but it was all too evident that she wasn't Marie's child.

Her father, poor dear, was always more concerned with his experiments than he was his household. Occasionally, he would ask Martha if she was happy and she would always answer yes.

When Gran came to live with them about five years ago, everything changed. She had a feeling that she had an ally, even though Gran had never said such a thing. She had, however, overheard her grandmother say a few unflattering things about Marie.

When Marie had left Griffin House for the entertainments of Paris, Gran had let slip her dislike.

"Perhaps I'm being too hard on her. If she hadn't been so greedy, Matthew probably would never have married again. She was aggressive, like a hunter who sees a wounded fawn. She went after him and he had no chance from the beginning."

She'd been surprised at her grandmother's revelations. Now she wondered if Gran knew Josephine had also inherited Marie's acquisitive nature. When Josephine wanted something woe to the person who tried to stop her.

Before she could confide further in her grandmother, the door opened and Josephine swept into the room. Her color was high, but her hair was perfect, as was her appearance. Josephine could walk through a mud puddle and emerge immaculate.

"Sedgebrook is simply glorious," she said in greeting. "Every room has something to recommend it. The duchess's sitting room alone will make you sigh. Everything is upholstered in a pale peach silk with tiny flowers embroidered on it. I understand it comes from France, of course. The walls are upholstered in the same peach silk. I wouldn't change a thing in the room."

Martha stared at her sister, uncertain whether to be aghast or embarrassed.

"How did you find out the fabric came from France? Did you ask the housekeeper?"

Josephine waved one hand toward Martha as if her questions were foolish.

"Of course not. Simply one of the upstairs maids. A knowledgeable girl. I had her unlock the Conservatory for me so I could see the inside of it."

No, she was both embarrassed and aghast.

"You can't simply go traipsing through Sedgebrook as if you own it," she said.

Josephine glanced at her and smiled. Someone else might interpret it as a sweet or maybe even a condescending expression. But she knew her sister well enough to know it signified something else. Josephine had something planned.

"I don't think you should . . ." she began, only to be interrupted by a knock on the door.

She expected it to be Amy, returning with another plate of biscuits, but instead, the duke stood there. He'd put on a jacket and was no longer attired in just a white shirt and black trousers. She preferred him in more casual dress, but regardless of what he wore, he was a strikingly handsome man.

He stood there for a moment, looking at Gran and Josephine. For some reason, he didn't look at her as he took a few steps into the room, his slow progress making her heart ache. Josephine, thankfully, found the view from the window suddenly fascinating. Gran, however, was studying the duke with sharp eyes.

"His Grace has a boathouse set up almost like Father's cottage," Martha blurted out, uncomfortable with the silence.

She'd intended to draw her grandmother's attention. Instead, she succeeded with her sister. Josephine's head whipped around so fast it seemed to be mounted on a swivel.

"It's quite large," Martha continued. "He has a great deal more space than the cottage."

"You've been busy," Josephine said, the words so soft she knew they were meant only for her.

"You mustn't mind Martha, Your Grace. She was Father's assistant. I can't tell you how many times she could be found up to her waist in the muck when she was tinkering with one of his machines."

The duke studied Josephine for a moment, his face expressionless. Instead of answering her, he glanced at Gran.

"How are you feeling, Mrs. York?"

"Much better, Your Grace. Thank you for your concern. And thank you, as well, for your hospitality. Everyone on your staff has been exceedingly kind and gracious."

He inclined his head. "Is there anything they haven't done? Is there anything you need?"

"Nothing at all," Gran said, smiling. "Except time, perhaps. Dr. Reynolds said I should rest for a few more days. Thank you for giving me the opportunity to do so."

He nodded, his face still not revealing what he felt. The expression struck Martha as being ducal, but he hadn't been reared for the role. He'd been a naval officer when he'd met her father. Had he commanded men? Had he been aboard ship?

She really should quell her curiosity about him.

"I'm afraid my confinement is tiresome for my granddaughters," Gran continued to Martha's horror.

"Unfortunately, we have no entertainments planned at Sedgebrook," the duke said.

Gran smiled. "Then perhaps they could join you and Mr. Burthren for dinner."

She couldn't look at her grandmother. Nor could she glance at the duke. Josephine, however, didn't have any such reservations. Her sister sauntered over to the end of the bed, only feet from where the duke stood.

"What a pleasure that would be, Your Grace," she purred, lowering her voice until it was a throaty contralto.

Martha almost rolled her eyes. She'd seen Josephine's behavior around men. It always reminded her of a cat's insistent charm just before it was fed.

She glanced at Hero still sunning himself. The cat lifted his head and returned her look. He seemed to raise one eyebrow as if to ridicule her concerns.

"Then perhaps you and your sister could join us for dinner," the duke said, bowing slightly.

Josephine smiled while Martha wished the floor would open up and swallow her whole.

"Miss York, were you able to speak to Frederick?" he asked Martha.

"Not yet," she said. "But I shall in a few minutes."

He nodded. "Then I'll expect you at the boathouse later," he said, turning to leave.

The minute the door closed behind him, Josephine rounded on her.

"What did he mean, Martha?" Josephine asked.

Twin lines formed between Josephine's brows. Her eyes narrowed and her lips thinned until they almost disappeared in her face. Any one of her many admirers would be surprised to see her now.

"I'm going to help him with his ship," Martha said. "It's what Father would have wanted."

"Gran," Josephine said, turning to their grandmother, "you can't allow this. It's scandalous. She and the duke will be alone. In the boathouse."

"If it makes you feel better, Josephine," Martha said, annoyed, "I'll ask for a footman to be in attendance. Would that satisfy your sense of decorum?"

She knew exactly why her sister was upset. She was going to be with the Duke of Roth and Josephine wasn't. But there was a difference between them. She had no intention of trying to charm the duke.

Besides, she wasn't Josephine. She wasn't as attractive. Nor did she have an affinity for flirting.

"I'll go with you," Josephine said, her smile once more restored. "I'm better than a footman."

Martha stared at her sister. The duke wouldn't be pleased. Unless, of course, she could convince Josephine to sit there in silence. Josephine would fill the air with chatter. If not about herself, then how dark the boathouse was, how much it smelled of the water, how boring she thought the silence was.

Perhaps her thoughts were unsisterly. Even more disturbing was the idea that maybe she'd been wrong. Perhaps she wanted to try to charm the duke after all.

Chapter 9

"Why are we going this way?" Josephine asked.

"There's no other way to reach the stables."

"I'm not going to the stables," Josephine said, stopping in the middle of the path. "We were going to the boathouse."

"We have to go to the stables first," Martha said, trying to push back her irritation. "I have to move Father's crates."

Josephine grabbed her skirts and mumbled something under her breath. Martha caught only a few words, but it was enough to make her frown at her sister.

"It's no good complaining," she said. "I'm responsible for Father's work."

"Not anymore," Josephine said. "You've given it to the duke and it's his now."

She didn't bother trying to explain what had happened. Her sister simply didn't care and attempting to make her understand would be a waste of time and effort.

Frederick had told her a footman would meet her at the stall and she could direct him to load the material into a handcart, the better to transport it to the boathouse. She hadn't, however, thought Josephine would be following her, punctuating every step with another complaint.

The smell was horrid.

The flies were abominable.

You would think Josephine had never been around horses before when it was just the opposite. She rode every day, taking one of her three favorite horses out around Griffin House. Josephine never rode with a companion, saying no one could keep up with her. Martha wasn't as good a horsewoman as her sister. She respected horses, but she could go for a long time without riding one.

Once inside the stables Josephine stopped to admire one of the duke's stallions. Martha glanced at the name above the stall: Ercole.

"Aren't you a beauty?" Josephine said, rubbing the horse's nose.

Martha continued on to the stall, catching sight of both the stablemaster and a young man in dark blue livery.

"His Grace said to bring everything, Miss York," the older man said. "Is there anything we should start with?"

She nodded, directing them to which crates she wanted loaded first.

Grabbing a small bag packed with the most recent notes she'd taken, she put it atop the handcart—a wagon pulled by a human being rather than a horse. Once the cart was filled, she followed the footman, a young man by the name of Ben, with bright red hair, a freckled face, and a pleasant smile, out of the stables and down the path to the boathouse.

Josephine had rejoined her by this time and was raving about the duke's horses.

"I'm going to ride that stallion," she said.

"You didn't bring your habit," Martha said. A second later she looked at her sister. "You didn't, did you?"

"If I did?"

She didn't know what to say. Had both Josephine and her grandmother planned for this visit to be something other than what she'd anticipated? This trip to Sedgebrook had been to carry out her father's wishes, not to parade Josephine in front of the duke.

She wasn't feeling betrayed as much as irritated by both her relatives.

"You're going to have to remain silent while we're working," she said.

Josephine didn't say anything, only sent her a quick look. She noted, however, that Josephine was also checking her appearance as they walked.

The dress her sister was wearing was a lovely blue on white print, the sash at her waist a matching blue. Her hat had a large brim to better shade her complexion from the sun and was secured by a ribbon Josephine had tied to one side under her chin.

She couldn't help but wonder how many dresses Josephine had packed. The original plan was to stay overnight at an inn after delivering the wagon to Sedgebrook. She'd brought only one additional dress, the pale lavender garment she'd worn this morning. Nor had she bothered grabbing her bonnet before leaving the house. A bonnet only made her hair worse. Nothing would stop it from curling, especially being so close to the water.

She was being silly, almost like Josephine in wanting male approbation. Her sister flirted with every man in sight, even the tradesmen who appeared at

Griffin House. Was it something she'd learned or inherited from her mother? Marie had been the same, exceptionally charming, but more so toward men.

It was as if she developed a separate personality when dealing with males. She'd seen Josephine change when a man walked into a room. The effect was startling and disconcerting. She was left wondering exactly which person was actually Josephine.

She had no doubt her sister would spend the whole time at the boathouse flirting with the duke. He would, no doubt, allow himself to be charmed like all of Josephine's conquests.

Once they were in sight of the boathouse, the footman pulled off the path and let them precede him. Martha grabbed the valise and led the way, ignoring Josephine's complaints about the weeds, the smell of the lake, and the blinding sun.

The door to the boathouse was open, but she knocked on the frame. When she heard the duke speak, she stepped inside, momentarily blinded until her eyes adjusted to the dimness.

"Your Grace?" Josephine called, her voice taking on the velvet tone she used when talking to men.

"Yes?"

Martha could finally see him, seated at the bench on the far side of the boathouse. He'd taken off his jacket again, revealing his white shirt, the sleeves rolled up to his elbows.

She'd never before admired a man's arms. What was wrong with her?

"I've brought my father's things," Martha said.

"Our father," Josephine interjected.

She sent Josephine a quick look, but her sister

wasn't paying any attention. Instead, Josephine had a smile on her face as she looked at the duke.

If he was still simply a naval officer, as he'd once been, would Josephine be so charming?

Pushing that disloyal thought away, she placed the valise she carried onto the workbench, opened it, and withdrew a sheaf of papers.

"These are the last of my father's notes," she said.

He nodded, but didn't reach for the notes.

"What a lovely place you've made this," Josephine said.

Martha glanced at her sister in disbelief.

The whole of the interior of the boathouse was shadowed. There were no flowers or other embellishments about the structure. The only thing "lovely" about the boathouse was its spaciousness and the lure of the bright afternoon in the glint of the sun off the lake.

Josephine, however, wasn't finished.

"Not only are you the Duke of Roth, but you're so clever, Your Grace."

The duke turned on his stool and regarded Josephine with some interest. Next, he would say something about her appearance, how she made the boathouse brighter with her beauty. Then he'd smile at her and the two of them would be encased in a special bubble of mutual attraction.

Meanwhile, she'd feel unwanted and invisible.

"Not as clever as your father, Miss York," he said. Surprisingly, he looked over at Martha. "I have your father's latest letters," he said, pulling a box forward. "Would it be any inconvenience for you to look through them?"

"You want to see if there's anything he told you that I didn't list in his notes?"

He nodded.

Actually, it was a wise idea. Her father meant to include ideas in his daily notes but sometimes forgot. She often had to ask him to fill in the gaps between days or even processes.

She took the box from him and looked around for a place to sit. He gestured to a stool not far away. She grabbed it with one hand, dragging it below a clear spot on the workbench.

"Well, I can certainly see you didn't plan on visitors," Josephine said on a trilling laugh. "Wherever shall I sit?"

Any of Josephine's admirers would have immediately stood and offered his stool to her. The fact that the duke blatantly ignored her sister was not only startling, but it evidently infuriated Josephine.

"Shall I just stand here, Your Grace?" she asked, her voice losing its seductive timbre and carrying a note of irritation.

"I'm afraid you're right, Miss York," he said, not looking in Josephine's direction. "I've not planned on visitors. Perhaps dinner would be a better place to converse."

Martha didn't turn when Josephine flounced out of the boathouse a few minutes later. She'd seen her sister's tantrums often enough to be able to picture Josephine's expression, the clenched fists on her skirts, and her stomping progress back to the house.

Neither of them spoke. The duke didn't offer any explanations for his rudeness. Nor did she attempt to excuse Josephine's behavior. Sometimes, silence was better than words.

Perhaps she should leave, too, demonstrating a loyalty to Josephine her sister honestly didn't deserve in this instance. She knew, when she next saw her sister, that Josephine was going to criticize her for all the things she should have said, but didn't. If she was going to bear the brunt of Josephine's anger, she might as well do what she wanted first, spend some time with the surprising Duke of Roth.

She was startled to find that her father had written Hamilton more often than she realized. Although she'd read each of the duke's letters, she'd rarely seen the letters her father had sent him.

Five years of letters were carefully arranged by date. Some letters were dated the same day. Each looked well-read. In addition, the duke had made notes in the margins. A great many times his comments had echoed her own thoughts. Sometimes he questioned things she'd never considered.

She found herself embarrassed about her father's praise. He wrote about her in almost every letter, but his words weren't limited to her assistance with his work. No, he even talked about her sense of humor, her penchant for laughing at the most awful jests, her frustration with being unable to make something work the way she wanted. To her horror, she discovered her father had even commented on her disastrous season.

I cannot think that Martha will find these entertainments to her liking. She does not suffer fools gladly, my daughter. She has, instead, a wish to engage people on intellectual pursuits and, in doing so, is often considered strange or odd.

She could only stare at the letter, the paper trembling in her hands just a little. Surely her father hadn't meant those words to sound so cruel.

Without speaking, the duke pulled the letter from her hands and read it.

"Your feelings are hurt, I take it?" he said. "Foolish of you, if so."

She glanced to the left and saw that he was studying her intently.

"Why foolish?"

"Your father obviously had the greatest admiration for you, Miss York. He merely meant you were too intelligent for most people. That's not an insult."

She blinked at him.

"Surely you've thought the same thing yourself," he said. "Or will you deny it? Have you never found yourself in a group and felt alone?"

"Yes," she said. "Not because of my great and magnificent intelligence, but because I was different."

"Ah, but don't you see? You're different because of your great and magnificent intelligence. It's been my experience that most people don't want to think. They simply wish to *be*. But being isn't enough, don't you see? We were given our brains—even women—to use them. They're not simply there to put a hat on and look pretty."

"You needn't say it like that. 'Even women.'"

He only smiled at her, the expression so unexpectedly charming she was silenced.

"He loved you," he softly said. "And he was proud of you."

"Thank you," she said, reaching out and taking the letter back.

She truly did appreciate his kindness, especially since she hadn't expected it.

"He had the greatest admiration for you, too," she added. "He always said how logical you were, how you made these leaps of thought that saved him days and weeks of worrying about a problem."

"I liked him," he said. "I respected him, but I found myself liking him, too. He had a sense of humor that showed in his writings. He was capable of poking fun at himself, which I found endearing."

She would not look at him, especially since she was trying, desperately, to blink her tears away. His words brought back her father so strongly he might have been there in the boathouse with them.

After clearing her throat she said, "I'm sorry I said what I did earlier. I shouldn't have. I know you would have been there if you could. I'm glad he had you for a friend. My father didn't have many friends. He, too, didn't suffer fools gladly."

She glanced at him to find him looking at her. She smiled and he responded in kind.

She really shouldn't be here alone with the duke. Not when her thoughts weren't entirely on her father's work.

JOSEPHINE AVOIDED THE worst of the brambles on the side of the path. This was a new dress, a garment her mother had sent her from France and she wouldn't have it ruined. At least she cared about her appearance and her wardrobe.

Gran wouldn't be pleased to hear how rude Martha had been. Nor had her sister done one thing to make the duke offer her somewhere to sit, or even ask her to remain. No, Martha had been insufferable and Gran would have something to say about her behavior.

What a pity Martha was too old to be sent to her room with only tea and crackers for supper. But if Gran was angry enough, perhaps she could keep

Martha from attending the dinner with the duke and his friend. That would mean she'd be alone with two handsome men.

If her sister was, somehow, allowed to attend dinner then she would simply have to regale the two gentlemen with tales of Martha's exploits. How Martha was not averse to wading into the lake with her dress tucked between her legs, trying to find something that had fallen off their father's silly ship. Or how many times Martha had come home with her face all red from the sun or her dress covered in mud, unconcerned about how she looked, or smelled, for that matter. How many times she had returned to the house stinking of one of their father's chemicals. Or, heaven forbid, with blistered hands from pounding copper.

Martha behaved just like a man and men didn't care for such behavior.

"You have a cat's smile. As if you've just eaten a defenseless bird."

Looking up, she saw Reese Burthren standing there, leaning against the gate. She would have to pass him in order to get to the house. She pushed aside her irritation and smiled brightly at him instead, ignoring his rude remark.

"Good afternoon, Mr. Burthren. Isn't it a lovely day?"

"Have you been visiting Jordan?"

She stopped in the middle of the path, clasping her hands together in front of her. Was he going to block her entrance to the walkway? If the price for getting past him was a few minutes of charm, she could certainly accomplish that.

"I accompanied my sister to the boathouse," she said. "We delivered my father's papers and experiments to the duke. Do you share an interest in his work?"

"Only tangentially," he said, smiling slowly at her.

He truly did have a lovely smile. Men smiled for different reasons than women, her mother had told her. A woman will smile to hide something, but men always smiled to reveal themselves, especially when they were fascinated with a woman.

She returned his expression, thinking if the duke wasn't around, she might reciprocate Mr. Burthren's interest. For now, however, her main occupation was Jordan Hamilton. If she wanted him, he was hers. He may not know it yet, but he would.

"You don't seem the type to be interested in torpedo ships," he said.

"I'm not. I think men are more suited to such things."

"Your sister doesn't feel the same way."

"No," she said. "She doesn't. Martha has no interest in feminine pursuits."

"Ah, but if she did she'd be competition, wouldn't she?"

His smile had changed character, become almost insulting.

"I'm sure I don't know what you mean."

Surely he could recognize that Martha was almost plain while she wasn't. If he expected her to say something along those lines he was going to be disappointed. Maman had always told her men prefer a modest approach. Besides, it was better to let them think they'd come up with an idea with careful coaching.

If she cared enough about Reese Burthren, she'd make sure he decided she was the prettier of the two sisters. However, she didn't, so his opinion mattered only a little.

"I understand you've been exploring Sedgebrook," he said.

"If I have? Why is it any of your concern?"

"I'm told you made a few interesting comments. Things like what you would change or not."

"How do you know that?"

She was not going to use Constance again if the maid told tales about her.

"Do you see yourself as the next Duchess of Roth, Miss York?"

She really did have to rid the man of his insulting smile.

"You are in my way, Mr. Burthren. I would like to return to the house."

To her surprise, he stepped aside, still smiling. She had the feeling he watched her as she passed, but she didn't look back.

Chapter 10

Martha decided it was best to put aside her father's letters for now. Perhaps she would revisit them later when her emotions were more stable and she didn't feel like weeping.

"How did you become interested in torpedo ships, Your Grace?" she asked.

"The same way your father did, I think," he said. "The Crimean War."

"My father didn't speak of the war with much fondness, Your Grace. I know he was appalled at the loss of life. Especially in the hospitals."

"And because of the mines," he said. "My first captain had been aboard a ship approaching Sevastopol, sailing directly into one of those mines. He considered them an abomination."

She tilted her head a little and regarded him.

"I thought of them as a challenge," he continued. "How could we defend against them? We had to have something more effective than men stationed in the bow as lookouts. Then, I became interested in the idea of a mobile mine we could develop. My first idea was for a type of weapon that could lower and raise itself, depending on whether the approaching vessel was friend or foe."

She smiled in admiration. "What an excellent idea. Have you done anything with it?"

"No," he said. "I proposed it to someone in the War Office. He told me about your father's idea, to make a moving mine. A torpedo ship."

"And that's when your correspondence began," she said, smiling. "I remember my father's reaction to your first letter. He was quite impressed. He came to me and waved it in front of me and said, 'Martha, here is a young man who wishes to learn. A naval man. He wants to know my thoughts, can you believe it?'"

"He was a great inspiration, Miss York. I found myself wanting to impress him, just to see him write, 'Hamilton, you have it!'" He shook himself a little as if to dismiss his reverie. "I don't think we'll see his like again."

"Oh, I don't know, Your Grace," she said, studying him. "Perhaps you're more like him than you know."

It wasn't a specious compliment she gave him. Jordan Hamilton asked questions few people asked. He saw the world as a curiosity, something offering up endless possibilities for change, adaptation, and even invention.

Her father had the same openness. He'd once told her, *To live with wonder, Martha, is to be given a great gift. To wake each morning and want to find out why—now there's a life's full pursuit.*

She'd felt that wonder working beside him. His excitement and enthusiasm had been infectious. She, too, wanted to know why something wouldn't work or, conversely, why it did. The idea that two minds could work independently on a problem to find a solution had always fascinated her. So, too, the easy sharing of ideas, like the letters between her father and Jordan.

"Did you like your time in the navy?"

She was curious about every aspect of his life, something she probably should hide.

He glanced at her and hesitated. Did he wonder why she wished to know? Or was he trying to find a way to keep information about himself private? Was he going to tell her to restrain her interest, that he had no attention of divulging details about his life to a woman who was little more than a stranger?

Except that he didn't feel like a stranger to her. She'd read his letters to her father until it felt as if she knew him like a dear friend. Not a comment she was going to make.

"I did, yes," he said, surprising her with his answer. "I liked the order, the symmetry of it. You knew what was going to happen from one day to the next, as far as routines and drills and duties. Granted, the world around you could change, but you knew a certain watch had to begin on time. Each man had his duties and everyone knew the rules and the punishment for not obeying them."

"Do you like rules, then?"

Before he could answer, she spoke again.

"I hate rules, myself. They seem to constrain thinking. At least creative thinking."

He studied her in the dim light.

"What rules do you find constraining?" he asked.

"Those doled out by society," she said instantly. "What sort of clothes and hats you have to wear. Who can speak to whom. What you have to say. I'm afraid society and I don't often agree."

"That's not altogether a bad thing," he said. "It leaves you better able to think great thoughts."

She smiled at him, delighted at his comment. "I doubt my thoughts are great," she said. "But I would rather think of anything but clothes and hats."

"Your sister is a fashionable woman."

"Yes, she is," she said, feeling a disappointment at his comment.

"Does she have many suitors?"

"She does. Probably too many to be considered proper. She hasn't yet had her season. I'll be sure to convey your admiration to my sister," she added. "I'm sure she'll thank you for it this evening at dinner."

Why did every man lose his mind around Josephine?

Why was she jealous when she'd only rarely felt the emotion? She certainly didn't want the Duke of Roth for herself. He was not for the likes of her. She had absolutely no desire to become a duchess.

First of all, she wasn't as pretty as Josephine.

Second, she had absolutely no interest in fashion, witness the plain lavender dress she was wearing. She hadn't bothered to order a new wardrobe after their mourning period had expired. Besides, Josephine had kept the seamstress so busy she probably didn't have time to work on any other garments.

Third, she wasn't interested in flirting or telling a man what she thought he wanted to hear. Let the truth suffice. Let there be a meeting of rational minds. Why must she bat her eyelashes and act coy? Why must she wilt against him like a fragile flower? Why must she talk in a breathy little voice as if her lungs were suddenly not working correctly in his presence? Why, oh why, did she have to say idiotic things to him as if she had no mind of her own?

She'd watched her stepmother act in idiotic ways around men. She'd heard Marie's admonitions to Josephine. None of those rules made any sense to her. The only time she'd expressed her reservations to her father he'd stopped what he was doing, put down the clock parts and magnifying glass, and studied her.

"I would prefer, Martha," he'd said in that somber tone of his, "if you'd remain just as you are. Yourself."

"I've been told I should never express my curiosity around a man. That it's off-putting."

He hadn't asked her the source of that advice. Nor had she ever confessed to him that Marie ridiculed her for reading so much and asking too many questions.

"A man who does not wish to hear what you have to say is not for you, my dear daughter."

Now his words came back to her. A caution she should remember. The Duke of Roth was not for her, even if he did want to know her thoughts occasionally.

No, she simply wasn't for him. Nor was he for her.

He was too good-looking. No doubt he knew how handsome he was. He probably looked in the mirror more than once a day or studied his reflection in the morning, marveling at himself.

He was too stubborn. She knew that from his letters. He refused to give up. While that might be an admirable trait in itself, coupled with his arrogance it meant that Jordan Hamilton had the potential to be insufferable. She needed to remember that.

She reached for the letters again, curtailing her curiosity. When the duke began to examine a group of gears and chains, she didn't ask one question. The afternoon passed in silence, the time strangely companionable.

The fact that she enjoyed his company even when

they didn't talk was worrying. She really shouldn't be here.

He wasn't for her. She wasn't for him.

Finally, she stood and walked to the door.

"I shall see you at dinner, Miss York."

"I am feeling slightly indisposed, Your Grace," she said, lying. "I'm sure you'll understand if I take a tray in my room."

She wished she could have frozen the look on his face to study it more closely. It was half-resigned, half-horrified.

"I doubt anyone would think it proper for your sister to attend dinner alone in the company of two bachelors," he said.

In addition, Josephine would hate her if she couldn't go to dinner with the duke. Worse, she'd complain endlessly.

"Very well," she said crossly. "Perhaps I'll feel well enough to join you for dinner."

"I look forward to seeing you both," he said, giving her a small bow.

She didn't say good-bye as she left, plus she pushed the door a little too hard so it made a resounding thud as it closed.

Her father should have warned her about him. He should have put a caution in the letter he left her, the one asking her to ensure the Duke of Roth had his bequest. In addition to explaining that he admired Hamilton's curious mind and questioning thoughts, he should have said something along the lines of: *Daughter, guard yourself. He is an extraordinarily handsome man who will cause you to think thoughts that are not necessarily maidenly. In addition, he will incite your curiosity as well as your compassion. You will find yourself*

wanting to know more about him and such curiosity could
be dangerous to your peace of mind.

Of course, her father had said nothing of the sort.

What a pity.

HE'D BEEN SITTING too long. Normally, Jordan stood every half hour or so, stomping through the boat-house to ensure his leg didn't cramp. But with Martha there he'd remained sitting.

For some reason, he was averse to demonstrating his weakness to her.

He didn't doubt she would have been compassion-ate if not genuinely concerned. The problem was he didn't want either her compassion or her concern. He didn't want her lovely brown eyes to soften in pity. Or her hands to reach out to help him in any way.

He wasn't an invalid, damn it, although it had been only a few months since he'd thought he would be one for the rest of his life.

He made it back to his room managing not to limp too badly. Henry was, blessedly, waiting for him.

"You've overdone it," the man said with the lack of tact for which he was renowned.

He didn't argue, merely made it to the adapted sofa in the dressing room. Henry had the carpenter raise the sofa, remove both ends, and create what was essentially a fainting couch. When he'd made that comment, Henry had disagreed, saying it was a mas-culine fainting couch.

At the moment he was damned close to fainting.

"I've overdone it," he agreed, removing his jacket. "The damned leg is making its displeasure known."

"Shall I get the elixir?"

"No," he said. "Not yet."

The concoction Dr. Reynolds had given him was for the worst nights, but he hated taking the stuff. It gave him horrendous nightmares and made him lose his sense of self. If he had to, he would take it, but only after he'd tried everything else.

An hour later he was sweating and exhausted, but Henry's manipulation of his leg had beaten back the worst of the pain. At least his leg wasn't cramping any longer. Nor was he afraid he was going to start whimpering out loud.

For tonight, at least, he wouldn't take the elixir. But neither was he going to push himself to attend dinner. The York women would simply have to do without him. Reese would have to take up the slack and be his usual charming self.

MARTHA SAT ON the chair beside the bed in her sister's room, wondering how much longer Josephine was going to take to get ready for dinner. To her surprise, Josephine hadn't yet said a word about the boathouse.

"The silk brings out the color of my eyes," Josephine said, preening in front of the pier glass. "But do you think it's too formal?"

Since Martha was still wearing the lavender dress she'd worn all day she couldn't find it in herself to answer. It was true, the lovely dark green of the dress was the exact match of Josephine's eyes, which was why her sister had approved the fabric.

"How many dresses did you bring with you?" she asked, looking at the discarded garments strewed across the bed.

Amy would be forced to hang them and, no doubt, ensure they were pressed first.

Josephine didn't say anything, but she hadn't really expected an answer.

Even though her sister had begun getting ready for dinner hours ago, there was every possibility they would be late.

Amy had done a beautiful job with Josephine's hair, allowing little ringlets to fall from an artful bun.

Her own hair was in dreadful shape, but it always was, especially when she was around a body of water. The humidity made it curl even tighter. The only thing she could do with it was pull it back at the sides and gather it up in a bun at her neck and cover the whole thing with a snood. With any luck it wouldn't escape and frizz all around her face.

"If you don't hurry we'll be late," she said.

If the duke thought Josephine lovely before, he would be in awe of her beauty tonight.

"We don't want to be rude," she added.

"Let him wait. He'll think it worth it." Josephine smiled at herself in the mirror. "It's a pity he's revolting," she said.

"He's not revolting."

"He's a cripple," Josephine said.

"He's been injured. He's recovering."

Josephine glanced at her in the mirror. "How protective you sound. How many hours did you spend together?"

"I left a little while after you did."

"Did he tell you to leave also?"

"He didn't tell you to leave," Martha said.

"He as much as did. He was exceedingly rude."

"He wasn't."

"You should have had a chaperone with you. A

maid, if nothing else. Gran wouldn't be happy if she knew you spent hours alone with him."

"It wasn't hours, and there was no need of a chaperone. We spent the whole time talking about Father's work. Or you."

"Me?"

"He thinks you're lovely."

"Does he? What a pity he's a cripple."

"I don't think you should call people names." Especially not Jordan Hamilton when he'd done nothing but offer his home to them and treat them like valued guests.

She was wise enough, however, not to say anything too complimentary about the duke to her sister. If Josephine knew how she felt about the Duke of Roth, she'd never hear the end of it.

"I APOLOGIZE ON His Grace's behalf," Reese said, meeting them at the bottom of the staircase. "He's indisposed this evening and won't be joining us for dinner."

"Is he all right?" Martha asked.

"His leg is bothering him," Reese said. "But Henry is with him."

"Henry?"

"His valet, but he's much more than a valet. Henry's from Sweden and has been educated in *sjukgymnast*."

At her look, he smiled. "It's manipulation," he said, "of injured limbs."

The fact that Reese had mentioned legs or limbs in their company was shocking, but she was grateful for the information.

Martha half expected to be led into a parlor where they would converse for a few minutes before dinner was announced. Instead, they were immediately shown to their places in the dining room, helped by two footmen who then promptly disappeared, leaving her and Josephine alone with Reese.

Reese had changed into evening clothes, making her wish she had something other than her lavender dress to wear. She looked like a drab older relative, someone who might chaperone the two of them.

She didn't care. She didn't even mind that Reese and Josephine talked over her the whole dinner. She sat quietly, lost in her thoughts.

After a butterscotch pudding was served for dessert, she started to pay attention to the conversation around her. The two of them were involved in a lively discussion of horses.

"Do you ride, Miss York?" Reese asked Martha.

"She doesn't," Josephine said. "Oh, she does, but not often. I, on the other hand, ride almost every day."

She was perfectly able to answer for herself, but she bit back her retort and finished the pudding.

"Perhaps I could show you the stables in the morning. His Grace has a selection of magnificent horses."

"I've already seen Ercole," Josephine said.

Reese only raised one eyebrow. "You do know your horseflesh," he said. "He's the prize stallion in the stable. His Grace has promised him to the Earl of Doncaster. He's due to be shipped out in a week or so."

"Doesn't His Grace ride?" Josephine asked.

"No," Reese said. "What time would be convenient for you to meet me at the stables?"

Something about his posture made Martha think he was more alert than he'd been earlier. Or maybe on guard.

What a curious certainty to have.

"Will the duke be joining us?" Josephine asked.

"No," he said, his eyes never leaving her.

Reese was evidently interested in Josephine, but he might be too worldly for her sister. For all her flirtations, she was still only a few years out of the schoolroom.

Something about Reese Burthren worried Martha. He had an edge to him, almost as if he was more daring than he let on, standing on the precipice of polite behavior. His gaze was shuttered like a man who had some practice with being who he wasn't. He was the duke's friend, but what else was he?

Josephine might hint at being shocking, but she suspected Reese actually was. He hid it well, however, almost like a spider who dressed like a fly.

Would Josephine listen if Martha warned her? What could she say that would make any sense? *Be careful? I think he fancies you?* Josephine would only laugh at her. Besides, it wasn't the first time a man had admired her sister. But no other man had given her the feeling he wasn't quite what he seemed, that he had secrets that might be dangerous to know.

Perhaps she should accompany them, but if she did it would mean she'd have to give up going to the boathouse. Or she could insist on them taking a chaperone, which would be a little hypocritical since she was going to be alone with the duke.

While she was trying to decide, the two of them arranged a time. Before she could say anything, Josephine stood, smiled at Reese, and turned to her.

"Shall we retire?"

She said her good-nights and accompanied her sister up the stairs, but at Josephine's door she hesi-

tated. She wanted to say something about Mr. Burthren, but before she had an opportunity to speak
Josephine closed the door in her face.

JOSEPHINE WAS ANNOYED that the duke hadn't been at
dinner, but perhaps there was still a way to institute
her plan.

She rang the bellpull and asked for Constance
when the maid appeared at her door. She'd already
paid for the girl's cooperation and she was willing to
pay even more if it meant learning where the duke
was. A little money passed about often paid great
dividends.

"He almost always retires to his library at night,
miss," Constance said when Josephine welcomed the
girl into her room and closed the door behind her.
A simple question about the duke's whereabouts un-
locked a flood of information.

"But not tonight."

"What makes tonight special?" Josephine asked.

"His Grace is suffering something terrible. It's his
leg, you see. He'll be with Henry."

Unfortunately, that information coincided with
what she'd learned at dinner. She was running out
of time. They'd be at Sedgebrook for only two more
nights, but it looked as if tonight was out of the question.

She slipped a coin in the girl's hand and thanked
Constance. The maid curtsied and took herself off.

Josephine closed the door and leaned against it,
thinking. Her objective was not thwarted as much as
delayed. She wouldn't see the duke tonight, but she
would put her plan into effect tomorrow.

Chapter 11

Jordan normally woke with the dawn. He'd always done so, eager to get a start on the day. In the past year, however, his early rising was because he hadn't slept well. Last night had been a difficult one because he'd refused to take the elixir that dulled his mind yet gave him a respite from the almost constant pain in his leg.

Dr. Reynolds had not, unfortunately, been able to give him any reassurance the pain would ease. But, then, he'd grown accustomed to ignoring a physician's recommendations or cautions. Therefore, he wasn't going to base his hopes on what Dr. Reynolds said or didn't say. After all, what did the man know? He wasn't supposed to walk again. The future was like a vast ocean in front of him. He was the one who would plot his course.

Thankfully, none of his servants were around to watch him descend the grand staircase in a slow but dogged fashion. What he lacked in coordination he made up for in determination. Finally, he was at the bottom and made his way to the Morning Parlor, only to be disconcerted by the presence of Josephine York.

"You're up early, Miss York," he said in greeting.

He would not allow himself to limp to his favorite chair at the head of the table, but it was close.

Her dress was a pale yellow, embroidered with bunches of pink-and-purple flowers. For someone who'd been unexpectedly waylaid by her grandmother's illness, Miss York had a varied and extensive wardrobe.

He couldn't help but wonder if Martha was going to wear her lavender dress today.

"Will your sister be joining us?" he asked.

The last thing he wanted to encounter first thing in the morning was Josephine's artificial brightness. She was like a great many women he'd met since ascending to the title. He'd been invisible to them as a naval officer, but the minute he became the 11th Duke of Roth, he was suddenly charming, witty, and erudite.

That kind of shallowness irritated him on a base level.

"I'm afraid not," she said, smiling at him. She gave him a sideways look, no doubt presenting her best profile. Was he supposed to be overcome by her attractiveness?

He supposed she was pretty, in a way that would fade quickly.

"Will Mr. Burthren be joining us?" she asked.

"I suspect not," he said. "Normally Reese avoids breakfast."

"A pity, then. We shall have to entertain each other."

He couldn't imagine a more hideous scenario. What was he supposed to say? Regale her with tales of the latest play he'd attended? He hadn't left Sedgebrook in a year. Was she bookish? Perhaps he should ask her what she'd read lately.

"I've seen Ercole," she said. "What a beautiful horse he is. Are you certain you want to sell him?"

He didn't want to discuss his brother's stallion.

"I can direct you to my factor," he said. "If you're interested in the horse."

His comment seemed to silence her, at least for the moment.

He served himself breakfast, his appetite gone.

Why the hell hadn't Martha showed up? At least with her he could discuss something that interested him. Even their silences were more comfortable than what he was experiencing at the moment.

Martha didn't simper at him, either. She didn't act coy. And she most assuredly did not stink up the room with some ghastly perfume smelling of dead flowers in a hothouse.

Had Josephine no idea of how overpowering the scent was?

"We missed you at dinner last night, Your Grace."

"Yes." He wasn't going to go into why he hadn't been in attendance.

But she, however, was not to be denied.

"I understand you didn't feel well."

Good God, was the woman going to pry even further? Common decency would have silenced most people before this, but Josephine evidently thought herself above the fray.

"Have you always been lame, Your Grace?"

He turned his head slowly, regarding her like he would if she was an experiment gone awry in a way he hadn't expected.

She was smiling faintly, her green eyes soft. No doubt she thought her beauty gave her license to say anything she wished. Had she no inner barrier? No sense of decency? Or, at the very least, no concept of decorum?

"No, Miss York," he said, the words spoken with studied care. "I haven't always been 'lame,' as you say. It's a recent acquisition of mine."

He stood, desperate to leave the room and be quit of Josephine York. This time, he didn't give a flying farthing if he limped because he held his walking stick almost like a club. If nothing else, if she approached him, he'd brandish the damn thing like a weapon.

MARTHA WOKE LATE, drank her tea in her bedroom, skipped breakfast, and went straight to the boathouse.

Her eagerness was unseemly, no doubt. If anyone had asked, she would've told them she wanted to help the duke. She might even say her assistance was something her father would've wanted.

The fact that the Duke of Roth was an extraordinarily handsome man did not enter into her thoughts.

Yesterday, he'd asked her questions and seemed to value her opinion. She had the feeling, if someone annoyed him, he would make his thoughts known, regardless of whether the individual was male or female.

Look at how he had behaved around Josephine.

When she was almost at the boathouse, her footsteps slowed. Would he be there? Or would his leg be paining him? Did he ever stop working because of his discomfort? Would he welcome her? Or would he ask her to leave?

She had too many questions and no answers.

Still, she was cautious when she opened the door and peered inside.

He was already there, sitting at the workbench, the

morning sun making the window beside him glow with golden light.

She stood there for a moment.

The lingering scent of water and fish perfumed the air. Another odor reached her, something reminding her of the flux her father used when closing a seam. There was no fireplace here, only a small unlit brazier in the corner.

He glanced toward the doorway.

"Are you coming in?" he asked. "Or are you going to stand there gaping at me?"

"I don't gape," she said, entering the boathouse. "I might stare," she added. "Or peruse. But gaping implies awe and I'm rarely awed."

He half turned to watch her walk toward him.

"Have you nothing else to wear? Your sister seems to have planned for this extemporaneous visit. She was in another dress at breakfast."

"You had breakfast with her?" she asked, surprised. "Josephine normally doesn't rise early."

"It's because I'm a duke," he said.

The comment startled her.

"You breakfasted with my sister because you're a duke?"

"She went out of her way to breakfast with me," he said. "It's the title. It has a life of its own. I often think of it as a ghost, a filmy specter folding around me like a cloak."

He glanced at her, his smile slightly crooked. "I haven't the slightest idea why I told you that. I've occasionally thought it, but I had no intention of confessing the notion. The fact is, people sometimes go out of their way to accommodate me, simply because of my title. I suspect your sister is one of those people. You aren't."

"How do you know I'm not? Perhaps I wasn't hungry this morning." She wasn't going to tell him that she woke late, that her night had been filled with dreams of him.

"By the fact that you're arguing and not trying to charm me," he said.

He really shouldn't smile at her. It did something to her insides.

And she has her sights set on you, Your Grace. Perhaps she should have warned him about Josephine, but what good would it do?

"Is that the only dress you have?" he asked. "Or perhaps you just like lavender."

"I have my dark blue traveling dress," she said, finding it odd to be discussing her wardrobe with the Duke of Roth. "It has an overskirt and a small bustle. It's fancier than this one, but if this dress offends you, I can always change."

"Oh, but that would be accommodating me. Perhaps even making an effort to charm me."

She couldn't help but smile. "True."

"Did you simply not plan for this extended visit?"

"No," she said, approaching the workbench. She pulled out the stool and sat on it. "But Josephine has a greater interest in fashion than I do. I'm not surprised she packed more garments than she needed. We only planned to visit with you long enough to deliver my father's bequest, then stay at an inn and return to Griffin House the next day."

He sent her a sharp look. "How is your grandmother feeling?"

When she'd seen Gran this morning, she'd been sitting up in bed, eating her breakfast with a hearty appetite.

"Better. I don't doubt we shall be leaving in a day or two."

Why did that thought instantly alter her mood and not in a good way?

"I wasn't arguing with you, by the way," she said. "I don't actually argue much. I'm normally amenable."

"I think you're wrong in your assessment of yourself, Martha. I think, perhaps, when you disagree with people you simply retreat into your own thoughts. Arguing is often a waste of time and I suspect you don't spend a great deal of time on idiotic pursuits."

Never before had anyone assumed a knowledge of her character. She didn't know how to respond.

When she remained silent, he reached over and put something in front of her.

"What is wrong with that?" he asked. "Can you tell?"

"It's part of a pendulum," she said.

She picked it up and studied it, turning it back and forth in her hand. "It's weighted differently."

"That it is. Your father and I had discussed whether or not it would matter."

She closed her eyes, the better to see the complex arrangement of gears, wires, and chains found in the guidance system. The pendulum was located in the middle, toward the rear.

Opening her eyes, she looked at him. "It would pull too far on the left rudder chain," she said. "It might even cause the ship to be nose-heavy."

He didn't say anything for a moment, merely studied her.

She wanted to ask if he really did object to the lavender dress. She had more freedom to move in this garment, but it wasn't fashionable. Yet she didn't want to have to worry about what she was wearing when it normally didn't concern her.

"You're an unusual woman," he said.

She'd heard those words before, but they hadn't been a compliment.

"Is it a bad thing? Are you saying I'm odd?"

He smiled again and although the expression didn't look mocking, she held herself still, waiting for his words.

"You know a great deal about forming copper, pendulums and the like, and compressors."

He reached out and grabbed her hand, turning it over to examine the palm.

"Your father told me about how you got this scar," he said, tracing a small mark at the base of her thumb. "You were trying to force a piston back into place when it slipped."

She pulled her hand free, embarrassed in a way she hadn't been for a long time. Ever since her season in London, as a matter of fact.

It was him, of course. She'd never met a man who was so supremely male. She felt fluttery and feminine when she was nothing of the sort. Once she was dressed in the morning, it was the last time she concerned herself with her appearance. She didn't stop in front of a mirror or worry about what she looked like.

Until she'd met him. Now she was all too aware of her flaws.

"I'm easily bored," she said, giving him the truth. "I haven't the slightest interest in fashion or how to arrange my hair. I detest shopping, except when it comes to material we need. It seems to me my time is better spent seeking sources of copper tubing and sheathing than in selecting hats and gloves."

"And for that I thank you," he said, startling her again. "I find you almost the perfect companion, Martha."

She stared down at the pendulum, picked it up again, and concentrated on it even though she was more focused on the man beside her. A bright happiness flooded through her, making the shadowed boathouse seem sun-filled.

Yes, she was being foolish. Yes, he was much more handsome than any other man she'd ever known. Yes, he was no doubt a danger to her peace of mind.

But she wouldn't have traded being here for anything.

"I DIDN'T THINK you'd come," Reese said, smiling at Josephine.

He turned back to Ercole's stall.

"Why shouldn't I?" she asked, moving to his side.

Ercole. This was the horse she wanted. What a beauty he was.

Reese glanced at her, surveying her from the top of her hair to the tip of her shoes. Her dress flattered her and he was smart enough to note it. Not perceptive enough, however, to make a comment on it. He should have praised her appearance at least.

Instead, he only walked across the stable to stand at another stall.

"This is Jessamine," he said, and recited the mare's bloodline.

"She isn't the match of Ercole," she said.

A faint smile played on his lips, making her wonder if he ridiculed her.

"I want him," she said. "I'm an excellent rider," she added. "I could control him."

"Do you always get what you want?" he asked, his laughter borderline insulting.

She didn't allow her smile to falter.

"He's already spoken for and I doubt you'll convince the earl not to take ownership of him."

"But as the duke's friend, you could change his mind, couldn't you, Reese?"

"Perhaps," he said. "If I cared enough to make the effort."

"If I promised to make it worth your while?"

"Do you make the same promise to all the men you know? Do they stumble over themselves to do what you want?"

"Most of them," she said, smiling. "If I let you kiss me, would you speak to the duke?"

He laughed, grabbed her hand, and kissed her fingers.

"No," he said, and then did the one thing she hadn't expected. He walked away, leaving her standing there looking after him.

JORDAN FOUND HIMSELF bemused by Martha York. He hadn't lied. She was unlike any other woman he'd ever known. She hadn't batted her eyelashes at him once. Nor had she pretended to be helpless.

Her voice was normal, neither breathy or high-pitched. A little on the low side, it was definitely fascinating. He found himself listening carefully when she spoke.

The first day they'd worked together she'd called him "Your Grace" a great many times. Today, he noted, she didn't, almost as if they were becoming friends. He had a feeling his title was an impediment to Martha and not an asset.

For the first time, he wished he'd met her when he was in the navy.

He found himself wanting to ask her opinion about a great many things. Did she think his boathouse was arranged in the most practical manner? From which sources did she acquire her materials? Would she be interested in helping him relaunch his ship when it was found?

All questions he might've asked of Matthew York if he was sitting here. But he doubted if he would have been as fascinated with the older man's appearance as he was his daughter's.

He shouldn't have mentioned her dress. But lavender didn't favor her. She needed to be attired in something bold, deep greens or blues, a shade to compliment her porcelain complexion and dark brown eyes.

She was wearing her hair in a bun again, but recalcitrant tendrils had escaped to frame her face. Her curly hair was another fascination. He wanted to touch it, see if it was as soft as it appeared.

He wanted, in a way unlike him, to hear her laugh, to see her eyes sparkle with humor.

All thoughts that had nothing to do with a torpedo ship.

He should have sent her away. In the past few months he'd gotten good at banishing people. All he had to do was act ducal and arrogant. Or dismiss them with a look. Instead, he worked beside her, discussing the merits of using brass versus copper, tooling methods, and various polishing formulations.

Matthew was quoted often in those hours, but they didn't discuss anything else of a personal nature. She didn't ask him why he changed position from time to time, as if she knew his leg was beginning to bother him. He said nothing about how often she patted her hair into place, as if it was an annoyance.

From time to time she propped her elbow on the workbench, supporting her chin on her hand. She'd be intently focused on his actions, whether it was cleaning a part or crimping the link of the chain, and sometimes comment on what he was doing incorrectly.

He retaliated by giving her some parts to polish and remarking on spots she missed.

They worked in perfect accord for hours, the passing time deepening what he was considering a friendship, one he'd never before experienced with a woman.

When the maid came, at noon, to bring him his meal as she did every day, she was obviously surprised to find Martha with him. When he would have asked Polly to fetch a meal for her, Martha demurred.

"I should be returning to the house," she said, getting up from the stool. "I need to check on Gran."

He found himself wanting to keep her there, but was constrained in his speech by Polly's presence.

"Will you come back?"

They exchanged a look. He wasn't going to beg her. The fact that he was close to marshaling his arguments was enough to keep him silent.

"I don't wish to be an imposition," she said.

"You're not. I've enjoyed your companionship. Not to mention your assistance."

She smiled, the expression lighting up her face. "Very well," she said. "I'll come back."

This afternoon her hair might come free of its punishing bun. She might laugh. The sun would tint her cheeks a soft pink.

She left the boathouse accompanied by Polly.

A thought occurred to him as he glanced over and saw the box containing Matthew's letters. Had she read all of his to her father? The thought was disturbing. He wished he could remember everything he'd divulged to Matthew over the past five years. No doubt some of his insecurities or his longing for his previous job. He'd enjoyed his tasks at the War Office. Few people knew he was *that* Hamilton, related to the Duke of Roth. Nor did he go around telling anyone.

The day he'd been informed of his brother's death had been strange and disconcerting. He remembered writing Matthew about how he'd felt. He and Simon had rarely seen each other in the past few years. His first thought was that the damn fool wouldn't have contracted cholera if he hadn't been in Italy. His second thought was amazement that he was the new Duke of Roth. He was so stunned by that realization that he could only stare at his solicitor for a few moments.

He hadn't wanted to be duke. He remembered writing Matthew that, too. He had delayed his arrival at Sedgebrook for weeks before finally feeling compelled to come home. The house was too big, echoing with memories of a boy who wanted to be noticed and appreciated and loved but who had been joyfully ignored. He probably would have been a different person had his mother lived. But he'd been reared by a nurse, a nanny, the tutor, and then rushed off to school.

His father had been a shadow during most of his childhood and when he died Jordan had attended the services in the family chapel feeling strangely cheated. Who had Harold Hamilton been? What was his personality? His likes, dislikes, acquaintances, and friends—all questions he had.

He tried, once, to ask Simon about their father. His brother had dismissed his curiosity with a wave of his hand. He couldn't help but wonder if Harold was a shadow to Simon as well.

If Martha had read his letters, she knew more about him than anyone else. He hadn't minded the revelations to Matthew. If anything, the older man had almost taken on the role of parent. But Martha knowing everything?

He felt more vulnerable than he'd ever felt. The boathouse was suddenly darker and the silence too deep.

He ate his solitary meal, abruptly aware of his own loneliness.

Chapter 12

$\mathcal{I}$n the afternoon they continued to work together in harmony.

Martha had taken up her father's letters again. From time to time she would press her fingers to Matthew's signature, carefully smoothing out the well-read pages. Did she think to capture her father's spirit? He wanted to tell her that Matthew would always live on, just not in a way she'd probably considered.

His ideas would incite interest in others, encourage thought, conversation, wonder, and speculation. Matthew York was a great mind, a thoughtful person, and a generous soul.

If he could be half the man Matthew had been, he'd count himself fortunate.

At the moment, however, he was concerned with just being polite.

His damnable leg was hurting, which always made him short-tempered. Martha did not deserve his irritation. Nor was he annoyed in any way with her. The past hours had been surprisingly pleasant in a manner he'd never expected.

However, he needed to move. He stood, walked around a bit, then made his way to the workbench and sat heavily, closing his eyes at the pain. Some-times it felt as if he was walking on a knife. The hilt was at his foot and the point his hip, the entire length of his leg sliced open with each step.

"Are you all right?" she asked.

He opened his eyes. "No, I'm not. I am, as your sister has so aptly stated, 'lame.'"

"Did she really say such a thing?" she asked, her tone one of horror mixed with surprise.

He turned his head to look at her. "She did. At breakfast."

"I'm sorry," she said, then startled him by asking, "Would you be more inclined to like Josephine if she hadn't made that remark?"

By being too damn wise, she added another layer to his conundrum. He'd not only shared his thoughts with the woman, but he was coming close to liking her. Perhaps even admiring her. No, the admiration had started the moment she'd begun talking about weight ratios and propellers. He would have been content to listen to her lecture him for hours.

"No," he said, answering her question about Jo-sephine. "I don't think I would. She isn't the type of female who interests me."

She pulled the stool closer to him, pulling her skirts aside so they didn't touch his trousers. How proper their clothes were, never touching or even daring to brush next to each other.

"Have you ever been disappointed in love?" he asked, the question so out of context that they both stared at each other.

"Why would you ask such a thing?" she said.

"Because I'm curious. I know about your season. When I read your father's words my first thought was that your emotions had already been taken. I thought you were pining for someone."

When she didn't speak he raised one eyebrow. "Then it's true. I've found when people refuse to answer a question it's because the answer's obvious."

"No," she said, frowning at him. "It isn't true. If you must know, I don't have much faith in love. It doesn't seem to be a kind emotion. Oh, it is when you say you love a dog or a horse or a kitten. But not people. When you love people, you're almost asking to be harmed."

How curious that they shared the same feelings.

"My stepmother, Marie," she continued, "says love is as necessary as air. It's the glue holding everything together." She glanced at him. "She's passionate about things. She wants to experience every moment of life to its fullest."

He didn't say anything for a moment, feeling his way through the maze of words.

"Your father didn't mention her often."

"I noticed," she said.

"I got the impression the marriage wasn't a happy one."

"I don't know," she said. "Marie liked to stay in London a great deal. Or travel to France. When she finally came home she always appeared to be happy to see Father. He came out of his cottage long enough to notice he had a family and a wife."

"Is that why you started to work with him? So he'd notice you?"

She shook her head. "He was the most interesting person I knew. He was always thinking different thoughts. He could think of something in the middle of the night and make it real by the next day. He always seemed to be doing something more interesting than needlepoint. Or talking about fashion." She smiled faintly. "He didn't worry about getting dirty. He waded through the lake. He invented things. Who wouldn't want to be around someone like that?"

"Have you invented anything?"

"A new propeller design," she said. "Nothing as important as my father's ship."

"Don't you worry about creating a weapon?"

"A weapon?"

"Surely you know the torpedo ship is a weapon? The nose will be filled with gunpowder. That's the reason why the directional capabilities have to be so precise."

"Of course I know the nose will be filled with gunpowder. It's just that I disagree with the label you've given it. The torpedo ship is a defensive piece of armament, a way to protect our ships. Better to use a torpedo than be rammed amidships."

The nautical term surprised him, but it shouldn't have. York Armaments was an important supplier of all types of weapons—however much Martha might dislike the label—and they furnished the navy with a great many cannon. She'd probably grown up knowing a vocabulary not shared by other young misses.

"So it doesn't bother you that you're creating something that can cause death and destruction?"

She thought about it for a moment, then answered. "Almost anything can cause death and destruction if it's used in the wrong way. A knitting needle. A kitchen knife." She glanced down at the workbench before picking up a sizable piece of slate he kept there as a paperweight. "I could throw this at you and strike you in the head," she said. "You could die from the blow."

His right leg chose that moment to send him a signal, lightning traveling from his hip down to his ankle. Just a reminder in case he forgot.

"You aren't going to throw that at me are you, Martha? I can't outrun you."

She dropped the slate back on the bench and looked at him, a woman with intelligence blazing from her eyes and determination in the set of her smile.

"Will you ever be able to run again?"

No one had ever come out and asked him such a question, one oddly similar to that he asked of his physician.

"I don't know," he said, giving her a gift of his honesty. With anyone else he might have said something like, *it's none of your concern*. Or he might have simply ignored the question completely. But she was a brave creature, one who saw nothing untoward with telling him when he was wrong, or at least when she believed he was wrong.

They'd already gotten into a number of arguments. He'd forgotten his composure and raised his voice. She'd done the same. Strangely, he liked arguing with Martha York. He found it to be exhilarating in the extreme.

He wanted to know a great deal about her, but he didn't tell her that his curiosity surprised him. He'd gone for months without feeling a scintilla of interest in another human being. The fact he could admit to his insularity shamed him a little. He'd been too involved in himself.

One day, not too long ago, he'd awakened feeling a bone-deep fatigue. He didn't want to think about himself, worry about himself, or even concern himself with any facet of Jordan Hamilton. It was the day he'd come back to the boathouse, immersing himself in his work.

It was also the day he'd finally read all the letters Martha had written him.

"Did you know that my father could make light follow a waterfall?"

He shook his head.

"He had one whole wall of inventions. Whenever I asked him why he didn't finish one, it was because he'd gotten word someone else was working on a similar machine or process. You're the only one with whom he ever corresponded. He didn't seem to mind you were mirroring his work."

"Not mirroring," he said, then wondered why he was so quick to correct her.

Was his pride so great he had to be first? Perhaps it was, an answer that surprised him.

"Maybe you're right," he said. "Some days I was behind him. Sometimes I was ahead."

She nodded. "I think you were almost at the same place," she said. "At least from his letters. I'm surprised he told you so much."

He noted that she didn't mention Matthew's comments about his family. His remarks were always said in fondness, but Jordan realized now how correct they were. Josephine was described as being overly concerned with the world around her while Martha never seemed to notice. Josephine wanted pretty baubles. Martha wanted answers.

Matthew had also mentioned his mother often in his letters, but strangely rarely commented about his wife.

How odd that he could remember almost everything his mentor had said about Martha. He wished, however, that Matthew had explained her a little more. What was her favorite color, her most treasured book? What annoyed her—other than anyone who slighted her father in any way?

She sat half in shadow. Behind her sunlight beckoned through the boathouse window. He wanted to study her for a while, but how strange would the request sound?

Stay right where you are, Martha, while I marvel at the perfect oval of your face and the direct, penetrating look from your brown eyes. You have the faint beginnings of a frown line between your brows, as if you've often contemplated something difficult to comprehend. And there's a small indentation at the right corner of your mouth leading me to think humor is not a stranger to you.

What would she say if he continued his thoughts aloud?

I like your curly mop of hair. I imagine it gives you fits and makes you long for something more fashionable. I like the dramatic arch of your brows that seem to convey your thoughts so easily. Right at the moment they're slightly elevated as if you're wondering at my interest.

I'm wondering, too.

I like that you cared so much for your father, that your grief is there in your eyes for anyone to see. I admire the patience you've demonstrated around your sister, but I suspect it's hard-won and often lost. I also admire your love for your grandmother, the care and concern you have for an old woman with the skills of Machiavelli.

Martha, your grandmother is lying.

I also appreciate that you're not wearing scent, other than what I suspect is your soap. A faint rose scent, if I'm not mistaken, but nothing else. Unlike your sister, who seems to drench herself in a perfume better worn by a mature woman of the world.

He wished he danced. He wished he could dance. He had the strangest wish to stand, take her hand, hum some waltz he'd heard, and whirl her around the boathouse. He wanted to see her smile, watch her cheeks blossom with color.

A sign of his incipient insanity. He should banish her from his presence.

He did no such thing.

"THEY'VE BEEN TOGETHER for almost the whole day?" Susan York asked her maid.

Amy nodded. "They seem to be quite companionable, Mrs. York. Of course, I heard raised voices, too."

"Oh, dear. You mean Martha was shouting?"

"Not just her, Mrs. York. It was the duke, too."

"Oh."

Susan wondered what to make of this development.

In the great reckoning to come—which wasn't, unfortunately, all that far off—she would be called upon to explain her actions. Namely, her numerous prevarications (her nature flinched at the word *lies*), her sloth in remaining in bed playing cards with her maid, and eating all sorts of delicious biscuits (she really must get the recipes from Sedgebrook's cook).

There was a reason for her actions, but she doubted the Almighty would excuse her easily. Wasn't there some parable about doing the right thing for the wrong reason? She wasn't certain, but surely she would be forgiven.

Being at Sedgebrook was fortuitous; she couldn't

overlook the opportunity she'd been given. How many times had she heard her darling son talk about the Duke of Roth?

Yes, she'd been guilty of planning. Yes, she'd taken the future into her hands. Yes, she'd no doubt abused the Duke of Roth's hospitality.

She'd arranged their meeting, just as Matthew had wanted. He'd often told her how alike Martha and the duke were.

"I am not the type to matchmake, Mother, but they have the same nature, the same kind of mind."

She'd promised him, on his deathbed, to somehow arrange a meeting. When the moment had come, she'd acted on it. And, from what Amy had learned—bless the woman, she could ferret out anyone's secrets—the duke and Martha were faring well.

Would it do any good to tell Martha about her father's thoughts?

"They'd suit, Mother. Both of them are determined, focused, and have a mind for mechanics. Jordan is as reserved as Martha and, I think, as lonely."

Had the duke known she was healthy as a horse? Susan suspected the doctor had, even though she'd acted faint and moaned more than once during his examination. She was not given to theatrics normally, but it seemed easy enough to emulate her dear mother-in-law. The poor woman had declared herself ill with so many different ailments that when she succumbed to heart problems it had been a true shock.

The only thing she hadn't done was plan Martha's wardrobe. The unfortunate lavender dress didn't bring out her delightful coloring. But, that could be construed as an asset as well. If the duke found himself entranced with Martha, she'd know it wasn't for her attire but despite it.

Should she hint at the fact that Martha was an heiress? No, she'd leave that little tidbit for later, just in case the duke needed some urging.

All she needed now was to give Martha and the duke a little time. And somehow curb Josephine's curiosity and more acquisitive tendencies. The girl coveted. That was the word for it. Despite never having to worry about money she sometimes wanted what other people had. Heaven forbid someone has a prettier dress or a more accomplished horse.

Unfortunately, from what Amy said, Sedgebrook had captured her attention. Perhaps she should move up her plans for Josephine's season. That would certainly keep her granddaughter occupied with thoughts of a new wardrobe and appropriate jewels.

As far as Martha, perhaps they should remain here a few more days than she'd originally scheduled. She could always relapse, feel faint again.

For now, she was content to allow nature to take its course.

She smiled and reached for her book and another biscuit.

Chapter 13

$\mathcal{M}$artha slid from the stool and walked to where her father's boxes and crates were stacked.

He stood. "You don't have to do that," he said, when she went to open the first of the boxes.

She glanced over her shoulder at him. "Who better? I packed them. I know what's in each."

He sat back down, watching her. She was looking for something. After taking out a sheaf of papers from the first box, she put the top back on and moved to a coffin-like crate.

"You'll have to help me with this one," she said.

Grabbing his walking stick, he moved slowly to her side, taking the precaution of grabbing a length of iron from one of the vertical bins against the wall.

She nodded at him approvingly as he bent and used the iron as a pry bar, lifting the lid from the box.

"I wanted to make sure it wasn't disturbed in the move," she said, helping him lift the lid.

"It's your father's prototype."

She nodded. "Bessie."

Mounds of shaved wood were pillowed atop and on the sides of the torpedo ship. She gently pushed it away, revealing a bullet-shaped vessel four feet long. The metal had changed from a copper color to verdigris in several places, indicating that it had been used on more than one voyage.

At least Matthew hadn't lost his in the bottom of a lake.

Placing the lid of the crate on the floor, she carefully lifted the ship from its nest.

When he moved to assist her, she shook her head.

"It's not that heavy," she said.

"I'm not an invalid, Martha," he said his voice stiff.

She looked at him, her eyes widening at his comment.

"Of course you aren't. I didn't decline your assistance because I thought you were unable to give it."

Her glance swept up his body and down again, leaving him to think he'd never been so thoroughly examined by a female.

"No," she said. "I most certainly would not consider you an invalid. A man in his prime, perhaps."

He felt the back of his neck warm.

"Besides, I've lifted Bessie myself numerous times."

As Martha carried the vessel to the workbench, he grabbed his walking stick and followed, silently cursing his lurching gait.

Once seated at his workbench he reached out a hand and placed it on the curved copper snout.

"It looks like mine," he said. "But that's to be expected, since your father and I exchanged drawings."

She nodded. "This is the one he was operating that last day. I still don't know what he did that was different. I've examined it and tested it myself numerous times, but I haven't discovered what changed. Perhaps you'll be more successful."

He didn't say anything, merely moved his hand carefully over the body of the ship and the seams where the three sections of the ship were joined together. If the prototype was true to Matthew's drawings, the engine run by compressed air was in the middle of the ship while the hydrostatic valve and pendulum were in the rear. At the bottom was the rudder keeping Bessie level and on course.

He wondered if it also controlled the depth at which the ship ran.

His fingers trailed over the copper vessel, hesitating on the spots of verdigris.

"Why didn't Matthew tell you what he'd done?"

"At first he wanted to share the secret with you," she said. "Later, when he realized you weren't coming, he was too ill and delirious."

He sometimes regretted what he'd done. This was one of the few cases where he wanted to make amends for an act he hadn't performed. Yet he couldn't have gone to Griffin House since he was in his own sickbed. Nor did he feel comfortable telling her that since it sounded as if he was begging for pity.

He reached out and touched her hand where it rested on the workbench, wordless comfort. Or perhaps an appeal for her understanding without him furnishing an explanation.

She turned her head and looked at him.

"Forgive me," he said. Did she realize that it wasn't the first time he said that to her?

She nodded, turning her hand over until their palms met. For a moment that's how they remained: her standing, him sitting beside her, their hands and their gazes touching.

A sliver of time in which he had the curious thought that they communicated without words. He felt her pain and loss and wondered if she could sense his regret. Or understand his bruised pride that, even now, dictated that he offer no excuse.

She pulled her hand free and reached out to touch Bessie, her fingers smoothing over the copper as if she felt for tactile differences in the vessel.

He had a thought that had nothing to do with torpedoes, one that would have probably offended her had she known it.

What would her hands feel like on him?

"I suggest you install a wire to the stern," she said, effectively cutting off his reverie. She pointed at the back of the ship where a small round circle had been welded. "I would have lost every single one of my vessels if I hadn't."

"A leash?"

"If you wish," she said, smiling.

If he'd thought to do that, he wouldn't have lost three of his ships and would've been able to reel it in when it sank. Nor would he have had to ask for volunteers among the footmen to dive for his vessel.

They treated the whole thing as a jest, which is probably how his entire staff viewed his preoccupation with a torpedo ship. The lame, penurious duke, attempting to recoup his family's coffers by inventing a metal fish. Yet it was no more laughable than his brother traipsing through Italy armed with his brushes and his painting teacher.

He turned away, staring at the empty bays where his prototypes once rested.

By her competence she put his own incompetence into relief. He felt inept around her, an emotion he'd rarely experienced. He'd known failure before, but never this sudden need to explain his shortcomings.

He wanted her approval, a thought that startled

him. He wanted Martha York to smile at him and say something in praise of his efforts or his thoughts or even his plans.

Matthew should have warned him.

My daughter is a treasure. He'd written those words more than once. He should have appended them. *My daughter will befuddle you, Hamilton. She'll make you laugh, shout, argue, and contemplate circumstances you have no business thinking.*

Perhaps it would be better if she didn't return to the boathouse. He'd muddle on without her. He'd examine Bessie at his leisure—alone—without her comments or constructive remarks. He'd done very well without Martha before. He could certainly do so again.

Why, then, did the idea of working by himself annoy him?

A pain streaking through his right side effectively silenced any contemplation of tomorrow. Smoothing his face of any expression, he moved his leg to stand. The knife had grown teeth over the past hour, gnawing into the muscles and bone.

He should have stopped working earlier. Hopefully, he hadn't left it for too long. If he didn't seek out Henry soon the pain was going to get worse.

Standing, he grabbed his walking stick, prayed that his leg would hold up, and looked at her.

"Shall we go?" he said.

He was being too abrupt, almost rude, but thankfully, she only nodded. Nor did she remark on the fact that his passage to the door of the boathouse was slower and more lumbering than before.

He didn't want to look lame in front of her, damn it.

Once outside the boathouse, he realized that the day was more advanced than he'd thought. The sky was darkening to the east, a blaze of orange and red streaking across the western sky.

"It's gotten later than I thought," he said.

She didn't look away, making him realize there wasn't any compassion in her gaze. Nor was there pity. Instead, she regarded him the way a friend might look at another, without judgment.

"I'll take you through the Duchess's Garden," he said. "It cuts down the distance back to the house."

She didn't say anything, merely joined him on the path.

The back wall of the garden was brick, with hornbeam hedges forming the other three walls. The entrance to the Duchess's Garden was through an intricate trellis arch. He stepped aside for her to precede him.

"This is one of the gardens featured in the prints in the Morning Parlor," she said.

He was surprised she knew that. Most people didn't notice what was around them, but he should have known Martha wasn't like most people.

"The garden was begun in the late seventeenth century as a kitchen garden, but now we grow our vegetables in the Potager."

At her look, he explained. "It's an ornamental vegetable garden closer to the kitchen. Here the area is set aside for roses, in honor of my mother. She was fond of roses, I believe."

She glanced at him and he answered her unspoken question.

"She died when I was three months old," he said.

"I always thought bringing you into the world led to her death," his father stated once. His offhanded remark had been like a weight around Jordan's neck for years, until he learned his mother had died of influenza. It wasn't the first time he'd experienced his father's casual cruelties and unconscious insults.

"It's like a separate world," she said, looking around her. "All these colors. And the scent of roses is almost intoxicating."

"It clings to you," he said. "If I spend any time here I can smell roses on my clothes hours later."

"How many types are there?" she asked, walking slowly down the path.

"I don't know," he said. "Once, there were over a thousand. I don't know if my brother added or subtracted from the number."

"Was he duke for long?"

"Ten years." Long enough to do his damage to the family coffers.

His father and brother evidently believed money was a natural province of a dukedom. Inherit one and the other magically appeared. It didn't.

"My mother died when I was a baby," she said.

Another commonality between them. He wanted to ask, but didn't, if she often found herself feeling adrift in her own family.

"Will you be joining us for dinner this evening?" she asked.

Had she noted his difficulty in walking? Or had his face revealed the degree of his pain?

"Yes," he said. Whatever it cost him, he'd be there, if for no other reason than to prove he wasn't an invalid.

He left her at the back entrance to Sedgebrook,

claiming a need to speak with his housekeeper. In actuality, he was going to use the servants' stairs to get to his room. That way, his painful ascent wouldn't be witnessed by his guests.

He wasn't *lame*, damn it.

Chapter 14

*M*artha was worried about Jordan, a fact she hid from her grandmother when she visited her. She hoped he'd been able to get some relief for his leg and was eager to go down to dinner to ask him how he felt.

Josephine, however, was running late again when she left Gran and went to get her sister.

This time, she was preening in front of the mirror attired in a dark blue patterned dress that was beautifully made with swaths of material in the train. Even though Josephine occasionally annoyed her, there was no disputing the fact that her sister was a beautiful woman.

When she complimented Josephine on her appearance her sister only smiled.

"Am I beautiful enough to be the Duchess of Roth?"

"What?" Martha stared at her sister in shock.

"What a pity he's a cripple. But I could always live in London like Maman did for a while," Josephine said, turning to survey herself once more in the mirror.

"You think the duke will offer for you?"

How odd that the words were so difficult to say. They clung to her lips like a dying man might to a life raft.

"Of course. He's a man. All I need to do is to be in the right place at the right time."

"What does that mean?" she asked, hoping that what she was thinking wasn't what her sister was planning. However, she knew better than to under-estimate Josephine. When it came to getting what she wanted, she could be ruthless.

Josephine turned to face Martha. Her smile had disappeared.

"Gran would be shocked to find me in a compromising position, wouldn't she? Angry enough to demand His Grace do something honorable."

"You wouldn't do that. It's calculating and . . . wrong."

Not, however, beyond Josephine's abilities to carry it out. From the moment she'd seen Sedgebrook, Josephine had wanted it. She was like a spoiled child with a treat held just beyond her grasp. She was going to engage in a tantrum—in this case, shocking behavior—until she got it.

"You wouldn't," she said.

"Oh, I would," Josephine said airily. "I don't suppose he'll send me away if he finds me in his bed. Cripple or not, he's a man."

She stared at Josephine, horrified.

"Hopefully, I can ply him with wine during dinner. We'll both encourage him to drink. He'll be a little confused when he finds me in his bed, but not enough to do anything about it."

"You expect me to help you?" she asked, finally able to speak. "You haven't thought this through."

"Oh, my dear Martha. Of course I have. Are you afraid I'll lose my virginity? That disappeared a year ago. However, I can always make the duke believe he's deflowered me. He'll have no other choice but to marry me, don't you see?"

"Please. You can't do this."

"Of course I can."

She moved to the door. "Then I'm going to tell Gran. She'll stop you."

"Go ahead," Josephine said smiling. "I'll deny it, of course. I may even cry. I'll ask Gran why you're being so cruel, how you can possibly say what you're saying. I might even hint that you're jealous and you want the duke for yourself. Do you, Martha?"

She'd never before seen that particular expression on Josephine's face, almost as if her sister viewed her as an enemy.

"Come, Martha, we'll be late. I'd hate to tell the duke it's because you were so slow."

She stared after her sister as Josephine left the room.

Josephine had always been interested in Josephine to the exclusion of anyone else. Nothing had ever stopped her from getting what she wanted. A stable of new horses? Fine. They'll arrive next month. A wardrobe filled with new gowns? As soon as the seamstress could finish them. Whatever she wanted was granted to her.

Somehow, she had to stop her. Not entirely for Josephine's sake, but also because it didn't feel right to harm a man whose only sin had been to take them in and offer his hospitality.

Jordan didn't deserve Josephine's scheming. Or her greed.

AT DINNER MARTHA began to believe that Josephine couldn't possibly have been serious. She had to be teasing—even if that teasing had bordered on cruelty—about seducing the Duke of Roth. Right now she was involved in batting her eyelashes at the duke, sending him simpering, idiotic looks, and generally making a spectacle of herself.

Did Josephine really think men succumbed to such behavior? Did she expect the duke to collapse on the snowy white linen and beg her to end his misery?

Oh, marry me, Miss York. Take my heart from its prison and set it free! Give me the peace only a look from your emerald orbs will grant. I beg you to release me from torment. Be mine!

True, Josephine had an effect on men. They tended to stumble around her. They stuttered. They fixed their gaze on certain portions of her anatomy and didn't seem capable of wrenching it free. They bowed. They looked longingly after her as she passed.

Martha only hoped Jordan was immune. He'd certainly ignored her from the moment she descended the stairs. It was as if the camaraderie they'd experienced for the whole day had vanished. Gone was the man who'd asked her questions, argued with her, and criticized her polishing only to reward her with a smile later.

He was not the man he'd been this afternoon. His face was set in stern lines. His gaze was flat as he surveyed the table.

Something was wrong.

Martha realized what it was a moment after studying him. Although he sat at the head of the table, he gripped the handle of his walking stick until his knuckles shone white. She knew, without him telling her, that he was in pain and doing everything in his power not to reveal it.

"Your Grace," Josephine said, "have you given any thought to our conversation about Ercole?"

He slowly turned his head and looked at Josephine.

Was Josephine blind? Anyone could see he didn't want to converse. She suspected that he was having a difficult enough time just sitting there.

"My compliments to your cook," she interjected in the silence.

"Mrs. Madison comes from France," Reese said, blessedly taking up the topic. "She's English, but was married to a Frenchman."

"While my mother was French, but was married to an Englishman," Josephine said.

Everyone turned to look at her. She angled her head slightly—in a way that flattered her—and smiled.

"Dear Maman returned to France after dear Papa died. I don't think she can bear to remain in the country with all its memories."

Josephine had never called their father dear Papa. Nor did her sister mention *Dear Maman's* letter and her gushing enthusiasm about her new suitor, a count with a château in the south of France.

Of course I'll send for you when it's time, my dear, she'd written to Josephine.

No doubt Marie thought to wheedle her daughter out of her share of the York fortune. What Marie didn't know was that Josephine was as greedy as her mother.

Had Josephine truly lost her virginity a year ago? Or had she only made the comment to shock her? She'd certainly accomplished that aim. Did Gran know? Is that why they were here? To find Josephine a husband before she was embroiled in some sort of scandal?

Surely Josephine didn't mean what she'd said earlier? This frozen-faced man was not ripe for seduction. Nor could she imagine the duke ignoring the fact that Josephine had called him lame. Or had her sister forgotten that? Did she think she could say anything just because she was beautiful?

"May I come to the boathouse tomorrow?" Josephine asked. "I promise to bring my own chair."

The duke didn't look at her. Nor did he answer. Instead, he was doing exactly as Josephine had hoped, drinking another glass of wine—his third. Was the man going to get sotted? That's all she needed, for him to be drunk enough that Josephine's plan might work.

As if he'd heard her thoughts, he turned to study Martha until she wanted to ask him to look away. His intent regard was embarrassing her, especially since the other two were joining the duke in staring at her.

Had some leek gotten caught in her teeth? Had she spilled some of her wine down her bodice? Was her abominable hair frizzing around her face?

She could feel her cheeks warm. She was not going to blush, not now. Not here, please God.

"Your brother was a talented painter," Martha said, determined to direct his attention elsewhere.

When he didn't say anything, she wondered if she'd committed a faux pas. Was the tenth duke not supposed to be mentioned?

"He was, wasn't he?" Reese asked, rescuing her once more from the awkward silence. "He only painted scenes from Italian cities, however, which was probably understandable since he loved Italy so much."

"Do you paint, Mr. Burthren?" she asked, grateful for his politeness.

"Me? I'm afraid not. I've no discernible talent in anything."

"Don't be fooled by his modesty, Miss York," the duke unexpectedly said. "He's one of the War Office's rising stars."

His words startled her. She'd corresponded briefly with several members of the War Office after her father's death. They'd been interested in the York Torpedo Ship and had been disappointed in the news it didn't work.

When dinner was over, she was surprised the men didn't remain behind to smoke their cigarillos. Instead, the duke and Reese joined them in the Crystal Parlor.

She wanted to ask who had collected all the examples of glass art, figurines of every sort from dancers to shepherdesses to animals: dogs, cats, goats, cows, and a bull with delicate-looking horns. Everything sparkled in the yellowish light of the crystal gas lamps.

The Crystal Parlor was another room Martha didn't care for, but it seemed to enchant Josephine. Her eyes were large as she took in the shelves of crystal statuary.

The maid assigned to this room must consider it a hellish task. Just moving toward the end of the sofa made Martha nervous. What if she accidentally swept the crystal tray off the table in front of her?

She kept a death grip on her skirt, wishing she was at least as graceful as Josephine. She sat, finally, looking up at the two men who'd taken up a stance by the fireplace with its crystal mantel.

The duke had a glass of brandy in his hand. What on earth was she going to do to stop her sister if Josephine was intent on seducing the duke?

Hadn't Josephine given this idiotic plan any thought at all?

If she was found out, news of the debacle could reach London. There were just so many sins a fortune could mitigate. No man wanted a wife who would bring scandal to their marriage. She could just imagine the tales.

Did you hear? Josephine York was found at midnight in her nightgown, wandering through Sedgebrook. I think she was intent on a tryst, don't you? Scandalous! Simply scandalous!

". . . don't you, Miss York?"

Josephine nudged her with her elbow, bringing her to the present. She glanced at her sister.

"The duke has asked you a question, Martha."

Oh, dear. So much for being a proper guest.

Looking up at him, she decided posturing was not going to help. Little got past that stern gaze.

"I do apologize, Your Grace, but I was thinking of something else. What were you saying?"

"Weighty thoughts?" he asked.

"Yes."

"About the York Torpedo Ship?"

He was more like her father than he knew. Not every thought, idea, or musing was about the ship.

Smiling, she shook her head. "I was thinking of something entirely different."

She was conscious of Josephine's irritated look and Reese's glance of amusement, but she wasn't going to be the first to look away.

"Care to share your thoughts?" he asked.

"They would only bore you," she said.

"I doubt that. Perhaps I should be the judge."

"In this, you'll have to take my word, Your Grace.

Unless," she added, "you don't believe a female can be trusted to keep her word."

"I hold no antipathy for females, Miss York. In fact, I quite enjoy their company. As to trust, is it singled out by gender? Or by character?"

It was exciting to be in a game of wits with him. She'd been reared to believe her mind was the equal of any man's, that ideas or insight was rewarded regardless of where it originated.

She smiled, thoroughly enjoying herself. "I would say character, but I suspect that is not an answer a man might give."

"Then you've probably not been around the right kind of men, Miss York, if you'll pardon the effrontery of my remark. Reese, for example," he said, glancing at his friend, "is of the same opinion as I am. A woman's word is the equal of a man's. Yet her dishonesty can be the same as well."

She inclined her head to grant him the point.

"Then you agree if I tell you my thoughts were unimportant?"

He smiled at her, an expression warming her entire body. Did he realize the power he held with one simple smile? She wouldn't be surprised if he did. She suspected beautiful people were aware of their effect on lesser individuals.

"I doubt any of your thoughts could be considered unimportant, Miss York. You seem to me to be a singular female."

"You mustn't say such things to Martha, Your Grace," Josephine interjected, a trilling laugh accompanying her words. "She isn't used to flirting. Why, she hated her season, can you imagine? She said she'd had her fill of people saying all sorts of things they didn't mean."

Was there anything more exasperating than being talked about as if you weren't sitting there listening?

"Another example of your uniqueness, Miss York," the duke said, punctuating his remark with a small bow to her.

Josephine was not to be outdone. Evidently tired of being ignored she said, "Do you not entertain at Sedgebrook, Your Grace?"

"I do not, Miss York," he said. He moved his right leg slightly, leaning heavily on his walking stick.

Why on earth didn't the silly man sit if he was in pain? The answer was just as swift. Because he didn't want to be seen as different from Reese. She frowned at the other man, but he didn't get her hint. If he didn't sit, the duke wouldn't, either.

"What about traveling to London? I adore London. So much to see and do. I don't think I've ever seen as many people in one place. And the fashions!"

If she didn't stop Josephine, she would go on and on and by the glazed look on the men's faces, she would succeed in boring them entirely.

She could either excuse herself and she and Josephine could leave—although she wasn't entirely certain Josephine would do so without an embarrassing verbal tug-of-war. Or she could come up with another topic. Weather? She couldn't think of anything to say. The days had been fair, not a cloud in the sky.

"Do you like to travel?" she asked when Josephine took a breath. "Have you done a great deal of it? What is your favorite country to visit?"

The two men looked a little bemused at the onslaught of questions, but thankfully the duke answered.

"I've done a great deal of it, although I don't think I prefer traveling over remaining at home."

"I have as well," Reese said. "I like it, unlike Jordan. My favorite country? It's a city, instead. Paris. I quite like the French."

Josephine smiled.

"Do you feel the same about Paris, Your Grace?" Josephine asked.

"It's not my favorite city, no," he said to Josephine's obvious disappointment. "Although it does have history to recommend it."

Should she ask about their reading next? Or simply give up, stand, and hope Josephine came along without an argument?

The duke saved her from having to make a decision.

"If you'll excuse me," he said, placing his half-empty snifter on the mantel, "I must leave you. I've correspondence I need to ready for the morning post."

With that, he headed for the door, leaving them all staring after him. Josephine evidently wanted to continue to charm him. As for her? She was glad he was gone. Truly. Perhaps now he would rest his leg.

She couldn't help, however, but anticipate meeting with him in the boathouse in the morning and wasn't that the height of foolishness?

HE DIDN'T KNOW what Josephine had planned, but Reese knew it was something. He knew that determined look. He'd seen it in his own eyes.

For some reason, titles attracted the venal and the amoral. Josephine, for all her youth, was both.

He liked her, though, and that surprised him. She was both greedy and unapologetic about it.

He wanted her, too, another surprise. He preferred mature women, those who knew what life was about. He suspected Josephine wasn't a virgin, but he doubted she was all that experienced.

She was doomed to failure, however. Miss York didn't understand that Jordan didn't give a flying farthing for grasping, mercenary women. Her sister had a better chance with Jordan only because she didn't seem to care about a ducal title or the fact that Sedgebrook was one of the great houses of England.

It was also one of the great millstones around Jordan's neck.

Just because she was determined didn't mean Josephine was without virtues. She was a beauty, he'd give her that. Plus, she intrigued him on several levels. He admired ambition. He had it himself. He also admired practicality. She was, if nothing else, eminently pragmatic. He had a feeling that she was willing to barter what she had to get what she wanted.

The question was: did it include her virginity? If she was a virgin, no doubt she guarded her virtue, knowing it was worth something in the marriage mart. Or perhaps he was wrong. She was one of those females who would always look innocent, but she'd be a whore in the bedroom.

Reese thought his mission was going to be a failure until the York women arrived. So far he'd not discovered anything he could take back to the War Office, but things could change. Martha York might help Jordan get his torpedo ship to work.

In the meantime, the younger sister might turn out to be a momentary—and pleasant—distraction.

BEFORE RETIRING FOR the night, she and Josephine went to check on Gran who was playing cards with Amy and looking hale and hearty. They took turns kissing their grandmother on the cheek before saying good-night.

As Amy was closing the door behind her, she whispered to Martha, "Could I talk to you, Miss Martha?" She glanced behind her, then added, "It's something I can't mention to your grandmother."

"Of course, Amy."

"I'll come to see you as soon as I get her settled for the night."

She nodded, concerned and curious, then caught up with Josephine before her sister could enter her room.

"You will be going to bed right away, won't you?" Martha asked. "You don't have plans to do anything else?"

"Of course. I don't understand what you think I'd do."

Josephine was the picture of innocence, but she'd witnessed her sister lying straight-faced before and wasn't fooled.

"So you've given up the notion of causing a scandal?"

"Oh, Martha, don't be foolish. I was only jesting. I have no intention of doing anything shocking."

Josephine's laughter wasn't the least bit reassuring. Neither was her sister's quick smile as she shut the door.

Was she a terrible person for believing her sister capable of such behavior? Possibly, but she couldn't trust Josephine. Last night the duke had been with his valet. Tonight she suspected Josephine was going to do something foolish.

She also knew she was the only person who could stop her sister.

For a moment she toyed with the idea of going to Gran and telling her about Josephine's plans. If she did, her sister would probably lie and pretend innocence. Besides, she might be wrong. Not about Josephine, but about Gran. Her grandmother might truly be ill and the last thing she wanted to do was make her condition worse and delay her recuperation.

No, she was going to have to handle this herself, even if she had to stand outside Josephine's room and stop her physically from doing something shocking.

Chapter 15

Jordan had already subjected himself to Henry's punishing session of exercise. The man had stretched his damaged leg until he wanted to scream. He hadn't, by sheer willpower and something else—his damnable pride.

It wouldn't do for his guests to hear shouts of agony emerging from his suite.

He'd overdone it today. First, he'd sat for too long on the stool in the boathouse. The position had caused the muscles in his leg to bunch. Second, he'd refused to take the elixir the night before, which meant that the pain had only grown in the intervening hours.

It wasn't coming in waves as it normally did. No, this time the pain was centered in his hip, arcs of cold traveling down the outside of his leg and remaining there as if he'd packed snow against his limb.

He'd excused himself from the Crystal Parlor because he was unable to mask his discomfort any longer. Slowly, he made his way to his library, closing the door behind him.

This room had never been a refuge for him. Ever since he was a child he'd chosen the boathouse as his sanctuary. Both his father and brother had left the imprint of their personalities here to the point that the staff felt an almost superstitious kind of hallowed reverence for the library.

No one would bother him here. Not one servant, from Frederick to Mrs. Browning, would dare to knock on the door.

He sat on the enormous desk chair behind the equally massive desk, leaning his head back and staring up at the fresco his brother had painted there.

A young and attractive satyr was summoning a bevy of male and female angels to him, stretching out one hand as if commanding by a single gesture. From the rapturous expressions on the faces of the angels, he needed even less persuasion than that.

As he did every time he saw the fresco, Jordan couldn't help but wonder if Simon had modeled the satyr on someone of his acquaintance. Had the man been as cleverly wicked as his brother had portrayed him?

The satyr reminded him vaguely of Reese, especially in the role he'd assumed for this visit, the ears and eyes of the War Office, but willing to be distracted by a beautiful woman.

Did his friend actually think he was that naive? Reese hadn't inquired about his well-being for months. Yet Matthew dies, he begins work again, and suddenly Reese appears at Sedgebrook? The connection was obvious even to a blind man.

He wondered if Reese would pursue Josephine. If so, he wished Reese well. He'd seen her type before, women who were basically self-centered, determined to live their lives according to their own wishes and to hell with anyone else.

Those type of women cared for others only as long as it benefited them. As companions they were amusing. As lovers they were inventive, but as friends or wives, they were disastrous.

Standing, he made his way to the bellpull and jerked on it. When the maid arrived, he gave her an order to prepare a few hot bricks for him. She only nodded, familiar with the process. Mrs. Browning would ensure the bricks were heated and wrapped in flannel. He'd called for them so often lately that he wouldn't be surprised if the housekeeper had orders to keep a few on the stove at all times.

He'd put them against his leg. The heat wouldn't affect the ache in his bones, but at least his muscles wouldn't tighten up and make the pain worse.

He slowly began to traverse the library on a well-worn path, one he'd made on other nights like this.

Today he should have stood every few minutes, explaining to Martha that if he didn't, his damnable leg would cramp. He'd wanted to appear normal to her, perhaps even stoic. He hadn't wanted to be weak, a half man whose injury made him do odd things.

The cold was getting worse, making it feel as if his knitting bones were freezing. He was afraid that the night ahead of him would be more than miserable. He was in for hours of agony.

He walked as far as the circular iron staircase, back to the door, up to his desk, retracing his steps. Movement didn't seem to ease the deepening ache. The knife sensation was back, making each step like striding on a sword point.

He wanted to whimper. He wanted to cry out, curse the world or himself. He'd damn himself with his words, as he had a hundred or even a thousand times over the past year.

Once the bricks came, brought to him by Mrs.

Browning, he sat at his desk, placing one against his hip and the next slightly lower.

"Is there anything else I can bring you, Your Grace?" she asked, her round face arranged in compassionate lines.

"Thank you, no, Mrs. Browning," he said, forcing the words from his lips. There, he didn't sound whiny, did he? No, he sounded like himself, in command of the situation. Stalwart. Dependable. A man who hid his weaker nature from those who depended on him.

He wanted her out of the library before the pain seeped through to his face.

"Shall I bring you some tea, Your Grace? Or some brandy?"

Please go. Just go.

Instead of saying the words, he pasted a smile on his face. He couldn't help but wonder how it looked. Did it appear as false as it felt? Was it a frightening expression?

"Thank you, Mrs. Browning," he said. "I require nothing further."

Nothing but your absence. Be quick about it. Please, for the love of God, will you leave?

Blessedly, she left, but not before glancing at him one last time. He kept his smile tethered to his face with difficulty until the door closed.

He leaned his head back against his desk chair and allowed a moan to escape from his clenched lips.

Just a few minutes, that's all. He had to wait until the heat from the bricks eased his muscles and gave a little warmth to his bones. He could endure this. All he had to do was wait.

He thought about the York Torpedo Ship and its bearer. Martha hadn't wanted to bring it to him. She hadn't been impressed by his consequence. Nor had she been pleased with his reception of her gift.

She was right; he hadn't behaved in an honorable fashion. But he'd tried to make up for his initial reaction to her presence by allowing her into his sanctuary.

She'd been a surprise, a companionable woman who didn't flirt with him, unless her forthright comments could be considered a type of flirtation. She didn't flatter, but she did convey her respect in an odd fashion. He felt a glow of satisfaction when she said something complimentary. It was all too evident she didn't utter falsehoods. When she gave him praise it was so simply done he knew she actually felt what she was saying.

She didn't seem to give a flying farthing that he was a duke. Nor did Sedgebrook seem to impress her. He recalled her expression when he'd come to the Rococo Parlor. She'd been fascinated but in a repulsed, rather than admiring, way.

What did summon her admiration? Other than her father, of course. What made her eyes light up in amazement?

How curious that he wanted to know.

The thought occurred to him like a whisper, cutting through his thoughts of Martha. *You have the elixir.*

He pushed the thought away, but it came back, throbbing along with his leg. Dr. Reynolds had concocted a potion of sorts—at least that's what he'd called it in the early days. The mixture was a combination of a few herbs and some opiates, but it effectively took away his pain. It also stripped him of his consciousness, not to mention his memories. He was left feeling as if he'd died for those few hours of being under the influence of the elixir.

He took it only when nothing else worked.

Right now, the exercise and heat weren't working. He didn't have many solutions. Alcohol didn't ease the pain. All it did was leave him with a raging headache. The elixir worked, but it stripped him of any control over his life.

For now he would simply endure.

He knew, from previous experience, that he and agony would be doing battle until dawn.

THE MINUTE JOSEPHINE closed the door to her room, she began to undress. Tonight she wouldn't ask for Amy's help.

Martha was so puritanical. She didn't understand that this was a perfect circumstance, one screaming at her to take advantage of it. Martha would have been satisfied to spend the rest of her life working with their father, fiddling with things that didn't interest most men.

She never even tried to tame that atrocious hair of hers. Nor did she dress fashionably. She was an heiress, too, yet she didn't seem to spend a cent of her money on herself.

Unlike Martha, she was not going to remain at Griffin House as if she was a novitiate at a convent. It was up to her to forge her own destiny, fix her future in the direction she wanted.

Her own dear Maman had always encouraged her to seize a likely opportunity.

"Women have to make their own way in life, my dear Josephine," she'd said. *"We can't simply sit in the parlor and wait for a man to call on us. No, we have to give him*

the idea, first. We have to pursue him with single-minded determination, all the while allowing him to believe it was his idea."

She had no doubt, whatsoever, that Maman would understand what she was about to do.

Josephine stared at herself in the mirror, pleased with her appearance. Her ivory complexion was enhanced with a delicate rose flush. Her eyes glowed with good health and her hair looked shiny and soft.

She was beautiful enough to be a duchess. Sedgebrook would be the perfect backdrop for her. She could entertain in style here. People would come from miles around. People would call her Your Grace. She might even add on to the Crystal Parlor with a few of her own pieces. She would most definitely change the Conservatory, perhaps add a few rooms to the house so anyone coming to Sedgebrook would marvel at the magnificent changes she'd made.

As to the lawn, she'd make some alterations there, too. Perhaps add in a few more topiary bushes and soften the approach somewhat so Sedgebrook wasn't so imposing from the front. With those twin staircases, it looked almost like a dragon's mouth stretched wide, ready to ensnare an unwary carriage. Or perhaps she might even have an architect redesign the facade.

The history of the Hamiltons would become hers. She would be immortalized in the Upper Hall where all of the portraits of the previous duchesses hung. She knew exactly where she wanted her painting to be placed: right beside the double doors so it couldn't be missed when someone either entered the room or left it.

Instead of waiting for Sedgebrook to settle down

around her, she was going to go to the duke's suite now. She'd be in his bed when he turned in for the night.

He wouldn't dare refuse her.

What man would?

INSTEAD OF UNDRESSING for the night, Martha remained in her lavender dress. Catching sight of herself in the mirror over the bureau, she sighed.

Regardless of how many minutes she spent with her hair, it was a disaster: curly, unmanageable, and definitely possessing a mind of its own. It was simply easier to allow it to do what it wanted. The humidity hadn't helped matters. Now her hair formed a corona around her head, making it appear she hadn't spent any time on it all day.

Sometimes she wished she could be more like Josephine with her beautiful hair that never seemed out of place.

How foolish. She was herself. Envying someone else would never fix her hair.

Sometimes, however, she wanted to know what it felt like to look in the mirror and be greeted by perfection. She certainly didn't have it. Her nose was slightly long for her face while her mouth was too large. She had a mole near her left eye and it always looked like a spot of dirt on her face. Her chin was too forceful, her jawline too sharp. Yet her eyes were a warm brown and possibly her best feature, being clear and direct.

Her father had once said she had a way of demanding the truth with her gaze, that no one could lie to her.

She would like, just once, for someone—a man—to

be swept away by her appearance. If he gazed into her eyes and wanted to see, not their color, but what lay beneath, to examine the person she hid from the world.

She knew full well she didn't want just any man to be attracted to her. She wanted it to be the Duke of Roth.

Josephine didn't see who he was; she saw only the title and Sedgebrook. Because Jordan had a physical impairment, she discounted his attractiveness. How could she overlook his beauty: the symmetry of his features, the perfect smile, those high cheekbones, and his striking deep blue eyes?

Of course, Josephine hadn't seen the way his hands moved, the care with which he touched her father's ship. His fingers had smoothed over the copper with almost a loving touch. The same gentleness he'd show a lover.

She stared at herself in the mirror, shocked. What was happening to her? She was thinking thoughts she'd never had before about a man who was nearly a stranger.

No, he wasn't that, was he?

She'd read every single one of his letters going back five years. She wept for him when reading about the death of his brother. The letters had grown more candid over the course of his friendship with her father. She knew the Duke of Roth wasn't wealthy, that Sedgebrook was expensive to maintain.

When Amy knocked on the door she opened it, letting the maid into her room.

"Thank you, Miss Martha. I didn't know who else to talk to about this."

Amy's hands smoothed down the skirt of her dark

blue dress repeatedly as she talked, a habit she had when she was nervous.

She motioned Amy to the chair, but the maid only shook her head, still standing by the door.

"It's your sister, Miss Martha."

What has Josephine done now?

"I've been listening to some of the other maids here, Miss Martha. They were talking about Miss Josephine. I'm afraid they weren't saying very many nice things about her."

Gossip went on in any house, but she could imagine the sheer size of the staff at Sedgebrook made gossip almost an industry. Add in the fact that Josephine was beautiful and wealthy and it wasn't surprising that she was being talked about.

Evidently, however, it wasn't her beauty or her wealth but rather her behavior that was under discussion.

"She's been asking for special favors, Miss Martha. Wanting to be treated almost like family I've heard it said. She's given one of the maids enough money that it's caused problems among the staff. She insisted on meeting with the cook this afternoon to revise the breakfast menu. And she told Mrs. Browning that some of the upstairs maids had been lazy. There was dust on some of the portrait frames in the upper hall."

Amy's usual pleasant face was contorted with worry.

"Mrs. Browning told one of the girls that if Josephine wasn't stopped, she was going to the duke himself."

She and Amy exchanged a look. Each of them knew that Josephine was nearly impossible to constrain. Gran was the only one who could do it. Even Marie had never tried.

What did they do now?

She went and sat on the edge of the bed, wrapping her arm around one of the posts. If she could, she'd magically transport them back to Griffin House where there was no hint of looming disaster.

Should she tell Amy what Josephine had planned? No, she wouldn't be able to keep the maid from telling Gran. There was a possibility Josephine had been teasing her, but after what Amy said, she was beginning to think Josephine was serious.

"I'll talk to her," she said.

She didn't have much hope that her words would be enough to change Josephine's behavior. But surely her sister could see that she was putting herself in jeopardy? Servants talked. Rumors spread like fire. Something that happened in a country house could easily carry to London. Josephine would be tainted by the aura of her own rudeness before she even had a season. Playing Lady of the Manor at Sedgebrook was hardly the way to ease her way into society.

"I'll talk to her," she said again.

She closed the door after Amy, wishing she felt more optimistic about the outcome of any discussion with her sister.

JORDAN TOLERATED THE agony for two hours. Two hours in which he paced the library, called for more heated bricks, and cursed himself for not moving more during the day. During those one hundred twenty minutes he ignored the siren call of the drug.

He sat in the chair staring up at the dome above the second floor noting the small cracks he'd been measuring for a year now. He'd have to find the money from somewhere to repair the dome before it crashed in and destroyed the library.

Perhaps he could sell some of the books surrounding him, volumes clad in leather with gilt lettering, pounds and pounds of books purchased by his grandfather and chosen for their colors more than their contents. The bottom tier was scarlet leather, topped by a sea green. On the upper floors the books were blue.

He couldn't attest to the fact, but he suspected most of them had never been opened. Despite the sheer number of books, he found Sedgebrook's library lacking in what he needed. But, then, he wanted to read about the latest advancements in science. No one had purchased a new book for the Hamilton library in years.

The curved iron staircase captured his attention for a while. He made note of the intricate ironwork connecting the railing, tracing the pattern from the base to the top of the twenty-seven steps.

At the end of the two hours, he reached into the bottom desk drawer and uncorked one of the three bottles of the elixir he'd secreted around Sedgebrook. The second was in the boathouse and the third in his bedroom.

He drank two swallows, knowing it would be enough to numb the pain and dull his wits. In a few minutes it would begin to take effect, giving him enough time to laboriously make his way up the stairs to his room where he would surrender to the elixir and lose himself.

Chapter 16

$\mathcal{J}$osephine crept out of her room, closing the door softly behind her.

"Beauty is a key." A comment Maman had often made. "It can unlock many doors, but you must be wise and choose exactly the right door."

She had every intention of doing exactly that.

There wasn't a footman at the end of the corridor, thank heavens, only a sconce flickering in greeting. She headed in the opposite direction. Her slippers were soundless against the carpet runner. Her grandmother had selected the thick cotton nightgown with its matching wrapper, both garments staid and old-fashioned. Once she was inside the duke's suite, she had no intention of wearing either.

A light in the foyer below sent shadows around the base of the stairs. Everything was silent but in her mind she heard the laughter of future guests.

She could see herself at Sedgebrook as the Duchess of Roth. When they entertained, which would be often, she would make a grand entrance. Here, exactly on this spot, above the stairs, she would wait until people congregated in the foyer below. Slowly, with great presence, she would descend the steps, smiling graciously. Everyone would look up and whisper about her.

Isn't she magnificent? Oh, my dear, she's the most beautiful duchess of them all. Sedgebrook is the perfect place for someone of her beauty.

She could feel their admiration as she hesitated on the bottom step, allowing them to come to her one by one. She'd nod and greet each person with grace and poise. For days they would talk about this moment, how they felt when first viewing her, how they couldn't forget the sight of her. They'd yearn for another invitation to Sedgebrook, if only to see her.

Smiling, she turned and walked to the family corridor. No one was awake. She was alone, as if she owned the great house and was privy to all its secrets.

REESE HAD TO hand it to her, Josephine had nerve. How was she going to explain her presence in Jordan's room? He didn't know, but he wasn't going to let her get that far.

She'd miscalculated and had worn something light. She looked like a ghost in the corridor, someone who might spark rumors of yet another haunting in the old house. He'd heard at least six stories since his first visit to Sedgebrook. He had deliberately cultivated friendships among the servants and now they felt free to tell him anything, from ghost stories to who was sleeping with whom and who wanted to work in London.

You never knew when a servant would come in handy. Plus, they were often the source of vital information such as timetables and habits.

Because of Jordan's money troubles, there weren't

many footmen at Sedgebrook. Otherwise, there would have been a few stationed at intervals throughout the house, especially at night. Their presence would have prevented Josephine from carrying out her intentions.

He was going to have to be the one to stop her.

She was a voluptuous creature and a gorgeous one. Of course, she knew her advantages and didn't hesitate to use her beauty when it was necessary. He couldn't fault her, since he occasionally utilized his own good looks. If he could charm a woman into giving him something he needed, thereby saving time and effort, all the better. Besides, violence had repercussions he disliked.

As a longtime friend, he'd been given a room not far from the ducal suite. Reese waited until Josephine was level to his door before grabbing her elbow with one hand. Except for a startled exclamation, she didn't make a sound as he pulled her into his room and closed the door behind him.

"Can't sleep, Miss York?"

"You scared me," she said, her hand at her throat.

"For a moment I thought you might be sleepwalking, since you're so far away from your room."

"I couldn't sleep," she said.

"And you thought to take a constitutional?"

"I might ask the same of you, Mr. Burthren."

"Reese, please," he said, his amusement surfacing. "It's after midnight. We're alone. You're in your night-clothes. It's not exactly a proper time or place, is it, Josephine?"

She took a step sideways, intending to slip by him, but he matched her movement.

Momentarily defeated, she looked up at him and

smiled charmingly. He didn't doubt she'd practiced the expression in the mirror.

"What are you doing awake, Reese?" she asked softly. "You can't sleep, either? Why, a guilty conscience?"

He bent his head until he was close enough to kiss her cheek.

"It's no good, Josephine. You won't trap him this way."

Placing her hand on his chest, she pushed at him. He didn't move.

"I don't know what you're talking about," she said.

"I'm sure that sweet and innocent look fools some people, but I'm not one of them."

"You're a truly despicable human being," she said.

"Ah, but I'm not the one haunting Sedgebrook, hoping to catch our host in a compromising position. Or are you going to pretend you weren't doing exactly that?" When she didn't answer, he continued. "You're wasting your time, you know."

"What do you mean?"

"Jordan has other things on his mind than a flirtation."

Her smile disappeared.

"Whereas I'm in the mood for a flirtation. Perhaps even more."

"Step aside, Mr. Burthren."

"Reese," he said.

"Step aside, Mr. Burthren."

"Reese," he repeated. "I'd like to hear my name on your lips."

"Reese," she said, accentuating the sibilant sound until it sounded something like a snake.

He admired a fiery woman.

"Reese," he said, stopping her from heading for the door by the simple act of pulling her into his arms.

He thought he might pass along a ghost story of his own, a tale of an outraged virgin. Or perhaps he would change it slightly since he was now almost certain Josephine was no longer a virgin. Perhaps he'd make her an avenging succubus roaming through Sedgebrook, intent on trapping men.

She'd let her hair down and it fell over her shoulders in dark waves. He wanted to thrust his hands into it. Her cheeks were pink, the color deepening as he studied her.

She stood there quivering with righteous indignation, biting her lip, and glaring up at him.

Damn, but he wanted to kiss her.

Before she had a chance to guess what was on his mind, he did just that.

Her mouth opened in surprise beneath his. He smiled when her outraged gasp turned into warm, softening lips.

She allowed the kiss to last a few long, enjoyable moments before placing her hands flat on his chest and pushing him away.

"How dare you!"

"Quite easily," he said, fingering the bow at her waist.

What a proper robe she was wearing. It was cinched tightly, as if to protect the nearly naked figure beneath. He pulled at the end of the belt and the robe fell open, revealing a proper cotton nightgown.

She grabbed the edges of the robe and held them together.

"What do you think you're doing?"

"Seducing you, I think," he said. "I hadn't intended to, but you are proving to be nearly irresistible."

Two tears fell down those beautiful cheeks of hers. She blinked up at him, her blue eyes deep with emotion.

"How could you treat me so horribly?"

He couldn't help but smile.

She was truly a magnificent actress.

"What did you think you were going to do, Josephine? Tell Jordan that same idiotic tale about not being able to sleep? Did you think to seduce him?"

She took a step back from him. Doing so put her close to his bed. He could reach out with one hand and push her gently onto the mattress.

"Afterward, you were going to do what? Scream in terror or do something to attract attention? Did you think being found in his bed would be enough for him to offer marriage?"

"You're insane," she said.

Her tears had dried up fast enough. She wasn't the pitiful virgin right now. He suspected the frown she was giving him was closer to her true nature.

"I'm leaving, right now," she said.

"Are you? Do you think I'm going to let you do what you'd planned?"

"Why shouldn't you? It's none of your concern."

He should have expected her arrogance. This woman was not going to be embarrassed or humiliated. Instead, she faced him down, almost daring him to do something.

He never wanted a woman as much as he wanted her, right this moment.

He smiled. "Oh, but it is. Jordan is my friend. He deserves better than your little games."

"Who do you think you are?" she asked, contempt dripping from every word. "The morals judge?"

He took a step toward her, until he was only inches away.

"No," he said. "I'm your lover."

She tilted her head back and stared up at him. "It's my decision who I take to my bed," she said, "and I don't choose you."

"Ah, but you have, by coming into my room and not making a sound."

He guessed her smile took a great deal of effort, but she somehow managed it.

"If you'd made it to Jordan's room you would have discovered that he wasn't there."

"Where is he?" she asked.

"Do you think I'm going to tell you? I wouldn't put it past you to wander through Sedgebrook looking for him. Better you should practice your seduction talents with me."

"I don't need any practice."

He pushed at her shoulders. The expression as she landed on the mattress was one he would always remember.

"Oh, I think you do," he said, joining her.

Chapter 17

*M*artha slipped outside her room, closing the door softly behind her. She stood there for a moment before crossing the hall and knocking softly on her sister's door.

When Josephine didn't answer she knocked again. When there was still no response, she grabbed the door handle and entered the room. The lamp was burning on the bedside table, but Josephine wasn't there.

In the time she was talking to Amy, Josephine had evidently put her plan into action.

Now what did she do? Dear God, what? She'd never been the type to panic, but she was cold with fear.

Had Josephine gone to the duke's suite?

She had to stop her.

She hadn't explored Sedgebrook like Josephine. She reasoned, however, that Jordan's suite would be among the larger bedchambers in the house, which meant they'd be at the end of the wing. There was no room at the end of this corridor, so she kept walking. Thankfully, she didn't encounter any servants as she passed the staircase and entered the other wing, coming to a set of double doors.

She tapped on the right door, but no one answered.

Her sister had behaved with forethought, determination, and cunning. But she doubted Josephine would be punished for this act or anything else. People like her sister never were. Instead, they were given excuses, their bad behavior accepted or brushed away.

As she waited, her fear turned to anger. She couldn't help but recall all those moments when Josephine had gotten away with something egregious. The excuses ran the gamut: *It's because she's so much younger than you, Martha. It's because Matthew rarely notices her. It's because she's half-French. It's because she has a less serious nature.*

What excuse would people give for Josephine's behavior tonight? She couldn't imagine one that made any sense, other than: *It's because Josephine was greedy. It's because Josephine saw something she wanted and she went after it.*

At another time, in another circumstance, she might have admired her sister's single-minded determination, but not now.

The duke wouldn't marry her; she knew that. Regardless of Josephine's behavior, it wouldn't result in her becoming the Duchess of Roth. Instead, her actions were certain to ruin her and cause gossip to swirl around the family.

Her stomach felt as if it was twisted in knots. Another emotion to lay at Josephine's feet. She didn't know if she was more afraid than she was angry or more angry than afraid.

She knocked again, her stomach churning.

Dear God, please help me do this.

Would God understand? Would He send a lightning bolt to strike them both, the sinning sister and

the one who wanted to sin? What was worse? To feel
envy? Or be bubbling with resentment against Josephine?

What was she going to say when the duke answered the door?

Is my sister here?

Have you seduced her yet?

She prayed the right words would come to her
when he opened the door.

Except he didn't.

Finally, she pushed down on the latch and entered
the duke's suite.

The sitting room was illuminated by a gas lamp
and, like the guest chambers, was adorned with a
mural. This one took up the whole of the far wall and
portrayed scenes of Rome she recognized from ste-
reoscope pictures of the city.

"Hello?"

No one answered.

Please, don't let them be in the bedroom, so occupied in their actions they didn't hear her. Could anything be worse than that?

Taking a few steps toward the closed door, she
wondered if it was wise to continue. Wondering, too,
in a self-examination proving to be acutely painful, if
she was here because of sisterly loyalty or womanly
jealousy.

It might be a little of both.

She crossed the room until she stood in front of the
door. She was trembling as she gripped the handle.
A moment later she drew back her hand, her heart
pounding so loudly she thought anyone on the other
side of the door could hear it.

She said a prayer, not unlike the ones she'd uttered

earlier. *Please, don't let her be here.* She was nearly sick to her stomach when she grabbed the handle again and made herself open the door.

The room was dark.

She didn't advance, merely stood in the doorway, her eyes adjusting to the darkness.

No one demanded she leave. No stern ducal voice questioned her presence.

The relief she felt at the sight of the empty bed, turned down for the night, was so overwhelming she was nearly faint.

Josephine wasn't here. Neither was the duke. She needn't explain anything. She didn't need to save Josephine. Thoughts she had for the expanse of only a few seconds, no more than that. The sound of a door opening sent her catapulting back into panic.

She didn't think, only reacted. She pulled the door closed and slipped behind a screen concealing the door to the bathing chamber, nearly tripping on a metal plant holder.

If Josephine wasn't with the duke, she would announce her presence and explain she had gotten lost. An idiotic excuse, but the only thing that came to mind.

At the moment, she wasn't thinking at all. She was only feeling. Terror, panic, regret, embarrassment, shame—they were all cascading through her.

Her heart was beating fiercely, her pulse racing. She could barely breathe. It wasn't going to be Josephine who made a laughingstock of the family. It was her. Rock-steady Martha, practical Martha, boring Martha who would rather study plans and calculate measurements than do anything shocking or untoward.

Perhaps one day she'd be exciting. Perhaps she'd

shock everyone who knew her by doing something entirely unlike her.

Not tonight, however. Please God, not now.

THE CEILING SHIFTED above him as Jordan made his way down the corridor to the staircase. Halfway up the long stretch of steps, the whole of the foyer abruptly altered position, causing him to grip the banister to keep from falling.

Perhaps it wasn't a good idea to take the grand staircase after all, but he didn't want to use the servants' stairs since so many of them were making for their beds. He didn't want to be seen weaving like a drunkard.

The elixir had hit him hard tonight. No doubt a result of the wine he'd had in the library while waiting for the bricks to work. What a fool he'd been for combining the two.

At least his leg wasn't hurting. He couldn't feel much of anything, including his nose. He couldn't test the theory, however, since his right hand was currently holding on to the banister and the left was carrying his walking stick.

Damnable thing, that. He hated the tangible proof of his injury. A constant reminder of his own fallacy. He'd been a fool to take Ercole out that day. He wasn't the horseman his brother had been.

He wasn't a lot of things his brother had been, including profligate and hedonistic. No, he was the proper son, the dutiful and honorable child of the wildly popular 9th Duke of Roth. A boy shuttled off to school when he got old enough, given enough funds to purchase a commission when he'd reached his majority.

He'd never done anything to attract the wrong kind of attention, but neither did he have that spark, that something that compelled people's interest. His father had it. Simon had it. Reese had it. Even the annoying Josephine York had it.

He wasn't dangerous or demanding or dictatorial. He wanted peace and contentment and order around him. He wanted to be able to give his mind room to breathe, to function, to examine and detect.

The landing abruptly tilted, making him idly wonder if he was going to tumble down the stairs. The Duke of Roth found at the bottom of the grand staircase, limbs shattered, mind lost, a fool dead before his time.

He gripped the banister even tighter, refusing to lose his footing. That's one thing he had for which he'd never been given credit—a stubbornness filling every part of him. He wouldn't give up. He would never surrender. Not to infirmity. Not to circumstances. Not to the mind-altering effects of the elixir.

Finally, he was done with the stairs, walking with some difficulty down the corridor. He stretched out his left hand as a guide, his fingers brushing against the wall to keep him centered on the runner.

He thought he heard laughter. Or it might be the elixir, bringing him taunting sounds and images as it normally did. He lived in a cloud of his own imagination when forced to take the stuff. He saw fantastical animals, colors, and shapes. Nothing was tethered to the earth but seemed to float slightly above the ground.

Not far now. Only a little way. Once in his room he would collapse on his bed and let the hallucinations continue. He'd allow himself to become part of them, the god on the clouds, Neptune of the sea, a bee buzzing in the Duchess's Garden.

Thank God he was almost to his suite.

THE BEDROOM WAS dark, the only light spilling in from the sitting room. She moved back behind the screen as the duke entered the suite. The door closed hard behind him, the noise loud in the silence of the night.

Was he angry?

She hoped not, because she needed to come out from behind the screen and announce herself. How could she explain being in his living quarters without him summarily banishing them tomorrow? Coupled with Josephine's outrageous actions, they'd hardly been the perfect houseguests, had they? Whether or not Gran felt up to the journey, there was every chance they would be asked to leave.

She heard halting footsteps near, so close she held her breath.

Now, Martha. Step out now and explain yourself.

"Who's there?"

His voice was odd, the speech slurred. Had he spent the time since dinner imbibing more spirits?

She peered out from behind the screen to encounter Jordan standing only a foot or two away from her.

His hand reached out and touched her, his fingers brushing against her bodice.

"What the devil?"

She swallowed with difficulty, but the words wouldn't come. Instead, they were trapped in her throat.

What could she possibly say?

He was suddenly closer. She raised one hand and encountered his shirt. In the past few hours he'd taken off his jacket, appearing as he had in the boathouse.

She was trembling. Could he feel it?

He took another step. His shoe edged hers, a curious mating.

He bent his head, his breath on her forehead.

"A dream," he muttered. "A fevered wish granted."

She didn't understand, but she thought he might be intoxicated.

Her heart felt as if it was skipping beats. She was breathless as if she'd been running in the past few minutes instead of hiding in his room.

Her hand moved, the fingers splaying. She closed her eyes, the better to sense him. Although she had sketched out her father's plans, she had no talent at drawing. For the first time, she wished she could take charcoal and paper and draw him as she felt him.

No doubt it was the influence of the mural of Rome, but she saw him as a gladiator, naked but for strips of leather, his eyes deadly intent. This man would fight for his life, would combat anything or anyone set against him.

He frightened her at the same time he excited something in her, a wish, a desire, a need to be someone different. Daring Martha. Beautiful Martha. Martha, who incited a man's yearning.

His breath was on her cheek now and she knew she should step away. Instead, she held herself still.

"Shall I kiss you, creature of my dreams?"

She should tell him who she was. She should inform him that she was the plain Martha with whom he had worked this afternoon. The same woman who'd been half in love with him before she ever met him.

His breath was on her lips now.

Josephine would have taken advantage of the moment. Josephine would have reached up, put her arms around his neck and opened her mouth to his kiss.

She wasn't Josephine.

But she did the same, standing on tiptoe, stretching both hands up to link behind his neck, waiting. Her first kiss and she desperately wanted it to be with him.

Suddenly, his mouth was on hers and she gasped in wonder. Every part of her body felt as if it was tingling, from her toes to the warmth inside her.

His lips tasted of wine, but that was only the first surprise.

No one had ever hinted about a kiss. Nor had anything she ever read explained it would harness your breath and send your heart catapulting. Your mind would be emptied of all thoughts until it felt as if light spread through you. Your body became a stained-glass window, vibrant colors appearing behind your closed lids.

Her hands tightened behind his neck as she began to tremble. His arms went around her, linking at her back, pulling her even tighter to him.

Could he feel her breasts?

She wanted him to touch her, which was only one of the shocking thoughts she had in the next few minutes. He didn't release her and she didn't struggle against him.

When he finally broke the kiss, they were both breathing hard.

"You feel real," he said, his voice different. Lower, perhaps, or slower, as if the words had been carefully considered and deliberately spoken.

She was shocking herself, but she didn't want to leave. Not yet. Give her a moment or two more of this bliss, please, enough to last her for a lifetime of memories.

"You can't be real."

Oh, but she was. More to the point, so was he. So real, so warm, and so close.

His fingers trailed over the edge of her collar. No one had ever told her that her neck would be so sensitive, or that a man's fingers would bring fire in their wake. No, not any man, only this man.

Had he had a great deal of experience in seduction? It seemed as if he had, because he bent to kiss her again and her whole body felt as if it was inflamed.

If anyone saw her now, she'd be ruined. Worse, she would be ridiculed. Who did she think she was? A true beauty, or a seductress—someone who could enchant the Duke of Roth? No, she was only Martha York, the girl who worked with her father, who could always be found out on the lake. Never in a ducal apartment adrift in passion.

She really had to leave. She had to escape, now, before anything else untoward happened. She was not going to continue to press herself against his body, marvel at his physique, or compare him to other men she'd seen.

She'd never been this close to a man or allowed one to take liberties with her. Not once had she encouraged a kiss or hoped he would touch her.

How shameful was she? She wanted to see him without his clothes. She chastised herself mentally for her forwardness but she didn't move away. She couldn't remember ever having that wish about anyone, but it seemed so natural and so right to want to place her hands on his bare shoulders, marvel at the play of muscles she could feel beneath the shirt.

Please, give her a few minutes to flatten her hands against his chest, allow her fingers to trail through the hair there, then dance across his flat stomach.

Her thoughts weren't the least virginal. She wished she had more experience instead of having only witnessed the act on a shadowed terrace.

A button on his shirt slipped free. Two fingers slid into the placket, her fingertips resting against the skin of his chest. By her actions she'd broken some kind of barrier, one of thought and will.

Slowly she undid two more buttons until her hand slipped inside his shirt. She felt as if she'd done this before, as if she knew him in an elemental way. As if kissing him was natural and so were her explorations.

His fast breathing was an echo of hers. Was his heart beating as rapidly? Were his thoughts as chaotic?

She knew what she was doing was wrong, could never be explained to another soul. Yet, at the same time, it felt right and ordained. She was supposed to be here with him in this shadowed bedroom. She was destined to touch him, ramping up the wonder and passion she felt.

He didn't move. She continued until all the buttons were open and she could push the edges of the shirt wide.

Stepping forward, she placed her lips on his chest, a kiss of benediction, of wonder, and possibly of supplication.

She knew what she wanted to do next, continue disrobing him, revealing him in all his beauty. She wanted to run her hands over his skin, rejoicing in the symmetry and perfection of his body.

She didn't get the chance.

Chapter 18

*P*rovidence had evidently felt charitable toward him tonight. *Here, Jordan, I grant you agony with your leg, but forgetfulness in the elixir and passion in the touch of a soft and welcoming woman.*

The room was spinning, but she felt real. She was his prize for having endured the earlier pain. He wouldn't remember her tomorrow or even a few hours from now. However, he was going to enjoy the hallucination as long as it lasted.

A waking dream, that's what he would consider it.

She was touching him and breathing in a way that made him think she was as aroused as he. If she was real, he'd thank her for making him feel as if he was whole and virile and man enough to please her.

But she was only a creature formed by his loneliness and the opiates in Dr. Reynolds's elixir.

When she'd kissed him, the top of his head went sailing somewhere among the stars. He wanted to kiss her again. He wanted to feel the desire she so effortlessly summoned.

Where had his walking stick gone? He'd dropped it somewhere after entering the bedroom and being confronted with this delightful dream made real. His hand reached out, pressed hers against his chest.

He threaded his fingers through the mass of her curls, feeling the softness of her hair as he bent to kiss her. A drumbeat began deep inside him, the rhythm slow but increasing, demanding.

How long had it been since he felt the touch of a woman? Too long. He'd been celibate for years, first out of necessity in the navy. Second, because after ascending to the dukedom the last thing he wanted was to find himself in a compromising position with a young miss.

His waking dream wasn't a virtuous female and he didn't have to worry about anything. She wasn't real. Neither was he, in the strictest sense. His mind was under the throes of the drug. His will was compromised. His needs were dominant.

He folded his arms around her, drawing her closer. In the way of all dreams she fit perfectly as if she belonged there.

She was tall enough she could place her lips against his throat, sigh against his neck, and make him grateful for the effects of the elixir.

He'd never before kissed a woman and felt like this. Not once in his experience had the world fallen away.

Until this moment he thought he knew passion. He didn't realize it had the ability to infuse him with joy. Or make him want to grab her and twirl her around the room in a thoroughly un-Jordan-like move.

He wanted to kiss her until dawn lit up the room. He wanted to touch her everywhere and find those spots that made her giggle or sigh or moan. She was only a waking dream, half wish, half need, created by the elixir.

Yet one kiss led to another and to another until he felt weak in the knees.

He was going to fall down any moment.

He stumbled backward, feeling the mattress against his back.

She didn't utter one compassionate word, thank God. This hallucination was not a creature crafted of pity.

He drew her with him and she went, her lips still clinging to his. Somehow they climbed onto the mattress, his delusion remaining with him.

He didn't say a word, terrified she would disappear and he'd be left staring at a twirling ceiling. Until he lost himself to the opiates, he would enjoy her touch and her mind-numbing kisses.

To his surprise, his waking dream was helping him disrobe. Not only him, but her. Her fingers flew over the fastenings, most of which defied his clumsy hands. Women's fashions were geared to making it as difficult as possible for a man to understand them.

Virtue maintained through confusion.

She slid from the bed and he stretched out a hand to stop her then clenched his fingers into a fist. Let her go. Let her disappear. What sort of fool was he to want to love a hallucination?

To his surprise, she wasn't leaving him after all; she'd only stood to remove her petticoat. When she returned to the bed his waking dream was attired only in a shift. With any luck she wouldn't leave until after they loved.

He might become addicted to Dr. Reynolds's elixir if it promised this kind of companion.

"You're not real," he said.

There, a bit of sanity in the midst of this fog. At least he was attempting to find some semblance of himself. His rational mind was trying to make sense of everything while his body merely wanted the pleasure.

Her finger pressed against his lips, followed shortly by her mouth.

His imagination had provided a dream who could kiss like a houri, who tempted him without a word spoken.

His leg prevented him from being completely mobile, but he could certainly sit up and remove his shoes, socks, and then his trousers. It had been years since he'd undressed in front of a woman, but it didn't matter because she wasn't truly there. She was a thought, a wish, something fervently desired and as amorphous as a cloud.

Her hands wrapping around his ankle was surprisingly erotic. But when her fingers trailed up his leg, he stopped her. The pain was there, dormant but waiting to be summoned from his mental fog. Not yet. He didn't want it to return just yet. Let him experience the miracle of this enchanting, unreal creature for a few more minutes before he surrendered to either the darkness or the agony.

He removed his shirt, lay back on the bed and allowed himself to fully enjoy the moment. His waking dream stripped him of every thought, of every worry. He felt only pleasure at her hands and unexpected joy.

Her hands stroked from his waist, all the way up his chest to his neck before bracketing his face. She lowered her head to kiss him again.

If she was real, he'd ask what gave her pleasure. Her excitement was evident from the soft exhalations of breath escaping her. When his hands stroked her, she softly moaned.

His imagination furnished her with the softest

skin, the smoothest curves, and plump breasts fitting his palms just so. She was perfect, created out of his most fervent fantasies.

Her skin was warmer than normal as if she had a fever. If so, it was another thing they shared, this dream creature and his besotted self. He felt as if he was in the middle of a conflagration, flames bursting from inside him.

Sliding to the center of the bed, he raised her over him. He did so with ease, his imagination making this seduction effortless. She didn't question why he put her in that position. Why would she? This female was an extension of himself, his wishes given the illusion of flesh.

Her shift was white in the moonlight, making her appear like a phantom. His body responded as if she was real. His heart was racing, his pulse jumping in concert. His breath was tight and fast.

Real or not he prayed the hallucination would last. Just for a few more minutes. He wanted her. He had to have her.

She bowed over him, placed her lips on his, and sighed into his mouth. For an eternity of moments he was lost in her kiss.

He needn't cajole her or charm her or even appear before her flawed and broken. She already knew him. She was part of him. He'd created her solely for these perfect moments. As she allowed him to pull her shift over her head, he realized his imagination was so much more powerful than he'd ever known.

She didn't see him as damaged or lacking. In this act of joining, they were simply two creatures lost in the throes of passion, rejoicing in the act of making love. Who cared if he was drugged and she wasn't real?

Her breasts filled his hands, the hard tips pressing into his palms. One hand at her back urged her down. He raised his head until he could mouth a nipple, smiling at the sound of her sigh above him.

He couldn't think, could only feel, desire overcoming any memory of pain. Ecstasy surged through him, numbing him to outside noises or even his own being. The creature of his imagination moaned above him. He lifted her until her heated flesh slid over his erection, teasing him with its wetness. He hesitated there, at her opening, then guided her into place. She was tight yet welcoming, clenching around him as he entered.

Her moan of delight changed slightly.

Damn him, he'd imagined a virgin.

She was a sweet innocent who needed to be soothed, treated with tenderness. In that next instant the cogent thought abruptly vanished, leaving him overwhelmed by pleasure.

Why had he imagined a virgin? A question lasting until she rose up over him. His hands on her waist urged her down again.

He opened his eyes to see her back arched, her head back. Her breasts, proud and large, were almost begging for his hands. He cupped each, gently pinching the nipples.

She moaned again and this time the sound was too real, almost piercing the fog surrounding him.

His hands left her breasts only for a moment to stroke from her waist, down her thighs, and back up to her breasts. He wanted to embed the touch of her on his skin for those nights when he couldn't summon her, when distorted images and frightening sounds took her place.

She rose and fell, rose and fell again, the rhythm one she began. She was making little sounds that accompanied her movements, soft breathy gasps telling him she no longer felt discomfort.

His vision grayed. The moment extended. Was this what dying was like, when you were conscious of every pore, every inch of skin, every beat of your heart even as you became separated from yourself? He felt, in that instant, as if he was being thrown out into the cosmos, only one more flickering star, and then gradually returned to his body, to his bed, and to the consciousness that his waking dream was weeping.

Surely he wouldn't have imagined such a thing? Was it the elixir? Or Providence, punishing him for having such an erotic dream?

She was vanishing, sliding from the bed, departing as he'd half expected from the beginning. The fog was returning, falling over him.

He was alone, the stark silence in the room expected yet troubling. The opiates had created a lover for him, one who'd given him immense pleasure, but she wasn't destined for permanence. She was only a temporary respite from his loneliness, a ghost created in his mind.

He heard the door close, as he allowed himself to fall, to spin downward into a drugged sleep.

"I'LL WALK YOU back to your room," Reese said.

Josephine glanced back at the bed where he lounged. "You haven't played the gentleman all night, why bother now?"

"A reward, perhaps?" he said, his voice amused. "A token of my appreciation for hours well spent? I trust you felt the same."

"You're a skilled lover, Reese, is that what you want to hear? That I nearly screamed?"

"As I recall, you did," he said, chuckling. "A good thing Sedgebrook's walls are thick, else you would have terrified the staff. Everyone would have run for the exits, thinking some type of banshee creature was loose."

She bent, retrieved a pillow from the floor, and tossed it at him.

"You are truly a despicable creature," she said, wishing she didn't feel so wonderful.

She was finding it difficult to dislike the man when her body was still thrumming with satisfaction.

"Am I?"

He propped himself up on one elbow and watched her as she looked for her clothing. He'd insisted on leaving the light on and she found it a heady experience being so openly admired.

Dawn would come shortly and the industrious Sedgebrook servants would be up and about. She grabbed her nightgown and wrapper and put them on, intent on returning to her room before encountering anyone. She'd come dressed for seduction, hadn't she? Just not in Reese's bed.

There was still time for her original plan. Gran didn't look as if she was ready to leave for home. There was always tonight.

"You're plotting something," he said. "I can see it in your eyes."

"I don't know what you're talking about," she said, standing.

"I'd put some cream on that spot on your chin."

One hand flew up, her fingers smoothing over her face.

"You marked me?" she asked, horrified.

"There and in a few other places," he said, grinning at her. "Your left breast, for example, bears the marks of my night beard."

She frowned at him, annoyed when he began to laugh.

Turning, she went to the door and listened for a moment. From the mantel clock, it was only a little after one, too early for the servants to be up and about.

She slowly pulled the door open, looked both ways, then slipped out into the corridor, closing the door behind her. Halfway back to her room, she realized she wasn't alone after all.

Martha was ahead of her, fully dressed, and hurrying to her room. Evidently, everyone was roaming Sedgebrook tonight.

What was proper, staid, and plain Martha doing out of her bed?

MARTHA ESCAPED FROM Jordan's suite feeling like God Himself was chasing her. What had she done? Why had she remained? It was clear he hadn't been himself. He'd thought she was a sylph, a spirit, someone he'd imagined.

He'd been real to her.

What could she say if anyone discovered what had happened?

He seduced me. Not entirely correct, was it? She'd had plenty of time to leave. She could have slipped from the room at any time, but she hadn't.

I was confused. She hadn't been. Instead, she'd been certain of what she wanted and it had been *him*.

I was innocent. True enough, but she wasn't now.

Her grandmother would say she'd lowered her bridal chances. *No man wants a well-used woman, child.* Gran had originally made the comment during her season, warning her about not being alone with one of her suitors. What would Gran say if she knew she'd not only been alone with the Duke of Roth but that she'd wholeheartedly participated in her own downfall?

He'd taken her virginity. She'd found discomfort and delight in his arms. An apt reason for wanting to burst into tears.

She didn't get the chance.

She'd just closed the door to her room when it suddenly opened again.

"Where have you been?" Josephine demanded. "What have you been doing, Martha?"

She didn't want to have this conversation now. Nor was she in the mood to take on Josephine. She wanted to think about the past few hours, about Jordan, and how she would act when she saw him in the morning.

Her sister, however, entered the bedroom, shutting the door behind her. Josephine advanced on her, stopping a few feet away.

"Tell me. Where were you?"

"It's none of your concern."

At that, Josephine narrowed her eyes.

"You've been with someone, haven't you? You've had relations."

The accusation left Martha staring at her sister.

"What are you talking about? Of course I haven't."

"Who was it? Did one of the footmen strike your fancy?"

"Will you leave?"

"No. Who were you with? Tell me."

When she didn't answer, her sister turned toward the door.

"Maybe I'll go tell Gran you've been wandering around Sedgebrook before dawn. She'll get it out of you."

Her stomach lurched at the thought of Josephine waking their grandmother with that kind of news.

"Leave Gran alone, Josephine," she said, biting back her fear.

Josephine glanced over her shoulder and smiled, the expression one she wouldn't have shared with the men who admired her. This smile had an edge to it.

"Tell me or I'll go right now," she said, turning. "You know I will."

Josephine was certainly capable of doing exactly that.

For a moment she balanced the thought of revealing where she'd been against Josephine's threat. Would the truth silence her sister?

She didn't have a choice, did she?

"The duke, all right? I was with Jordan."

The attractive pink of Josephine's cheeks deepened to become a splotchy flush spreading down to her neck. For a moment she didn't say anything, just stared at Martha.

"You couldn't have," Josephine finally said. "He wouldn't have looked at you."

Hurt crowded out any fear she felt. Martha took a deep breath and somehow managed a smile.

"If it makes any difference, he didn't. He was besotted."

"Was he?" Josephine asked.

She nodded. "I don't think he even knew it was me." She sat on the end of the bed, wishing it wasn't the truth.

"How interesting. Did you seduce him? Did you go to him in hopes he'd make your maidenly dreams come true? How was he? Did that leg of his interfere with his manly charms?"

"I'm not talking about this," she said, standing and moving past Josephine to the screen in the corner. She wanted to bathe.

"You're right to want to wash the scent of him off you, Martha."

She loved Josephine, but there were times—like now—when she didn't like her much.

After she washed, Martha peered out from behind the screen to find Josephine had left the room. Staring at the closed door, she wondered if her sister had gone to see Gran. Would she tell their grandmother anything? Or would Josephine simply go back to her room and forget everything she'd learned?

That was a foolish wish, wasn't it? As long as she was wishing, then perhaps Gran would feel well enough to travel a day early and they could leave Sedgebrook.

Please, God, let her go home to Griffin House. Now before anything else happened.

Chapter 19

At dawn, Susan York was abruptly awakened from a perfectly beautiful dream. Her youthful self had been holding hands with the young man she'd loved all her life and the two of them were strolling through a lush and overgrown garden.

The bees were buzzing and she heard the sound of singing, making her wonder who was serenading them. She was turning to say something to the man she loved when her youngest granddaughter grabbed her hand and anointed it with tears.

She blinked up at the ceiling, trying to make sense of what was happening.

Josephine was sobbing, her face buried in the mattress at her side.

"Oh, Gran, I'm so sorry. I made such a mistake."

What had Josephine done now?

What a pity Josephine couldn't join her mother in France. Unfortunately, she didn't hold out much hope for that happening. Her granddaughter was a beautiful girl. Marie was an aging woman who was as vain as Josephine. She suspected the last thing Marie would want around her was youthful competition, even if it was her daughter.

"I was a fool, Gran, but he was so persuasive. I didn't know what I was doing."

There was nothing else to do but to wake up and face this newest catastrophe, whatever it was.

Slowly, Susan sat up, rearranging her pillow behind her.

Josephine was seated at the side of her bed, weeping.

"I didn't mean to, Gran. It was a terrible mistake. A terrible mistake. Now I don't know what to do. What will happen if I'm with child?"

Now she was definitely wide-awake.

"What are you talking about, child?"

"The duke. He seduced me."

Hopefully, Amy would be bringing her strong black tea shortly, the better to cope with this situation.

"You had better begin at the beginning, Josephine," she said, feeling a sense of dread probably not out of proportion to the circumstances.

Josephine's eyes were red, her hair askew. Her cheeks were flushed and there was a mark on her face Susan remembered from her days of being kissed senseless by her night-bearded husband.

In short, her granddaughter looked as if she'd been engaged in pursuits designed to better occur after marriage than before it.

She wasn't a fool. She knew quite well that couples occasionally made it to the bridal bed before the minister said the vows. On a few shocking occasions, the bride was even pregnant before the ceremony.

She had her suspicions about Josephine. The girl seemed a little more knowledgeable than she should have been. Plus, she didn't hesitate in trying to charm every man she saw, from the stablemaster to any number of shopkeepers who visited Griffin House.

At the moment, however, it didn't matter how much she'd flirted. If the story she was telling was true, they had an enormous problem on their hands.

Had the duke truly seduced her?

"Go to your room," she said now.

For the past several years, ever since coming to live at Griffin House, she'd watched Josephine carefully. If she had a choice between a falsehood or the truth, all things being equal, her granddaughter sometimes chose to lie.

Had she lied about this?

"What are you going to do, Gran?" Josephine asked.

She didn't know. Dear heavens, she didn't know.

"Go to your room right now. I will think on it."

"What if I'm with child?"

"Shouldn't you have considered that earlier, Josephine?"

The girl smiled, an expression out of place for this moment and her earlier tears. She wasn't entirely certain she believed her granddaughter, but she had to act on the information regardless.

She watched as Josephine left the room. When Amy arrived with her tray, Susan swung her feet over the side of the bed and addressed her maid.

"We have a problem, Amy. A problem I hadn't anticipated, but I think it's going to change everything."

JORDAN HAD A blinding headache on waking, but that was often the result of taking Dr. Reynolds's elixir. The concoction might ease the pain in his leg, but it left him with wild dreams and a morning headache mimicking the worst hangover he'd ever had. He was also nauseated but that symptom eased once he had something to eat.

Something else was wrong. Not pain, exactly, because his leg always felt better after taking the elixir. This was a sensation almost like a mental itch, reminding him of something he needed to remember, a feeling that things weren't right.

He'd never experienced it before, but then he'd never seen blood on his sheets, either. It corresponded to a memory cloaked in a grayish white shroud. His dream lover had been a virgin.

But she hadn't been a dream.

He pulled the sheets from the bed and shoved them into the bottom of the armoire, then pulled them out and stared at the pile of linen. He'd never felt the burden of his dukedom as much as he did now, wishing to dispose of the evidence he'd deflowered a woman he couldn't remember. His servants would find the sheets, talk among themselves. He might even be visited by Mrs. Browning who would want to know why he'd accosted one of the maids.

What the hell had he done last night?

What the hell was he going to do now?

He dropped the sheets back on the bed. If anyone asked—and they wouldn't—he'd simply tell them he had a restless night. And the blood? The blood wasn't necessarily a sign he'd bedded a virgin. He could have cut himself somehow when he was under the effects of the drug.

Good God, he was now lying to himself. Practice for lying to the world, no doubt.

What the hell had he done last night?

"It was bad, then?" Reese said when he joined him for breakfast.

Although he valued Reese's friendship, he didn't want to see the compassionate look in the other man's eyes. He didn't need anyone's pity.

"Manageable," he said, smiling lightly.

He had every intention of going to the boathouse, but the Yorks' maid was suddenly standing in the doorway.

"Your Grace?"

"Yes? What is it?"

Had Mrs. York's condition worsened? That's all this ruination of a morning needed.

"Begging your pardon, Your Grace, but Mrs. York would like to meet with you on a matter of some urgency."

His first thought was that she'd decided to leave. If so, she'd take Martha with him. Where had that sudden regret come from?

"Tell her I'll call on her within the quarter hour."

The maid nodded, performed a slight curtsy and disappeared, leaving him sitting there, his appetite suddenly gone.

Perhaps they would be leaving today. Or perhaps she simply wished to convey her thanks to the staff. Or request a certain meal to tempt her appetite. Nothing about the request should have summoned a sour feeling in his stomach or a dread making his extremities feel suddenly cold.

Standing, he placed his napkin beside the plate, nodded to the maid who entered the room with a fresh teapot, and made his way up the stairs.

The journey was, as it had been for the past year, a slow one and more than a little awkward. Yet each week brought about progress. He was at least able to mount the steps without assistance. He no longer needed to be conveyed about on a stretcher.

At the top of the staircase he took a few minutes to steady himself, annoyed to discover his hands were trembling. An effect of the exertion, and one he hoped would ease in time. Or maybe it was just simply the anticipation of the meeting to come.

The dread was increasing, coupled as it was with the discovery he'd made this morning. Something had happened last night. Something that hadn't been a dream, a hallucination, or an effect of the elixir. Something was terribly wrong and as he turned left, heading for Mrs. York's room, he felt as if he was walking to the gallows.

She wanted to see him on a matter of some urgency.

He'd bedded a woman last night. A virgin.

His memory strained to recall how she'd spoken. Was she well educated? He couldn't remember. Was she quick-witted? Had she amused him? He couldn't recall. Had they spoken of anything other than their base needs, some conversation to give him a clue to her identity?

Who the hell had she been?

A woman had been in his room and he'd taken her to his bed. He hadn't been capable of convincing her, so she would have come of her own accord. Why had she even been in his room?

Was it Martha?

His honor would demand that he do the right thing. Perhaps, at the base of it, that's why he hadn't sent her away. Maybe his drugged mind had realized what it meant to take her to his bed. She understood his work.

She had a fascinating mind. There was something about her that was arresting, some ability she had to summon his gaze. It was the way she spoke. He liked watching her lips enunciate the words. Or perhaps her expressive eyes. He suspected that if Martha thought you were an idiot, she'd leave you with no doubt of it.

She didn't think he was damaged.

She had a quick wit, was loyal and kind.

He could do worse for a wife. In fact, considering that she was an heiress, he couldn't think of another candidate for the position who would be so ideal.

She had, even virginal, been eager to explore passion. He'd been caught up by her, enchanted, and nearly overwhelmed.

Would she want him? He had a suspicion she didn't give a flying farthing if he was a duke or a footman. Would she be miserable if her grandmother forced her to marry him?

The next few minutes would tell, wouldn't they?

He made his way down the corridor to the guest chamber and knocked on the door. The Yorks' maid opened it and stood aside for him to enter.

Mrs. York sat up in bed, commanding the room with the aristocracy of the queen. Josephine sat on the chair beside the bed.

Martha was nowhere in sight.

He nodded to Mrs. York.

"Are you feeling well?" he asked.

"No, Your Grace, I find I'm not. In fact, I'm feeling disturbed and disappointed."

That comment put to rest any thought that this meeting might be for an innocuous reason. No doubt the tension in the room was natural, given the circumstances.

"I've been forced to ask you to attend me because of your behavior and that of my granddaughter."

Was that why Martha wasn't in the room? To shield her from any humiliation? If such was the case, why was Josephine here? As an unmarried woman, it was hardly proper for her to be present at this meeting.

"Josephine has confessed all," she said.

He stared at the woman.

He was having trouble marshaling his thoughts, no doubt a residual effect of the elixir.

"What?" It was, in his defense, the only word he could think of to say.

"My granddaughter has told me you've taken her virginity, Your Grace. Do you deny it?"

He looked at Josephine, trying to reconcile her image with the one he'd already formed in his mind. His waking dream had been Martha. Hadn't it been her?

He'd threaded his fingers through her hair, marveling at how it had curled around his hand. He'd kissed her lips, lips that were fuller than Josephine's. Her breasts had filled his palms. He'd heard her soft, throaty voice in his ear.

Or had it all been wrong, his mind's wish to make less of a disaster of the circumstances? Because that's what this was, a bloody, undeniable catastrophe.

"Do you deny it, Your Grace?"

Josephine suddenly gave out a sob, then dabbed at the corners of her eyes. He'd never before caused a woman to weep. Or if he had he was unaware of it.

Words were impossible. They would simply not make the journey from his brain to his lips. He felt as if he was still under the effects of the elixir, the room hazy and not entirely in focus. Sunlight streamed in through the window and it was too bright, almost glaring. His thoughts were chaotic, unformed: the only word making itself known was simple and declarative. *No. No. No.*

He looked at Mrs. York, caught by her sharp gaze, held aloft by the strength of her will.

When he'd first surfaced after his accident, he'd been told he'd broken his leg and pelvis. He'd never be the same. He would never walk again. He would be in constant pain. His life, as he'd always known it, was over. He'd heard those words with the same disbelief he now heard Mrs. York's.

His concept of himself, whole and unbroken, had had to endure a new birth, one taking place over months of learning to walk again, pushing himself from one milestone to another.

This transition—a new birth as well—took only minutes, but instead of hope he felt something in him die. An excitement, an enthusiasm, a need he'd not even known was there.

Martha wouldn't be his wife. He wouldn't make her the Duchess of Roth. Instead, his lust, his weakness, his need for the elixir had done the worst thing, delivered up to him a hideous choice: to defy his honor or take as his bride a woman he distrusted and disliked.

"Your Grace? Are you going to say anything?"

Josephine's weeping intensified.

"Yes," he said, the word forced from his mouth and coated with reluctance.

"Yes, what?"

He was being upbraided as if he was in short pants, except his sin was one of a mature man. He shouldn't have bedded her. He should have called for Frederick or Mrs. Browning or summoned one of the maids or a footman or two and had her summarily ejected.

He shouldn't have taken Dr. Reynolds's preparation. His damnable leg had led to all of this. And his pride had led to the injury to his leg. In other words, the responsibility for last night led straight back to him.

Her look was impatient, but it didn't matter. Not when he was having to extract every syllable from his lips with a pincer.

"Evidently, given the evidence, I seduced your granddaughter."

Only it wasn't Josephine. In his drugged state he'd replaced her with another woman, one he'd wanted. One he respected and admired. One, if the truth served any purpose at all at this moment, he felt as if he'd known for years.

"What do you suggest we do about the situation, Your Grace?"

The point of his honor sharpened, spearing him to the wall.

"There's only one thing to do, isn't there?" he said.

No, there were several things, none of which would serve him well. He could banish all the York women from his home. He could explain about the elixir. He could take himself off to Italy, like his brother did whenever anything difficult happened.

Or he could simply bow to circumstances.

"Will you do me the honor of becoming my wife, Miss York?"

There, honor was satisfied. Nothing else mattered, did it? Not even this horror filling the whole of him.

He heard her answer from far away, said something else in response to her grandmother's words, managed to act in a semicoherent fashion until it was done, over, complete, only the details to be arranged.

When it was finished, when the noose was laid around his neck and he was led to the gallows—with instructions to step lively, man—he left the room knowing that, once again, his life had changed. Only there was no hope this time.

Regardless of what he did, he could never make this situation bearable.

Chapter 20

*W*hen Martha went to the boathouse the next morning she found it empty. Jordan was nowhere in sight. Nor was there a note explaining his absence.

She sat there for a half hour, feeling increasingly uncomfortable.

Was the duke deliberately avoiding her? Was he ashamed about last night? Did he wish it had never happened?

What could she possibly say if he felt that way? Nothing, of course. She would simply have to pretend that his regret meant little to her.

She returned to the house to discover that Gran was meeting with him, an event that had her stomach plummeting to her toes.

Josephine had said something. Gran had summoned Jordan. Her world was about to explode in a firestorm of recriminations.

She retreated to her room, feeling a cornucopia of emotions. Fear, perhaps a little of that. Dread—yes, that, certainly. Shame? Society would say she should be ashamed. It was a rule, one of those she didn't particularly like. Perhaps she should try to summon some regret. She didn't want to hurt her grandmother or Jordan in any way. Embarrassment? It was there in large measure. How could she possibly be expected to talk about last night in front of other people?

Perhaps she could go back to Griffin House with the wagon driver if he hadn't left, anything but be subjected to that.

She sat in her room for an hour until Amy knocked on the door.

"You're to come to a meeting, Miss Martha," Amy said. "Your grandmother says it's important."

"A meeting?"

The maid nodded and gave her directions.

She was to go to yet another of Sedgebrook's parlors, this one called the Veldt. When she arrived, she realized the room was most definitely not a woman's chamber, not with the spears and shields painted in wild slashes of brown and black and arranged along the pale green walls.

Fearsome masks, some round, some elongated until they stretched at least three feet, were mounted on a far wall.

The room was on the second floor and no doubt filled the function of an office, due to the desk sitting by the window. She wondered if the duke had chosen it for that reason or for the fact that it didn't require her grandmother to descend the steps. She had a feeling it was the latter, because he'd always struck her as being considerate of others, even when it wasn't convenient for him to do so.

Look at how kind he had been to Gran, as well as the hospitality he'd shown them.

She was the first to arrive, and wanted to ask someone if the masks and weapons came from Africa. Unfortunately, the next person to enter the room was Josephine.

They hadn't spoken since last night.

She wasn't surprised to see that Josephine's sparkling green eyes were pink. Someone who didn't know her well would think she'd spent the intervening hours crying. Or that the dark circles meant she was feeling ill.

She knew her sister and had seen Josephine redden her own eyes with a mixture she'd purchased in London. A tiny bit of soot would explain the dark circles. Josephine was not above dulling her beauty if it meant succeeding in manipulating people.

"Why are we here?" she asked.

No one had told her. While Amy said it was important, she hadn't added any additional information. When Amy didn't want to say anything further no amount of coaxing would get her to speak.

"Gran wishes to make an announcement," Josephine said now, studying the room with an almost acquisitive look.

She needed to speak to Josephine about her behavior, but now was not the time.

Besides, she was getting the feeling she was about to be called to account for her behavior last night. The fact that Josephine refused to look at her, instead choosing to studiously examine the masks, was a form of premonition.

Why here, though? Why hadn't Gran summoned her to her room? Was it because she was also going to ask Jordan to be in attendance?

Please, no.

She sat on one of the dark brown overstuffed settees with a rosewood frame carved with horns and animal faces. Josephine sat on the opposite settee.

Her sister was wearing yet another dress, this one

a dark blue with a white-and-blue striped sash. The fabric of the skirt was drawn up from the hem, revealing a white-and-blue striped underskirt before meeting in a bustle at the back. She'd never seen the garment before and under normal circumstances she would tell Josephine how lovely it was. However, she wasn't feeling charitable toward Josephine at the moment.

Amy had done miracles with Martha's dress, sponging off the dirt at the hem, freshening up the bow at the bustle, but it was the same lavender dress she'd worn for days.

Why was she worried about what she was wearing? Did her appearance matter?

She didn't want to be here, dread settling over her like a warm blanket.

"Did you tell anyone?" she asked Josephine.

Her sister wouldn't look at her.

"Josephine, please. Did you tell Gran what happened last night?"

Her sister only smiled at her, a small, almost pitying expression that only increased Martha's anxiety.

Her sister had betrayed her, a fact that unfortunately didn't surprise her.

The clock on the mantelpiece struck the hour. Both she and Josephine glanced at it, each other, and then away.

The tale would be spread to London, she was certain. People liked to talk about the York family. York Armaments was an important institution, both for the government and the military. She could almost hear the gossips' words.

Martha? The older one? Oh, the spinster girl. Oh yes, Martha. You say she did what? How droll. You wouldn't think it of her, as plain as she is. Studious, though, isn't she? A bluestocking, I hear. She works on weapons, can you imagine? But to go to the duke's bed? What did she think to accomplish by her actions? Other than shaming herself, of course. Did she actually think the duke would offer for her? Well, she isn't that smart after all, is she?

Hopefully, none of them would realize that she'd lost her mind, that she'd been so taken by Jordan's looks, by his manner, by the way he spoke she'd lost all sense around him. Or that she'd been so filled with desire—a word heretofore meaning absolutely nothing to her—that she hadn't given any thought to her reputation, or any other ramifications, for that matter.

She deserved every single bit of gossip anyone might say about her.

She knew when the duke entered the room, because Josephine whipped out a handkerchief and began dabbing at the corners of her eyes. She uttered a choked sob, patted her chest with one hand, then sighed loudly.

"If you would put the tray there, Sarah," he said.

The maid who followed him put the tray on the table between the two settees with a second maid replicating her actions. Both trays were laden with teapots and plates filled with delicacies both savory and sweet.

Evidently, refreshments were to be served at the scene of her humiliation.

Josephine stretched out one trembling hand. "Shall I pour?" she asked, her voice sweet, demure, and faint.

The duke glanced at her. "If you wish."

"Don't you think you should wait for Gran?" Martha asked.

Josephine looked toward the duke, smiled tremulously, and said, "It's up to you, Jordan. Would you like a cup now?"

"I'm content to wait on your grandmother, Josephine."

He walked to the desk, turned one of the chairs in front of it toward them, and sat. He couldn't be any farther from them unless he left the room.

She couldn't look at him. She couldn't even look in his direction. Perhaps she should just scrawl a confession on a note admitting to everything and leave. She hardly needed to be here.

Nor was she in the mood to witness Josephine's theatrics.

"I apologize for my tardiness," Gran said.

Martha turned to see her grandmother standing in the doorway, looking healthy, hale, and as autocratic as a duchess. Her gaze touched on Jordan, then Josephine, and finally lit on Martha.

She nodded, as if coming to some kind of decision.

Martha straightened her shoulders, placed her hands flat on her knees, and stared at the tea set. They had a similar set at home that they rarely used since silver didn't hold the heat well. But their service didn't have a crest on it, this one belonging to the Hamiltons.

She wasn't certain the Yorks could trace their lineage back as far as the duke's family could.

Why on earth was she reflecting on tea sets and lineage? Because she'd rather think about anything but what Gran was about to say. She'd have to be courageous, admit to her behavior, and somehow endure the chastisement of those present.

When Mr. Burthren entered the room, followed by both Mrs. Browning and Frederick, she was shocked. Amy was the last to arrive, taking up a place beside the door. Evidently, she was going to be publicly excoriated. Martha took a deep breath and readied herself.

Gran squared her shoulders and looked at all of them one by one.

"I have something to tell you," her grandmother finally said. She let a moment elapse before she continued. "It is my pleasure to announce that the Duke of Roth and my granddaughter, Josephine, are to be married."

Martha had never before considered the act of blinking. What an absolutely marvelous cooperation of brain and eyes. Her eyelids closed and then opened again on their own. Her heart beat and she breathed the same way, too. Each separate function was performed without her conscious thought. A good thing, because she was suddenly incapable of it.

Her heart beat, another automatic function. She would have swallowed, but there seemed to be an impediment in her throat.

There was nothing wrong with her hearing, however, or her sight. She watched as Mr. Burthren crossed the room to shake Jordan's hand. Amy proffered her congratulations as did the housekeeper and the majordomo, each of them stiffly proper.

She wanted to ask for clarification or explanation. Nothing made any sense whatsoever.

What had her sister done? How had she gotten the duke to offer for her? What had happened in the hours between Martha's returning from Jordan's room and this meeting?

"We shall leave tomorrow morning, return to Griffin House, and prepare for the wedding," her grandmother was saying.

Josephine was going to be wed. Josephine was to marry the Duke of Roth. Josephine had gotten her wish—she was going to be a duchess.

She should turn to her sister now, paint some kind of smile on her face, and say something.

While her heart might beat, her eyes blink, and her lungs work, her capacity for speech had suddenly ceased.

"When is the ceremony to be held?" Mr. Burthren asked.

Good, someone else had asked. She didn't need to push the words past her numb lips.

"There's no reason to wait," Josephine said, smiling brightly. "In a month."

She was going to be ill.

Jordan glanced at Martha and for a moment their gazes held. She was the one to finally look away, only to see Josephine's triumphant smile.

A month from now her sister was going to marry Jordan.

The York family consisted of numerous cousins and second cousins. Their side of the family would make up for any lack from Jordan's. They could fill a church easily. Add in all the inhabitants from the two villages not far from Griffin House and there would be an overflow crowd at the church.

How was she going to endure this?

Josephine had called him lame. She hadn't seen the man behind the injury. She cared nothing for Jordan's character or his questioning mind. His curiosity didn't impress her at all. All she wanted was the title and the house.

Somehow, Josephine had managed to get exactly what she wanted.

MARTHA WAS IN the parlor, but she sat there unmoving as if turned to marble, a sculpture of a woman in repose. He saw her blink, breathe, look down at her hands folded in her lap, but moments after her grandmother made the announcement, she still hadn't spoken.

His bride-to-be accepted the well-wishes of his staff and Reese with the sort of noblesse oblige that might've amused him under any other circumstance.

He was finding nothing about this situation remotely humorous.

He wanted out of the room, away from his guests, his friend, and his staff. He wanted to be alone where he could occupy his mind on something other than himself and this idiotic situation.

At least he'd had the sense to bed an heiress. Sedgebrook would be saved, but at what cost?

The price was too damn high.

Chapter 21

*W*ell played, Josephine. How did you manage to convince Jordan to offer for you?"

Josephine held herself still, determined not to let Reese know he'd surprised her. He leaned against the brick gate to the garden, his arms folded, a mocking smile playing on his lips.

"I came to the garden for a little solitude," she said. "Not to be insulted."

"Solitude? I would think you'd still be holding court, accepting congratulations from the staff."

She frowned at him.

Holding court? Hardly. Jordan had left the parlor in indecent haste without a word to her. Martha had stared at her intently until it was uncomfortable. And the staff? Mrs. Browning had been distant, her well-wishes bland and lacking in enthusiasm. Nor had Frederick looked eager to accept her as his mistress.

If they didn't change their attitude, she would be replacing them shortly.

"I'm not insulting you," he said. "I admire your nerve. How did you do it? I watched you. You didn't go to Jordan's room. How did you convince him that you had?"

"Does it matter?" she asked.

He studied her for a moment, so intently that she grew uncomfortable.

When he put out his arm and would have wound it around her waist, she pulled away.

"What did you do?"

"I'm sure I don't know what you're talking about."

"He took the elixir last night. I know that much. I also know that it makes him forget whole chunks of time. How did you convince him that he seduced you?"

"That's between Jordan and me."

"I don't think so," he said. "Especially since you were in my bed."

He continued to look at her as if she was a bug he was studying.

"Does it matter? Why are you so interested? I'll make him a good wife."

"I frankly doubt that," he said. "I think you'll be one more millstone around his neck."

"A wealthy millstone."

His laughter was irritating.

"You really do know your own worth, don't you? You've sold yourself to be a duchess, and I don't doubt you'll wring every penny from the bargain. If I let the marriage happen, that is."

He tried to put his arm around her again and once more she stepped away.

"What do you mean?" she asked, disliking that trembling feeling in her stomach.

"What do you think would happen if I told him you were in my bed last night?"

As a threat it was effective.

"You aren't going to say anything," she said.

"Why not?"

"Because you would have already. You needn't worry. I'll be a solicitous wife."

"I doubt Jordan wants anyone solicitous. Perhaps someone with the milk of human kindness running through her veins. I have a feeling yours has curdled."

"You didn't think so last night," she said. "Are you jealous?"

She gave him one of her best smiles, the one she reserved for men who'd done something worthy of her praise.

He didn't seem affected, if his grin was an indication.

"Not in the least. I have a feeling that, should I visit Sedgebrook after the nuptials, the bride might well occupy my bed. Just to ensure she doesn't suffer from boredom."

This time her smile was genuine.

"Perhaps something like that could be arranged," she said.

His grin vanished and his eyes went flat.

"Or I could tell Jordan where you were last night."

She heard a bargain in his threat. She was good at negotiations, especially if she had no other choice. In Reese she recognized a person who saw a situation for what it was worth and took advantage of it. They were not unlike in that trait.

The question was: What would she have to give up to keep him quiet?

"What do you want?"

"You're leaving tomorrow," he said. "Come to my bed tonight."

She blinked at him, her smile fading away.

"Are you insane? What if Jordan finds out?"

His smile was back, an almost paternal, patronizing expression that irritated her.

"He won't if you're careful."

His smile slipped a little, but his eyes hadn't changed. They were still hard and a bit more calculating than she liked.

Perhaps she should have allowed him to embrace her after all.

"Do it, Josephine. Or I'll go to Jordan."

"You wouldn't," she said. "He's your friend."

"That's exactly why I should," he said.

Once again, she didn't like either his tone or his look.

"Are you so desperate for female company you need to bargain for it, Reese?"

"Let's just say you amuse me. One last night isn't too much to pay for a lifetime of silence, is it?"

"But will it be a lifetime of silence?" she asked, her fingers trailing up his jacket front.

He didn't answer her. Instead, he asked, "What shall I give you as a wedding gift? A silver vanity set? Or an urn, perhaps?"

"A tea set," she said. "So when I'm entertaining my friends, I'll think of you."

He smiled again. He was almost as adept at his expressions as she was.

Reaching out, he pulled her to him and this time she allowed him to wrap his arms around her.

"Be careful, Josephine. I'm not one of the boys you play with. I'm a little more poisonous."

She'd already figured that out. Drawing back, she smiled up at him.

"Then you'd better let me go so that no one sees us. If you want one last night with me."

She wouldn't look at him as she turned and walked away, but she knew he was watching her. Well aware, too, that she was playing a dangerous game. She could easily be caught going to Reese's room.

The lure of the forbidden had always been exciting, however.

MARTHA DIDN'T GO to the boathouse after the meeting. She didn't want to be around Jordan. How could she possibly put into words her confusion or her feeling of . . . the only word was *betrayal*.

How foolish. He owed her nothing, not even constancy. She was the one who had appeared in his bedroom. She could have left at any time. He didn't restrain her. He didn't try to cajole her. If anything, she was the one who'd taken advantage of the situation. Not him.

She'd known something had been wrong. As she told Josephine, she thought he was under the effects of alcohol.

Even so, why hadn't he remembered her? How had he gone from bedding her to offering for Josephine?

She spent the afternoon in her room, sitting by the window and staring out at the lake, trying to understand the past twenty-four hours. Finally, she bathed her face and tried to do something with her hair. A moment later she gave up, deciding her appearance wasn't going to change.

She'd never be as pretty as Josephine.

She tapped on Gran's door and when Amy answered, slipped inside the room.

Amy took one look at her face and said, "I'll go and get tea, shall I?"

Martha nodded, grateful for Amy's tact.

Gran was sitting in the chair beside the window. She was still dressed as she'd been this morning, her bearing familiar. She'd always been a strong woman, but this past year had been a test of her strength.

Her father had been Gran's only child. Their relationship had been more than mother and son. It had been evident to anyone looking at them that they respected and genuinely liked each other.

His death had hit Gran hard, but she'd rallied to help all of them, issuing dictates carrying them through the first difficult days.

"Matthew would want you to remember him with a smile, Martha. Not your disheartened look."

"Matthew would say you're working too hard, Martha. I insist you come and rest in the parlor with me. We'll read one of the newest novels together."

Gran had made those terrible months bearable.

Now she was hoping the older woman would do the same with this situation.

"What is it, Martha?"

She sat on the edge of the bed, folded her hands in her lap, and faced her grandmother.

"I don't understand," she said. "Josephine has never spent any time with the duke. How did this marriage come about?"

Gran looked down at Hero, the cat having found his way to the room once more. Again, he'd found a spot of sunlight and was sprawled on the carpet, revealing his furry white belly.

After a space of a few minutes, she almost asked the question again, something that would have just irritated her grandmother. Whenever she'd been impatient for an answer, Gran said something like, *"I'm not feeble, child. I haven't forgotten what you asked."*

She remained silent, summoning her patience even though it was hard. Gran might not answer her at all.

Instead, she could say something like, *"Is it any of your concern?"* Or: *"Curiosity is a good thing, child, but there must be limits to it."*

Finally, Gran looked at her and sighed.

"It's a conundrum, isn't it? Josephine is happy, that's for certain. The duke?" She shook her head. "I don't believe he's as pleased. However, you reap what you sow and His Grace is learning that difficult lesson."

Her stomach tightened and she forced herself to say the words in a disinterested tone.

"What did he do?"

Gran looked at Hero again before shaking her head. "Let's just say it was something they did together. More than that I'm not comfortable saying, Martha. You are, after all, a single woman and a virtuous one."

Martha wished her grandmother hadn't used those exact words.

She gripped her hands together. What would compel her grandmother to tell her what had happened? She'd have to choose her words carefully. She knew Gran. Nothing could sway her once she'd made up her mind. If Martha pushed too hard, it was conceivable that her grandmother would simply refuse to speak about it and the topic would be forbidden in the future.

"Please, Gran," she said. "Could you explain?"

To her surprise, Gran's face softened in compassion. "You like him, don't you?"

Was that the right word? It didn't feel complete.

"I've come to respect him," she said. Part of the truth, but not the whole of it.

"Your father thought the two of you would suit," Gran said.

Surprise kept her silent.

"If anyone is to blame for what happened, it's probably me," the older woman continued.

"What do you mean?"

Gran sighed again, stretched out one hand toward Hero and wiggled her fingers at the cat. He disregarded her summons with some disdain, seeking out the dwindling square of sunlight.

"I thought, if we remained here for a time, you and he would form some kind of attachment."

"You feigned illness," Martha said.

Gran smiled lightly. "I didn't feign fatigue. I've found the last few days relaxing."

She wasn't the least surprised about Gran's confession, but her father's thoughts had been a revelation.

"What did Josephine do?"

The idea that occurred to her was so wrong that she was willing to irritate her grandmother in order to verify it.

"Did she go to the duke's room?" she asked.

Her grandmother's look was a combination of discomfort and annoyance.

"How did you know? Did Josephine tell you?" Gran shook her head again. "I would have thought she'd have more sense than to brag about her foolishness."

Josephine's treachery sat like acid in her stomach. She shouldn't have been surprised that her sister had manipulated the situation to her advantage, but she was. Josephine had put herself in Martha's place, leaving Jordan with no other option.

"And the duke offered for her," she said. "Because it was the honorable thing to do."

Martha was so certain she was right that her grandmother's reluctant nod was anticlimactic.

He hadn't known it was her in his bed. He hadn't

known. Which was worse? Realizing what Josephine had done? Or that Jordan had been too sotted to know which sister had been in his bed?

"We'll be leaving in the morning?" she asked, sliding from the bed. Dear God, she couldn't wait to get home, to leave this place, to put Sedgebrook and the Duke of Roth behind her.

Her grandmother nodded again.

The sharp look Gran gave her was a warning. She forced a smile to her lips.

"It will be good to get home," she said, moving to the door.

"Is something wrong, Martha?" Gran asked.

She shook her head. "I'm feeling a little nauseous," she said, which wasn't a falsehood. "In the meantime, I'll take dinner in my room. Perhaps a good night's sleep is all I need."

"I do hope you're not sickening with something," Gran said, her look troubled.

"Nothing that going home won't cure."

Once again, she smiled, the effort more difficult than Gran would ever understand.

Chapter 22

$\mathcal{M}$artha didn't go down to dinner and thankfully no one came to the door urging her to be sociable. She heard laughter from far away and wanted to hate the person who was so filled with joy.

Above all, she didn't want to see Josephine.

When Sedgebrook settled down for the night she left her room, intent on the Duchess's Garden.

Moonlight spilled over the brick wall, casting shadows over the rosebushes, making them appear like shrouded, hulking figures. If she had been more imaginative, perhaps she might have felt a little unease. But nothing could be more disturbing than the tenor of her thoughts.

She didn't follow the path to the boathouse. She wouldn't go there again. In the morning they'd leave for home. Once at Griffin House, she'd devote herself to experiments on the prototype she'd created on her own.

She would never correspond with the Duke of Roth. In fact, she would destroy every one of his letters to her father, the selfsame letters she'd read repeatedly until she'd memorized his words, knew his handwriting by sight.

Everything she knew about Jordan Hamilton would

have to be expunged from her mind. Every single emotion she felt would have to be washed clean. He would be her brother-in-law, a relative by marriage. She could never feel for him what she felt last night and even memories of those hours would have to be erased.

"Can you not sleep, Martha?"

She held herself still, wishing in that instant he would think her a shadow as well.

Go on past, make your way to the boathouse, ignore me. Above all, leave me alone.

"No," she said, her voice faint. "I can't. I might ask the same question of you."

He didn't answer her, merely moved out of the shadows. He was leaning more heavily on his walking stick and she wanted to ask if his leg was paining him.

She didn't, knowing he probably wouldn't answer such a question. He didn't refer to his injury easily and he certainly didn't solicit sympathy. It was as if he wanted everyone to treat him as though he'd never had an injury.

Didn't he realize she didn't see him as infirm? With his determined refusal to solicit sympathy, he was even more attractive.

How could he marry a woman who'd called him lame?

"The stars look close tonight," he said, tilting his head back to examine the night sky.

He was right. There wasn't a cloud to be seen and the moon was like a bright white orb she could almost pluck by merely reaching out her hand.

The silence in the garden was absolute except for the sound of the lake just beyond, the water lapping at the shore. Not a bird spoke from its nightly roost.

Not an insect chirped. No sound came from Sedge-brook, settled down for the night. Even the wind had calmed here in the secluded garden.

It would serve him right if she burst into tears. She almost wanted to leave him as confused and disoriented as she felt.

"You're leaving in the morning," he said.

"Yes."

"They've found my ship, but you won't have a chance to examine the vessel."

"No," she said.

"Perhaps it's a good thing. It's covered in mud. It'll take me some time to clean it out."

"Will you put a tether on it from now on? So you don't lose it?"

"I think I shall," he said. "It's a good idea."

How polite they were being.

She walked to one of the backless benches and sat, moving aside the skirts of her lavender dress in case he chose to sit. He did, joining her a moment later.

He held the walking stick with his right hand as he stared out at the shadowed rosebushes. The air was thick with scent and almost heavy.

Words hung unsaid between them. *How could you not remember me? How?*

She couldn't say that to him.

"Is your leg paining you? Is that why you're not asleep?"

"Yes," he said, "but it's something I'll endure."

"How were you injured?"

She would not have asked the question normally. Perhaps it was because they were alone in a moon-lit garden. Or because in the past two days they'd become friends, of a sort.

Not only did he answer her, but he did so with a candor that was even more surprising.

"My brother was always better than I was in a great many things. Speaking languages, being cordial to perfect strangers, painting. He even knew most of the plants we're growing in our greenhouse and he was an expert horseman. I was a better marksman, but he was a better rider. One of his last acquisitions in Italy was Ercole, an irritable, nearly wild stallion."

He stood, walked some distance, then returned, standing in front of her.

"The day my solicitor called on me and let me know to what degree my brother had attempted to ruin the family financially, I found myself enraged. I thought a good ride might take the edge off my anger as well as prove to myself I was his equal in horsemanship."

His chuckled mirthlessly.

She wanted to comfort him with words or even touch. She only looked at him standing there, baring himself to her.

His hair was askew, a lock tumbling down over his brow. She wanted to push it back into place with her fingers.

"All I proved to myself was that pride goeth before a fall, isn't that the expression? I was a fool and it was a mistake I'll pay for every day of my life."

"Have you nothing to ease the pain?" she asked.

"I do, but I'll not be taking it. Because of that damned elixir—begging your pardon for my language—I'm about to become a bridegroom."

"I don't understand," she said.

Slowly, he returned to the bench.

"It's why I'm marrying your sister."

She turned her head toward him.

"Sometimes, the pain is so great that I don't think I can endure another minute of it," he said. "On those nights I take the mixture my doctor prepared. Unfortunately, it makes me lose a connection to the world around me. I feel drugged and unlike myself." He took a deep breath. "It's as if something takes hold of me," he added. "I become someone not myself."

He didn't look away. She wished she could see the expression in his eyes. She had the strangest feeling he was asking for forgiveness.

She didn't say anything in response. What could she say? That she'd witnessed his behavior up close? Last night she'd thought him affected by the wine he'd drunk, not drugged. Otherwise, she would have left him in his suite and returned to her room still a virgin.

Still, she'd known he wasn't himself. Yet she'd stayed.

"You took the elixir last night," she said. It wasn't a question and the words chilled her like winter rain.

"Yes."

"And you think you took advantage of Josephine," she said, speaking the words slowly.

"Yes," he answered. "It shouldn't have happened."

It hadn't. Josephine had somehow convinced him it had, and he'd done the right thing, the proper thing, the honorable thing.

She stared out at the shadowed rosebushes. From this moment on she knew she'd never be able to smell the scent of roses without also feeling this horrible sense of loss.

Now was the time for her to speak, to turn to him and say, *"It wasn't Josephine in your bed. It was me."*

How, though, did she explain that she'd remained with him, even thinking he was inebriated? How could she explain that she'd been fascinated with him, that she'd wanted him to touch her and introduce her to passion?

Would he hate her if he knew? After all, her behavior had put him in this position.

She pressed a hand against her waist, the other at the base of her throat, almost as if to keep herself mute.

Didn't you know it was me? Don't you know now?

She wanted to tell him the truth, but she remained silent. Perhaps a miracle would occur and he'd suddenly realize that it had been her who'd held him, who'd kissed him, who had given him her virginity.

Instead, the silence stretched out thinly between them. No miracle occurred.

He hadn't known. He didn't know now. She was the only one who knew the truth, the only one who could keep this disaster from happening.

At what cost?

Everyone at Sedgebrook was aware that the Duke of Roth was going to marry her sister. They were probably all aware of the circumstances as well. She could just imagine what would happen if she spoke now.

This morning she'd been stunned into silence, but she'd had hours to consider the ramifications of coming forward.

Gossip would swirl around them like a miasmic fog. The York name would be synonymous with derision. She and Josephine would be laughingstocks. They might be heiresses, but scandal would still follow them, probably until the ends of their lives.

She couldn't imagine Josephine recanting her story,

not when she was so close to becoming a duchess. It would be a case of her word against her sister's.

Did you hear? Both York girls say they were in the Duke of Roth's bed! Can you imagine? No wonder the mother escaped to France. It's a wonder their grandmother hasn't had apoplexy!

She'd lost her sister. She'd never be able to look at Josephine without knowing what she'd deliberately done. Josephine had wanted a title and Sedgebrook more than anything else. More than family.

And now she had the same choice.

How much did she want the truth to surface?

When she woke this morning her first thought was that she was going to see Jordan. She wanted to help him make his torpedo ship a success, a mission completely separate from what she might feel about him personally. It wasn't, after all, his fault she found him attractive. Or that she'd wanted to experience passion and had, at his hands.

Everything had changed this morning. Lives had been altered. None of them would ever be the same.

She sat there in silence, gradually coming to a decision. She wasn't going to be like Josephine. She wasn't going to manipulate others to get her way.

She'd made a terrible mistake. First, by staying with Jordan. Second, by not realizing the lengths to which Josephine would go.

If she had remained with Jordan until he woke, none of this would have happened. If she had taken responsibility for her actions the entire house would have been scandalized, but at least it would have been better than this outcome.

But she hadn't and now they needed to go their

separate ways, the Duke of Roth and his onetime lover, the spinster Martha York, heiress and oddity.

Yet the words still wanted to be spoken. *It was me. Can't you see? Can't you tell? Shall I kiss you and have you say, oh yes, I see it now, it was you, Martha.*

How foolish she could be sometimes.

"I hope you have a safe journey home," he said.

"Thank you," she responded, taking a deep breath. This farewell needed to be done, as quickly as possible. "I wish you luck on your trial voyages. Shall I write you if I come up with any new ideas?"

"I'd like that," he said.

"Would you let me know about your own observations?"

If nothing else, perhaps they could have a correspondence. She would come to treasure his letters to her as much as she did his letters to her father. She would press them against her chest as if to inhale the words or somehow feel him through the ink and paper.

"Thank you for your kindness," she said.

"When you arrived, you didn't think I was particularly kind."

"Then you must forgive me. It was an error in judgment. I'm sure my father wouldn't approve of what I said."

"He was always in favor of your strong opinions. 'Martha knows her own mind.' I remember reading his comment many times."

She didn't know her mind now. Or perhaps she did, but she couldn't do anything about her thoughts or her wishes. She wanted to throw her arms around his shoulders, place a kiss on his cheek, perhaps invite him to turn and embrace her. They would kiss and she would show him, wordlessly, how she felt.

It was too late. The time to be honest with him was last night. Before he'd pledged himself to Josephine this morning. Before the announcement that was, no doubt, even now finding its way to London.

In her defense she'd had no idea Josephine would insert herself as the harlot of this piece.

What did she do now? What could she do now?

Nothing. Absolutely nothing. Any explanation she offered, any truth she said would only bring scandal down upon all their heads.

"I've enjoyed our time together," she said. There were so many words she shouldn't say, but she'd say what she could. "I think my father was right in liking you."

"That's a great compliment," he said, "but I'm not sure I'm worthy of it."

Oh, he was. He was the most honorable man she'd ever met yet honor had proved to be a burden, hadn't it? Still, she was glad she'd gone to his room. There, the truth, perhaps never to be revealed to another soul.

She stood and looked at him one last time, one long and steady look to last her for the rest of her life.

She smiled, then said, "Good-bye, Your Grace."

My love.

Chapter 23

$\mathcal{M}$artha finished packing her lone valise and looked around the room she'd occupied the past few days. She'd already left a small gratuity with Mrs. Browning, along with her thanks.

How strange that the chamber felt familiar and comfortable. It wasn't Sedgebrook she would miss. It was *him*. Jordan of the letters. The arrogant man who'd touched her heart so easily.

It was time.

She hadn't known him before arriving. Perhaps she'd been curious about him from reading his letters, but that's all it was. It certainly wasn't fascination. Making love to him was only because of that same curiosity: she'd wanted to know what passion was like.

What a terrible series of lies she'd just told herself.

Moving to the window, she stared out at the lake. Would she ever feel the same about another man as she did Jordan? Probably not. Never again would she allow herself to feel as much. Never again would she be as free as she'd been that day only three days ago when they'd first arrived at Sedgebrook. Never again would she look at a man the way she'd looked at him, with her breath tight and her pulse racing and tears too close to the surface.

She was standing in a sunbeam. That was the only reason her entire body felt warm.

From here she could see a tiny corner of the boathouse. She wouldn't go and say good-bye. She'd already done that last night.

Their carriage was being readied. She'd been told they'd leave within the hour.

She looked down at her dark blue traveling dress, wishing she had something else to wear. But it was a choice between this and the loathsome lavender and she couldn't bear to wear that garment one more day.

She'd already helped Amy prepare her grandmother and watched as the footmen devised a chair-lift to help Gran down the stairs.

Once at the bottom of the grand staircase she greeted her sister with a nod, ignoring Josephine's almost proprietary glance around Sedgebrook. Almost as if she was saying: *This is all mine and in a few weeks I'll come back and claim it.*

Martha was more than ready to go home; she was almost desperate to reach Griffin House. She knew herself there. There were no secrets being revealed just when she least expected them. She would not be challenged by a handsome man who also touched her heart and made her dream of things that could never happen.

In the past three days he'd revealed himself to be truly Jordan of the letters. A man who'd so captivated her heart it hurt to think of leaving him. Especially knowing that when she saw him next he'd be her sister's husband.

"You didn't see His Grace," Gran said.

"You should have said a proper farewell," Josephine offered, pulling on her gloves.

"I'm sorry," Martha said to her grandmother. She was not going to address Josephine. Nor did she offer that she and Jordan had seen each other last night. The time in the moonlit garden was hers, not to be discussed with anyone else.

"When will the carriage be ready?" Josephine asked.

"Only a few minutes from now," her grandmother said.

She turned away when the two of them began discussing plans they would make as soon as they reached Griffin House. She didn't want to hear about the wedding preparations. She didn't even want to think of the coming ceremony.

The journey home would be miserable. Being around Josephine was uncomfortable especially since she wanted to shout at her sister, demand an explanation even as she knew nothing could explain away the viciousness of Josephine's actions.

Every mile they traveled away from Sedgebrook, she would feel worse. She hadn't known him long enough to yearn for him. She didn't know him well enough to feel this kind of grief. Yet it felt as if she had. Five years of letters, sometimes two a week, had given her an insight into the man, probably more than he wanted.

He'd been her friend, too, although he'd never known it. She and her father had talked about him often, wondering what he'd think about a certain modification to their design. She'd marveled at his instant understanding of complex concepts.

At least she had copies of her father's notes. She'd already replicated his vessel, calling her ship the *Goldfish*. She hadn't given up trying to understand the final test that had so overjoyed her father.

She would do that—finish her father's work independent of Jordan Hamilton. Yet in a way, working each day on the same project would make her feel close to him.

The carriage was brought around and she waited until Josephine and Gran had settled before she entered the vehicle.

She studiously ignored Josephine, which was difficult since her sister hadn't stopped prattling about the wedding arrangements.

She pressed her hand to her waist. Would anything happen from that night? Was she going to have a child? She almost wished she would, and wasn't that a shocking thought?

Would it be enough to stop this hideous wedding?

JORDAN STOOD AT the head of the twin staircases leading to Sedgebrook's iron front door.

The York carriage had been brought around to the front. He'd instructed Mrs. Browning to lead Susan York through the small corridor to the exterior door beneath one of the stairs. The passage wasn't often used, but today it would eliminate the need for the older woman to have to descend one of the staircases.

The younger York women were already there. Josephine glanced up at him and smiled. Martha didn't turn.

Shortly, the carriage would make its way toward the main road. From his vantage point he'd be able to see them for nearly a quarter hour, at least until they made a left turn, dipping behind the strip of trees bordering the front of his property.

Martha still didn't turn.

Leaning heavily on his walking stick, he watched as they entered the carriage.

From now on he would take better care of himself. He wouldn't overdo, at least not until he healed a little more. He would take frequent breaks since he'd no longer have a boathouse companion he wanted to impress.

His damn leg was a constant reminder of not only his limitation but his failings. He had flaws and frailties and wasn't the paragon he should have been. He wasn't anything like his father or Simon, for example.

Nor as charming at Reese.

In a few days Jordan would write a note to Mrs. York, expressing his hopes that the journey had been easy and she'd regained her health. That would be the polite thing to do even though they both knew she hadn't been all that ill. He'd have Mrs. Browning send along a batch of the biscuits the older woman had liked.

Martha said she would write him from time to time. He would let her know if her suggestions worked. He could change the hydrostatic valve and adjust the pendulum and test it out.

He'd known her for only a matter of days. There was no reason to feel this sudden sense of loss, as if he'd miss her.

He would be wiser to leave now and get back to the boathouse.

Only an idiot would stand here until her carriage was out of sight.

She was gone.

Three days ago, she'd mounted the steps and stared at him accusingly. What had been her first words to him? Something about him not having any choice about her being there. He couldn't help but smile at the recollection.

Martha was everything Matthew had said she was: stubborn, opinionated, determined, fiercely loyal, kind, generous, witty, and intelligent.

The next time he saw her, it would be at the wedding. She'd be his sister by marriage.

That thought was enough to sour his mood.

"Interesting women," Reese said at his side.

"Yes."

"I never thought you would offer for her," Reese said.

Jordan's mind made the adjustment between sisters. He didn't want to think about Josephine.

"Was she able to help you?" Reese asked.

Another adjustment back to Martha.

"Yes," he said. "I think she was. I have to finish the modifications and test them out, but everything she recommended made sense." He smiled despite himself. "She also recommended I put a leash around the ship so I don't lose it. I can call it home like a lost puppy."

"Intelligent woman."

"Yes," Jordan said. "She is. Remarkably so. I was able to discuss the problems with my compressor with her and she told me what to do to fix it. She has an affinity with machines I've never found in a female. Rarely in a male, for that matter."

"In other words, she tinkers like you do."

"She invents," Jordan corrected. "She attempts. She proposes and dares and postulates."

"It sounds as if you and Martha are better suited than you and Josephine."

He had nothing to say in response. What comment

would be appropriate? That he was sickened by the thought of marriage to Josephine? That he couldn't remember a damn thing about two nights ago? Lust and only lust had guaranteed this union, but it was fueled by the elixir, not his wishes. He was damned if he was going to take it every night in order to feel something for his bride.

Maybe she could be convinced to go and visit her mother in Paris for an extended time. She could flaunt her new title as he fixed the roof on the north wing, both of them getting what they'd earned.

What would marriage to Martha have been like? Now that was a surprising question. Why had he even contemplated it? He pushed away the thought, although it was difficult to do so.

"What a pity Martha isn't as attractive as her sister. I have a feeling she probably won't marry." Reese shrugged. "Not that she needs to. Wealthy women don't need husbands."

"She's attractive in her own way," Jordan said, feeling a surge of unexpected irritation. "Her eyes are warm. Her face is a perfect shape and wonderfully expressive. Her hair is a soft cloud."

His words faded away. How did he know her hair was soft? He could almost feel it curling around his fingers.

"It sounds like you should have offered for the older sister," Reese said, and added to the remark by patting Jordan on the shoulder.

He heard the door close as Reese entered Sedgebrook. He stood where he was for too long, well after losing sight of the York carriage.

He couldn't dismiss the thought—even though he tried—that Reese had just swerved into the truth.

Chapter 24

"A letter's come for you, miss," Sarah said.

Josephine handed the girl another stack of fabric swatches to carry before taking the letter from her.

According to her grandmother, she didn't need her own maid until she had her season or was married. Consequently, she used the services of Martha's maid, a silly girl who was forever smiling and giggling in an annoying way. She couldn't do proper hair and she had no sense of style whatsoever. The only thing she did well was take things from one place to another. Oh, and tell stories, which made her halfway valuable.

Because of Sarah she knew what was going on at Griffin House, which wasn't much, all in all. The tradesmen came when Gran summoned them. The church elders were always there with their hands out. The roof needed repairing; the altar should be refurbished. The organ required new pipes and the baptismal font had sprung a leak.

The church elders had better ensure her wedding ceremony was magnificent for all the money the Yorks had provided over the years.

She glanced at the letter, half expecting it to be from her mother. The letter to Maman informing her of her upcoming marriage had been one of the first ones she'd written.

Although Maman would be pleased she was marrying a duke, there was always a small possibility her mother would not return for the wedding. Josephine was under no illusions as to her mother's maternal instincts. They'd always come behind Marie's self-interest. She'd discovered that fact when she was nine years old and her birthday celebration had clashed with her mother's wish to visit London.

To her surprise, the letter wasn't from Maman. She frowned at it before telling Sarah to take the swatches to the parlor.

"The seamstress will be here any moment. Tell her I'll be with her shortly."

The maid nodded and took herself off, leaving her to open the letter from Reese.

How dare he have the temerity to write her? He was still at Sedgebrook and would remain there for a little while, but he would be attending her wedding.

Did she know of any advances her sister had made on her ship?

What did she care about that stupid ship?

Another blessed benefit of her wedding. She would never have to listen to anyone talk about vessels or ships or engines or navigational systems. If Jordan thought to fill her ears with such topics, she'd simply eat her meals in another room or take a tray in her own sitting room.

She had no intention whatsoever of sharing a suite with her new husband. Not as large as Sedgebrook was. The idea of doing so was, frankly, revolting.

She needn't see Jordan much. Perhaps she would live in London. As a married woman, she could travel to Paris. She would finally have her own maid, a French girl. Maman always said the best servants came from France.

Martha had made it so easy for her. Josephine didn't even have to bed the duke right away. Of course, there was every possibility he would insist upon it sooner or later. She would have to bury her aversion and go to his bed. After all, she would be responsible for producing the next duke.

"Motherhood will destroy a woman's body if she allows it," Maman had once said. They'd been talking about a neighbor, a woman who'd had four children and had a figure resembling a bag of flour with a sash around the middle.

She had no intention of letting her looks go.

Not like Martha. She could be quite attractive if she applied herself. However, Martha was more inclined to putter around the cottage than she was to address her hair or her wardrobe.

At least she didn't have to see Martha often once she was married. She needn't pretend any longer. Other than compulsory family gatherings, when to do otherwise would draw attention, she could simply ignore the York family.

For now, she dismissed any thought of Martha or Jordan or Reese in favor of meeting with the seamstress. After all, she had a trousseau to plan, garments appropriate for her new role as duchess.

REESE FOUND HIMSELF missing Josephine. Damned if he wasn't sorry to see the minx leave. She was one of those women who burrowed into your skin, made you want to scratch an itch.

She'd never be docile. You could never take her for

granted. He wasn't sure you could ever trust her completely, either. If he had any sense at all, he'd forget about her and concentrate on his mission. Later, he'd see if he could find himself a decent woman with a sense of morals and values he was sure Josephine didn't possess.

He'd written her but he wasn't surprised when she hadn't answered. She probably thought herself safe with her ruse, being so close to her wedding.

In five days he'd accompany Jordan to Griffin House and watch his friend get married.

He'd have a chance to see Josephine again before she became the Duchess of Roth. He hadn't lied to her; he suspected she wouldn't remain faithful after her marriage. A damn shame since Jordan wasn't going to get the wife he probably deserved.

For that matter, he hadn't gotten the friend he deserved, either.

Reese's conscience was an annoying burden and one he tried hard to ignore most of the time. Lately, however, it was grating on him. Especially after witnessing how doggedly Jordan was trying to make a go of his torpedo ship.

Ever since the York women had left, he'd haunted the boathouse. When Reese went in search of him, it was the first place he looked.

This morning was no different.

"You might as well sleep here," he said, seeing Jordan hunched over the workbench.

"There are two bedrooms upstairs," Jordan said, without glancing at him. "I've used both of them from time to time. I'd recommend the east room. The mattress is firmer."

He wouldn't have been surprised to discover that

Jordan had used the boathouse as a hiding place, of sorts. He hadn't gotten along well with his father, and there were enough years between him and Simon that they were almost strangers.

Jordan didn't collect people like his older brother had. Nor did people want to surround Jordan the way they had the 10th Duke of Roth. He'd heard Jordan described as icy and aloof when the truth was that Jordan was bored by things that interested most people.

He had no interest in gambling, since one of the first discoveries after becoming the Duke of Roth was how much of the family fortune had been decimated over the past two decades. He wasn't fond of horses, especially after his accident. He didn't drink to excess. Cards didn't interest him. Nor was he adept at social chatter. He didn't give a flying farthing about the weather or the politics of the day.

Talk to him about the Crimean War, however, one of the things he'd studied in depth, and he could talk your ear off.

Moving to the workbench, Reese watched as Jordan fiddled with a small flat object in the rear of the vessel that had recently been recovered from the bottom of the lake. Not only had the copper changed color, but there was a black sludge covering the interior mechanisms.

"How did Josephine do it?" Reese asked, his conscience rearing its ugly head again.

"Do what?"

"Convince you that you took advantage of her?"

Jordan didn't say anything, only reached for another tool on the bench, adjusting what looked to be the controlling mechanism of the ship.

"You're so damn honorable, Jordan. You'd do something wrong for the right reasons."

Jordan still didn't answer him.

If he was a true friend, he'd confess about Josephine. Instead, he managed to subdue his conscience after a moment or two. His mission for the War Office came before his friendship with Jordan.

He could always tell Jordan what they wanted, but to what end? The powers that be wanted to own the idea behind the torpedo ship, any patents, and all the inventions that had gone into making it work—if it could work. All without paying for the privilege, or being forced into negotiations and haggling.

Some people might think his mission was to cheat a fellow Englishman and friend out of a monetary reward for his efforts, but they'd be cynics. He chose to think of himself as a patriot, one whose mission was to procure a new weapon for his government with the least possible effort.

"What are you doing?" he asked.

"I'm adjusting the pendulum," Jordan said. "I've been told it's in the incorrect position."

Reese bit back his smile. "Martha told you that? I'm glad to see your collaboration bore some fruit."

Jordan nodded, put down his screwdriver and directed his attention toward Reese.

"Did you time your visit to be here when the Yorks arrived?"

Reese smiled. "I didn't know they were coming," he said. "Although, if I had, I might have planned to be here. If, for no other reason than to meet Josephine York and watch you make an idiot of yourself."

Jordan looked past him to the door, almost as if

he was willing Reese out of the boathouse. His next words proved that guess.

"I have no intention, either now or in the future, of discussing that night with you. Or with the War Office. You can go back to them and tell them I haven't succeeded in making my torpedo ship work. Not yet, but I will."

Surprise kept Reese silent for a moment.

"Did you know from the moment I arrived?" he finally asked.

Jordan had always been an intelligent man. Until, of course, he'd been outmaneuvered by a woman.

"That it wasn't just a friendly visit? Or that you had an ulterior motive? We're friends, Reese, but we worked for the same organization. Did you think I'd forget it?"

Reese didn't have a comment. He couldn't argue with the truth.

The two men remained silent, Reese watching as Jordan tightened the chain on the pendulum.

"Are you sure about that night?" he asked as he turned to leave. "You're not yourself when you've taken the stuff. You've admitted as much to me. What if you didn't take Josephine to your bed? Would you now be contemplating marriage to the woman?"

All it had taken was a little observation. Martha York had left Sedgebrook silent and obviously miserable. Had she been the one in Jordan's bed? He was beginning to suspect she had. He knew damn well it wasn't Josephine. Yet he didn't understand why Martha had remained silent. Had Josephine blackmailed her somehow? Or had Martha been terrified of the potential scandal? That was something that hadn't bothered Josephine. She was more than willing to trade her good name for becoming a duchess.

Maybe it was his conscience prompting him to say what he had. Or perhaps it was a sliver of altruism. At least he'd satisfied his conscience's requirements by sowing a little doubt in Jordan's mind.

The problem was Jordan's sense of honor. Even if he remembered the night as it had been, would it be enough to get him to alter the course of his future?

Reese hoped so, for his friend's sake.

Josephine might be a fascinating woman, but he wouldn't wish marriage to her on his worst enemy.

MARTHA SLOWLY WALKED through the small building attached to her father's cottage, inspecting the compressor as she'd been taught. The machine fueled the prototypes with compressed air, making it possible for each ship to be self-contained.

Once she was certain everything was in working order she returned to the cottage, sat at the table in the middle of the space, and wrote her findings in the journal. The tasks of inspecting the compressor and recording what she'd found were things she did every day, relaxing in their routine and repetition.

In a way, it was as if she kept alive all the various bits and pieces of her life with her father.

She could almost expect him to come walking in any moment, carrying a piece of toast in his right hand and his mug of tea in the other, pushing the door closed with his hip.

"It looks to be a bright and beautiful day, my dear Martha," he'd say as he did every day, regardless of the weather.

Strangely, most of the days with her father were

bright and beautiful. He had such a sunny personality it put everyone around him in a good mood.

The cottage had been built to specifically house Matthew York's experiments and inventions, a two-room structure where he could tinker and test, then perhaps take a nap in the loft reached by a ladder in the corner. The second room was used for storage, the space nearly empty now that most of the inventions had been taken to Sedgebrook.

The cottage still smelled of his tobacco and she found it comforting. In the afternoon the sun streamed in through the windows on the west side, making her think she needed a cat like Hero to take advantage of the squares of light.

The whitewashed walls in this main room had once been adorned with plans and sketches, notes and reminders. She'd rolled up all the plans, copied what she wanted to save, and packed the originals up for the duke.

When her father was alive, the table where she sat had been strewed with drawings and occasionally metal fastenings and copper parts. Now the only thing on it was her journal and the *Goldfish*, the prototype she'd made using her father's design.

Over the past weeks the *Goldfish*'s copper sheathing had changed color. Now it was a greenish hue, indicating corrosion. The final vessel, once she'd solved the problem of the steering, would have to be covered in another metal, something that wouldn't add significantly to the weight yet keep the corrosion to a minimum.

She'd been studying the experiments Sir Humphry Davy had made on the degradation of copper by seawater and was leaning toward cast iron. The problem was it would have to be forged; she wouldn't be able to simply pound or twist copper sheets into the final shape of the ship.

Today, however, she decided to put aside the problem of the corrosion and work on the steering mechanism again.

Few people came to the cottage, one of the reasons she'd been coming here every morning in the past weeks and staying until dark. She didn't want to see Josephine. Nor could she talk to Gran.

Her father had the idea she and Jordan would suit. The thought made her both sad and happy. She wasn't angry at Gran for trying to fulfill his wishes.

How, though, did she forgive Josephine? She was no closer to answering that question today than she'd been weeks ago when they'd left Sedgebrook.

Ever since then they'd spoken only a few words to each other and those said in Gran's company and only for her benefit. Otherwise, she and Josephine avoided each other.

She didn't want to hear about the wedding plans. She didn't want to have to pretend any type of happiness for her sister. What Josephine had done was wrong, deceptive, and . . . her thoughts stumbled to a stop. She couldn't call her sister evil, but she couldn't help but think what Josephine had done was cold, calculating, and spiteful.

Only one other time in her life had she felt more miserable than she did now—when she'd held her dying father's hand and watched as he left her. She wanted to believe he'd seen her mother at the end, that their long-awaited reunion had been the reason for his smile.

This situation, the circumstance she found herself

in, was not unlike those dark days. Eventually she would learn to live with missing her father, but how did she endure the pain of watching Josephine marry the Duke of Roth?

The upcoming wedding wouldn't be the celebration of a union as much as a public announcement that Josephine York was becoming the Duchess of Roth.

Jordan was simply incidental to the process.

Even though Josephine would much rather the wedding take place at Sedgebrook's baroque chapel, her grandmother had insisted it happen here.

Josephine acquiesced without much of a fuss. Marrying in the church they'd attended for years would mean everyone from the nearby villages would attend, in addition to their friends in London. Afterward, everyone would come to Griffin House for the enormous reception being planned.

Each day that passed Martha castigated herself for not saying anything. But it would have been pointless, wouldn't it? She would have made the situation even worse. Two York sisters claiming the duke had taken their virginity and Jordan being unable to remember any of it.

What had Reese said? That Jordan was surfeited by honor. Well, he'd certainly acted with more honor than anyone else, offering to marry the woman who'd accused him.

What she couldn't forget—or forgive—was Josephine's triumphant smile.

The marriage was taking place in indecent haste. No doubt Josephine had given their grandmother some sort of excuse, or claimed that she might be with child.

At least that was one thing Martha didn't have to worry about.

She put the journal back with the rest of them on the shelf above the table and retrieved the ship she'd made, the exact duplicate of the one she'd taken to Sedgebrook. The only difference was the name etched on the stern: the *Goldfish*. The ship looked exactly like a goldfish when it wiggled below the surface of the water.

Pulling up a stool, she examined it, seeing the original vessel in her memory. Once again, as she had so many times, she wondered what her father had changed to make the guidance system work. Something small, perhaps, a simple turn of a screw, a change in linkage. Some tiny alteration she'd never noticed.

She gently pried off the back of the *Goldfish*, her fingers tracing the complex web of pulleys, gears, and chains. She'd launched her ship every day since returning to Griffin House. The mystery still tantalized her and would until she solved it.

Today, however, the sight of the *Goldfish* brought on a surprising feeling of sadness. She was more than just her inventions, more than her calculations, her notes, and her experiments.

Even her father, who'd made this cottage his hermitage, had been married twice. She'd known, from their conversations, that he'd adored her mother. She'd often wondered if he loved Marie, but it wasn't a question she would have asked. Still, he'd ventured out into the world and found someone to love before retreating into his work.

Some people might say she'd done the same, but in an abbreviated manner. In actuality, she'd only allowed circumstances to dictate her actions. She'd never, like Josephine, gripped Fate with both hands, shaken it, and demanded it behave as she wanted.

Where had Josephine gotten her confidence? Martha had never felt such self-possession and poise. Did it come from being beautiful? Of being assured people would notice your appearance, remark upon it, and praise you as if it was something you did? What happened when you aged or if your beauty faded?

Her looks had never before mattered to her. She'd been grateful she wasn't completely plain, but she'd never wanted to turn a man's head, at least until now. She didn't want the attention of any man. Just one.

She'd been thinking of Jordan, not the ship's guidance system. Her left hand hesitated on a twisted chain. She examined it closely, realizing it had slipped from the rudder.

When she'd created this prototype, she'd duplicated her father's guidance system exactly, down to the links of the chain and the placement of every component.

Now she stared at it realizing that while the gap wasn't large enough that she would have noticed it normally, her fingers had registered the deviation.

Standing, she walked to the shelves where all her father's tools were stored and picked up a pair of crimps. Once back at the table, she began to make an adjustment by pulling off the forward part of the rudder. She stared at it for a moment, remembering the day more than a year ago when she'd first examined her father's ship. She'd thought that retrieving it from the lake and bringing it back to the cottage had caused the chain to come loose from the rudder.

But what if it hadn't? What if her father had removed it on purpose? Doing so would cause the rudder to drag slightly in the water, but maybe the drag would also aid in its steering.

She put the crimps down without using them.

Instead, she carefully returned the *Goldfish* to its crate and replaced the top.

Tomorrow she'd fuel the ship from the compressor and try another run. Maybe, just maybe, this small change might mean the guidance system worked.

If she succeeded, if the *Goldfish* hit the target, she would have a reason to write Jordan. Or she could just wait until he arrived.

How could she bear watching him marry Josephine?

She would simply have to.

Chapter 25

$\mathcal{J}$ordan asked his driver to stop for a few moments on a hill overlooking Griffin House. Behind him, Reese's carriage did the same. Reese sat with him while the other vehicle contained his valet, Henry, and his trunks.

In two days he'd be wed to a woman he didn't know and wasn't certain he liked. He'd delayed until the last possible moment before leaving Sedgebrook. This journey was the first time he'd left his house in nearly fourteen months.

Griffin House surprised him. He'd expected a manor house, square and solid on the landscape. What he saw was a sprawling estate, nearly the equal of his own home.

The main part of the house was a four-story Palladian building in dark red brick with white columns and cornices. Two wings stretched on either side of the structure and behind those were smaller buildings. A scaffold erected on the western side of the house was a symbol of the York wealth. He couldn't afford to do any major repairs to Sedgebrook, but money was no consideration to the York family.

Behind the house, surrounded by a good-sized

forest, was a lake. Matthew had described it better than his home.

"Impressive place," Reese said from beside him. "At least she's an heiress."

He glanced at Reese but didn't answer. Yes, at least Josephine was an heiress. That fact didn't ease the discomfort he felt about his coming marriage, however.

After giving the signal to the driver to continue on, he settled back against the seat and clenched his hand around the top of his new walking stick, a wedding gift from Reese. The gold top of the ebony wood cane was formed in the shape of a griffin, the body of a lion topped with the head and wings of an eagle. He wondered if Reese knew the mythology, that the griffin was the king of all creatures and responsible for guarding treasure. Or had he merely procured the walking stick as a bit of irony considering the name of the York home.

Regardless, he'd brought it with him and he clutched it now, girding himself mentally for the arrival at Griffin House and his reunion with the York women.

He'd been unable to stop thinking of one of them ever since she'd left, but it hadn't been his soon-to-be bride. Instead, Martha had filled his thoughts. Every time he'd begun work on the new leveling device for his ship he'd seen her smile. Whenever he was working on the pendulum, he heard her voice, low and seductive.

He pictured her in different places throughout his home: in the dining room, her eyes wide at something outrageous her sister had said. He couldn't remember Josephine's words, only Martha's startled expression.

Or standing on the landing at Sedgebrook's entrance, trying to hide the compassion in her eyes and failing miserably.

He'd never thought his memory to be perfect, but he'd been able to remember each of their conversations, how she charmed him when he was certain she hadn't meant to, or annoyed him when he was sure that had been her intention. She amused him and challenged him and made him wish circumstances were different and he could retrace his steps in time.

If so, he would never have taken the elixir. Nor would he have seduced Josephine. He wouldn't have placed himself in a compromising position, one requiring he be sacrificed on the altar of honor.

Martha was loyal and kind. She was also irritating, didactic, fierce, and opinionated. But she wasn't his fiancée and wishing things were different didn't change them.

As they approached Griffin House he was more impressed by what he saw. Even Reese remained silent beside him, taking in the sheer size of the house and the grounds.

Jordan knew, from things Matthew had said, that the majority of the York wealth came from York Armaments. The family had become as rich as Croesus after the Crimean War, and had diversified their investments into transportation, including ships and railroads.

They needn't worry where the money was going to come from to pay the annual salaries of the servants. Or how the roof repairs were going to be made.

If nothing else, the wealth Josephine would bring to their marriage should have given him some enthusiasm for the union. Unfortunately, it didn't.

Josephine had written him once in the past weeks, informing him of certain activities planned around the ceremony. Her handwriting had been juvenile, the many misspellings, inarticulate grammar, and almost bluntly worded demands giving him an indication of what his future was to be.

It wasn't enough that he brought a title and Sedgebrook to the marriage. He suspected he was going to be reminded, often, that she was an heiress. Frankly, he was ready to let Sedgebrook crumble around his ears rather than sell himself.

If he hadn't taken her to his bed, he would have never offered for her.

As it was, every night when he entered his bedroom, he got a flash of memory, something making him smile. It made no sense, but he remembered being happy. Feeling as if the moment, the interlude had almost been ordained.

On retiring, he sat on the edge of his pristine bed, remembering how rumpled the sheets were after they loved, the spot of blood declaring her virginal.

In his memory he heard her soft voice and it caught in his chest, almost as if she'd reached in and placed part of herself there.

He couldn't rationalize those memories with the woman he was going to marry.

THE DAY WAS a lovely one, the sun passing directly overhead. Not a cloud marred the piercing blue of the summer sky. Sunlight glittered on the surface of the lake, making the scene appear as perfect as a painting.

To the north, however, the sky was darkening, promising a storm shortly.

Martha walked from the cottage down to the dock,

carrying the *Goldfish* in her arms. A soft, warm breeze carried the scent of the water as she approached the lake.

The dock was wide and had been constructed three years ago. The boards had already weathered to a pale gray, but they were even and didn't bounce beneath her feet as she made her way to where she normally launched her ship.

Kneeling, she placed the *Goldfish* on the boards, unbuttoned her cuffs, and began to roll up her sleeves.

"Miss Martha?"

Martha turned to see Amy standing at the end of the dock. She watched as the maid approached her.

"Your grandmother sent me to tell you His Grace's carriage has been spotted. He should arrive momentarily."

She knew Jordan was coming today. She just hadn't expected him to arrive right now. Nor had she expected her pulse to suddenly race at the news that he was here.

Part of her wanted to rejoice that she would see him. She'd be in the same room with him again. She'd be able to talk to him. Another, more rational part, reminded her that he was going to be her brother in marriage.

In the past few days she'd been behaving like one of those besotted females she'd met in London. She'd reread each one of Jordan's letters to her father. Several of them she'd placed in a special pile because they'd revealed his character. His sense of humor was in those letters. So, too, the warmth and affection he felt for her father.

"I can't possibly leave now," she said. "A storm is coming and I wanted to get in one test beforehand."

Amy walked a few feet closer, her hands smoothing her skirt.

"I'm to tell you that your grandmother expects you to welcome him, Miss Martha."

Martha stared down at the *Goldfish*.

No, she couldn't. She couldn't be there when he arrived, not when she was certain Josephine would make a scene. She could just envision it now.

Her sister would come sweeping down the stairs, her face lit with happiness, a bright smile—one of her better expressions—curving her mouth. She'd embrace Jordan, act as if her life had been dull and gray without him instead of what it had been, weeks of Josephine commanding everyone and having a wonderful time doing it.

"I'm not dressed for visitors," Martha said, which was the truth.

She was wearing her oldest dress, a faded blue cotton only requiring one petticoat. Otherwise, it was too short. The cuffs were frayed as was the collar.

Her hair was frizzing around her face and she knew her cheeks were pink from the sun. She had a blemish on her cheek. She hadn't slept well in the past week and there were dark circles beneath her eyes. These weren't from soot, but rather sadness.

She would look even worse next to Josephine who was probably dressed in one of the new garments in her trousseau.

"Your grandmother was insistent, Miss Martha."

Standing, she turned to face Amy.

"Tell her I'll be there for dinner," she said. "But I can't possibly become presentable in time to welcome him. Plus, if I'm not going to test the *Goldfish* I have to empty her engine compartment."

Amy looked as if she wished to say something but changed her mind. Turning, she walked back to shore, her shoes making clomping sounds on the dock.

How was she supposed to do this? From where did she get the strength to watch Josephine marry a man she so much admired? Or was it just admiration she felt? Was it more? It couldn't be more. She couldn't feel anything stronger for Jordan Hamilton.

Besides, what did it matter how she felt? No one cared, least of all Jordan.

She would concentrate on the only thing over which she had any control: her own actions.

Perhaps she should move away, take up residence somewhere else. Or travel. If she hired a companion, travel would be acceptable. She would go to Germany to take the waters. Or perhaps even to Scotland. She would go somewhere where there was no talk of Josephine, where no one knew Jordan. Where news wouldn't come of him.

Anything but subject herself to more of this pain.

JORDAN AND REESE were warmly received from the moment they stepped inside Griffin House. A major-domo about half Frederick's age directed them to a sunny parlor overlooking a formal garden.

"Mrs. York will be with you shortly, Your Grace. In the interim, I'll direct your trunks to be taken to the Queen's Rooms."

He only nodded, assuming the Queen's Rooms was a suite set aside for visitors.

"And your trunks as well, Mr. Burthren," the majordomo continued, bowing slightly to both men.

Evidently, the staff had been fully informed about their arrival.

Less than a minute later Mrs. York sailed into the room.

"Welcome to Griffin House," she said.

"You look well," he said to Mrs. York.

He wasn't exaggerating. The woman looked at least twenty years younger than she had playing the invalid at Sedgebrook. Today she was wearing a black dress with a coral cameo at her neck, her white hair arranged in a crown of braids.

She gestured to the comfortable-looking chairs in front of the windows. Once she sat on the facing sofa he and Reese each took a seat.

"I had no idea Griffin House was so large," Reese said. "It's nearly the size of Sedgebrook."

"But without the history," she said. "Most of the house was completed in the last hundred years. My husband was the last to build anything and that was Matthew's cottage. You must see it while you're here."

He smiled politely, wanting to ask about Martha, but keeping silent. The room faced the east side of the house, but didn't have a view of the lake.

For the next several moments they skated atop the glassy surface of politeness. All of them were careful not to say anything too personal or intrusive.

Mrs. York served tea and whiskey. He wanted to decline both, but sat holding a cup and saucer for a few moments before placing it back on the tray.

"I'll send for Josephine, shall I? She's with the seamstress right now, but you haven't seen her for a few weeks. We'll give you two a few minutes alone," she added, glancing at Reese.

"That's not necessary," Jordan said.

The last thing he wanted was to be alone with Josephine. In a matter of days he'd have a lifetime with her. The thought made him wish he hadn't declined the whiskey.

"Then I'll let you get settled and we'll all meet each other at dinner. Like you, we keep country hours."

Another few moments of conversation made him grateful for Reese's command of a hundred different topics. His were limited to the scientific journals he'd recently read or the correspondence he'd exchanged with friends in London.

Reese knew about current events, fashion trends, and, most important, gossip. He and Mrs. York talked companionably like two middle-aged women.

"Oh, but we're boring you," Mrs. York finally said, glancing at him.

Evidently, he hadn't been able to hide what he was feeling. Either that, or Mrs. York was extraordinarily perceptive. He had a feeling it was a combination of the two.

She stood. "We have you in the Queen's Rooms," she said. "A project of my husband's. He invited Queen Victoria to come and visit after they were finished."

"Did she?" Reese asked.

She smiled brightly. "Yes, she did, but only once. She came with her entire brood on the way back from Scotland." Turning to Jordan who'd also stood, she said, "But since there isn't any hope of her making another visit, poor thing, I feel safe in placing you there, Your Grace."

He said something innocuous, one of those tedious phrases he'd had to learn as a child. He was adept at those—saying nothing while saying something, appearing pleasant and conformable while wishing you were anywhere but where you were.

As his eyes swept up and around Griffin House's

curving staircase, he realized climbing those steps was going to be a challenge.

"If you wish, Your Grace," Mrs. York said in a whisper, "I can convert one of the parlors to your use. It would mean not having to mount the steps."

He was damned if he was going to sleep in one of the parlors. He'd master Griffin House's stairs or die in the attempt. At least, then, he wouldn't have to marry Josephine York.

"I'm looking forward to seeing the Queen's Rooms," he said, taking the first step.

Chapter 26

As they waited in the parlor for Martha to join them for dinner, Susan was doing everything in her power to dispel the tension in the room.

A stranger coming upon their group would have thought Reese was Josephine's fiancé. He laughed at her quips. His gaze was appreciative and he solicited answers from her by asking inventive and complementary questions. Jordan, on the other hand, rarely spoke.

"How was your journey?" Josephine asked, batting her eyelashes at the duke.

Jordan didn't seem entranced by Josephine's flirtatious behavior. Ever since the man arrived it was obvious he didn't want to be at Griffin House.

Right now his bearing was as stiff as it had been this afternoon. His shoulders were straight and rigid beneath his black suit, almost as if a board was strapped to his back. His right leg was stretched out before him. Near one perfectly polished shoe was the end of the walking stick he was using. His hand was clasped around the top, so tightly Susan could see his white knuckles.

He hadn't smiled since Josephine had appeared

a few minutes earlier, greeting him with a high-pitched—and strangely annoying—laugh.

Reese Burthren was much more personable, addressing himself to Susan with a distinctive charm before greeting Josephine.

Susan had the feeling Jordan was pretending Josephine wasn't sitting opposite him attired in one of her new gowns, this one a dark green to set off her lovely eyes.

Josephine was difficult to ignore when she was attempting to be charming. The girl had a way about her, especially around men. She made the butcher stutter and the gardeners blush. Nor were the footmen exempt. Many times she watched the hunger in a man's gaze as he followed her granddaughter's walk across a room.

Jordan was proving to be an exception, however. Josephine might as well be one of the upholstered footstools.

Amy entered the room, giving the duke a perfectly executed curtsy. She could always depend on Amy for being proper.

Where was Martha? They couldn't go into dinner until she appeared.

"Begging your pardon, Your Grace," Amy said before turning to her. "Miss Martha sends her apologies, ma'am. She says she'll be here as soon as possible."

"Where is she, Amy?"

"In her room, ma'am, but she's just returned from the cottage."

Before she could say anything further, Josephine leaned toward Jordan.

"You truly don't wish to see her when she's been playing in the water, Jordan," Josephine said. "She smells of fish and her face is sunburned. Martha cares nothing for female pursuits."

Josephine added a charming laugh to her description of her sister, but it didn't make her criticism any less caustic.

She really did need to talk to the girl. Regardless of whether she was soon to be a duchess, she should show some loyalty to family members.

Before she could decide what, exactly, to do— either to go in to dinner without Martha or convince the others to wait longer—her granddaughter appeared in the doorway.

Josephine was right in one instance. Martha's face was red from the sun. Her hair was also curling around her face. There was an expression in her soft brown eyes Susan couldn't read, but she didn't have the chance to ponder anything before Martha spoke.

"I'm sorry," she said. "I had every intention of being here immediately, but I needed to expel some of the *Goldfish's* air. I'd fueled her for a test earlier, you see."

"No one is interested, Martha," Josephine said, interrupting her with a soft laugh.

Josephine stood, went to stand beside the chair on which Reese was sitting. He would escort her into the dining room while the duke would see Susan to her chair.

She didn't have a good feeling about this dinner, especially since Josephine was being insensitive. Martha had subsided to a hurt silence. The duke was being taciturn, while Reese was obviously compensating for everyone's bad behavior.

Susan almost turned around and went back upstairs.

"DO YOU LIKE the Queen's Rooms?" Josephine asked.

"It's a magnificent suite," Jordan said.

Martha stole a look at the duke. She'd always thought the Queen's Rooms were like being inside an abattoir. There was just too much crimson fabric used in the suite.

Crimson was also one of Josephine's favorite colors. Perhaps she should warn the duke not to allow her sister to redecorate any of the rooms in Sedgebrook.

"The suite is reserved for the queen normally," Josephine continued. "Of course, the queen has only been here once, but we're prepared just in case."

"Then I feel doubly honored, and I promise to vacate the premises if Her Majesty does come calling."

Josephine's trilling laughter would have been truly charming had Martha been in a mood to appreciate it.

She'd wanted to take a tray in her room, but she'd been forced to attend this dinner in the formal dining room because Gran's orders were never disobeyed. Besides, she'd always been lectured that she was a York and Yorks are studiously polite.

Very well, she would be polite even though she wanted to be anywhere but here. Any other place in the known world would have been better than sitting at the long mahogany table and watching as Josephine tried to charm both Reese and Jordan.

Jordan hadn't smiled once since approaching the table. He'd been gracious to everyone, but he'd focused his attention on the meal as if he was a man who'd never before seen lobster bisque, roast beef, or the other courses being served.

His one recent contribution to the conversation was to comment on the china pattern, saying it was similar to one at Sedgebrook his mother had preferred.

That statement led to Josephine asking, "Has your mother been dead for a great many years?"

Martha caught Gran's wince out of the corner of her eye. In her new role as duchess, Josephine was going to have to be more tactful and phrase her questions in a kinder way.

"Yes," Jordan said. He didn't elaborate, which was a clue to anyone that he had no interest in speaking about his mother.

"How terrible for you," Josephine said. "I don't know what I would do without Maman. She is so charming and sophisticated as well as well traveled. She would be here now, but she much prefers France."

Jordan only nodded, leaving Reese to say something complimentary about the French.

Martha glanced at her grandmother. There was every possibility Marie would not return for her daughter's wedding. Gran gave a slight shake of her head, a sign that she either hadn't heard back from Marie or her stepmother had, indeed, conveyed she wouldn't be able to make it back in time for the ceremony.

However, it was difficult to muster any compassion for Josephine, given her actions in acquiring the duke as a husband.

Most of the conversation related to the wedding ceremony to be held in a matter of days. The village church was going to be beautifully decorated. A choir comprised of village children would welcome the wedding guests. The ceremony would be officiated by the bishop, not their usual minister. Josephine had insisted on it since she was marrying a duke.

Notices had been sent throughout the two nearby villages. Every single villager was invited to Griffin House for a reception to honor the bride and groom.

They were expecting a few hundred people at least, which was why the kitchen staff had been increased and everyone was industriously working. Martha couldn't walk from her sitting room to the library without smelling something delicious like Cook's meat pies or the chocolate biscuits she loved.

She'd already decided that she would make the obligatory appearance at the wedding, school her face into a quasi-happy expression, then attend the reception for a few moments. She'd stroll through the lawn, or under the tent if the weather became inclement, say hello to those people she knew before spending the rest of the day in her room. Above all, she didn't want to have to say farewell to Josephine and her new husband. She didn't want to have to wave as the ducal carriage stopped at the crest of the hill. She didn't want to imagine Josephine and Jordan arriving at Sedgebrook and having their wedding night.

Dear God, anything but that.

Would Jordan take his elixir? Would he somehow know the woman in his arms was not the same one who'd been there weeks ago?

Did he ever think back to that night? Of course, it had been a momentous night for her while it had only been a drunken dream to him.

The three of them—Gran, Reese, and Josephine— kept the conversation going. Did they even notice she and Jordan didn't say more than a word or two?

She really didn't want to be here and felt almost as petulant as a child. Perhaps she would invent a fever, something to keep her in her room until after the wedding. Illness wouldn't be far off from what she truly felt.

Thunder suddenly rumbled overhead. Martha looked up at the ceiling. When she was a little girl, she'd thought thunder was God's way of demonstrating his anger. Evidently, she and God were in the same mood tonight.

She really didn't want to talk about ribbon and fabric and song selections and trays of biscuits. Everyone knew Josephine's wedding and reception would be lavish despite the short notice. All the shopkeepers from here to London had been pressed into service. They'd hired dozens of extra servants. Heaven knows what they'd spent.

She just wanted it all to stop.

"I think I've discovered what my father did," she said when Josephine took a breath.

There, that stopped the talk of the wedding. The two men turned to look at her. Jordan even put his fork down, his attention on her.

Josephine started to say something, but it was Gran who lifted her hand to silence her. Surprisingly, her sister subsided into a pout.

"I think it has to do with the rudder," Martha said, and explained in more detail.

Jordan nodded thoughtfully while Reese looked on.

"Have you tested it yet?" Jordan asked.

She shook her head. "No, not yet, but if it's a fair day tomorrow I will."

"I absolutely refuse," Josephine said, ignoring Gran's look. "Must we have talk about that silly ship at the dinner table?"

There was so much wrong with her comment that Martha was silenced. *That silly ship* was the reason their father had died. *That silly ship* was of great interest to the man she was going to marry in a matter of days.

Standing, Martha forced a smile to her face. "If you'll excuse me," she said.

Without a glance toward her grandmother, she left the dining room, making her way back upstairs. Until the wedding, she was going to eat in her room, regardless of the York reputation for politeness.

Chapter 27

$\mathcal{M}$artha hadn't been able to sleep well. Part of it was the knowledge that Jordan was beneath Griffin House's roof.

He was as handsome as he'd been weeks ago. She wanted to stare at him at dinner, mark the changes in the past few weeks. He looked tired. Did regret strip him of his sleep? Now she couldn't stop herself from recalling everything she noticed from her quick glances: how his hair was longer and how much easier he seemed to move. Was his leg improving?

Finally, when the sky was light, she rose, but didn't ring for her maid. Instead, she dressed in one of her oldest dresses, something suitable to her intentions for the day.

She wasn't trying to impress anyone. Jordan wouldn't be stunned by her beauty or silenced in admiration of her grace and poise. She was only herself, Martha York, and this morning she was going to prove her father's invention worked.

JORDAN HAD THE strangest sensation he'd been here before, seated in a large library on the other side of a desk presided over by an officious-looking gentleman.

The man was not unlike the Hamilton family solicitor. He had bushy muttonchop sideburns, a whitish-gray head of hair, and an air of competency. The only thing he didn't have was a funereal expression. That's because, no doubt, he was accustomed to smoothing the way for copious amounts of York money to be transmitted to various places and personages.

Jordan's solicitor had presided over one thing: the announcement of the deplorable state of the Hamilton funds.

He was hard-pressed to keep his face from betraying his astonishment. Although he'd known the York women were, by anyone's standards, heiresses, he had no idea it put them among the richest women in not only England, but the Commonwealth. Josephine could spend outrageous sums of money every day and not make a dent in her principal.

The fact that he was made privy to this information wasn't surprising, but the presence of Josephine and her grandmother was.

Also slightly astonishing, given that he'd thought he'd have to go to Josephine for funds for Sedgebrook's upkeep, he was informed his house now had an allowance, of sorts. So did he. The bulk of Josephine's inheritance was placed in a trust for her to use, with twenty percent of it held over for their children.

He suspected the allowance was an addition from Susan York, since it freed him from having to ask Josephine for money. In the same fashion, he could spend the funds for Sedgebrook as he saw fit—to repair the roof or work on the chapel altar or a dozen things worrying him. In addition, the funds would be renewed every year.

In other words, he would never have to worry about money as long as he lived.

He should have been overjoyed.

He should have had a sense of liberation.

Instead, a small voice whispered to him that nothing ever came without a price. Josephine was the price. Perfumed, pampered, flirtatious, and coy, she was to be the Duchess of Roth and from the moment in the church she would carry the title to either the Hamilton glory or their eternal shame.

After signing where he was told, he sat back in the chair and looked at Susan.

He suspected she'd lectured Josephine sternly and, for the time being, it had made an impression. He'd never seen the woman behaving so demurely. Nor had Josephine ever been as silent.

Martha was nowhere in sight, but then she wouldn't be. The arrangements for him to sell himself had been made among those most involved. Susan as matriarch. Mr. Donohue as financial matchmaker, and the bride and purchased groom.

"You said something about Matthew's cottage. Would it be possible to see it?"

Did Mrs. York know how desperately he wanted to be out of this room? How much he needed air at the moment? She stood and smiled at him, offering him a lifeline if she only knew.

He grabbed his walking stick and stood.

"I'll have one of the footmen show you the way," she said, opening the door and motioning a tall young man inside the room.

His request had evidently made Josephine angry, because when she looked up at him her smile thinned. Josephine had a honed kind of beauty, aquiline features, pointed chin, and a mouth thinner than Martha's. She could easily go to mean: the eyes narrowed, the lips turned down in constant disapproval. With the years her jawline would probably become even sharper, her nose longer.

"I'm not going to the cottage, Jordan. Besides, it's not a short distance. Are you sure you can manage it?"

He pushed down the comment he normally would have made, nodded to the solicitor, managed a smile for Mrs. York, and left the room as quickly as he could.

Behind him, Josephine said something. Jordan deliberately blocked out her voice.

MARTHA FUELED THE *Goldfish*, the process taking nearly two hours. Biting back her impatience, she remembered her father's words: *"Most important things in life take a bit of time, Martha."*

She'd never spoken to him after his death, but she did now, addressing her soft words to his spirit.

"I'm going to do it, Father," she said. "I'm going to prove that you made it work."

She wound a long wire around the retaining hook then wrapped the excess into a circle, carrying it with the *Goldfish* to the dock.

Once at the end of the dock, Martha slowly dropped to her knees and gently lowered the vessel into the water. The ship's nose bumped to the surface before settling.

She waved to Sam, one of the stableboys who was manning the rowboat that was acting as the target this morning. He often helped her, being eager to learn and more than willing to exchange his duties in the stables for piloting the boat.

She raised her arm then lowered it, a signal she was ready to begin. Her shoulders tightened.

Her father had died for this. He'd been exultant in

those final hours, overjoyed that his vision had been accomplished, the task of his later years done. If she could recreate the moment it would be like fulfilling a promise to him.

She felt almost as if he was standing there, his spirit blessing her as she unwound the wire. If the *Goldfish* sank she would still be able to retrieve it.

Had Jordan started using a *leash* for his vessel, too?

No, she was not going to think of Jordan right now, but it was difficult. He'd featured in so many of her father's discussions. Now he was here, at Griffin House.

He was going to marry Josephine.

He'd never known she'd been in his bed.

She was *not* going to think of him. Instead, her thoughts should be focused on what she was doing.

If the changes she made to the guidance system worked, the *Goldfish* would reach the rowboat. In an armament test, the nose would be filled with explosives, but only after she'd proved the vessel design was both seaworthy and accurate.

The *Goldfish* bobbed in the water, buoyant and eager. Stretching out on the dock on her stomach, she reached into the water and placed her hand on the rounded hull of the ship. After saying a quick and fervent prayer, she turned the lever midpoint on the ship.

Air bubbles exploded on the surface as the *Goldfish* took off, racing beneath the water. A few seconds later she lost sight of the ship as the wire tightened.

Where was it?

She rose to her feet, brushing off her skirt. No air bubbles were visible between the dock and the rowboat. Either the *Goldfish* had sunk or it had gone off in another direction.

She'd been wrong. The changes to the guidance system hadn't worked. The disappointment was sharp and painful. Blinking back her tears, she began to pull on the wire to retrieve the vessel. Only then did she hear Sam's screaming.

"Miss Martha! Miss Martha!"

He was nearly overturning the boat by leaning over the side. Any caution she might have shouted to him was silenced when he retrieved the *Goldfish* and stood, his face split by a wide smile.

She'd been right. She'd been right. No, her father had been right. The *Goldfish* had made the journey from the dock to the target as straight as an arrow. It had dived deeper than she'd planned, but it had made it.

She clutched her arms to her chest, bit her lip, and didn't try to stop the tears from flowing. A moment later, overcome, she flung her arms outward as if wanting to embrace the whole world at that moment. Exhilaration filled her even as she wept. Tears mixed with her laughter.

She did it!

DESPITE HIS IRRITATION at Josephine's words, Jordan discovered she was right; it was some distance to the cottage. By the time he reached it he was limping badly, twinges in his leg warning him he'd overdone it. Any discomfort, however, was forgotten when he caught sight of Martha at the end of the nearby dock.

Her arms were flung out, her skirts belling around her as she twirled like a child. Her hair was a cloud around her head as she laughed.

Beyond her was a boy standing in a rowboat holding a ship resembling Bessie.

Jordan reached the dock, getting halfway to the end before she noticed him. Then she surprised him by picking up her skirts in both hands and racing to him.

"It works!" she said, her voice bubbling with joy. "Jordan, it works. It hit the target. It works!"

She nearly knocked him over in her enthusiasm. He steadied himself by reaching around her waist with one arm and holding her tight.

"Oh, Jordan," she said, tipping her head back to look up at him, "it works!"

He was immediately bombarded by two emotions: excitement that she'd figured out the problem and disappointment that he hadn't been the one to do so.

He wanted to ask what she'd done. He almost formed the words before they simply vanished. Her smile captivated him. Staring down into her warm brown eyes, he found himself lost in her happiness.

Her hands flattened against his chest, then crept up to his shoulders as the smile melted from her face.

Moving closer, he bent his head, his gaze never leaving hers. The bright glow of excitement on her face faded as did every caution in his mind. All he knew was that he had to kiss her. It was as vital as drawing breath, drinking water, something elemental to life itself.

Her lips were soft. She gasped as she opened her mouth to him. He wished he had two free hands to embrace her, but one was still holding on to his walking stick to retain his balance. The other pressed against her back, bringing her forward.

He could feel the shape of her long legs through the thin dress she wore. Her breasts pressed above her corset. He knew her body, the curve of her waist measured by his thumb, the indentation of her back where his palm pressed.

She smelled of copper, a distinctive metal tang, sunlight, and water. All scents so normal to him that she could have been an extension of himself. But she wasn't. She was all woman, irresistible and soft. His hand relinquished its possession of her waist to rest on the edge of her jaw, his thumb stroking the delicacy of her heated cheek.

He moved his head slightly, took command of her mouth, his tongue darting in to taste her. She sighed and the sound speared through him, making him feel as if he was the conqueror and she the vanquished.

He wanted her.

He knew her in a way he didn't understand but had to accept at this moment.

Reason left him.

He wanted her in his bed, her body bowing beneath his, her screams of joy silenced by his lips on hers. His hand speared into her hair, feeling the softness of the curls winding around his fingers. This, too, was something familiar to him.

Slowly he pulled back, his body screaming at him to continue this seduction.

Her lips were pink. Her eyes were dazed, the feathery lashes revealing them reluctantly. He pressed a kiss to her forehead, just above her perfect nose. He tried to calm his breathing, all the while lecturing himself to step back, away.

"How charming. One would think, looking at the two of you, that you were the ones to be married."

He dropped his hand, turned, and faced Josephine standing a few feet away. He hadn't heard her approach, but then he hadn't been paying attention to anything but Martha.

Words failed him. Not one excuse came to mind to explain his behavior. Not only did he owe Josephine an apology, a fact that irritated him, but he should also say something to Martha.

Before he could speak, Martha picked up her skirts and moved around him, brushing past Josephine without a word.

Chapter 28

Martha had successfully avoided her sister in the past weeks, but there was no chance of escaping Josephine now. There was going to be a confrontation. Martha just didn't want it to take place in public.

Josephine followed her all the way back to the house.

She made it to her room, but she didn't even get a chance to close the door. Josephine grabbed it, slammed it shut, and rounded on her.

"How dare you! He's going to be my husband. Mine!"

Given that nothing occurred to her as an acceptable answer, Martha remained silent. Josephine was right. She shouldn't have kissed Jordan. It didn't seem fair, however, that her sister now had a reason to be justifiably angry when Josephine had been underhanded and devious from the beginning.

She took a few steps back, erring on the side of caution. Josephine looked angry enough to strike her. Her cheeks were florid, her mouth twisted. Her eyes were narrowed and filled with rage.

"Why were you kissing him?"

Because she lost her mind around Jordan. She lost all thought of who she was, the circumstances, the day, the witnesses, everything. On the dock all she'd been feeling was an exhilarating joy.

It felt right and proper that he was there to celebrate with her. The kiss was just a natural extension of her mood.

How, though, did she explain that to Josephine?

Could she say that the moment felt special and worthy of a grand gesture? Or that she was moved to tears by being able to replicate their father's success?

"It just happened," she said, walking to the window.

The view was of the lake, but from here she couldn't see the dock. She would never tell Josephine it would remain a special place for her, the location where she realized what she felt for the Duke of Roth was more than friendship.

She loved him. An emotion she'd never thought to have, a feeling now forbidden.

First, she'd been curious about Jordan. Then, a little envious of her father's praise of him. Later, as she'd read his letters, she began to admire his mind. Finally, she got a sense of the man himself not only from the words he wrote but those things he carefully left unsaid. By the time she arrived at Sedgebrook she was already interested in him. Sparring with him, challenging him, being near him had somehow pushed her the rest of the way.

None of which she'd confess to Josephine.

I love him. I love him. The words ached to be said. She'd never utter them. Not to Josephine. Never to Jordan.

"I was just excited I made the *Goldfish* work," she said. She glanced over her shoulder at Josephine. "You'll be glad to know I found what Father had discovered."

Josephine's lips twisted. "I don't care about those ships, Martha. I want you to leave Jordan alone. He's mine."

"Why pretend you feel something for him?" Martha asked, turning. "We both know you don't. The only allure Jordan has for you is the fact he's the Duke of Roth and he owns Sedgebrook. If he were still a naval officer, you wouldn't notice him. Oh, you might glance at him long enough to ridicule him, but you certainly wouldn't contemplate marriage."

"But he isn't a naval officer, is he? He's a duke. He's my duke. Just remember it."

"You would do anything to become a duchess, wouldn't you?"

Josephine's smile was unnerving, the expression of a woman much older than she was, someone skilled in manipulation and deceit.

"Yes, Martha, I would do anything. I'd be a fool not to."

"What did you tell Gran to make her believe it was you?" A question she'd never asked of her sister but one she considered every single day.

"I just confessed to being in the duke's bed."

She could just imagine the scene. Josephine weeping with remorse, her grandmother aghast yet pragmatic.

"You weren't."

"You and I know what happened, Martha, but no one else does. You should thank me. Because of me, your reputation remains unsullied. You can go on to become a spinster and no one will know the duke took your virginity.

"Leave him alone," Josephine continued. "I don't even want you in the same room with him. In a matter of days I'm going to be the Duchess of Roth and you're not going to ruin it."

Martha stared at her sister as she left the room. She shouldn't have kissed Jordan, but she couldn't summon any regret. Not when it would be the last time.

Was this how it felt when your heart broke?

"No doubt Marie is finding some excuse not to attend the wedding," Mrs. York said, frowning at the envelope before giving it to Amy to take to Josephine. "She is probably overjoyed that her daughter is marrying a duke, but envious at the same time. Marie does not handle envy well."

Amy didn't say anything, but then she normally remained silent. Mrs. York didn't require agreement with her comments, only discretion. However, in this instance, she thought the older woman was right.

Marie York was not the right example for any young girl. The woman disregarded propriety, acted on impulse, and did what she wished most of the time.

Unfortunately, Josephine was taking after her mother. Look how she'd caught a duke for herself by acting in a shocking manner.

Taking the letter, she went in search of Josephine, only to see her marching back to Sedgebrook after her sister, an expression on her face that warned Amy now might not be the best time to encounter the girl. Perhaps she'd just leave the letter in Josephine's room.

A task she had every intention of fulfilling except for the sound of raised voices coming from Martha's room.

Amy listened, torn between her better nature decreeing such a thing was wrong and an overriding curiosity. What she heard both horrified her and explained so many things. Why Martha's demeanor had changed since their visit at Sedgebrook. Why the girl was quiet all the time and looked to be miserable, especially when the upcoming marriage was mentioned.

Josephine loved being the center of attention, so the ceremony was always the prevailing topic of conversation.

What she didn't understand was how the duke had been fooled.

She opened the door to Josephine's room, dropped the letter on the bureau, and was leaving when Josephine stormed across the hall.

"What are you doing here?"

"I've left a letter from your mother," Amy said, pointing to the bureau.

Josephine didn't say a word, just slammed the door in her face.

Amy headed for the Summer Parlor and Mrs. York.

SUSAN YORK STARED at her maid, words failing her.

"Tell me what you heard again," she said, her fingers massaging her throat, the better to urge the words up from the block of ice that had become her chest.

Amy repeated everything. Nothing sounded better the second time.

"Oh dear."

"Josephine was taken with Sedgebrook, ma'am. Couldn't stop talking about all the rooms, the Conservatory, and the ornamental ponds in the garden, too. She was even saying what she wanted to change when she became duchess. She made quite an impression with the staff, but it wasn't a good one."

"In other words, the girl would have done anything."

Amy nodded.

Susan glanced toward the open door of the parlor. Without being directed to do so, Amy slid it closed. She patted the sofa next to her. A moment later Amy sat beside her.

"She seemed so sincere that morning," Susan said. "Almost terrified. I would never have imagined Josephine to be lying about such a thing."

It wasn't the first time she'd spoken of delicate subjects with her maid. Amy wasn't in the first blush of youth anymore, plus she'd always had a level head on her shoulders. Her greatest asset, however, was a ferocious loyalty.

Josephine had a tendency to overlook Amy, treating her with no more notice than a footstool or a cabinet. Her mother had been the same. Was arrogance inherited? She'd never thought so until Marie and Josephine entered her life.

What had she done? Why hadn't she factored in Josephine's greed? Her youngest granddaughter unfortunately had the heart of an asp.

For the first time in a long time, she felt genuinely ill.

Her mother had often told Susan that she interfered too much in other people's lives. Even as a child, she was interested in the happiness of her siblings. Thanks to her, her brother had met his wife and her sister a husband. She'd also been instrumental in smoothing out rough patches between spouses, interpreting difficulties in communication. Yes, she interfered, but mostly to the betterment of those people involved in the situation.

Until now.

She'd never expected to fail so spectacularly in this one thing.

Dear God in Heaven, what had she done?

She should have seen how affected Martha was by the duke's presence. The girl bit her lip, clenched her hands together until the knuckles whitened, and spoke in a faint voice unlike her.

It was all Susan's fault. No one could say otherwise. Her machinations had borne fruit, but not exactly as she'd planned. She'd hoped that Martha would attract the duke's attention, especially given everything that Matthew had told her about the man and about how he wished the two of them might one day meet. All she'd wanted was to generate a little interest between them.

She had a scandal of epic proportions, one prevented by a quick wedding. Except, of course, that the wrong people were getting married.

What on earth did she do now?

MARTHA DIDN'T APPEAR at dinner or afterward when they adjourned to the parlor. Jordan wasn't unduly surprised. He hadn't seen her since their kiss.

He felt as if the moment on the dock had been one of déjà vu. She felt familiar in his arms. Or maybe it was just that it felt right to hold her.

Josephine hadn't said anything to him about the situation, but he knew she was angry. Her smile had a different flavor to it tonight and she wasn't paying as much attention to him as she was Reese. He'd also caught Mrs. York glancing at him from time to time. Did she, too, know about the kiss?

Perhaps he should just stand and issue a blanket mea culpa. *Yes, I kissed her. Without thought to my role in life, my upcoming marriage, or anything else, I kissed Martha.*

He'd wanted to go on kissing her as well, which was something he wasn't about to confess.

Perhaps it's a good thing she hadn't appeared. He might not be able to conceal his thoughts. Or the sudden longing he felt—as troubling an emotion as his reluctance about his wedding.

"I'm sorry Miss York is feeling ill," Reese said. "I wanted to ask her about her discovery this afternoon."

Evidently, Reese had put out feelers among the staff. Someone—a maid, a footman, maybe even a stableboy—had already told him everything about the *Goldfish's* successful voyage.

If the rumors were true, the Topographical & Statistics Department was becoming the Intelligence Branch of the War Office. Reese was already well on his way to making himself invaluable.

"Did she really get her ship to work?" Reese asked.

Jordan didn't say a word. Nor did Josephine, but he wasn't sure if it was ignorance on her part or just a dislike of the subject. He hadn't been alone with Josephine much but when he was it was obvious she wanted the conversation to be centered around her.

He had a lifetime of boredom ahead of him.

No, it wasn't his imagination, Mrs. York was most definitely glancing in his direction. If they'd been alone, he would have asked her forgiveness for his behavior.

His priorities had never been so skewed before, but then he'd never been as confused as he was now. The woman he was about to marry was a stranger and the woman who should have been a stranger felt like someone he'd always known.

Part of it was Matthew mentioning his daughter in his letters. He'd grown accustomed to Matthew's observations about Martha, knowing what she'd said or how she felt about a certain situation. The older man had also passed along Martha's thoughts about improvements to the vessel, most of which Jordan found insightful and practical.

Plus, his talks with Martha at Sedgebrook had been unusual, at least for him. He'd never divulged as much to anyone, feeling a trust with Martha that he'd only experienced with her father.

He didn't feel that same trust for the woman he was about to marry.

He'd been trapped into this marriage by honor. Wouldn't it be interesting if he could withdraw from it for the same reason? He'd kissed Martha. Would it be enough for Josephine to release him?

He doubted it. Even now Josephine was holding court by chattering on about events planned around the marriage ceremony. He didn't care. Just get it over with. He would take Josephine back to Sedgebrook and involve himself wholeheartedly in his work.

Would Martha tell him how she fixed the guidance system? Or would she rightfully retain the knowledge so her father got the credit for the York Torpedo Ship? If so, he would have to find something else to occupy himself, a few other inventions that had interested him in the past.

What the hell was he going to do with his life? What was he going to do about this marriage?

He was going to do his duty. He was going to be the 11th Duke of Roth, damn it.

Everyone was looking at him expectantly.

"Josephine was just complimenting your stable," Mrs. York said.

Why the hell did the woman keep mentioning those damnable horses? Wasn't she aware of the accident? Or perhaps she didn't know why he wouldn't be able to walk without a limp for the rest of his life.

"My brother is to be thanked for the stable," he said.

"You won't have to sell Ercole now," she said, deigning to finally smile at him.

He almost wanted to sell the damn horse to spite her. He studied her for a moment in silence, then simply nodded.

He caught Mrs. York's eyes on him and looked away.

SUSAN YORK WATCHED Josephine and Jordan, a sinking feeling growing in her stomach. What a horrible set of circumstances, and how like Josephine to have taken advantage of the situation.

Her granddaughter had lost no time circulating the news she was to wed the Duke of Roth. Susan had never seen Josephine write so many letters in such a short time, and most of them to their London friends.

Had it not been for the flurry of correspondence—and she suspected that was the exact reason Josephine had written everyone she knew—Susan might have tried to stop the wedding.

Why hadn't the duke spoken up? Why hadn't Martha said anything? Shame? Humiliation? Perhaps she didn't want to be put in the position of having to marry the duke while Josephine was more than happy to do so.

Susan didn't know the answer to any of those questions. She said a quick prayer, hoping the Almighty would understand her request: she wanted a way out of this marriage, some divine intervention that would result in happiness for those who deserved it.

At the moment she was out of ideas.

Chapter 29

$\mathcal{M}$artha didn't venture out of her suite for three days. Staying in her rooms was the only way she could avoid people, namely Gran, Josephine, and Jordan.

Sam sent word that he'd put the *Goldfish* in the cottage. A good thing he'd been so conscientious because she'd forgotten to take care of the vessel, the scene on the dock taking her mind from her responsibilities.

Gran came to check on her every day, but she didn't urge Martha to emerge from her hermitage. She was well aware that Gran was looking at her strangely. Did she know what had happened at Sedgebrook? Did her grandmother know her heart was breaking?

On the evening of the third day, desperately tired of her own company and wanting a respite from drawing plans and reading, she went to sit on the terrace.

The hour was advanced; it was late enough that people would have retired after dinner. Even the servants were preparing for bed.

The brick-walled terrace was her favorite spot on a summer night. Beyond lay the forest, now only shadows.

She sat on one of the built-in benches, looking up to

see the magnitude of the heavens spread out for her to witness. All the stars made her feel infinitesimal. What were her minor worries in comparison? Her petty annoyances, even her accomplishments, felt so minor in view of such a display. She was only a sigh in the Almighty's consciousness, nothing more. Yet sometimes when she sat here, especially in the past year, she had the feeling she wasn't alone. Something or someone cared about her, guarded her, looked out after her. Perhaps it was God or the spirit of her parents.

She missed her father terribly and would have missed her mother, she was sure, if she'd had a chance to know her. But she'd died when she was three and little remained of Martha's childhood memories.

Her father told her stories, especially when they worked late at the cottage. She'd sit there enthralled, her pen poised above the journal where she was transcribing his words.

"She liked greens," he said one night. "And I liked lamb. It wasn't one of her favorite dishes, so we would dare each other. I would eat some of her greens if she would have some of my lamb. I'm surprised Cook didn't just deliver our dinner on one plate."

He'd smiled then, his eyes soft with the recollection.

She, too, would have memories, only not of a spouse. But she would carry to her grave the moments she and Jordan sat together at the workbench in his boathouse. Or when she was in his bed.

After tomorrow Josephine and Jordan would be married. They'd go back to Sedgebrook to live out their lives and she'd remain here at Griffin House, intent on another task she would set herself. She'd find something to occupy her days, to challenge her mind, and to keep her thoughts from Jordan.

Only a matter of hours were left. Perhaps she should count them, tick them off in her journal. Record them somehow so she was prepared for the wedding. Anything to keep herself going, enduring, and surviving until he left.

He had been, even without knowing, a large part of her life. When a letter came, her father would always hand it to her and ask her what she thought. Often, she reread the letters or quoted parts to her father, especially when Jordan had sent calculations.

She would simply have to grieve for him, just like she had her father. She'd treat him as if he, too, had died. She'd grow accustomed to never hearing from him again.

Only a few more hours.

Only a little while until he went to the church in his ducal carriage, accompanied by Reese. He'd be dressed in formal wear, the picture of a proper duke. She wouldn't be surprised if there were a great many women in the congregation who would sigh in longing when first seeing him.

How could Josephine only view him as lame? How did she not see him as the most handsome man in the world?

Only a few more hours.

"Do you mind if I join you?"

She looked up, startled. Gran stood there watching her.

"I've been wanting to talk to you and now seems as good a time as any."

She scooted over on the brick bench to make room for her grandmother. Susan came and sat with her usual grace and economy of movement.

They both stared off in the direction of the forest

for a few minutes. The shadows and shapes of the trees had been reduced to black, earthbound clouds, their tops tinted silver by the moon.

"I let you hide in your room," Gran said, "because I know what it's like to have acted the fool about a man."

Startled, Martha glanced at her grandmother.

"When I was a young girl," Gran said, "I fell in love with a young man who was not, according to my parents, my equal either in rank or birth. My parents refused to entertain the suit."

There was just enough light to see her grandmother smiling softly, as if she was reminiscing.

"I told my parents I would always love him, that nothing would ever change my feelings for him."

"He wasn't my grandfather?"

"No," Gran said. "His name was Matthew."

"You named your son for him," Martha said, surprised.

Gran nodded. "It was a York family name, so no one ever knew the difference."

"Nothing changed your feelings for him?"

Gran smiled. "No, but I began to respect your grandfather and then to feel fond of him. Later, fondness turned to love. He made my days pleasant as well as my nights. I learned that I could love someone else almost as much as I loved Matthew."

"What happened to Matthew?"

"He's still living a bucolic existence on his farm," she said. "He married, too, and had seven children."

She knew there was a reason her grandmother had told her the story, but she wasn't certain what it was. Unfortunately, she wasn't left in doubt for long.

"Just because you've lost your virginity to one man doesn't mean you can't fall in love with another."

She stared straight ahead, unable to look in her grandmother's direction.

Several long minutes passed. The shriek of a fox and the rustle of undergrowth in the forest were the only sounds.

"How did you know?" she asked, only one of several questions coming to mind.

"Amy overheard you and Josephine a few days ago."

"Oh."

"If I'd known the truth, I would have stopped this marriage. As it is, I don't know how to keep it from happening now."

"I'm sorry, Gran," she said. It wasn't enough of an apology, and she knew it even as the words were uttered.

"What shall we do about the situation?"

She sank back against the bench, closed her eyes, and wished herself anywhere but here.

"Is there anything to be done?"

"You could find a husband," Gran said.

"I don't want to marry anyone."

"Don't resign yourself to life as a spinster, child. You could experience love with someone else."

She didn't want anyone else. She wanted Jordan. Perhaps her feelings would change in a few years. Perhaps when she didn't feel this great yawning emptiness inside.

"He doesn't seem to have an affinity for Josephine," Gran said.

She didn't say anything.

"Is there a possibility you could be with child?"

"No," she said. "There isn't."

"Well, thank heavens for that."

They remained silent for another few moments. Her grandmother placed her hand on Martha's wrist.

"Why on earth didn't you say something? Why did you just sit there and allow her to win?"

A question she'd asked herself hour after hour.

"At first I was too shocked to say anything. I didn't understand why Jordan had gone along with Josephine's story. Then I learned he'd taken a medicine. He genuinely didn't know the identity of the woman he was with."

She glanced at her grandmother. "You mustn't blame him. I'm the one who was in his room."

"I expected to have problems with Josephine, my dear girl, not you. Why were you there?"

"Because of Josephine," she said, and told her what her sister had planned.

Gran had no comment other than a muttered oath, one she'd never heard her grandmother use.

"How do you feel about him, child?" Gran asked a moment later.

"Does it matter now?"

Her grandmother sighed. "No, I guess it doesn't. This is a terrible situation, my dear girl, and I haven't the slightest idea how to cure it."

Neither did she.

"I wish you'd fought for your happiness, Martha. Like it or not, Josephine does. You let others dictate your life."

Martha turned and looked at her grandmother.

"You've been defined by those around you, my dear girl. You were your father's daughter, Josephine's sister, Marie's stepdaughter, even my granddaughter.

It's time to stand up for yourself and decide what you want."

What if she wanted the Duke of Roth? How did she accomplish that?

She didn't ask the question of her grandmother. There wasn't, after all, an answer.

Gran left her with a kiss to her cheek and a pat on her shoulder.

"We'll get through this, my dear girl. I promise."

She'd always believed her grandmother, but she wasn't altogether sure Gran was right in this instance.

How was she to get through this? At this time tomorrow, Jordan would be married and legally her brother. How was she to have sisterly feelings for the man who'd been her only lover?

"Miss Martha?"

She looked up to find Mr. Haversham standing there, faintly lit by lights from the parlor windows. She and the stablemaster were cordial, but she rarely saw him. Unlike Josephine, she wasn't an avid horsewoman.

The stablemaster had bushy white eyebrows so long the hairs sometimes fell in front of his eyes. She wondered how he never noticed them. Or did he like looking through a forest at the world? His mustache was a match for his eyebrows in color and thickness. His beard, however, was neatly trimmed and the color of his hair, a mix of black and white. A stocky man, he had a bearing revealing his previous military service.

Charles was there as well, peering over the man's shoulder. She hadn't seen the carriage driver since they'd arrived home from Sedgebrook.

Charles had been with them nearly a decade and was as tall and thin as he'd been as a half-starved lad in London. He'd never quite lost his London accent, but thank heavens he had finally stopped looking terrified all the time, his eyes darting back and forth as if afraid someone was going to steal the shirt from his body.

"What is it, Mr. Haversham?"

Charles stepped forward; the two men looked at each other and then at her.

"It's a problem we have, Miss Martha. One we thought it best to bring to you."

That was curious. She knew nothing about the stables or about the maintenance of the horses. She probably rode about three times a year. Otherwise, she preferred more sedentary occupations.

"How can I help you?"

Charles pulled the cap off his head, turning it round and round in his hands. If there was more light she'd be able to see the expression on his face. Since he was staring down at the terrace floor she could only surmise it was one of reluctance.

She decided that encouraging his speech would do nothing. Better to simply remain silent and let the two men find their way to an explanation.

"It's about the torpedo ship, Miss Martha."

"What about it?"

The two men looked at each other again.

"Well, I was having my dinner," Mr. Haversham said. "One of the girls brought me some of the stew from tonight. Did you have a chance to taste it, Miss Martha?"

She bit back her impatience and answered him. "Yes, I did. I've always thought it was one of Cook's best recipes."

"I feel the same," he said, his voice sounding as if

he smiled. "Well, I was eating my stew and thinking of how it reminded me of my mother's cooking when Charles climbed the stairs and opened my door without a hint of a knock."

"I didn't want to be heard by the thief," Charles said.

She wasn't understanding, but she didn't like the words *thief* and *torpedo ship* spoken in the same story.

"What happened, Charles?" she asked, hoping the man was a little faster in his recitation.

"I was checking on the springs of the carriage, Miss Martha. The one we're going to use for Miss Josephine. Underneath it, I was. I don't think anyone could see me. Maybe just the toes of my boots, but they didn't seem to be looking."

Once again, she tried to be patient.

"It's not right, Miss Martha," the stablemaster said. "Nothing either of them could say would make this right."

Mr. Haversham had been in the military and was a stiffly proper gentleman. All the lads employed in the stable were inspected in the morning as to their appearance and sent back to their rooms to change if something was amiss with their shirts or trousers. No swearing was allowed, and anyone who broke the multitude of rules he'd established was severely reprimanded and given extra duty. Strangely enough, there were always applicants for any available position. Mr. Haversham was as well-known for his loyalty and support of his staff as for his strictness.

"I thought it best you know."

"Unfortunately, I don't know what you know, Mr. Haversham. Is someone stealing something? Something to do with the torpedo ship?"

Both men nodded at the same time.

"Your sister, Miss Martha. And His Grace's friend. They put your ship in his carriage, under one of the seats."

"You saw Josephine do that?"

Charles nodded. "Yes, miss. She was helping His Grace's friend."

Josephine had already betrayed her. Now she was stealing from her?

"He'll be leaving in the morning after the ceremony, Miss Martha, and he's all for taking the torpedo ship with him."

"No, he won't," she said, standing. "Thank you for telling me, both of you. I won't forget your kindness and your honesty."

"What shall we do, Miss Martha?"

"Right now, just watch the carriage. Make sure he doesn't leave early."

She straightened her shoulders. She could confront Reese herself. Or she could simply retrieve the *Goldfish* and place it under guard, never discussing the issue with either Josephine or Reese. Or she could demand an explanation from Josephine.

None of those alternatives seemed to fit the situation.

Instead, she was going to ask for help from the one man she should avoid at all costs.

JOSEPHINE WOULD HAVE slipped away had Reese not stood between her and her bedroom door, advancing until her back was against the wall.

"Thank you for helping me acquire the ship," he said, his voice low. "The War Office will be grateful for your assistance. What a pity you're getting married. I think you would have been an asset to the Intelligence Branch."

Josephine smiled back at him, but there was an edge to her expression.

"Are we done now? No more threats to tell Jordan anything?"

All he'd done was go to her and ask if the rumors were true. Had Martha discovered the answer for the guidance system? Josephine had responded by demanding he never mention Martha's damnable ship again. When he suggested that he could put the prototype to good use, she'd not only shown him where the ship was stored in the cottage, she'd accompanied him to the stables where he'd secreted it beneath one of his carriage seats.

This time he hadn't threatened to tell Jordan anything. Everything Josephine had done was of her own volition.

"Did you miss me in the last few weeks? I found myself thinking about you, a bit more than I wished." He propped his arm on the wall, leaning over her. She didn't, as he knew she wouldn't, move away or show any discomfort at all.

"You're a damned courageous woman," he said.

"Is that supposed to be a compliment?"

"Nothing scares you, does it? You see something and you go after it without a second thought."

"Why does that sound like an insult?" she asked.

He leaned down to brush a kiss against her forehead. She didn't move away.

"Believe me, it isn't. I'm the same way."

"What a pity you aren't a duke, then," she said.

She laughed, a soft little chuckle that did odd things

to his nerves. He wanted to kiss her, to press his body up against hers, to pin her to the wall until she admitted she had missed him, that she'd thought about him, and she was happy he was here now.

Instead, he cupped her cheek with his left hand, leaned down until he was only a breath away from her lips.

"I miss you in my bed, Josephine," he said.

She pulled away, putting a few feet between them.

"You're not a bride yet," he said, smiling.

"What does that mean?"

He shrugged. "It's not too late for Jordan to realize his error. He's marrying the wrong sister."

A dangerous woman, one whose smile didn't quite reach her eyes. He reminded himself to never get on Josephine's bad side. Or at least always have something about which to blackmail her.

"You'd be a lousy wife, Josephine. Jordan deserves someone who at least likes him. Someone who doesn't just covet what he has."

She studied him for a long moment. He didn't look away, wondering what she was thinking. No doubt it was a cunning plan featuring her as the victim. Poor Josephine with her emerald eyes swimming with tears and her kissable lips pouting.

"You'll be wasted as a wife," he said, surprising himself with the truth. "You truly should work for the War Office. No doubt there's a great deal you could ferret out from the unsuspecting man."

"I have every intention of being the Duchess of Roth," she said.

"Why? You don't love him. You don't even like Jordan. Is it because you want Sedgebrook so much? Or is it because Martha wants him?"

"I don't know what you're talking about."

"Just watch Martha's eyes when she looks at him. She loves him, Josephine. It's as plain as the sky is blue."

When she didn't say anything, only continued to look at him unblinking, he smiled.

"That's part of it, isn't it? You get to be a duchess and you get to take away the man Martha loves. Do you hate your sister so much?"

"Why do you care?"

He was damned if he knew. But there was something about the girl that intrigued him. Something calling to his darker nature.

"I want you in my bed, Josephine."

She inclined her head slightly. He recognized the gesture as one of surrender. She hadn't figured out how to silence him yet, so she'd come.

"I'm going to be married tomorrow."

"Then it's the last time I can have you, isn't it?"

He pulled her across the hall, opening the door to his room.

Seconds later she was in his bed.

SUSAN PRESSED HER ear against the door, listening. A good thing she was blessed with insomnia from time to time. Almost as if nature was warning her: you don't have many years left. Why spend them in sleep?

Her granddaughter was acting according to her nature. A sad thing, but true. She should have been watching Josephine closer since it was certain she was becoming more and more like her mother.

Susan had disliked Marie from the moment she met her, but there was nothing she could do. Matthew hadn't stood a chance against Marie's determination.

Perhaps it had been a good thing. Martha had needed a mother after dear Barbara had died and she supposed the woman fulfilled that role in some fashion. What she hadn't been was a good wife.

Matthew had been so involved in his projects, inventions, and discoveries he never noticed when Marie seemed exceptionally happy. When she took a lover, at least twice a year, Marie nearly danced around Griffin House. Everyone was a beneficiary of a quick kiss and impromptu hug. She could even be heard singing. She left off her needlework for collecting bunches of flowers to arrange in bouquets around the house. She visited the cook, ordering Matthew's favorite meals. She read to Josephine, fanciful stories of beautiful princesses and the princes who loved them.

These periods were always offset by other, darker times when the affair ended. Susan thought Marie's conscience occasionally troubled her, which was why she was the one who sent the man away. They'd lost a gardener and two footmen, not to mention that more than one shopkeeper looked yearningly toward Marie.

The woman was not the least bit discriminating. She would bed anything in pants and it looked as if her daughter was following in her footsteps. Nor did she expect Josephine's behavior to change after she married.

This marriage was going to be a disaster. It was going to make more than one person thoroughly miserable, but she doubted the bride would suffer.

What on earth was she to do? Would it be terrible to wish that something happened to the sanctuary roof? That might prevent the ceremony. She could, perhaps, come down with another illness, but she doubted anyone would believe her. Would the Almighty take kindly to a prayer for guidance at this late stage? She moved to her bed, sat on the side of it, and folded her hands, trying to think of some words that would be convincing as well as contrite.

She truly needed a miracle at this point.

Chapter 30

$\mathcal{I}$t was late, past midnight, hardly the hour to wake a guest. If the circumstances were different, Martha would never consider disturbing Jordan. Yet someone had to stop Reese and confront him. Who better than his friend?

She knocked on the door to the Queen's Rooms, faintly at first and then louder when he didn't answer. Perhaps he was asleep. After all, tomorrow was his wedding day.

If he didn't respond, she would return to the stables, retrieve the *Goldfish*, and face down Reese herself.

She was turning to walk away when the door finally opened.

She glanced back to see Henry standing there, worry in his eyes.

"Miss York."

She was surprised to see him. Normally, he would be asleep in the servants' quarters on the fourth floor. Unless, of course, Jordan needed him for some reason.

"Is something wrong?"

"No, Miss York," he said, his voice lowered to a whisper.

She didn't believe him.

"Is His Grace all right?"

He glanced back toward the suite, then shook his head.

"May I see him?"

"He doesn't like visitors at times like this, Miss York."

She was hardly simply a visitor.

"Is it his leg? Has he taken the elixir?"

He looked startled at her question.

"No, miss," he said. "He refuses."

"I need to see him."

"He isn't dressed, Miss York. It wouldn't be proper."

At the moment she didn't give a flying fig for propriety. Being proper wasn't at all rewarding.

She pushed past him and entered the sitting room designed for a queen. Everything was upholstered in crimson. The carpet was woven in a design of roses and peonies in shades of pink, crimson, and green. Even the curtains were crimson.

The queen had visited Griffin House only once. How had Her Majesty tolerated the color? It was like walking into a bloody beast.

Jordan was sitting on a chair opposite the settee, attired in a blue-and-silver patterned dressing gown. She could see his bare throat and the upper part of his chest.

He had his head back, eyes closed. His pale face was illuminated by the lamp on the table.

"I'm sorry," she said. "I didn't mean to wake you."

"I wasn't asleep," he said. "I haven't been able to sleep."

"Is it your leg?" she asked.

"Yes."

The answer was short, declarative, and almost angry, revealing the depth of his pain.

"Henry says you haven't taken any of Dr. Reynolds's elixir."

"No."

"Why not, when it's all too evident you need it?"

Henry closed the door and moved to the chair. He dropped to his knees, reached out, and began massaging Jordan's right leg with practiced expertise.

Jordan closed his eyes again, his lips thinning as his face stiffened.

"Are you using camphor oil?" she asked the valet.

"No," Jordan said, answering for him.

"Would you be amenable to finding our housekeeper?" This remark, too, she addressed to the valet. When Henry glanced at her, she continued. "My father had a back injury and she concocted something for it. It has camphor and some other things and it's similar to liniment. I think it might help."

The last comment she addressed to Jordan.

"I don't think anything will help."

"If you feel that way, then you need to take your elixir."

"The damnable elixir is the reason I'm here now," he said. He opened his eyes. "My apologies for the language."

"Well, you can't do anything worse when taking it now," she said. "Your wedding is tomorrow."

"Thank you for the reminder," he said. "I haven't forgotten. I just hate the stuff. It puts me in a stupor."

"Then we should start with the housekeeper's lotion."

"Very well," he said, looking at Henry. "Go and wake the housekeeper. Give her my apologies."

"You needn't be so reluctant," she said as Henry

left the room. "I'll bet it will do wonders for you. But I still think you should take the elixir."

"I hate the nightmares it gives me. I feel as if I'm hallucinating."

"Take it anyway," she said. "I'll stay with you."

For a moment they simply looked at each other. His eyes revealed the extent of his pain. What did hers show? That she wanted to help him and give him peace? Or that she felt too much for a man who would become her brother-in-law tomorrow?

In the valet's absence, she knelt in front of Jordan.

"What are you doing, Martha?"

"I used to massage my father's shoulders when he'd been hunched over his workbench. My hands are strong."

What she was doing was untoward and forbidden. A single woman never entered a man's room. She certainly didn't lay hands on his bare limbs. In fact, she was never in his presence when he was so scantily dressed.

When her hands surrounded his ankle, Jordan closed his eyes.

"Does the pain reach down to your foot?" she asked, surprised.

"It enfolds me," he said softly. "I become one with it. It's some sort of drug-induced monster, a creature of hallucinations, and it controls me."

"I won't let it," she said.

Gently, she began to massage his ankle with both hands, then inch by inch she traveled upward. His face stiffened as if he was trying not to flinch.

Was she making his pain worse?

"Take the elixir, Jordan," she said. "I'll stay with you, I promise."

"My Joan of Arc," he said. "Will you beat back the monsters, then?"

"With my shield and sword," she said, smiling.

"The bottle's in my trunk," he said. "The one from my navy days."

Standing, she walked into the bedroom where the trunks were stacked next to one of the large armoires. She recognized the one he mentioned immediately. It had an emblem of a ship on the lock.

She opened the hasp, feeling strange about delving into his personal belongings.

At the bottom of the trunk was a small square wooden box with a tooled top. She opened the box to reveal a corked bottle and metal spoon with a curved handle. The bottle was labeled and gave instructions for the dosage.

Returning to the sitting room, she sat in front of him. Remembering his words, she halved the dose, then halved it again.

He still sat with his eyes closed as she touched the spoon to his bottom lip.

"You promise?" he asked, his voice fainter than before.

She felt as if pain had become an invisible enemy, surrounding Jordan, keeping anything from helping him.

"I promise," she said, knowing she was a fool to give her word. Remaining in his room with him, alone, would be scandalous. Right at the moment, however, she cared less for scandal than she did his health.

He didn't complain. He didn't describe the depth of his agony. He was matter-of-fact about it, almost distant, but she could feel how much it consumed him. He was alone in his fight. She knelt at his feet again, needing to touch him, needing to do something to let him know she was there and that she cared.

"Miss York?"

She looked up to see Henry returning, carrying a brown bottle with a stopper.

She should have stood and let him take his place—his rightful place—before Jordan. Instead, she only held out her hand. He extended the bottle to her before glancing at the table and noting the small curved box.

"You will call me if you need me?" he asked, looking at her.

She nodded, watching as he crossed the room to the door, closing it softly behind him.

"We will shock your family," Jordan said, his voice slightly slurred.

"Yes," she said. They probably would. But she wasn't going to leave.

She began to massage his leg again starting at the knee this time and working her way down. The liniment, for lack of a better label to call it, was pungent with spices and camphor. She smelled lemon, too. Even though the housekeeper was generous to anyone who asked for a bottle of her special lotion, she was also secretive about the recipe.

Jordan extended his leg a little. Another good sign was the fact that his face seemed to be relaxing.

"I may hire you," he said. "Not only to be my Joan of Arc, but my manservant. How are you at shaving?"

She wasn't going to tell him the only time she'd done so was preparing her father's body for burial. She'd done the duty to spare Gran, a small gift of love to both her grandmother and her father.

"How are you feeling?"

"I'm about to enter a long gray tunnel," he said, his

voice sounding as if he'd imbibed too many glasses of wine. "I hate the tunnel," he said. "It's scary and I'm alone."

She placed both her palms around his bare knee.

"You're not alone, Jordan. I'm here."

She would not leave him.

"I don't want to die," he said. "It's the one thing I remember when I think about the accident. I was lying there on the ground with this damnable stallion above me and all I could think about was he was either going to kill me or I was going to die of my injury right there."

He reached out his hand and she took it, holding on to him as if he needed the touch of another human being.

"You're not going to die," she said, but he ignored her comment.

"It was a beautiful day, with the sky above so brilliantly blue it almost hurt to look at it. I was thinking I hadn't done anything with my life. Not really. Not like your father. He had invented so many things."

"Not that many," she said.

"But important things. He was an important man. I'm not."

"I think you're important," she said.

"Because I'm a duke?"

"I would say despite the fact you're a duke," she said, giving him the truth.

"You don't often address me correctly," he said. "I like that you don't call me Your Grace all the time."

"You started calling me Martha early on," she said. "It was only fair."

"You noticed that."

"I did."

"You aren't wearing lavender, are you? I grew to hate that lavender dress of yours."

"I feel the same," she said, smiling. "No, I'm not wearing lavender. I'm wearing a dark blue dress with white-and-blue cuffs and collar."

"You've been gone," he said. "Where have you been? Were you really ill?"

"No," she said.

"I missed you. I've missed you for weeks."

That was surprising. So, too, the fact he held her hand firmly.

"You should get to bed," she said. "You need to straighten your leg."

"Come to bed with me, Martha."

For a moment she couldn't breathe.

Had he suddenly remembered? Had he realized it was she who had been in his bed all those weeks ago?

"You can help me to my bed," he said, "and then leave before anyone knows you're here. I would hate to cause you any problems."

Standing, she reached down and gripped his hands, helping him to his feet.

"Lean on me," she said.

"Dearest Joan."

She really shouldn't be so pleased at his words, especially since he had taken an opiate.

Placing her arm around his waist, she helped him the two dozen feet or so into the bedroom.

He was right. If anyone knew she was there, it would cause a great many problems. Still, she had no intention of leaving him even as he slept. She had promised to be there as a bulwark against his nightmares.

The palatial bed built for a queen was set up on a dais. For a second she wondered if it was worth the effort to reach it, but the only other piece of furniture was an ornate fainting couch that was hideously uncomfortable. He wouldn't be able to stretch out his leg fully if he lay there.

They made it up the two steps of the dais by Jordan leaning on her heavily. Three more steps up to the bed. Jordan half fell on top of the mattress, but sideways.

She gently manipulated his leg until he was lying in the correct position, placed a pillow beneath his head, and rolled him to his left side so he wouldn't be putting any pressure on his bad leg.

The dressing gown parted, revealing a scar from his knee all the way up his thigh. Instead of quickly covering his nakedness, she reached out and pressed her palm against his scar, wishing she could impart some healing to him.

The elixir had worked quickly. He was asleep or nearly so. At least she thought he was until she stepped back. He reached out and grabbed her hand.

"Stay with me, Joan."

She knew it was wrong, even as she crawled up to the mattress and arranged herself beside him. She lay on her side, facing him, free to study him as she'd never before been.

His face was relaxed now, his mouth curved in a half smile. The nightmares had evidently not come yet. Was he dreaming of something pleasant? She hoped he was, scenes from a carefree past or hopes for an easier future.

Josephine would make him miserable and he deserved so much better. Not because he was a duke or the owner of Sedgebrook, but because he was a decent man, kind and caring.

He revealed himself slowly to people, as if he was

afraid to be too vulnerable. He offered himself tentatively, almost as if he would cup his hands to give someone a drink of water.

If she had any sense at all, she would flee from this room. She would scamper back to her own suite, grateful she had rejected temptation.

Around him she had no sense of decorum or practicality, only contradictory emotions. Her heart felt close to bursting with feelings she'd never before had. Tears were too near the surface. She wanted to laugh at the same time she wished to weep. She was grateful for knowing him while wishing she'd never met him.

He'd given her passion and joy yet being with him had been horribly improper, shocking behavior she'd never imagined of herself.

What would her life be like if she was the one to be the bride later today?

Slowly, so as not to disturb his sleep, she placed her hand against his cheek, his night beard abrading her palm.

Jordan.

She spoke his name in her mind and then repeated it.

She would never be as close to him again as she was right now. Her lips would never hover over his, a kiss just a thought away. She would never lay on a mattress with him, the memories of the first time they'd done so still fresh and new.

Slowly she drew back, resting her head on the pillow, her hand on the mattress between them, content to watch him for a while.

Chapter 31

*J*ordan awoke lucid, staring up at the ceiling, two thoughts uppermost in his mind. He wasn't in pain and he wasn't alone.

Slowly, he turned his head to see Martha there, her eyes closed in sleep, lashes brushing her cheeks. He studied her for long moments, measuring her soft breathing until he became aware he was matching his breath to hers.

The past few hours were hazy, but he could recall enough to put the pieces together. She'd taken Henry's place. She'd massaged his leg, easing the pain. She'd stayed beside him as she promised.

He needed to send her away. He should protect her virtue just as she'd protected him in the hours just past. She'd stayed when he asked her to. She'd understood when no one else ever had.

How the hell could he marry her sister?

How could he marry anyone else when his heart expanded as he looked at her?

Slowly, he reached out a hand and touched her hair, feeling as if his fingers knew the soft curls. He'd done this before.

He rolled to his side, grateful not to feel any pain

from his leg. Now he was so close her breath was on his cheek. This, too, was familiar.

His hand formed a fist, knuckles grazing the soft skin of her temple. A surge of protectiveness almost stopped his heart for a moment when she sighed.

What did she dream about? Sailing her torpedo ships? What captured her mind in her sleep?

He should wake her and send her from his room now, right this moment. Otherwise, he might be tempted to kiss her. A forbidden kiss and one he shouldn't even contemplate.

He cupped her cheek, the delicate edge of her jaw fitting against his palm in a way that made him think he'd done this before.

When?

His thoughts about Martha had occupied him, but when had he touched her? He'd thought of bending over her just as he was doing now and gently kissing her half-smiling mouth. When had he done it?

Her lips were warm against his. Her lips quivered a little, the half smile disappearing as she made a sound. Just a small sound, really, one of welcome, relief, joy. Was he being foolish?

No, she was turning to him, her arms stretching out to encompass his shoulders.

He knew her. This woman with her generous nature, with her surprising mind, was no stranger. She'd never been a stranger.

He knew her as he'd known no other woman.

MARTHA AWOKE WITH Jordan's lips on hers. The pleasure was so intense that for a moment she thought it was only a dream. But then, he pulled back and looked at her, his eyes clear in the light from the bed-side lamp.

There was no confusion in his gaze. Nor was there any pain.

"It was you," he said. "It was you, Martha. That night it was you."

She remained silent.

"Do you deny it?" he asked.

"No." The word was so softly spoken that he bent closer to hear it. His breath was on her temple, his hands gentle on her shoulders.

"It was you," he repeated.

"It was me." A confession she uttered on a sigh. "It was me."

"I dreamed of you," he said against her ear. "I could never understand why my dreams were filled with you. Now I know."

Heat filled her. She shouldn't have made her own confession, but she couldn't hold back the words.

"I dreamed of you, too," she said.

In each of those dreams, the result was the same. He woke knowing it was her.

He was suddenly kissing her again, just like in her dream. She wrapped her arms around his shoulders, knowing it was the worst thing she could have done.

In only a few hours he was going to marry her sister.

He kissed her mouth and then trailed a path across her cheek to her ear and then down to her throat, murmuring words that made her heart swell.

"It could never have been anyone but you," he said.

Just a moment. Only a moment and then she would leave. She would go with only the gift of his words to hold for the rest of her life.

She reached out both hands, framed his face, and kissed him back.

For a moment she couldn't hear anything but the rush of the blood in her ears, the pounding of her heart as he kissed her. Just like before, time seemed to slow and stop. Only the two of them existed in the entire universe. They were the only ones who mattered, who breathed and lived and touched.

Her arms wound around to his back, his dropped to her hip.

He was her lover. Perhaps her only lover. The only man who'd ever touched her naked skin. The only one to know the shape of her breasts, her limbs. He'd taken her virginity and given her something precious in return, a taste of pleasure and bliss. A knowledge of fulfillment she'd hold dear for the rest of her days.

Oh, how hard it was to leave him. She never wanted to move, wanted to go on kissing him for as long as she drew breath.

She should slide off the mattress and leave the Queen's Rooms as quickly as possible. With any luck, no one would know she'd been here.

This instant. She was going to leave any second. But if he could just kiss her once more beneath her jaw, or perhaps in front of her ear. On her lips, please. A deep kiss that explored her mouth and conquered her without a word spoken.

He wasn't drugged. He wasn't under the influence of an opiate. He knew who she was. Neither of them had an excuse.

She would never feel for another man what she felt for Jordan. She knew it somehow, the knowledge seeping through her bones. No one would ever matter as much or be capable of hurting her so easily.

Yet no one could ever stir her simply with a look or a quick smile.

What kind of person was she to contemplate making love under the circumstances? She'd never before considered herself hedonistic, but it seemed as if she was, especially when he touched her just that way.

Suddenly her petticoat was gone, thrown to the floor. Her bodice was loosened as was her corset.

She should sit up and put herself to rights. She should gather up her scattered clothing, lace her corset, and be gone.

He slipped a sleeve off her shoulder, kissing his way down to her elbow. She'd never known an elbow could be such a source of pleasure or that she could feel the touch of his lips there so acutely, the sensation traveling to her core.

"Jordan," she said softly, his name so easily tumbling from her lips. "Jordan." She'd meant to utter a caution, but his name sounded more like an endearment.

She really should leave. She really should. This very moment before she lost any more of her clothes.

But, oh, the temptation was too much. This was the reason mothers cautioned their daughters against passion.

This might be the last time in her life she tasted it. Here, now, with Jordan, might be the last memory to last her for years and years of yearning.

She wasn't going to leave. She wasn't going to pull away from him.

If anyone caught her here, she would claim she was half-asleep, or that she'd been seduced against her will. No, she wouldn't blame Jordan. The responsibility lay with her. Perhaps she would tell anyone who asked that she'd taken some of the elixir and was the one who was drugged.

"Jordan," she said again.

"Martha." He pulled back, smiling down at her.

He wasn't drugged unless passion could be considered an opiate.

She reached up with one hand and placed it against his heated cheek.

"I should leave."

"Yes," he said. "You should. After one more kiss."

"I shouldn't."

"No," he said, bending to kiss her throat, "you shouldn't. But I've just found you. How can I lose you again so soon?"

Oh, how she wanted to remain in his arms, to feel his body against hers, to marvel at the magic of lovemaking, how it could transform two people into one. She wanted to throw her arms around his shoulders and hold on as bliss overwhelmed her. She wanted to be carnal and adventurous and seductive, but her conscience was awake and demanding she do the right thing.

He kissed her again, one hand on her cheek, the other spearing through her hair.

"I love your hair," he said. "It's like a cloud surrounding you."

She should have left then, but she didn't. He was himself and he knew who she was. She wasn't a figment of his drugged state. She was Martha and for these few hours, his lover.

This afternoon she would stand in the church and watch him marry her sister, but for now he was hers.

Her clothes seemed to melt away from her body, testament to his skill at seduction. Perhaps another

time she might be jealous about who had taught him
to manipulate the busk of a corset or remove a shift
with such expertise, but not now. Not when time was
against her and the passing moments marched him
inexorably toward his wedding vows.

Let him love me. Just for now. Just minutes out of a
busy life.

She would ask forgiveness at a later date. Perhaps.
She would confess her sins and await God's censure.
But not now.

She couldn't stop the tears. They seemed perfect
for this moment. She couldn't hold everything she
was feeling inside. It slipped out as soft weeping
when he kissed her again.

"Why are you crying?" he asked, pulling back.

She could only shake her head. How did she tell
him? It was sadness that these moments could never
be replicated. She'd lived most of her life without him,
but she would know his loss for the rest of her days.
It was also joy, because she would always have these
memories, this forbidden time in his arms.

Slowly, sweetly, tenderly, he kissed each separate
tear. She placed her hands on the side of his face,
closed her eyes, and memorized how his bristly
cheeks felt against her palms, the softness of his hair
as she threaded her fingers through it.

His shoulders were perfect, the muscles in his
arms well developed, his chest with its light dusting
of hair attracting her attention and her kisses.

She rose up over him, her knees on either side of
his hips.

His hands held her breasts, teased the nipples,
then pulled her down for a kiss.

"How is your leg?" she asked.

His laughter reassured her, banished her tears, and made her smile.

"I care more about another appendage at the moment," he said.

She lay against him, her arms stretched out on either side of his head, her breasts pressed against his chest. She wanted to absorb the feeling of him, the heat of his body, the perfection of his form.

The words almost escaped her, but she held them back at the last moment. They weren't appropriate, not now. She had no right to say them, but she said the words silently as she rose up to kiss him.

I love you.

I love your strength and your courage.

I love your determination and your ferocity.

I love your pride and your persistence.

I love you.

I love you, Jordan Hamilton, for all the people you are and all the roles you play. I love you in pain and anguish. I love you in laughter and joy. I will love you until the end of my days.

"You should leave," he said, his voice even.

She bent to nuzzle at his neck, placing kisses over his throat.

"You're right," she answered. "I should leave."

But he neither pushed her from the bed nor did she move of her own accord. Instead, she rose up gently, slowly, allowing him time to reprimand her or alter their positions.

All he did was watch her, his eyes intent on hers, his hands gripping her hips.

She wanted him inside her. She wanted to claim him one last time. She wanted the bliss once more.

Condemn her as a harlot. Point her out in the village square. Castigate her in whatever manner you chose. It didn't matter. Nothing mattered but him.

When he filled her, she closed her eyes for a moment, a gasping sigh leaving her. Was there anything so perfect as this surrender, this joining that had been ordained since time began?

She opened her eyes to find that he was still watching her, his gaze almost another penetration. He could see inside her soul, witness everything she felt for him.

She wouldn't be able to see him after tomorrow. She couldn't be in the same room with him without wanting to be embraced, without needing a kiss. Her entire body would go hot at his gaze and she would be able to recall this exact moment when he filled her, his hands caressing her breasts.

She wanted him to remember her. She wanted him to recall this moment, forbidden, sinful, and glorious.

Let him dream of this. Let her fill his nights.

No, she shouldn't wish that for him. She didn't want him miserable. Nor did she want him lonely. Then, perhaps, it would be better to wipe her memory from him, grant him forgetfulness. She would take on the burden of memory for both of them.

She would never forget.

When her body trembled with pleasure and she collapsed with her face beside his, tears came again and this time she didn't try to stop or even hide them.

His hand reached up and cupped her wet cheek, soothing her. She turned her head, their lips meeting softly, gently. The tenderness in those moments was almost her undoing. But somehow, with the strength she didn't know she possessed, Martha moved away from him, gathered up her clothing, and dressed behind the screen.

Neither of them spoke.

Only when she was about to leave the bedroom did he say something.

"Why did you come to my room that night at Sedgebrook?" he asked.

She looked at him, then away again.

"Must I pose the question again?"

"I thought Josephine had gone to your room," she said. "I was trying to prevent her from doing something stupid."

"I take it Josephine's aim was to place me in a compromising position?"

She nodded.

"Are you certain the two of you are sisters?"

"Because she's so much prettier than me, is that what you mean?" she asked, an edge to her voice that hadn't been there earlier.

"I meant no such thing. I find your looks to be preferable to those of your sister's, especially your hair."

"My hair?" Her hand went up to tuck an errant tendril back into place.

"I'd like to see an end of that bun of yours. Do you ever release the mass of it to spring around your head?"

She stared at him, bemused. He liked her hair?

"And your lips. I think your lips are perfect."

She pressed her fingers to her mouth. She'd never thought to hear a compliment about her lips.

"Besides," he said, "looks fade. What will keep you beautiful is your mind. I find your mind absolutely fascinating, Martha."

"You do?"

He nodded.

What on earth could she say? She could tell him she thought he was the most handsome creature she'd ever seen, that his smile made her heart race. She'd never before felt what she did when he looked at her like he was doing now.

"You were a virgin that night. Was I a halfway decent lover?" He threaded his fingers through his hair. "Why am I asking you that question? You wouldn't know." He glanced at her. "Now I'm butchering any conversation we might have over the matter."

"I was quite pleased," she said. How did she tell him she'd enjoyed every moment of her seduction?

She'd always remember the sight of him now naked and unashamed, propped up on his elbow, his hair askew, his cheeks ruddy with color.

"Thank you," he said. "For caring for me. For being my Joan of Arc. Why did you come? How did you know I was in pain?"

She'd forgotten. Everything had flown from her mind when she'd seen him. She hadn't remembered why she'd come to his room.

"Reese has stolen the *Goldfish*," she said, telling him what Mr. Haversham had said. "It's in his carriage. I didn't know what to do."

He swung his legs slowly over the side of the bed, reaching for his dressing gown at the end of the mattress.

"I do," he said. His eyes went to the mantel clock above the fireplace. "Time enough to rectify the situation. I've no doubt Reese thought he was doing something good for the War Office, but he isn't going to steal your discovery."

The rush of warmth she felt had nothing to do with passion.

"It wasn't just mine," she said. "It's my father's and yours as well."

"Regardless, I'm not going to let Reese steal the *Goldfish*."

"What can I do?"

"Leave," he said gently. "Before anyone sees you."

"Should I summon Henry?"

He shook his head, his smile surprising her. "That would be unwise," he said. "I'll do it. You just get back to your room."

"No," she said. "Under normal circumstances, I would agree, but this is my ship. I have some stake in this."

"Martha," he said gently, "do you trust me?"

As much as her father or Gran, and more than Josephine or Reese.

"Yes."

"Then let me handle this. It would be difficult to explain your presence at this hour of the morning."

He was right. Annoyed nevertheless, she left the Queen's Rooms.

Chapter 32

Shame should have rooted him to the spot, but instead Jordan was curiously enthusiastic about the day. At two o'clock he was to be married. A little more than nine hours from now. Nine hours—time enough to divert the course of his life.

He rang for a servant, surprising the young maid who answered the bellpull with an apology.

She blinked at him several times, giving him the impression of a sleepy kitten.

"Oh it's no bother, Your Grace. I'm on night kitchen duty, in case anyone wants anything. It's what I'm here for."

"Would you fetch my valet for me?" he asked.

Henry had evidently introduced himself to the staff, because the girl's round and shiny cheeks turned pink and she bobbed two or three curtsies in a row.

"Of course, Your Grace. I'll go and get Henry right this minute."

Ever since Henry had come to work for him, Jordan had noticed the man's effect on women. More than one member of his female staff grew flustered in his presence. Even Mrs. Browning was known to giggle around his valet from time to time. No doubt it had something to do with Henry's height and the bulging muscles that could be detected through any of his shirts.

He thanked her and she grinned brightly at him, revealing a wide space between her two front teeth. Despite the hour and his errand, he couldn't help but smile back at her.

His entire outlook had been changed and he knew exactly why.

When Henry arrived, he told the man he wasn't ready to dress in his morning coat for the ceremony quite yet. Instead, he was content to wear a white shirt and black trousers.

His valet only nodded. Henry wasn't without curiosity, but his tact was greater. He didn't say a word about the messed-up sheets or the fact that Jordan couldn't stop smiling.

"Is your leg better, Your Grace?" Henry asked after he was shaved and dressed.

Jordan nodded, the question taking him aback. Not because Henry had asked it, but due more to the fact that this was the first time he'd given his leg any attention.

"Yes," he said, hearing the surprise in his own voice.

Before he left the room he gave Henry instructions about the preparations for his wedding. He would be at the church exactly at two o'clock.

He headed for Reese's room, certain his friend hadn't awakened yet. He knocked twice and waited.

Reese had always been ambitious as well as patriotic. Perhaps he should have expected his friend to do something as outrageous as steal Martha's ship.

He could understand ambition. He'd had his share of it when attached to the War Office. Each man was desperate to make his mark and attract the attention of his superiors.

But Martha wasn't working contrary to the interests of her country. As one of the heirs to York Armaments, anything Martha devised or invented would probably be turned over to the company. They had a long and prosperous working relationship with the British government.

Reese, however, evidently believed he could circumvent proper channels and make a name for himself at the same time. No doubt his superiors in the War Office would be interested in a self-contained ship that could, without incurring casualties, target an enemy vessel. All the better if they didn't have to work to get it.

He knocked a third time and the door was finally opened by a blinking Reese dressed only in trousers.

"Can't sleep?" Reese asked, threading his fingers through his hair. "Matrimonial nerves?"

"More like preventing a theft," he said, pushing against the door. "Or are you going to deny you've stolen the *Goldfish*?"

Reese stumbled back.

"A goldfish? What the hell are you talking about, Jordan?"

"Martha's ship, the newest York Torpedo Ship," he said. "I hear you've stashed it in your carriage. Is it true?"

"You can't come in here," Reese said, glancing toward the bed.

For the first time Jordan realized the other man wasn't alone. There was a person-sized lump in Reese's bed, but the woman had burrowed beneath the covers until not even her hair showed.

"Seducing the maids, Reese?"

"There's a plethora of attractive females at Griffin House," he said. "I would advise you to do the same at Sedgebrook, but I suspect your bride will only allow you to hire ugly women."

Although he would have preferred to have no witnesses to this encounter, Jordan had no intention of leaving until he got some kind of answer.

"Well? Are you going to admit it?"

"Why should I? You've evidently already discovered it."

"Is stealing the *Goldfish* worth losing my friendship?"

"It has nothing to do with you, Jordan."

Reese's words irritated him.

"Like hell it doesn't. It has everything to do with me. I didn't figure out the guidance system fast enough, so you had to steal Martha's work. There's no need for you to remain for the ceremony, Reese. I'd prefer you leave for London immediately. Without the *Goldfish*."

Before Reese could say anything else, he left the room, heading down the stairs with greater ease of movement than he'd felt the day before.

He'd always believed he was an honorable man. Honor had been as near to him as his skin. He couldn't peel it off and dismiss it when it became too onerous. He'd always believed that, given any set of circumstances, he'd choose the correct path.

He hadn't acted that way around Martha.

His world had been shaken on its axis. He'd awakened in the middle of the night without the blinding headache, feeling refreshed, and, even better, out of pain.

Even half-asleep he'd known the truth long before

he'd consciously accepted it. Why else would he have dreamed of her with such regularity over the past weeks? Why would he have felt a sense of acute loneliness on waking?

He'd known who she was immediately. It hadn't stopped him from seducing her.

No, he'd definitely not behaved with honor around her, a fact he was going to rectify as soon as he took care of securing her torpedo ship.

Dawn lit the eastern sky, tinting it pink and blue, promising a fair summer day.

He headed in the direction of the stables. He hadn't been around horses since his accident over a year ago. He carefully avoided the stables at Sedgebrook, but now, at Griffin House, he had no choice but to enter them.

It wasn't that he'd developed an antipathy for horses. Yet every time he saw one, he couldn't help but relive the moment when Ercole had refused to take the fence, and had, instead, thrown him onto it.

Today, however, was the perfect time to confront his weaknesses, especially if he was going to do the right thing, the proper thing, the act that honor itself demanded of him.

His future depended on what he did in the next few hours.

One day, he might walk without a limp. He might even be able to throw away the detested walking stick. If and when that day came, he wanted the rest of his life to be bearable. No, more than bearable. He no longer wanted to live a hermit-like existence. He didn't want his life to feel shadowed and gray as it did when he took the elixir. He wanted to live wholly, completely, and experience happiness.

Perhaps he didn't have as many talents as Simon. He knew he didn't possess his father's effortless conviviality, but neither was he a spendthrift. He didn't ignore the future; he planned for it. In addition, he had the ability to focus and concentrate and apply himself to a situation and a problem until its answer was found.

He was dogged and determined and refused to quit. When Dr. Reynolds said he would never walk again, he hadn't listened.

He was going to use that same determination today.

First, however, he was going to locate Reese's carriage and retrieve Martha's ship. Then, he'd take care of the rest of his life.

"ARE YOU A bedlamite?" Josephine said, popping her head out from beneath the covers. "He almost caught me!"

"Jordan is too much a gentleman to insist on knowing the identity of my partner. Shouldn't you be leaving? You have a role to play, that of innocent young bride."

He tilted his head a little and inspected her in the most insulting way possible.

"Will you be able to manage the charade?" he asked. "However will you explain your expertise?"

"That's nothing you have to worry about," she said.

Sitting up, she didn't even bother clutching the sheet to her bare chest. Let him look his fill. Today, as she married another man, let him wish the circumstances were different.

"You don't love him," he said.

"Love has nothing to do with this marriage. It

doesn't, in most cases. I simply found a way to advance myself. Do you fault me?"

"Actually," he said, coming to sit on the edge of the bed, "I don't. Your frank amorality is almost refreshing."

When he reached out and touched her shoulder, smoothing his hand down to her elbow, she slid away from his grasp.

"There's no time for that now," she said.

"It's barely dawn."

He pulled the sheet free until her entire body was revealed. She made no move to cover herself. After today, she would have to maintain a certain decorum, at least for a little while. She would be the Duchess of Roth and expected to behave in a certain manner.

There would be no taking of mongrels to her bed.

"I know you don't love him," he said. "But I suspect you feel something for me."

She allowed herself a small laugh. "Gratitude," she said. "Last night was pleasant."

"Is that all?"

Was that disappointment in his eyes? Or was he just teasing her? She had the feeling Reese was quite adept in handling women. She found she didn't want to be just another conquest. Instead, she wanted to remain in his mind and memory for a long time.

When he reached for her, she planted her hand against his chest.

"You don't seem upset about Jordan finding my sister's ship."

He shrugged. "There's always a way to get what you want, if you really want it."

She moved her hand to the back of his neck and pulled his head down for a kiss.

There was time, before she dressed as a bride, to enjoy herself once more.

MARTHA SAT IN her room, reliving the events of the past hours. She didn't feel as guilty as she had the first time she'd loved Jordan. Did sin become natural after a while? Did you lose all perspective of whether you were committing a shocking act?

Why didn't it feel scandalous? Why wasn't she ashamed?

It hadn't felt wrong. What felt wrong was Jordan's marriage to Josephine later today.

Yet he'd said nothing to her about changing his mind. He couldn't, could he? He was obligated to carry through with the ceremony, just as she was to attend it.

If she could, she'd find a reason not to be in the congregation. She'd come down with a sudden fever, perhaps, or a stomach upset. Something she could claim might be contagious. From the information she'd overheard, most of the inhabitants of both villages were going to attend either the ceremony or the reception or both.

But she had to be there for Gran's sake and because she was a York.

Would hundreds of eyes be on her? Would they be speculating as to her feelings?

The girl didn't have a good season, did she? How does she feel to have her younger sister marry before her? Is she destined to be a spinster?

Not one of them would know she'd spent the night in the groom's arms, that she bore the marks of Jordan's night beard on her breast.

She really should be ashamed of herself.

Instead, she wondered if Jordan had met with Reese. Had he recovered the *Goldfish*?

What on earth had inspired Josephine to help Reese steal the vessel? Did her sister hate her that much? Didn't she realize that making the *Goldfish* work wasn't Martha's victory as much as proving their father's success? If nothing else, she'd get the answer to that question today.

She left her room, intent on talking to Josephine.

Chapter 33

Josephine wasn't in her bed. Martha was surprised since her sister had never been an early riser. She knew Josephine was not briefing the housekeeper or visiting with Gran who did have a tendency to wake with the sun.

Had wedding nerves kept her awake? Was she walking in the garden? She doubted Josephine had gone to the library to select a book. Another point on which she and her sister were different. Josephine didn't like to read. In fact, she even commented that while Martha was content to read about adventures, she preferred to have them.

The maids would be in here shortly to straighten the room, close the jewelry box, collect the wadded handkerchiefs on top of the bureau, hang up the clothing strewed over the bed, the floor, or on various pieces of furniture. Josephine always left proof she'd been somewhere, as if she was a whirlwind.

Sarah and Amy both would probably be pressed into service to help her in a few hours.

A few hours. Only a few hours until the wedding.

The wedding dress was hanging outside the armoire, no doubt to prevent any wrinkles. Martha glanced at the gown, away, then back again.

The pale yellow garment was elaborate and festooned with lace, a work of art the seamstress and her four helpers had labored over for weeks. The lace was French, of course, as was the nightgown and peignoir for the wedding night, a fact Josephine had expounded on at length. No doubt they were packed in the trunk sitting beside the vanity. Another tangible bit of evidence that the wedding would be held today and the bride would depart Griffin House with the groom.

Martha removed some clothing from one of the chairs and sat, waiting for Josephine to return, deliberately not thinking of the wedding any longer.

A quarter hour later, Josephine slipped through the door, stopping abruptly when she saw Martha sitting there.

"Have you come to check on me, sister?"

Josephine's hair was mussed, her lips slightly swollen. She looked as if she'd come from a lover's bed.

"Do you need checking on, Josephine?" she asked.

Josephine only smiled.

"I came to ask why you did it."

"Did what?" Josephine walked into the bathing chamber separating their two rooms.

Martha stood and followed her. "Stole the *Goldfish*."

"I'm sure I don't know what you talking about, Martha."

Josephine bathed her face and carefully blotted it dry.

"Reese didn't know where I kept it. You had to have told him or even shown him. Why, though?"

Josephine returned to the bedroom, sat at the vanity, and began to take down her hair, one gold pin at a time.

"It wasn't just my work, Josephine. It was our father's, too. Did you think so little of him to simply let someone steal it?"

Josephine half turned on the vanity stool, pointing her brush at Martha.

"Not our father. Yours."

"What?" Martha frowned at her sister.

"He was your father, but he wasn't mine."

She felt as if she was suddenly encased in a bubble. The world outside was normal, the servants already stirring, excitement building about the big day. In hours hundreds of people would be at Griffin House but now, inside the bubble, time was slowing then crawling to a stop.

"Tell me what you mean," she said, feeling as if even her speech was stretched out, each separate word pulled thin.

"He wasn't my father," Josephine said, turning back to survey herself in the mirror. "That's what I mean."

Martha stared at her in the silence. Was she going to explain?

Finally, Josephine spoke again. "Maman told me when I was thirteen."

Martha sat down on the chair she'd occupied minutes earlier, focusing her attention on the well-polished andirons in the fireplace.

She'd known her father's marriage hadn't been idyllic, but surely Marie hadn't cheated on him to that extent.

"I don't believe you," she said.

Josephine shrugged. "It's not important if you believe me or not."

"Why would Marie tell you such a thing?"

"It was a present," Josephine said.

Martha looked at her.

"When you went off to London and everyone could only talk about you. How pretty Martha was. How talented Martha was. How smart Martha was. She knew I wasn't happy and she wanted me to know you weren't my sister. We aren't related at all."

The worst part wasn't Josephine's comment, but the evident enjoyment with which she announced it.

"Does birth matter?" Martha finally asked. "Father treated you like his daughter. Gran treats you like her granddaughter. I've always seen you as my sister."

"It matters to me," Josephine said. "My father was an important man. A titled man. He didn't fiddle with inventions all day long."

"The man you so easily dismiss left you a fortune," Martha said.

"Payment, don't you think, for enduring this family? For putting up with your oddness and your father's? For listening to all of Gran's rules? Once I'm married I never have to see any of you."

The words were said with a tight-mouthed hatred. What reason did Josephine have to feel vengeful? She'd always been the spoiled darling of the family, the princess who was never refused anything.

Martha couldn't think of a thing to say. Not one word came to mind. Standing, she faced the woman she'd known as her sister.

Josephine had always been more concerned with herself and what she wanted than anyone else, but she'd never been actively cruel. She had more than a few saving graces. She adored her mother. She was pleasant to the servants. She ignored people who didn't interest her instead of going out of her way to make them miserable. At least until now.

"Why did you help Reese?"

Josephine shrugged. "Why not?"

She pushed back the pain of Josephine's betrayal and asked, "Why does he want the ship?"

"You should ask him, Martha. I don't care."

"Then why did you do it? Why did you tell him where the *Goldfish* was?"

"To keep him quiet," she said, an edge to her tone. "He knew I wasn't with Jordan that night at Sedgebrook."

"How did he know that?"

"Because I was with him," she said.

Martha stared at her sister, unsurprised. "And you were with him last night, too."

Josephine smiled.

She sometimes thought Josephine had the appearance of a cat, especially when she cocked her head just so and glanced at you out of the corner of her eye. Now her expression was of a particularly satisfied cat, one who'd devoured a saucer of cream or a tasty songbird.

"I wanted to make sure he didn't say anything to Jordan. Tell me," she said, "you've had him, is Jordan halfway decent in bed? Or is he lame there, too?"

Martha didn't answer her. Instead, she said, "He knows. He knows it wasn't you that night."

She'd never seen anyone's face change so quickly. The smugness in Josephine's expression vanished.

"How does he know?"

It was her turn to smile. "Because I told him."

She looked down at Josephine.

Martha had always tolerated Josephine's occasionally rude behavior. She'd made excuses for her sister and had endured her complete disregard of the wishes of others. She'd gone behind Josephine to try to repair hurt feelings and broken relationships. She'd reached her limit. Josephine's actions were like a poisonous liquid spilling out over the top of her cup.

"I've known you since you were born. I protected you. I looked out for you. I read to you. When you were little, I endured your following me everywhere. I loved you. Now it doesn't matter if we have the same blood or not. I'll never think of you as my sister again."

Turning, she walked out of the room.

"I DO NOT have a good feeling about this, Amy," Susan said, sighing. "I'm afraid a mistake is about to happen yet there is nothing I can do to stop it."

Amy didn't answer her, merely continued to help with her new hat. It was a pretty piece of confection and one flattering her aging face, but not even a new hat could cheer her up at this moment.

"Are you feeling well, ma'am?"

Susan glanced at her. "I don't suppose the word is *ill*, exactly. Disheartened, probably. Aghast, most certainly. Both my granddaughters have proven to be harlots. Last night, alone, the traffic through the halls was enough to rival a bordello."

"No one knows, ma'am. Other than the few of us. No one else knows why the duke offered for Josephine. What's to prevent you from calling off the wedding?"

"I'm afraid it's not my purview," Susan said. "That's for the duke to do. From what I understand about the man, he has a surfeit of honor."

Amy stepped back, surveying her results.

"Would he sacrifice himself, ma'am, for his honor?"

"That's the question, isn't it, Amy? What matters more to him? His honor or his happiness?"

"Does he feel the same about Miss Martha, do you think, as she feels about him?"

"Another excellent question and one for which I don't have an answer. I think only His Grace knows for sure."

Unfortunately, the next few hours would tell the tale. Would Jordan Hamilton choose his position as the Duke of Roth over anything else? Did he love Martha? Was the emotion strong enough to overcome what he would have to face if he called a halt to the wedding at this late hour?

She didn't want to cause a scandal. She certainly didn't want to endure one. However, a few months of whispers and outright conjecture were much better than a lifetime of regrets.

If she'd been brave enough and strong enough, she would've defied her own parents. She would've run off with Matthew and the rest of her life wouldn't have been plagued with what-ifs and if-onlys.

She'd been happy enough, so she had no complaints, but should a person be given only so much joy and no more? She had her family and they had, for the most part, been an unending source of happiness. Her son had been the best child any mother could ask for. His first wife had been an absolute treasure. Martha was a constant joy. If Marie and Josephine brought discord into her life, it was a small price to pay for the rest.

But this, this union between Josephine and Jordan was wrong. Based on a lie, a falsehood and a deliberate deception, it cried out to be corrected.

Chapter 34

Griffin House was built of a red brick that probably looked almost black in the rain. The stables were, to his surprise, built of stone that looked almost white in the morning sun. The style was Palladian, however, to match the house.

Jordan hesitated at the entrance, then pushed himself forward to the carriage staging area. He had to pass a line of stalls, some of which had interested occupants peering out to see who passed. Or, more likely, checking to see if he'd come armed with some sort of treat.

Instead of searching out Reese's carriage, Jordan stopped at the stablemaster's office, a small square space filled with papers and all matter of equipage either ready to be mended or newly purchased.

Unlike the stablemaster at Sedgebrook, Mr. Haversham probably had no budget. Nor a need to mend tack until the leather fell apart in the stableboy's hands. The man wasn't in his office, but he wasn't surprised. He located him in the yard to the right of the main stable building.

Haversham was inspecting a coach, no doubt the one to deliver the bride to the church. Two stableboys stood at the ready, each armed with a white cloth to buff out any spots on the shiny black lacquer.

As he approached, the stablemaster turned and addressed him.

"Your Grace," he said. "What can I do for you?"

"I'm here to retrieve Miss York's torpedo ship," he said.

Surprise flickered over Haversham's face before the expression disappeared.

"Miss Martha told you, then?"

Jordan nodded. "I can only apologize for Burthren's behavior, Mr. Haversham."

"Well, and it's not like you did it, did you, Your Grace?"

"No, but I brought him here."

The man only nodded.

"Aye, then."

Haversham led the way to where the carriages were stored, each bay spacious and well lit. His carriage had been pulled out as well as another almost equally fine. No doubt it was going to be Mrs. York's vehicle to travel to the church.

Reese's carriage was still in one of the bays. He opened the door and would have lifted the seat had it not been for the stablemaster. The man pushed his way past Jordan and hauled the crate out of the vehicle.

"Where do you want it, Your Grace?" he asked.

He liked the man's assertive behavior, but he didn't need to be coddled. However, since he had another few tasks to perform before he had to get to the church he decided to let the man help.

"In the cottage," he said.

They walked in companionable silence around Griffin House, heading toward the lake.

"Hear tell you fiddle with those ships as well, Your Grace."

He smiled. "I do. But it was Miss York who made this one work."

Haversham nodded again. "Smart she is. Always has been. I can still see her as a little girl following her father around like a baby duck. It hasn't been easy for her this past year, Your Grace. I didn't like to see people taking advantage of her."

He wasn't certain if Haversham was referring to Reese trying to steal the ship or something else entirely. He decided that it would be prudent not to ask.

Once at the cottage, he reached out, opened the door, and stepped aside so the stablemaster could enter. Once he'd done so, Jordan entered.

"Should I put it here on the table, Your Grace?"

He nodded.

"Did that fellow take the ship to get credit for it, Your Grace?"

"Maybe not for devising the ship, but certainly for acquiring it."

Haversham nodded. "It do take all kinds in this world, doesn't it, sir?"

"That it does," Jordan said. "That it does."

"Is there aught I can do for you?"

"Nothing, thank you."

"Then I'll be getting back, Your Grace. I've the final inspection of the carriage before the ceremony."

Jordan didn't say a word as the man walked out the door. The fact Haversham didn't seem concerned about leaving him alone was a compliment of sorts.

He'd never been here, but it seemed familiar. Matthew had described it over the years. Over there was the storage room where he kept his other inventions. On the far wall was his tool rack. The table that occupied the middle of the space was where he made adjustments to his torpedo ship.

Jordan placed his hands on the smooth wood, wondering how many times Matthew had done the same.

He'd met his friend in London on only two occasions. Why hadn't he made the trip to Griffin House before? Why, for that matter, had he not invited Matthew to Sedgebrook? Probably because he'd thought there was all the time in the world in which to do so.

Time was getting away from him once again.

He opened the crate. Someone had burned the name *Goldfish* into the wood.

He carefully removed the top and set it aside. The copper vessel gleamed as if it had been recently polished. He knew, from working beside Martha, that she saw to every detail. She noticed things he wouldn't have seen.

Her mind was as fascinating as her character.

"I wasn't at liberty to speak before," Reese said from behind him.

Jordan turned, regarding the man he'd known since his school days. He had a great many acquaintances, but few friends. Today, he had one less.

"Is that why you're here? To plead your case? It's too late for that. Or perhaps you're here to explain. While you're at it, perhaps you could share why the woman I'm to marry today was in your bed this morning."

He'd never seen that startled look on Reese's face before, and it was the only enjoyable moment in this scenario.

"Perhaps we could revisit your definition of friendship one of these days, Reese. In my world, it doesn't mean stealing. Should I check the silver at Sedgebrook?"

"You know damn well I didn't steal anything from you."

Jordan marched on him, finding it remarkable that his anger kept him advancing on Reese without an appreciable limp. Evidently all he needed to not appear lame was to be enraged.

A foot away from Reese he stopped.

"You don't realize, do you? If you steal from her, you steal from me. If you hurt her, you hurt me. Damage her in any way and it's as if you've taken a sword to me."

"So it's like that?" Reese asked.

"It's like that," Jordan said, finding it strange that articulating his feelings for Martha had suddenly come so easily.

Yet once the words had been spoken, they wouldn't be beaten back. They demanded to live with the same fervency he had this past year.

"Yet you're still going to marry Josephine?"

He had no intention of voicing his plans for this afternoon, especially not to Reese.

"I wish you well, then," Reese said, turning and leaving the cottage.

Jordan stared after his friend. An abrupt farewell, but perhaps not even that. In a few weeks he'd probably receive a letter from Reese filled with gossip about the War Office and tales he shouldn't be sharing. There'd be no reference to this morning's actions or this scene in the cottage.

Reese had crossed over the line, even though he

probably had no idea he'd done so. Jordan would be pleasant to the man in the future, but he could never again trust him.

A few minutes later, he replaced the top of the *Goldfish*'s crate and left the cottage.

JOSEPHINE HAD MADE no secret of her plans, informing Jordan and others in her family exactly what would transpire on the day of the wedding.

For the first time, he was grateful for her self-absorption. She'd decided her grandmother would go on ahead, accompanied by her sister while she rode alone like a queen in the more luxurious carriage.

Jordan waylaid her before she could enter the vehicle.

"If we could speak," he said, placing his hand on her elbow. He turned and walked up the short flight of steps to the main entrance of Griffin House again, giving her no chance to refuse.

"Jordan, what are you doing?" she asked, her voice filled with outraged indignation. "We'll be late for our own wedding."

"There isn't going to be a wedding, Josephine."

She pulled her arm free, facing him.

"What do you mean there isn't going to be a wedding?"

When Josephine tilted her chin up like that and narrowed her eyes, she lost all pretense of prettiness. Her face grew hard, almost old. He wondered what she would look like as she aged. Almost a crone, nearly witchlike—especially if her character was anything to go by.

"We both know it wasn't you in my bed that night at Sedgebrook," he said.

"Does it matter now? The whole of England knows we're about to marry. Would you cause a scandal?"

If she'd asked the question of him a year ago, the answer might have been different. Honor had been a watchword, a definition of his character, perhaps. Now he knew that honor wasn't enough. It might define his life in some narrow fashion, but he also wanted more.

He never wanted to experience the past year again, feeling adrift and isolated from others, alone in his anguish and knowing only his will kept him going.

His servants respected him because he found a way to pay their wages and they were, perhaps, in awe of their surroundings. His London acquaintances liked the fact he'd become a duke. The hangers-on clung to him for any referred power they could attain. Little did they know he didn't wield any power. Not even the ability to keep himself upright without limping.

Even Reese had used him.

There was only one person who'd offered him boundless friendship with no conditions. She'd given up her knowledge selflessly. She wanted nothing from him. In fact, she'd effortlessly excused his behavior, granting him understanding and compassion he hadn't deserved.

What he felt for Martha was different and special, something he'd never before experienced. He'd admired certain women in his past, but he'd never thought one of them might hold his future happiness in the curve of her palm.

He wanted to be happy. He wanted someone to appreciate his work. He was, damn it, more than his role as the Duke of Roth, more than the sum of his ancestors. He was himself, alone and individual. He wanted to be important to someone, not because a great house had been entailed to him. Not because he bore a title. Not even because he had a mind lending itself well to invention and discovery. He drew breath. He lived, therefore he mattered.

"Oh, yes," he said. "It matters. I'm not going to marry you, Josephine. Not now. Not ever."

"Don't be ridiculous, Jordan. You can't beg off now."

He studied her, noted the pursing of her lips, the frown line already beginning to show between her eyes. Was she going to stomp her feet in a tantrum? Throw herself to the ground, shrieking and tearing at her hair? He could almost envision her doing exactly that.

"Yes, I can," he said. "And I am."

"What are you going to do, Jordan? Leave everyone sitting in the church waiting for me?"

He'd already made plans. Whatever the payment was for escaping this marriage, he'd do it and willingly. In addition, the honorable thing was to offer to offset any of the Yorks' expenses of this wedding, although how he was going to pay the bill he had no idea.

"My reputation will be in tatters," she said. "I'll be known as the woman the Duke of Roth spurned."

"You should have considered your reputation before you lied, Josephine. I'm sure you've always gotten your way," he added, certain of it. "Just not in this instance."

He turned and walked away, heading toward the stables. The sooner he got to the church, the better.

Chapter 35

Gran and Amy sat opposite her in the carriage while Sarah had remained behind to assist Josephine in her final preparations.

All the way to the church, the carriage wheels rolled along the road, singing a refrain echoing in Martha's mind.

No more.

No more.

No more.

She had to do something. She could not allow this marriage to continue. She didn't care how she did it, but she was going to stop this ceremony. Jordan deserved better. He deserved his share of happiness, too.

Inside, Josephine was hollow, the space filled up with possessions, acquisitions, and a sense of power she'd cultivated ever since she was a young girl. Although she now spurned the relationship, she was a York, and it brought enough attention on its own. Plus, she was ethereally beautiful. She could charm any man she wanted and did, if it suited her purpose.

But being wealthy and beautiful was not justification for destroying a man's life. Martha knew, without a doubt, that that's exactly what Josephine would do.

Somehow she had to stop her, even if it meant

acting the fool. Even if it meant bringing the brunt of society's disapproval down around her head.

Both Gran and Amy glanced at her from time to time, their looks strangely compassionate. Did they know what she was thinking? Could they sense the level of her misery?

She was going to horrify the villagers, not to mention their friends from London.

When the carriage rolled to a stop in front of the church, both Gran and Amy looked wide-eyed at the crowd of spectators waiting to greet them. Martha only sighed inwardly. This debacle was evidently going to be amply witnessed. The stories would continue for years.

She straightened her shoulders, took a deep breath, and waited until Gran exited the carriage first. Amy startled her by reaching across and placing her hand on Martha's arm.

"I just wanted to say how lovely you look today, Miss Martha."

"Thank you, Amy," she said, grateful for the maid's kindness.

Her hair had been unmanageable this morning and she knew it had already escaped its careful styling. The dress she wore was new and horribly uncomfortable, requiring the corset to be tighter. The bustle was heavy, pulling at her waist and back.

She was much more comfortable in the hated lavender dress she'd worn at Sedgebrook.

Gran greeted numerous people as they made their way up the steps of the church. Amy was there at her side, in case she needed some assistance, with Martha following behind.

When she entered the church she found it, too,

filled with people. Congregants were even along the outside aisles.

Most of the staff at Griffin House had been released to attend the ceremony. Since the reception was not going to be held until two hours after the wedding, they had more than enough time to return home and make the final preparations.

Would Gran want to continue with the reception? She wasn't sure. Perhaps her grandmother would want to retreat to Griffin House and barricade the gates, remaining in isolation until the gossip died down.

She was about to shame the entire family. That day at Sedgebrook she should have stood, denounced Josephine's lie, and admitted to her own behavior, taking responsibility for it.

She should have, but she hadn't. Now she had to make this right.

They took their place in the York pew, the first one on the right side, facing the altar. Behind them, the congregation continued to talk until the choir began. The little boys in their starched round collars looked and sang like angels.

She clasped her hands together to keep them from trembling.

Five minutes passed, then five more. The choir was replaced by organ music, the selections no doubt chosen by Josephine and designed to give an imposing feeling to the ceremony. She found them more suited to a funeral and wished the choir would begin singing again.

She hoped Gran would forgive her. If not, the lecture she was sure to receive would be something along the lines of: *"Perhaps it's a good thing your father wasn't alive to witness your behavior, Martha."* Or: *"Matthew would be rolling in his grave, child. Whatever possessed you to do such a thing?"*

Love? Was it reason enough? Honor? Her own sense of decency and propriety? Respect? For Jordan and herself. Revenge? The thought stopped her.

No, she didn't feel vengeful, but she was angry. Not only about Josephine's manipulation but her callous disregard for anyone else's feelings. No one was more important to Josephine than Josephine.

Martha had never been miserable in her life, not until going to Sedgebrook. Then, it was as if someone peeled away part of her she'd never known existed. A shield, a blanket, a way of keeping her from looking at the world as it truly was. Or maybe her father's death had changed her. She'd been left bereft and grieving, unable to connect with anyone and finding friendship in a man's letters and perhaps a bit of imagination as well. No, not imagination. She'd created a picture of Jordan from his own words and he'd turned out to be exactly as she hoped.

What had Gran said? That she was always someone's something: her father's daughter, Marie's stepdaughter, Gran's granddaughter. Josephine's sister.

Jordan's lover.

When was she simply going to be herself because of herself? When was she going to be whole and separate, asking more of the world than she had in the past? At what point did she refuse what she'd been given and demand a greater share of happiness?

When? Right now, this exact moment.

The choir began singing again, only to fade off when the double doors opened and Jordan entered the church.

Every single person turned his head and watched Jordan's approach. He must hate being the center of attention, especially since he was still dependent on his walking stick.

A few days ago Josephine had informed her of the details of the ceremony. She wouldn't walk down the aisle. She would have no attendants. She and Jordan would emerge from the door beside the altar and present themselves to the congregation before turning to face the minister who would begin to officiate.

She hadn't known at the time why Josephine had cut out everyone from the ceremony, but now she did. Josephine didn't consider herself a member of the York family. Instead, she saw herself as a stray dog that had somehow wandered into their kennel. That stray dog had become an heiress thanks to the generosity of her father, a man she rebuffed on her mother's word.

Perhaps Josephine had made another change to the ceremony and would follow Jordan down the aisle, the better to make an entrance.

It didn't matter. Martha couldn't allow the wedding to continue one more minute.

Her grandmother suddenly stood, the congregation's attention moving from Jordan to Gran.

"Jordan Hamilton," she said, her voice carrying over the abrupt silence, "do you love my granddaughter?"

Jordan stopped, half a church away and regarded Gran.

Before he could speak, she continued. "Not Josephine, but Martha."

His gaze veered to where Martha sat, her eyes wide. Every thought had flown from her head at her grandmother's question.

"Yes, Mrs. York, I do."

Martha's gaze flew to his.

This was not going at all the way she'd planned. She had thought she would scandalize the entire congregation, perhaps even be sent from the church in disgrace. She'd no idea Gran would suddenly act like an avenging archangel or that Jordan would shock her with a declaration of love.

He loved her? He could have mentioned that earlier.

"This marriage can't go on," Gran said, further surprising her.

"I agree," he said, making his way to the pew and standing in front of Martha, his expression solemn. "It's why I came. To make an announcement that the ceremony has been canceled."

Martha was teetering between a bone-deep joy that he'd said he loved her to a terrifying certainty that she was dreaming all of this. Any moment she'd wake up in her bed with this interminable day to be gotten through.

Perhaps she'd taken some of Jordan's elixir.

But would she have imagined Gran and her question? No, she couldn't have envisioned that. Nor could she have foreseen Jordan looking at her as he did now, as if he was memorizing her every feature.

Gran sat down beside her. Evidently she was retreating from the fray, leaving Martha to carry on. She straightened her shoulders, took a deep breath and stood.

She had planned to declare her love for him, tell him that if he needed an heiress, she was one. She'd gone over and over the words she would say in her mind. She'd utter them quickly, before anyone could interrupt her.

Yet now, with what felt like the whole world waiting, she couldn't form one coherent sentence. No, not one word would escape, let alone a few of them strung together.

All she could do was stare at him.

"You can't marry Josephine." There, finally, words had passed the portal of her lips.

"I agree," he said. "I can't."

He turned, his gaze encompassing the congregation.

"Please accept my apologies," he said, his voice sounding formal and ducal. "There will be no wedding today."

He looked at her once more. "Shall we go?" he asked, stretching his hand out to her, palm up. "I think we need to have a conversation."

Bemused, she placed her hand in his and walked with him from the church.

HE DIDN'T GIVE her a chance to balk, just grabbed her hand and pulled her down the aisle with him. Hundreds of eyes followed their passage from the church.

Martha didn't have to struggle to keep up. If anything, she had to slow her pace to his. Damnable leg.

He glanced at her, unsurprised to see her face flushed. The situation was rife with embarrassment, humiliation, and some degree of dishonor.

Why, then, did he feel so damn good?

Holding her hand would have been a damn sight easier if he didn't also have to wield this idiotic walking stick. The problem was without it, he wasn't sure he could maintain his balance.

Damn it all.

He stopped at the church door.

"Shall we proceed?" he said, glancing toward the carriage.

"Where are we going?"

"Back to Griffin House for the moment," he said. "I want to propose marriage to you," he added. "Without so many witnesses."

She only stared up at him, her expression one that made his heart lighter. She looked as stunned as a child presented with a magical present. Happiness lit up her eyes and her mouth was slightly open.

He couldn't help himself. He bent and kissed Martha in front of hundreds of people.

Let them talk. Let them tell the tale of the duke who came to announce that one wedding wasn't going to take place while proposing to another woman on the steps of the same church.

Nor was that the only shocking thing he did. He kissed her again and she kissed him back.

REESE PACKED HIS valise and looked around the room, paying special attention to the rumpled bed. Josephine would be married shortly. Would being the Duchess of Roth be everything she wanted or expected? He doubted it.

Most of the staff had already left for the church to witness the exchange of vows. How long would it be before Josephine broke hers? A month? Longer?

He wagered that Jordan would be faithful until the end. Or maybe he wouldn't even make it to the church. He wouldn't fault the man if he grabbed Martha and hied off to Gretna Green.

To his surprise, his carriage had been brought

around to the front of the house without his order. Not only had it been readied for him, but it seemed as if he had a traveling companion.

He entered the vehicle to discover Josephine sitting there, dressed in a brilliant blue traveling dress and jacket, a jaunty blue hat with a bouncy feather completing her attire.

"Should I ask what the hell you're doing here?" he said. "Or shall I just congratulate you for escaping a loveless marriage?"

"Don't be ridiculous," she said. "Most marriages are loveless."

"There are a great many, I understand, that are the height of companionship, not to mention passion."

She sent him a look no doubt designed to singe him to his toes. He was not so easily cowed. Perhaps she would learn that fact in time.

"I've been thrown over," she said, the words said with less venom than he expected. "Jordan has decided he doesn't want to marry me."

After her announcement, she glanced at him.

"You knew," she said.

"I didn't, but I'm not surprised."

"You might have warned me."

"Did you blame him?" he asked. "He knew it was you in my bed last night, by the way."

Her eyes narrowed. "Was that why?"

He shook his head. "I suspect it was because he wanted Martha more than he wanted you." Daring words. He half expected her to fly into a rage.

She surprised him by smiling and the expression look almost genuine.

"They belong together, don't you think? They'll

always smell of the lake. Perhaps their children will be little goldfish."

He couldn't help but chuckle. She had a way about her when she wasn't being manipulative.

"You said something intriguing."

"Lucky me," he said, leaning close. "Dare I get an appreciative kiss for my brilliance?"

She put both hands on his chest and pushed him away.

"No. You said something about my working for the War Office. Would it be a possibility, do you think?"

He sat back and regarded her with some interest.

He and Jordan both had begun work at the Topographical & Statistics Department, collating military statistics. Recently, however, the department had begun assimilating other duties and taking on other missions. As such, perhaps women could be utilized. Hell, maybe they were being used now and he just didn't know.

"You're an heiress. Why do you feel the need to work?"

She made a little moue of dissatisfaction. "I've always envied Martha. She's always had a goal, something to achieve. Other than a new wardrobe, I haven't."

He studied her for a few moments, wondering if she knew that with every new aspect of character she revealed he became more fascinated.

"It's worth a try," he said. "Shall I ask and let you know?"

She shook her head. "I'm afraid I've become *importun* at Griffin House," she said. "I'm traveling to London with you."

"Are you?"

She nodded.

He gave the signal to his driver and they pulled away, gravel pinging on the undercarriage.

"I have a present for you," she said, reaching across the seat.

Only then did he realize there was something hidden under a blanket in the corner. He stared at the crate with the name *Goldfish* on it in amazement.

Slowly, he began to smile.

"It seemed only right they lose their precious ship."

"How did you get it in the carriage?" he asked.

"It's not heavy. Besides, the only person in the stables was Brian and he would do anything for me."

He had a feeling most men would.

"Perhaps I should emulate Jordan," he said, bowing slightly. "Shall I offer to make you an honest woman, Miss York?"

"Don't be ridiculous," she said. "I have no intention of marrying you."

Of course not. He didn't possess a title. Perhaps he should tell her about his elderly uncle and how he would probably inherit an earldom in a few years. Or perhaps he would simply keep the information to himself. It would always be better to stay one step ahead of Josephine.

ONCE IN THE carriage Martha still held on to Jordan's hand.

He smiled at her in such a way she lost her breath. Thankfully, he hadn't smiled at her earlier. She might have fainted at his feet. But she couldn't just sit there staring at him like a loon, all the while holding on to his hand as if it was a life rope.

"You have a tendency to do something wrong for the right reason," she said.

"I do?"

She nodded. "Is this one of those situations?" she asked.

"Do you mean am I aiming to make reparations for my behavior by marrying you?"

She nodded again.

"I want to marry you because I want to marry you," he said.

She only stared at him.

"Although I admit I wasn't certain it was you in my bed until last night. I kept seeing you in my dreams. It makes sense now why, but not at the time. I thought I was just longing for you."

The most wonderful thing about this moment was that she wasn't imagining it.

"You told my grandmother you loved me."

"I believe I made the declaration to the entire church," he said.

Her heart was beating so fiercely surely he could hear it. The birds flying overhead could probably hear it, too, looking downward for that strange thudding noise.

When he extended his leg slightly, she glanced at it.

"How are you feeling?"

"Remarkably well, considering I've had little sleep."

She could feel the blush creeping up to her neck. Should he really be commenting about that?

She glanced away, feeling as if she'd become someone else in the past few minutes. She wasn't entirely certain she knew who this Martha York was. Surely she wasn't this tongue-tied, silly creature who felt inept and incapable of speech?

"Despite the fact I announced it to the whole of the

church," he said, "I didn't say it directly to you. Martha York, I love you."

That announcement certainly didn't make it easier to speak.

She could only stare at him. "Oh, Jordan."

HE HADN'T EXPECTED Martha to be terrified by his announcement.

She stared at him wide-eyed. Nor did she say a word in the next few minutes, the silence stretching out long enough to worry him.

All he had to offer her was a title and an albatross of a house. He suspected she didn't care about titles and Sedgebrook didn't seem to fascinate her, not as it had Josephine.

"Do you think me an invalid?"

He studied her eyes, certain he would be able to tell when she was lying. She was open about her emotions, something else differentiating her from her sister. Josephine used what she felt to manipulate other people. Martha didn't.

To his surprise, she frowned at him.

"Why on earth would I think you an invalid? Because of your leg?"

He nodded, once.

"Don't be ridiculous."

"I might always limp."

She tilted her head and regarded him, still with a frown. What did she see when she looked at him? He found he wanted to know. Or perhaps it would be better if he didn't.

"Does it matter to you?" she asked.

"It simply is. The fact does not require me to approve it or not. But it might be distressing to those around me."

"Do you think people would call you names or whisper behind your back?"

"I've known a great many kinds of people, Martha. I don't doubt they'd come up with a name for me. Something like the Damaged Duke, for example."

"Would you care?"

"Perhaps."

"Do you expect me to come up with a name for you?"

He studied her. "I doubt you would," he said.

"I could, if you want me to. Something like the Daunting Duke. I find you daunting a good deal of the time. Or even the Dangerous Duke if your eyes get any steamier."

"Steamier?"

"They're positively boiling with emotion right now," she said.

He was, in fact, trying to fight the impulse to kiss her. She was sitting there with her face pale, her lips tremulous. He wanted to calm her mouth, place his on it until she sighed against his lips.

"I've been trying to think of an inducement to make you marry me," he said. "And I'm coming up with little to offer you. You don't seem to care about Sedgebrook. Do you want to become a duchess?"

"Not particularly," she said.

"Then I have little to offer. I could give you half the boathouse. You could do your work on one side while I worked on the other."

"Would I get lunch there, too?"

"Absolutely. Perhaps we'd even have wine from time to time."

"Would you balk at my expenditures for copper or a new compressor?" she asked.

"Hardly, since you'd make it possible for Sedgebrook to get a new roof."

"There's my ruined reputation," she said. "That's a good reason to marry as well. But I doubt marriage will save either of our good names after today. I think we're destined to be shocking to a great many people."

"Then it's settled?" he said. "We'll marry? Not, however, at Griffin House, unless it's a private ceremony."

She sat back against the seat. "Not a proposal steeped in romance," she said.

"On the contrary. It's extraordinarily romantic, given I've declared myself to you and you've done nothing of the sort. I'm working on the assumption that you'll find yourself smitten with me in due course."

"The Darling Duke," she said, startling him.

"I beg your pardon?"

"That's what I'll call you," she said. She smiled at him, which lightened his heart immeasurably. "You could offer me you. It's all I really need. I love you, too. I think I fell in love with you long before we ever met in person."

He reached over and pulled her onto his lap, desperate to kiss her. He found, to his immense relief, his leg didn't object at all to Martha being there.

"I love you, too," she said once more.

He pulled back and looked at her. "You really are my Joan of Arc, you know."

She was not going to weep at the look on his face or the expression in his eyes. He was letting her see all his vulnerabilities, everything he held back from other people.

She was well aware of what a great gift he'd given her.

Instead of weeping, she decided it was time for another kiss.

Chapter 36

The reception for a wedding that never happened became a celebration for a marriage just announced.

Jordan Hamilton, the Duke of Roth, was to marry Martha York in a fortnight, the ceremony to be held at the bride's home, the minister presiding. Only the immediate family would be in attendance, which meant Susan York.

Josephine had taken herself off to London, the whispered rumors said. Not only had she left Griffin House with no maid, but she'd done so in the company of the duke's friend. People couldn't decide whether they were shocked, horrified, scandalized, or simply fascinated by the tale.

No further reception would be held at Martha York's wedding, so the villagers took advantage of this one, drinking their fill of ale, wine, and whiskey and eating all the wonderful treats offered up for their palates.

Susan York's name was mentioned often, but not as much as the Duke of Roth's. Wasn't he a handsome man? Didn't he have an air about him? And Martha York, when had she become so attractive? Maybe it had something to do with love, being as she was seen standing so close to the duke during the whole of the reception. Did you notice how the two of them were always holding hands?

Two hours into the reception, Martha wanted to escape all of it. From the look in Jordan's eyes, he felt the same. Plus, he had a carefully neutral expression on his face, one that meant his leg was paining him.

The whole of Griffin House had been turned over to the celebration. People were wandering throughout the parlors while the staff was furiously filling up trays and carrying barrels and casks out to the serving tables.

The only place to escape was the cottage and they headed there as quickly as they could.

"We can lock the door and no one can bother us," she said.

"You just want more kissing."

She glanced over at him and smiled. "Well, there is that," she said. "But more important, you can sit for a while." A moment later she shook her head at him. "Don't frown at me. You know you want to. It doesn't mean you're an invalid. Besides, I'd rather you keep your strength for other things."

"And what would that be?"

"Launching the *Goldfish* again," she said. "Recording our distance trials."

His laughter was contagious.

She opened the cottage door and did exactly as she'd promised, closed and locked the door behind them. Once that was done, she turned to find herself in his arms.

"You do want kissing," he said.

Sometime later, they surfaced to smile at each other.

She'd never been as happy as she was at this moment. Yet her joy was tinged with sadness. Her father wasn't here. She couldn't help but think he'd be celebrating both the *Goldfish's* successful launch and her coming marriage.

Martha's relationship with Josephine was filled with question marks and possibly always would be. For now, she wasn't going to think about Josephine or what she tried to do.

"The *Goldfish*," Jordan said, staring beyond her. "It's gone."

He circled her, going to the cleared table. She followed him.

"I had it brought to the cottage," he said. "Evidently, Reese stole it again."

The surge of anger she felt was not unexpected. What was strange was Jordan's smile. When she questioned his amusement, he turned to her and kissed her lightly.

"I had a feeling he'd try to grab it again," he said, turning and walking to the cabinet in the far wall. "Reese is ambitious. The *Goldfish* would do a lot to elevate him in the War Office."

He opened the cabinet door, retrieving what looked like the entire stern section of one of her vessels. To her surprise, it belonged to the *Goldfish*, containing all of its guidance system, rudder, and propeller.

When she looked at Jordan questioningly, he smiled.

"I just replaced it with a section from another one of your prototypes."

She stared at him in amazement. "Then what he has won't even float."

"I know," he said, grinning at her.

Outside the cottage two groups, situated on either side of Griffin House's expansive lawn, offered up entertainment: a string quartet that played cultured and refined selections and another, more raucous ensemble of village musicians with fiddles and flutes. People danced to one or the other or congregated in groups, smiling and talking about the scandal they'd witnessed that afternoon.

Inside the cottage, Jordan and Martha ignored them all, being involved with reciprocating engines, bending copper, buoyancy rates, and kisses.

Author's Note

The Topographical & Statistics Department (also known alternatively as the Department of Topography & Statistics) began in 1854 as an organization collating military statistics as well as creating maps of sensitive locations. Later, the T&SD became the Intelligence Branch of the War Office. However, since the book takes place in 1871, I've imagined that the structural and mission changes were already beginning in the T&SD and put Reese in the middle of those. Learning of advances in military art and science—such as the York Torpedo Ship—would have been of intense interest to the T&SD.

The stationary mines used by Russia in the Crimean War were called torpedoes. The self-propelled definition of the word *torpedo* is from the twentieth century. The Whitehead torpedo, developed in 1866 by an Englishman named Robert Whitehead was the first successful torpedo as we currently understand the term today. As a self-propelled vessel it used compressed air as an energy source.

Sedgebrook is loosely based on Castle Howard, located about fifteen miles northeast of York in England.

In 1813 the Royal Central Institute of Gymnastics was founded in Sweden. A physical therapist in Sweden is a *sjukgymnast*—or someone involved in gymnastics for those who are ill. I like to think Henry's training helped Jordan achieve the ability to use his damaged leg.

Don't miss the next breathtaking
romance from
New York Times bestselling
author Karen Ranney!

The American Duke

Coming November 2017!

*G*ive in to your Impulses!

These unforgettable stories only take a second to buy and give you hours of reading pleasure!

Go to *www.AvonImpulse.com* and see what we have to offer.

Available wherever e-books are sold.

AVONIMPULSE